FIELDS *of* FIRE

FIELDS of FIRE

Linda Hudson-Smith

NEWSPIRIT

FIELDS OF FIRE

A New Spirit Novel

ISBN-13: 978-0-373-83027-5
ISBN-10:   0-373-83027-0

www.kimanipress.com

Printed in U.S.A.

This novel is dedicated to my amazing husband
and best friend, Rudolph Smith.

And our loving children:

Kristina, Kevin, Greg and Scott.

And our adorable grandchildren:

Joshua, Keraishawn, Gregory III, Om'Unique and Scott II

You guys mean the world to me. I am so blessed
to have each of you in my life!

Thanks for all the unending love and support you give to me.

ACKNOWLEDGMENTS

I want to thank each and every one of you for all the encouragement and support you've given me during the year. It has meant so much to the continued success of my literary career.

Evelyn Moore—Borders Express, Fox Hills Mall—Culver City, California
Stephanie Kuykendall—March Air Force Base—Riverside, California
Jennifer Johnston—Feldheym Central Library—San Bernardino, California
Denise Noe—Waldenbooks, Moreno Valley Mall—
Moreno Valley, California
Karen Ferraro – Waldenbooks, Inland Center Mall—
San Bernardino, California
Wallace Allen—*Westside Story Newspaper*—San Bernardino, California
Beverly Jimerson
Daylin Philyaw
Bob Jenkins
Willie Brown and Woody
Judyann Elder
Ken and Debra Ross
Melville, Etona, Evonte and Elexus Campbell
Carlos, Kevin and Kelsey Ortiz
Leilia Jones
Bonnie Holman
Bill and Renita Anderson
Ralph Shepperson
Kerri Rowan
Kay Averette, Stark County Library,
Community Center Branch—Canton, Ohio
Sharon Combs—Lupus Foundation of America—
Canton, Ohio, Chapter
Charita Goshay—Writer—Canton, Ohio
I Rise Book Club—Canton, Ohio
Delta Sigma Theta Sorority—Canton, Ohio
The Martin Luther King Commission
Bob and Devera Fisher—Akron, Ohio
Elaine and Lawrence Williams—Akron, Ohio
Robert and Renee Green—Akron, Ohio
Maggie Holmes—Akron, Ohio
Marcy Zitron Lupus Support Group—Columbus, Ohio
Dollean Harmon—Marcy Zitron Lupus Chapter—Columbus, Ohio

Chapter 1

It appeared as if a fireball from hell had come to claim a middle-class town house community located in the southeast portion of Houston, Texas. Bright orange, red, blue and yellow flames licked ferociously at the moderately priced wood-and-brick structures. Standing ready to gobble up everything in its heated path, the nearly out-of-control fire raged on as fiery flames appeared to leapfrog in a single bound from one structure to the next.

Black, strangling smoke was as thick as the midnight hour, making visibility for the firefighters even more of a superchallenge. As the fire grew in intensity, it was getting hard for the fire crews to see their hands in front of their faces. Station 51 was in a rescue mode, at the same time praying there'd be no need to execute a recovery mission.

It had already been a major effort just for the fire crews to get inside the town house complex. The wrought-iron security gates had to be forced open by panicked residents after the remote control mechanism failed, causing a serious delay in getting the fire trucks and ambulances through.

This early summer Texas day had been hot and overbearingly muggy. The wind conditions were very bad, hardly serving as an ally to the firemen in the raging firestorm. The Southeast Houston Fire Department employees were busy evacuating residents as quickly and as safely as possible, taking special precautions with the elderly.

This four-alarm fire was the worst Stephen Trudeaux had seen in months. As he assessed the situation, his autumn-brown eyes drank in the blazing destruction happening all around him. He expected that more firefighters and trucks might eventually be needed. There were already numerous fire vehicles in the area, but it didn't appear to be enough, not as far as Stephen was concerned. The cause of this blazing fire had yet to be determined, but that sort of investigation normally came after all the smoke cleared.

Upon hearing a woman screaming at the top of her lungs, Stephen made his way toward the piercing howls. A hand suddenly reached out of nowhere and grabbed his arm, causing him to turn around with a start. The look of sheer terror on the young African-American woman's face told him she was in deep trouble, both physically and emotionally. "What is it, ma'am?"

Looking as if she was about to collapse, Marsha Anderson fell down on her knees. "Please help me," she cried. "My two-year-old son Nathaniel and my five-year-old twin girls, Kelly and Karla, are still in the house. I couldn't get to where they were sleeping for all the smoke. I did my best, but I couldn't rescue them. They're in the very back of the place. Please save my babies, sir, please."

As Stephen looked at the burning structure Marsha was pointing out to him, his heart skipped several beats. He then immediately sent up a quiet prayer on behalf of the entire family. The mother had managed to get two of her children out with her, a boy and a girl who looked to be around seven and eight. Since the front of the place was nearly a fireball already, he couldn't imagine anyone surviving the inferno.

Marsha's gut-wrenching pleas for Stephen to save her children made him see that he had to at least give it his best shot.

Stephen began to tear up the grassy knoll as he made his way toward the town house. Fear was all over him and he couldn't shake it. Despite his fears, he knew what he had to do. He also darn well knew that he shouldn't enter that house alone, but the thought of small children being trapped inside there kept him moving forward. Stephen had taken an oath to preserve life.

These young children hadn't had a chance at living yet and Stephen wanted them to have every conceivable chance at a good life. He heard the surrounding shouts of his fellow firefighters, who were busy on risky assignments of their own, which further convinced him to go this alone, though the rules didn't mandate it. Everyone else's hands were already full.

Stephen's determination to try to save the kids propelled him to move on. Disobeying orders could get him into big trouble, but firefighters often went with their gut feelings despite the consequences. If he saved the children, the disobedience would be addressed, but then quickly forgotten by the powers that be. If he didn't try, he'd never know for sure. Stephen actually believed he had a good chance of saving these little children. He had to believe it.

Although he'd only been engaged less than a year, Stephen hoped to soon marry and then have children with his beautiful girl, Darcella Coleman, whom he lovingly referred to as Darcy. Lately they'd been talking a lot about starting a family right after marriage, though he'd sensed some reluctance on her part during the intimate conversations. Stephen wasn't quite sure he'd been reading Darcella correctly, so he hadn't said anything to her about his suspicions.

Darcella was a registered nurse, a darn good surgical one, and she took her important job seriously. Caring for people was something she loved to do. She had always felt that taking care of the sick was one of the most important jobs on the planet. As a small child, she'd had dreams of wearing the prestigious whites and working in a big-city hospital. Darcella had never let go of her dreams, eventually accomplishing what she'd spent countless hours on, preparing herself to enter into the career field she was most interested in. Thinking of Darcella kept Stephen calm.

Then Stephen thought of his twin sister, Stephanie, whom he loved like crazy. The two of them were inseparable. Their mother, Doreen, had taught them to always have each other's back. When she'd died, they were all each other had left, until they'd eventually been reunited with Malachi Trudeaux, their estranged father. Malachi had come into the lives of the twins not long after their mother's death. The twins had never seen him before.

Although the initial meeting between Stephen and Malachi was bitter, they had reconciled their differences, but the father and son still had a long way to go despite the fact they'd been in each other's lives for nearly two years now.

Without looking back at Marsha, the mother of the children, or at his comrades, Stephen began to pray fervently, trying to completely ignore the dangerous signs all around him. In the next instant he began to shut down emotionally. He had a job to do. This was what he'd been trained for. If anyone could save the kids, Stephen felt that he could make a success of it.

Even though Stephen Trudeaux was very confident in his firefighting abilities, he knew that he'd never accomplish this mission without God there to guide and direct his way.

Stephen didn't enter the house from the front door because the fire was too intense. As he reached the backyard it appeared that the flames hadn't yet consumed the lower rear rooms. He didn't see fire in the back part of the upper section, either. Marsha had said the children were in the very back of the house. Stephen finally entered the home through the French doors off the patio, after he'd broken one of the windowpanes and had then reached inside to unlock the door.

Stephen made sure his face was covered before he began to make this way through the house. His tools of the trade were all intact. Finding the staircase would come first. When he saw the set of steps leading up from the kitchen, he assumed the place probably had two stairways. Slowly he inched his way up the steps. The closer he got to the top, the thicker the smoke was. His lungs had already begun to feel like they were on fire, too. As he reached the top of the landing, he got down on his belly and began to crawl toward the rooms in the back. Tamping down his fears, Stephen quickly maneuvered his way down the seemingly endless hallway.

What Stephen heard when he got to the very back of the house set off all his internal alarms. The anguished cries of a baby were very distinct. The little one was alive. He thanked God as he continued to inch his way to the door where he'd heard the cries coming from. Fear gripped him hard. He didn't know what to expect once he opened the door. The doorknob wasn't hot to the touch, which more than likely meant that the fire hadn't reached this room. What he feared was a back draft. What might happen when he opened the door had him very concerned.

Before turning the knob Stephen sent up another anxious supplication. Just as he entered the room, he looked behind him and saw that the flames had now reached the upper floor. After making a mad dash to the crib, he scooped up into his arms the wailing infant. Now that he had the child safely in his arms, he had to figure out a way to get him out of the house and into the safety of his mother's loving arms. The tension inside of him was mounting rapidly.

Stephen carefully tucked the baby under his thickly padded jacket as he made his way to the staircase he'd just come up. He was prepared to save these three children at all costs, hoping the twins hadn't fallen to harm's way. He'd look for them next.

Stephen had a gut feeling that the other stairwell had already been compromised. Then he heard rather than saw what sounded like a portion of the structure collapsing. They were probably trapped, he surmised. The only way out for them might be from one of the windows in the bedroom he'd just come from. After quickly retracing his steps, Stephen once again entered the room. In order to open the window, he had to lie the child back down in his crib. He then left the room in haste to go in search of the other children. It was now or never. Time was precious.

As Stephen stood at the door of the next bedroom, he used the same prayer as he'd done before entering the other room. Just as he opened the door, black smoke began to pour out, nearly overtaking him. He then felt the intense heat of the fire, which caused him to back away from the door rather quickly. Knowing there was no way for him to enter that room, deep regret filled him to the brim. If the twins were inside that room, he feared it was already over for them. However, once he got the baby to safety, he planned to come back and make a recovery attempt.

Seconds later Stephen stood at the window of the first bedroom, holding up the baby in front of the glass in hopes of someone below seeing him standing there. Time was running out on them. His screams couldn't be heard above all the other loud noises. Stephen thanked God with heartfelt emotion the moment they were spotted. He watched intently as his team went into action, providing a ladder for him to climb down from.

Little Nathaniel hadn't made a sound since moments after he'd first scooped him up again, which concerned Stephen a lot. He was also beginning to feel nauseated and very dizzy. As Stephen looked back, he saw plumes of smoke starting to creep under the bedroom door.

The climb down was taken with every precaution known to Stephen. His biggest concern now was falling off the ladder. The spinning inside his head had him seeing double. *Careful,* he told himself quietly. *You're almost at the bottom, champ. Marsha is awaiting baby Nathaniel. Then you have to go back in for the other children. Darcella and Stephanie will be waiting at home for you. You can do this, God willing. You can't give up now.*

Loud cheering and yelling broke out as Stephen slowly managed the last rung of the ladder. Then he heard a female crying out the baby's name over and over again. Then she began screaming the names of her twins, causing Stephen to rush back toward the ladder. After telling the fire crew that the other two children were still trapped inside and that he needed help to get them out, he started back up the ladder, only to be pulled away by his comrades. As he looked upward, he saw that the rooms he'd just escaped from were now fully engulfed in flames.

"There's no way we can get back in there, Trudeaux. It's over," his comrade told him. "The fire is too intense to make another attempt. This one is now a recovery mission."

Stephen looked horrified, deep regret and blinding tears awash in his eyes. He suddenly felt like a total failure. He had failed to save two small lives, had failed miserably. "It can't be," he cried, yet knowing it *was* over and done with. It wasn't humanly possible for anyone to be alive inside that fire-and-smoke-consumed hellhole. The twins were now with God.

Right after Stephen first handed Nathaniel to Marsha, his head had begun to spin around and around. Now, his eyes rolling to the back of his head, nausea was busy taking his stomach hostage. As Stephen hit the ground hard, he heard several of his comrades shout out for immediate medical assistance. Then darkness rushed in and instantly claimed him.

The heady scent of fresh flowers was overpowering to Stephen. As he tried to make sense of where he was, his burning eyes scanned the rather large, sterile room, which he quickly deduced was inside a hospital. The oxygen tube in his nose was more of an indicator as to where he was than anything else. When he tried to lift his head, he slowly lowered it back onto the pillow in hopes of easing the throbbing pain.

Relieved to see her fiancé finally awakening, Darcella, a dark-haired, five-foot-six stunner, with medium-brown skin, leaned over the bed and kissed Stephen on the forehead. "Welcome back, sweetheart," she said, her voice thick with emotion. "You really had all of us worried. You've been out cold for a couple of days. How're you feeling this morning, Stephen?"

Stephen tried to smile at Darcella, but even that caused him to wince in pain. "Terrible," he rasped in a southern drawl, which was normally smooth. "What happened to me, baby?"

"Smoke inhalation, Stephen. You were completely overcome by it. Your lungs have taken a serious pounding."

As it all came back to Stephen with crystal clarity, he felt like crying. Although he didn't know how many lives had been lost during the fire, he knew of two certain deaths, deaths that had occurred on his watch. Perhaps if he hadn't gone inside alone the twins might've been saved.

"Did you know that you're being touted as a hero in the media and among your peers?"

Stephen's brow furrowed. "A hero! For what? Doing my job? Are you folks forgetting that I couldn't help the two children that died in the fire?"

Darcella smiled with sympathy. "I'd say you did a little more than just your job. You *did* save a life. A tiny little life that only had you to depend on, Stephen. You're going to receive a medal of valor during a huge ceremony as soon as you get out of this place. The whole station wants to celebrate your heroism. I'm so proud of you, and you should be proud of you, too. I need to go and get your nurse so they'll know you're finally awake."

Stephen gingerly nodded his approval.

Stephen had a hard time believing what he'd just heard Darcella say. Medals and celebrations were so far from what he needed or wanted in his life it wasn't even funny. He got paid a salary to do a job he absolutely loved, and he'd simply tried to do it to the best of his ability, though he'd failed to rescue the twins. Yes, he'd taken certain above-the-call risks, but they'd been necessary. Fighting fires was a risky business in itself. There was no question about that. Stephen felt like anything but a hero.

The attractive African-American nurse, Nancy Goddard, came rushing into the room with Darcella right on her heels. After taking Stephen's vital signs, she smiled and then let the couple know everything was just as it should be. After telling Stephen and Darcy she had to phone Dr. Harmon Sykes, Stephen's private physician, she quietly left the room.

Stephen took a hold of Darcella's hand. "I have to stop the department from doing this hero thing, Darcy. I don't want any celebration or a medal. Lives were lost. I don't deserve anything akin to that. The brave young military men and women who are serving in the Middle East are the real heroes. They're the ones putting their lives on the line every minute of every single day. Save all the honors and revelry for their bravery and their homecomings."

Darcella looked at Stephen with tears floating in her bourbon-colored eyes. "I understand how you feel, honey. But if you reject the department's way of rewarding you for your bravery, they may see it as you being ungrateful. Just roll with it, Stephen. Your comrades need and want to honor you in this way. The twins' mother is so very grateful to you for saving her smallest child and she also wants to thank you and celebrate your heroism."

Stephen shook his head in dismay. "I don't like it. I see your point, but that's not going to stop me from fighting this thing. I just don't want a hero's celebration. Has the doctor told you when I'm getting out? I'm ready to go home. I miss it, especially when we're there together."

Darcella patted Stephen's hand in a calming manner. "Soon, Stephen. You took a lot of smoke into your lungs. You've been receiving inhalation-therapy treatments twice a day."

Tears sprang to Stephen's eyes. Thinking about the twins and the baby whose life he'd saved had gotten him all emotional. His pain was deep over the lost lives, but he vividly remembered how warm the small child had been when he'd held him close to his body. It was the kind of sensation that he didn't think he'd ever stop wanting to feel again and again. No one but Stephanie knew how much Stephen wanted children of his own.

Until Darcella was ready for parenthood, too, Stephen knew he'd just have to wait patiently. She had asked him to give her a year to make up her mind about having kids once they'd gotten married. His father hadn't been around for him during his youth, though not of Malachi's own choice, but Stephen planned on spending all his free time with his family.

Stephen loved spending time with his fiancée, though they didn't have a lot of quality time together because of demanding jobs. They were on totally different work schedules, where often one was coming as the other one was leaving. The few days they'd have off at the same times were always put to good use, but this wasn't what Stephen expected out of marriage.

Stephen looked up at Darcella. "Stephanie. Where is she and how's she handling this?"

Darcella pointed at the recliner chair stationed across the room. "Your sister has stayed in that chair all night long ever since you were admitted. She just left minutes before you woke up. She went home to take a shower and change clothes. You can bet your bottom dollar she won't be gone long."

Stephen's emotions resurfaced. "Gregory was supposed to visit her this weekend. Did he make it in?"

"Gregory got in early yesterday evening. He was up here with Stephanie all last night. He's gone back to his hotel. He plans to take a short nap. He hasn't had any sleep since he arrived here from New Orleans. Gregory's really concerned about how Stephanie's holding up."

Stephen grinned. "Mr. Saxton will soon learn how tough that old girl is. She's one of the strongest women I know, present company included. Their long-distance relationship keeps them from experiencing the everyday trials and tribulations dating couples go through on a regular basis. However, they've really gotten to know each other pretty well despite only seeing each other two weekends a month. Do you think the sound of wedding bells is in the air?"

"Definitely! They're positively crazy about each other, Stephen." Darcella grew quiet for a moment. Then she looked down at Stephen. "Your dad is on the way here. He called me on the cell to let me know. He's really worried about you, honey. Are you okay with him visiting?"

Stephen blinked hard. "Of course I'm okay with it. Had I known he was coming, would I have tried to stop him? *Yes*. I don't want him driving all the way here from New Orleans just to see me lying in a metal hospital bed. I'm sure Dad has enough to do in running that huge company of his. But you know what? I can hardly wait to see him. It's been nearly a month since we last saw each other."

Darcella was extremely happy about Stephen's last remarks. Stephen and Malachi had grown a lot closer over the past two years, but there was still a bit of tension between them from time to time. It always seemed to grow tense for the two men when the conversation turned to Doreen. Stephen had adored his mother every bit as much as she had treasured him, which made him fiercely protective of her even though she was no longer alive.

Bitterness had a tendency to arise in Stephen when he thought of all that Doreen had gone through to raise her kids without the benefit of their father. The Trudeauxs had lived poorly, yet with dignity. Then Stephen had to remind himself that Malachi had taken good care of his children financially and that he would've also been there physically had he been allowed.

Doreen had chosen not to use a good bit of the child support money Malachi had so generously provided her with, which had later been willed to her children upon her death. Stephen hated that his mother had played clever poker games with her children's lives, all the while making Malachi believe there was still a chance for them to reconcile. Had he not seen proof in black and white, in his own mother's handwriting, he wouldn't have ever believed it. The proof that his father had never stopped loving his mother was always evident in his eyes.

Although Stephen was now armed with the truth about his parents' silly separation pact, which had said that Malachi could only be involved in the lives of his children in a covert manner, there were times when he thought his father should've done more through the courts to win visitation rights with his kids. He had desperately needed Malachi in the days of his youth, especially when he'd been involved in several different sports. As it was with most teenage boys, Stephen had needed a male role model he could look up to, preferably his own father.

Looking fresh and pretty in a crisp white shirt, burgundy pullover V-neck sweater and denim jeans of the same color, Stephanie Trudeaux hurried through her makeup session, consisting of a light foundation to her sienna complexion, a corn-silk powdery sealant, a dab of blush to her cheeks, and a generous amount of a dark red-wine-colored lip gloss.

Although Stephanie hadn't gotten nearly enough sleep cramped up in the recliner chair in her twin brother's hospital room, she felt better than she had when she'd first arrived home. The hot shower had helped to revitalize her.

Soon after freshening up, she'd called her clients and canceled the in-home appointments she had scheduled for the next couple of days. Stephanie was an interior decorator who owned a steady, booming business.

As Stephanie thought about the odd feelings she'd initially had about something bad happening with Stephen, she trembled slightly. Her heart had nearly dropped from her chest once her twin's peril had been confirmed for her. The recent phone call Darcella had made to Stephanie had come right when she'd needed it the most, since she'd almost driven herself crazy with worry. Knowing that Stephen was finally awake and alert had Stephanie ecstatic. There was a time when she'd hated her brother's career choice, but he loved it so much that she'd stopped arguing with him over it a couple of months after his intense professional training was over.

A smile came to Stephanie's full lips when she thought of Attorney Gregory Saxton, her steady beau for nearly two years. Well, she mused, that's if you can call seeing each other twice a month "steady." Gregory, her father's godson and legal adviser, lived and practiced law in New Orleans. However often they saw each other, their relationship was an exclusive one. She and Gregory also saw each other during coordinated vacation times and special holidays.

Although Stephanie had met the dashing young attorney just before the Thanksgiving holiday almost two years ago, it was on that very night, after a grand feast at her father's home in New Orleans, that she and handsome Gregory had decided to begin dating only each other. Possessing eyes the color of smoked topaz and a clean-shaven mocha complexion, the intelligent corporate lawyer had practically swept Stephanie off her feet when he'd come knocking on her door to deliver letters to her and Stephen from Malachi.

Stephanie not only loved Gregory, she actually liked him, a lot. Even his sense of humor was intriguing. He could make her laugh as if she'd never laughed before. His vast knowledge on a slew of topics often astounded her. Although he was somewhat of a bookworm, there was nothing dull or uninteresting about him. She was so sure she'd learned something new from him each time they were together that she eagerly looked forward to the lessons.

Gregory was also a respected resident of his New Orleans community and a very active member in the church he attended. He sat on so many boards that it was hard for Stephanie to keep up with his array of duties. The one thing she positively loved about him was his love for giving back to the community. Gregory also took on his fair share of pro bono cases, always eager to help out those who couldn't afford to pay the Saxton & Saxton high legal fees.

The telephone rang at the same time Stephanie reached for the front doorknob. Eager to get back to the hospital to see Stephen, she debated whether to answer it or not. That it might be Gregory calling ended the few seconds of deliberation. A smile lit up her autumn-brown eyes the moment she heard the voice that never failed to turn her on. "Hey, Gregory! You sound much stronger now. I trust that you got some sleep."

Gregory chuckled. "Slept like the dead, Stephanie. But I'm wide awake now. What about us getting together for lunch?"

Stephanie looked at the time on her cell phone. "I'd love to, but I'm off to the hospital at the moment. Stephen is awake and alert. What about one o'clock, or are you really hungry?"

"One is fine, Stephanie. If you don't mind, I'll just meet you at the hospital. No point in me sitting around at the hotel when I can be with you. Had you heard that your father is on his way to Houston?"

"I have heard. Couldn't be happier. His visit will be so good for Stephen, a continuing affirmation on how much he cares about his kids. My brother still allows doubts to set in on him from time to time. I'll see you at the hospital whenever you get there. Be safe, Gregory."

"You, too, my love. See you soon."

Gregory had learned more and more about Stephanie with each passing day. When they weren't together, the telephone and e-mail messages were their constant form of communication. He loved how she sent him an inspirational e-mail each morning and another one before she turned in for the night. He'd only used the Internet for business purposes before Stephanie had come into his life. They also exchanged a host of friendship and romantic greeting cards via the Net. That each of them took time out of their busy schedules to send loving messages made them feel very special. Gregory was already convinced that Stephanie was *the* one.

Family was very important to Gregory, even though the Saxtons were often at odds with one another. His mother, Aretha, had left his father, Gregory II, for a much younger man. His dad was still pretty bitter about his wife's illicit affair, yet he tried to keep peace with her for the sake of their two sons. Gregory's brother, Grant, was once a miserable man, one who had loved to have lots of company when he'd throw himself a pity-party. He was doing much better now.

Gregory was still amazed that Stephanie had seen right through Grant the first time she'd met him, having refused to allow herself to get all caught up in his psychotic mess. Grant was extremely jealous of Gregory and often rivaled him every chance he got, believing that Gregory was the favorite son. Gregory and Grant's relationship had been strained most of their adult lives, but things had gotten somewhat better between them in the past couple of years. However, the two Saxton brothers still had a long way to get back to being loving siblings.

Stephanie embraced Darcella the second she stepped into the hospital room. Pleased to see Stephen looking so healthy and chipper, she leaned over the bed and kissed her brother on both cheeks. "How're you feeling, big brother?"

Stephen grinned. "I don't know. Since I'm getting so much pampering, I'm reluctant to let you ladies know that I feel great. When Dr. Sykes gets here, I'm going to press him to send me home with my beautiful girl. She can take care of me in the comfort of my own place."

Stephanie frowned. "Don't rush it, Stephen. You need a lot of rest and your lungs need more time to heal. But we'll continue to pamper you no matter where you recuperate."

Stephanie turned to Darcella. "Think you can talk some sense into your fiancé?"

Darcella positioned herself next to Stephanie at Stephen's bedside. "Don't worry, Stephanie, he's not going anywhere until the doctor decides to release him. My adorable fiancé is just blowing his usual smoke rings. I personally think he's enjoying being waited on hand and foot. It's rare for him to get anything like this at home, other than an occasional dinner or two cooked by me. Where else can you get all your meals served in bed, Stephen?"

Stephen grimaced. "Okay, ladies, you win. I won't bring up leaving this place until the doctor says I can go. That's a promise."

"That's a real good idea, man," Gregory said from the doorway. "That way my lady can get a lot more rest." Gregory smiled broadly as he took Stephanie into his arms and kissed her thoroughly. "You're looking much better, my love. I'm glad you went home and got some rest. He then turned his attention back to Stephen. "How's it going for you, brother?"

Stephen reached out his hand for Gregory to shake. "All is well, man, except the deep regret I have over the death of the twins. I don't remember much of anything that went on after I handed the mother her baby."

Stephanie grimaced at the pain in Stephen's voice. "That's 'cause you fell flat on your face right after that. All lights were out for you, pal. We all just thank God it wasn't any worse than it was. I'm sure Darcella told you about the department's decision to honor you. How about that for good news, hero?"

Stephen sighed hard as he turned up his nose. "Please, don't go there, darling angel. I don't know any hero who faints dead away like some little sissy." "Darling angel" was the endearing nickname Stephen had dubbed Stephanie with when they were small children.

A light suddenly went on inside Darcella's head. She now knew the real reason why Stephen didn't want any recognition for bravery. *He felt totally inadequate.* It bothered her that he let Stephanie in on way more of what was going on with him than he did her—and she was his fiancée. Stephanie was Stephen's true confidant. He trusted his sister with everything, including his life. All twins or other multiples weren't so seriously dedicated to one another, but these two were. Darcella often wondered if she'd ever have it like that with her man.

Darcella loudly clucked her tongue like a scolding mother hen. "You didn't faint, Stephen. You collapsed. Big difference. Your lungs were filled with smoke, so please don't downplay what happened out there on the line. You're no different from any other firefighter who's collapsed after being overcome by smoke. Keep in mind that you blacked out after you saved the baby, not beforehand. That could've been disastrous for both of you."

A slight smile of apology formed on Stephen's lips. The tone of Darcella's voice had let him know his remarks had distressed her. "I know, sweetheart. I'm sorry if I upset you. I didn't mean to make light of what went on that night. I know it was serious."

Stephanie loved how sensitive Stephen was to his fiancée. He hated to see her upset. For a man who hadn't seen or experienced any sort of relationship between his parents, he was doing very well in his relationship. Even though it had taken him a long time to fully commit to Darcella, he'd finally done so. He'd totally changed his views on commitment after he'd found out that Malachi had cheated on Doreen. It was now Stephen's belief that no woman deserved an unfaithful man, especially when he had a faithful woman that loved him.

Stephen had once told Stephanie that he'd flirted with many women and had even taken their phone numbers while involved in a love affair with Darcella, but he'd chickened out when an actual date had been set up. Stephanie had constantly told him how unfair he was to his girlfriend by not committing himself to her. Stephen had later come to realize he'd been dead wrong in not holding sacred his relationship with Darcella. Shortly after the enlightening revelation regarding the infidelity issues in his parents' marriage he'd asked her to marry him.

Knowing that Stephen was doing just fine had Stephanie breathing a lot easier. Despite how close she and Stephen were as siblings Stephanie made sure to give him and Darcella plenty of space, always showing the utmost respect for their relationship. Out of her deep respect for Darcella Stephanie called Stephen first before going to his place and she was mindful not to call her brother on the phone as much as she had before he'd gotten engaged. Stephanie had also learned to solve many of her own problems. Leaning hard on Stephen had become a thing of the past, but she knew without a doubt that her brother would always have her back.

Sensing that her brother and his fiancée needed some time alone, Stephanie looped her arm through Gregory's. "I'm ready to take you up on your offer of lunch, Gregory. I'm in the mood for some serious chicken and dumplings. What about your taste buds?"

Gregory's eyes held undeniable adoration for Stephanie. "Chicken-fried steak for me, girl. We can get both dishes at Cracker Barrel. Is that okay with you?"

"Yummy! Their dumplings are the best, but not as good as our mama's were."

Stephen moaned in protest. "Stop it, you two! You're killing me over here." He looked up at Darcella. "Think you can hook me up with some dumplings when I get out of here?"

Darcella laughed heartily. "That and anything else your stomach desires, boo."

Everyone exchanged warm hugs and light kisses before Stephanie and Gregory left the room, bound for the closest Cracker Barrel restaurant.

The silence between Stephanie and Gregory was not without a distinct voice, as the couple waited for a server to deliver their orders to the corner booth. Eyes and gesturing hands communicated quite effectively. She knew that she was cared about without him speaking a single word.

The wordless communication between Stephanie and Gregory was interrupted for a few brief moments when the waiter appeared with their food orders. Heads were bowed without question once the waiter left the table. Each voiced a soft prayer of thanks to the Creator.

Minutes into the meal the dramatic rolling of Stephanie's eyes told Gregory how much she was enjoying the chicken and dumplings. Gregory smacking his lips told her how he felt about his tasty meal. After Gregory reached over and wiped the corner of her mouth with the linen napkin, Stephanie smiled sweetly, grateful for the sweet gestures he often showered her with. She loved his sensitivity and his thoughtfulness.

Gregory laid his napkin down and then rubbed his stomach. "I'm full," he said, finally breaking the half hour or so of silence derived only through body language. "What about you?"

Stephanie shook her head in the negative. "I could eat another bowl of these fluffy dumplings. But I won't. Don't want you to think I'm a greedy pig," she teased.

Gregory shrugged. "Don't mind me. If you want more, you should order it." His eyes slowly roved her figure. "Besides, I've never seen such a beautiful, slender, shapely pig. Never!"

Stephanie chuckled. "I think I'll take out what's left on my plate. I don't want to get that overly full feeling of discomfort, especially since I plan on getting dessert. As you already know, the blueberry cobbler here is divine."

"I *do* know, Stephanie. It's one of the best berry cobblers I've ever had." Gregory quickly summoned the waiter. He then winked at Stephanie. "Two blueberry cobblers coming right up."

Stephanie and Gregory lapsed into silence again, once the dessert orders were delivered.

Right after Malachi vigorously shook Gregory's hand, he smiled at Stephanie, opening his strong arms to her. Stephanie beamed at Malachi, rushing into his loving embrace. The affectionate exchange between father and daughter took a couple of minutes. Malachi loved the warm feeling he always received from Stephanie. Though she was a grown woman now, to him she'd always be daddy's little girl. All the years they'd missed out on couldn't be reclaimed, but it prompted him to make as many new memories as he possibly could, as often as he could. A little over two years was the full history of their time together.

Seeing Stephen lying in the hospital bed had choked up Malachi when he'd first stepped into the room. Hugging his son had come easy for him despite the awkwardness they sometimes experienced. Both men had been making a supreme effort in getting to know each other.

Malachi couldn't wait for the day to come when his children would take over his multimillion dollar New Orleans–based company, SSM Trudeaux Incorporated. His kids were filthy rich on paper, as Malachi had made them partners in his company while they'd been mere babes in arms. The company was a family business long before his kids had ever met their father.

Malachi tenderly kissed the dead center of Stephanie's forehead. "You're looking well, my dear. How are you?"

Smiling beautifully, Stephanie lovingly stroked Malachi's smoky-dark cheek. "I couldn't be better, Dad. How was the drive down from New Orleans?"

Malachi affectionately squeezed Stephanie's fingers. "Uneventful, my dear. It was actually a very pleasant drive. Hardly any traffic at all on the roads."

Malachi, a tall man with an incredible physique for someone his age, encompassed both of his children in his dark gaze. "It's great to see both of my kids." His eyes softened as he looked at Stephen. "I thank God that you're not as bad off as I had imagined." Malachi's eyes then fell on Darcella. "You couldn't have a better nurse than your beautiful fiancée, Darcy. I'm glad you two have each other to depend on."

Darcella blew Malachi a kiss. "Thanks, Mr. T. I'm glad, too. I still have a hard time believing my guy has finally decided to ask me to meet him at the altar."

Malachi's eyes misted at the beautiful memories of their engagement day. His son had asked him to be his best man at the family gathering, right after Darcella had agreed to marry him, and he'd accepted. That offer had surprised the heck out of Malachi and everyone else close to him and Stephen. It was a day that none of the family members would ever forget.

Darcella noticed that Gregory had his arm around Stephanie's waist, while Malachi, who stood at her left side, held on to her hand. A wild streak of jealousy shot through her once again. Her sister-in-law-to-be was one of the luckiest women she'd ever known. She had not only one man who loved and adored her, she had three great guys at her beck and call.

Stephanie was at the very center of Stephen, Malachi and Gregory's universes. Even when his sister wasn't around, her fiancé seemed to talk about her all the time. Darcella didn't like feeling envious of Stephanie, but she had everything that had so far eluded her. The type of relationship she had with her father, Reginald, and two brothers, David and Daniel, wasn't the least bit healthy. They saw very little of one another—and when they did get together, dissention ruled. Her mother, Patsy, couldn't find time to spend with Darcella because all of her precious time went to the three men in her life. Darcella felt that her engagement party was only a success because of all the energy she and Stephanie had spent in making it a wonderful day.

Darcella had finally been the center of everyone's attention on that special day, wishing she were able to experience those exhilarating feelings of being queen for a day every day for the rest of her life. Darcella wanted Stephen and Malachi to adore her the way they did Stephanie.

Stephanie looked up at Malachi. "Are you staying with me, Dad?"

Malachi smiled. "I sure hope so. Sorry I didn't call ahead and ask if it was okay."

"You're welcome to stay at Stephen's place, Mr. T.," Darcella chimed in. "His home is much closer to Clear Lake Regional than Stephanie's."

Stephanie looked a little surprised by Darcella's offer, since Stephen wouldn't even be at home. Then she thought that Darcella was probably trying to bring them even closer together. Although she'd rather have her father stay with her, Stephanie decided not to protest. More than likely it would make Stephen happy to have his father feel more comfortable in his space.

Malachi looked between Darcella and Stephanie. "Thanks for the generous offer, Darcy. I plan to split my nights with Stephanie and Stephen. I've been away from my children so long that I don't want to miss out on a single opportunity to spend more time with them. I'll also be here at the hospital with you and Stephen on and off throughout the day. However, I'll stay with Stephanie tonight. I hope that's okay with you two."

"Of course it's okay with us," Stephen said. "But since I plan to be out of here very soon, hopefully today, maybe you can come stay with me tomorrow night if I do get out."

"I'd love to, Stephen. I'm going to stay in Houston until

you're out of here. Your uncle Max will be here sometime tomorrow. He's anxious to see how you're doing for himself, so much so that he's flying in instead of driving."

Just another of Stephanie's doting fans, Darcella thought churlishly. Maxwell Trudeaux, Malachi's only brother, couldn't love his niece any more than if she were his very own daughter.

Her offer to Malachi had been generous and had come straight from her heart, but she wasn't that surprised he'd all but rejected it. Darcella was hurt by the subtle rejection, but she'd get over it. She always did since she was used to being constantly discarded by her own family.

Malachi strolled over to his daughter-in-law-to-be and brought her to him, hoping to make her feel as important to the family as everyone thought she was. His gentle hand to the back of Darcella's head guided it to his chest. She looked so unhappy, but he didn't think it was all due to Stephen's plight. He'd sensed the restlessness in her spirit the first time they'd met.

"Look at us," Stephen said, a huge smile on his face. "We're now one big happy family. Once I'm out of here, we have to get a portrait done. There's a lot of love in this room."

Malachi silently prayed that Stephen would never have a reason to think otherwise.

As Dr. Harmon Sykes stepped into the room, all eyes rapidly turned on him. The doctor greeted everyone with a cheerful hello and a bright smile. Once he'd asked Stephen a few pertinent questions, he then went to work on thoroughly checking out his patient. After listening to Stephen's lungs with his shiny stethoscope, he then listened to his heart, nodding his head in an approving manner. "Everything seems to be in good working order, Stephen. Your lungs sound clear. You're a blessed man. How would you like to go home today?"

Already knowing how Stephen felt, everyone laughed at

the way he vigorously shook his head in response to the doctor's question.

Dr. Sykes laughed, too. "Okay, I get it. You've been ready to go. I'll get the discharge papers worked up ASAP. However, I'm putting you on disability for a few weeks."

Stephen frowned. "Is that really necessary?"

Dr. Sykes nodded. "It's a must. You need to get more rest. I know you're eager to get back to your job, but you'll be no good to yourself or anyone else if you don't heal properly. Getting back to work too soon could land you right back in here in just a few days."

Darcella stroked Stephen's hair. "The doctor's right, you know. I agree with him."

Stephen still didn't look too comfortable with the decision. Sitting around home for several weeks wasn't his bag. He liked to stay active. "What about getting back into the gym? Can I at least work out an hour or so a day?"

Dr. Sykes shook his head in the negative. "Complete bed-and-couch rest. You're to do nothing strenuous at all, Stephen. That's how it has to be for now."

Stephanie walked over to the bed and took hold of Stephen's hands. After smoothing his hair back, she kissed his cheek. "Dr. Sykes knows best, Stephen. Two weeks isn't all that long. I promise to drop by and keep you company when Darcy's unable to. Deal?"

Stephen grinned broadly. "It's a deal, darling angel."

Upset that Stephanie had once again gotten her man to agree to something she herself hadn't been able to get him to do, Darcella clenched her teeth, warding off the urge to scream out of sheer frustration. That he hadn't put up the least bit of resistance with his sister had her fuming. Darcella was sure that Stephanie could talk Stephen into flying up to the moon.

Dr. Sykes patted Stephen's shoulder. "Since we have all the important issues settled, I'll get started on getting you out of here. I want to see you in my office next week, Stephen.

Call and make an appointment." The doctor gave a pleasant farewell as he left the room.

Because she was nearest to him, Stephen hugged Stephanie before reaching out his hand to Darcella. "Did you all hear that? I'm going home. Hallelujah!"

Chapter 2

Stephanie and Darcella quickly dressed the king size four-poster bed in fresh linens while Malachi and Gregory kept Stephen occupied downstairs in the family room. The two women worked well together to try to get things done as rapidly as possible. Getting Stephen into bed and comfortably settled down was their top priority. The one thing that the two women definitely had in common was their love for Stephen.

Stephanie plumped one of the king pillows before placing it at the head of the bed. "I'm sure you're glad to have your fiancé back in his home, Darcy."

Darcella chuckled. "Ecstatic. It's been pretty lonely without him. I can't wait until we're married so I won't have to live alone any longer."

Stephanie smiled softly. "I'm happy for you both."

Darcella turned a curious eye on Stephanie. "Are you really?"

Stephanie arched an eyebrow. "Am I really what?"

"Happy for us?"

"Of course, Darcy, but why would you think otherwise?"

Darcella shrugged with nonchalance. "Not really sure."

Stephanie found Darcella's last statement to be downright injurious. "You said that for a reason, but based on *what* is what I want to know."

Darcella scratched her head. "Well, for one, you don't get to spend as much time with your brother as you used to, that is, before he got engaged to me. I'm more of a priority for him now. I'd think that would somehow bother you, Stephanie."

"Why should it? As his wife-to-be, you're supposed to be Stephen's number-one priority. Perhaps it's my brother's close relationship to me that is bothersome to you, Darcella."

"That's a crock, and you know it. However, you two *are* extremely close."

Stephanie had grown impatient. "I'm happy for my brother, Darcella. I'm happy for you. I hope you don't say these sorts of insensitive things to Stephen. His health is enough for him to deal with at the moment." With that said, Stephanie left the master bedroom, obviously dismayed by what had transpired between her and her brother's fiancée.

Stephanie hated what had just occurred. Darcella had managed to put their relationship on a totally different footing. The conversation had been disturbing to say the least. Perhaps Stephen's woman was guilty of exactly what she'd accused her of. It seemed to Stephanie that Darcella was the unhappy one, the only one portraying dark signs of jealousy.

Up until a few minutes ago Stephanie had had no reason to be anything but happy for her brother and his lady. Now she wasn't so sure if she should be as thrilled as she'd been before. Darcella hadn't ever before exhibited toward Stephanie this type of negative behavior. She'd certainly felt it in spades on this day. This issue might've made sense after the marriage, since she and Stephen were so close, but the wedding had yet to take place. Stephen was to marry Darcella and vice versa. Now wasn't the time for Darcella to feel envy or to feel left out. She was to be a part of the Trudeaux family, Stephen's wife, no less, and Stephanie loved her, too.

The more Stephanie thought about it she came to realize that Darcella had more to worry about from Stephen than from her. Her brother had very little tolerance for insecure women. Stephanie prayed that this was just a one-time occurrence, born from an unexpected onslaught of fear. The last thing she wanted was to cause trouble between her brother and his loving lady.

Darcella had sat down on the side of the bed right after Stephanie had walked out on her, wishing she hadn't put her foot all up in it. Her sister-in-law-to-be had been nothing but kind, loving and sisterly toward her from the moment they'd met. She really hadn't deserved what she'd received in return. Darcella was certain Stephanie was hurt by her snippy attitude with her.

If Stephanie told Stephen about this senseless incident, though Darcella didn't think she would, there'd be some tall explaining for her to do. Her husband-to-be wouldn't be too happy about how she had treated his sister, especially without just cause.

How to make it up to Stephanie was heavy on Darcella's mind. Although Darcella was sorry for what had occurred, she couldn't help how she felt about things deep down inside.

A man's woman should be his best friend and confidant, not his twin sister.

Malachi had noticed Stephanie's discomfited posture as soon as she'd stepped into the room. If he wasn't mistaken, he was sure the red puffiness around his daughter's eyes had come from crying. *But why? What had upset her?* Darcella instantly came to his mind, making him wonder if she had acted out toward Stephanie in a negative manner. Darcella's jealousy issues weren't lost on him. He'd noticed it before, when they'd all been together, but he seemed to be the only one concerned about it. Malachi knew exactly what the color of envy looked like.

Stephanie went over to Gregory and slipped her hand into his. "I think we should go now. Stephen needs his rest."

Gregory nodded. "You're right." He studied Stephanie a moment, sensing that her spirit was troubled. Deciding to find out what was wrong later, when they were alone, he slid his arm around her shoulders. "I'll follow you back to your place unless you're too tired for company."

Stephanie smiled gently. "I didn't have you drive all the way from New Orleans just to have you spend time alone in a stuffy hotel room. I'm never too tired to be with you."

Happy with Stephanie's response, Gregory kissed her on the tip of her nose.

Stephanie then announced her and Gregory's intention to leave. After giving Stephen a hug, each of them said their farewells. Malachi told his daughter he'd be along shortly, wanting to give her and Gregory some time alone. At any rate, he wasn't going to be in the way. As soon as he got to his daughter's place, Malachi planned on taking a long, overdue nap.

"Aren't you going to wait until Darcy comes back?" Stephen asked Stephanie.

Stephanie shook her head in the negative. "We've already had our say." Stephanie felt that she should leave it just like that, because it was the truth. More was probably said between her and Darcella than should've been. Stephen didn't need any more drama in his life.

The chicken and dumplings that Stephanie had consumed earlier at lunch were long gone. The loud growling let her know her stomach was running on *E*. Unsure of what she had on hand to make a quick meal out of, Stephanie went into her brightly decorated kitchen to take a look-see. Although she had leftover dumplings, she had nowhere near enough for three people. Since Gregory had run out to the store to restock her supply of Aquafina, her favorite bottled water, she had enough time to find something appetizing to cook for him and her father.

As Stephanie thought about all the different foods Malachi had told her he liked, she checked in her freezer to see if she had any of his preferences. After spotting the frozen jumbo shrimp, she pulled out the plastic freezer bag and placed it on the counter. Shrimp was one of her father's favorite seafood. Now all she had to do was check and see what other ingredients she had to make a simple shrimp dish. A quick survey of the refrigerator's fresh vegetable bin and then the pantry let her know she had what was needed for a zesty shrimp-and-snow-pea stir-fry.

After Stephanie retrieved all the recipe ingredients, she set aside the chicken broth, soy sauce and white wine. The recipe also called for cornstarch and minced fresh ginger, but she only had dried ginger to use as a substitute. She pulled out from under the counter a stainless-steel wok and then poured into it the suggested amount of peanut oil. While the oil heated in the wok, she thoroughly washed the snow peas and green onions. Once Stephanie had opened the eight-ounce can of water chestnuts, she set on the burner a pan of water to boil the white rice in.

Stephanie was proud of the tasty Chinese-style dinner she'd made for Gregory and Malachi. Throughout dinner the two men couldn't seem to sing her praises enough. Even though most folks probably thought candlelight was for lovers only, she had gone on and lit the candelabra in the center of her formal dining table, which made for a nice, cozy atmosphere. The guys had also complimented her on creating a warm, homey ambience for them to dine by.

The large white ceramic bowl Stephanie had served up the stir-fry in was practically empty. Since it probably meant that her guests enjoyed her cooking, she was very happy. Although her father and Gregory were two of the kindest men she knew of, she was sure they wouldn't eat something they didn't like just to spare her feelings. Besides that, the two guys had hardly come up for air while darn near inhaling the delectable meal.

Malachi smiled at Stephanie. "As the old saying goes, 'I hate to eat and run,' but I'm in dire need of a nap, my dear. Will you two young people excuse this old guy for a short while?"

"Of course," Stephanie and Gregory said simultaneously, laughing at themselves.

Stephanie got to her feet and then held out her hand to Malachi. "Come on, Dad, let me help get you tucked into bed comfortably. The guest room is all ready for you."

Taking hold of Stephanie's hand, Malachi chuckled. "I think I'd like that, Stephanie." Malachi then looked over at Gregory. "If I don't get up before you return to the hotel, I'll see you tomorrow, son. How long are you planning to stay in Houston this time around?"

Gregory stroked his chin. "I decided to make it an extra-long weekend. I plan to return to New Orleans on Tuesday evening. Dad's got everything at the office under control."

Malachi grinned. "I'm sure of that. As we all know, your dad *is* the man."

Inside the softly decorated guest room of cloud-white and whisper-soft pastels, Stephanie pulled back the comforter on the queen-size bed. After turning off the bright overhead lights, she touched on the bedside lamp. Malachi was already in the bathroom putting on his pajamas, so she sat down in the rocking chair to wait for him. Her father had decided to get dressed for bed because he wasn't planning on going back out this evening.

Toting his neatly folded clothes under his arm, Malachi stepped out of the bathroom. Once he'd placed his clothing bundle on the dresser, he walked over to the bed and sat down. He then looked at his daughter with concern. Malachi didn't liked how quiet and subdued she'd been since leaving Stephen's place. "What happened between you and Darcy?"

In a show of surprise, Stephanie jerked her head back. "Whatever do you mean, Dad?"

Malachi ran his hand over his chin. "I think you know exactly what I mean, Stephanie. You went into that bedroom in good spirits, but that's not how you came out. You can trust me with any confidence. I hope you know that."

Stephanie sighed hard. "I see that I can't get anything by you. Dad, it's complicated, but I don't understand why it should be." She went on to tell Malachi what had transpired between her and Darcella. That the ordeal pained her something awful was crystal clear to her father.

Malachi nodded with understanding. "I'm sorry to hear that, my dear. It isn't that abnormal for women to clash, but it usually starts with the sister being jealous of her brother's love interest. That's clearly not the case here. I'm just surprised that it's taken so long to surface. Do you know if she felt this way about your relationship with Stephen before now?"

Stephanie shrugged. "If she did, I guess I've been missing all the signals."

Malachi got up from the bed and walked the short distance to where Stephanie sat. He then knelt down in front of the chair. "I wish I could resolve this for you, but we both know I can't. Hopefully it'll work itself out. Can you forgive Darcella's hurtful comments?"

"I already have. I just don't understand why she feels this way or why she hasn't mentioned it to me before now." As Malachi stood, Stephanie did the same. "Let me get you all settled in, Dad. I need to get back to Gregory. We can resume our talk over breakfast."

Malachi smiled gently. "That sounds like a good idea, my precious girl."

* * *

Stephen gestured for Darcella to come and sit on the bed with him. She had been pacing the bedroom floor for several minutes now. She looked upset, making him wonder what was wrong. Even though he was safe and back in his home, he thought that the aftermath of the fire might still be haunting his lady. It always haunted him, too, days and days afterward.

As a nurse Darcella had seen many victims of fires, but she really didn't understand the major life-threatening firefighting missions Stephen often got caught up in. She thought the heavy action firefighters saw might somehow be exciting, but Stephen knew she'd feel differently if she'd ever have to experience it firsthand. Darcella had no idea what it was like to be out there on the fiery front line, other than through the drama she'd heard from him.

Smiling weakly, Darcella made her way over to the bed, removing her shoes before she sat down. Nestling in Stephen's arms was one of the things she lived for. Her love for her man was deeper than any ocean floor. Losing him would be her undoing. While she didn't think their relationship hinged on how well she and Stephanie got along, Darcella knew Stephen desired them all to have loving family-ties type relationships. His twin sister only meant the world to him.

As Stephen stroked Darcella's hair, she drew in closer to him, basking in the warmth from his strong muscled body. He hadn't been away from her all that long, but to her it had seemed like an eternity. The time she and her fiancé had to spend away from each other because of the different work shifts were hard on both of them. "How *are* you feeling, Stephen?"

Stephen tenderly ran his knuckles down the side of Darcella's face. "Pretty good, Darcy. The worst of it is over. I'm really glad to be home. How about you, honey? Are you okay?"

"I'm fine, Stephen. Extremely fatigued, though. I've hardly slept since this whole ordeal began. Just having you here beside me is therapeutic. Welcome back home, sweetheart."

"Thanks," Stephen said drowsily. In the next instant he was dead asleep.

Smiling with empathy for her man, Darcella pulled the covers up around Stephen's shoulders. If only she could go out just like that. Stephen often fell asleep as soon as his head hit the pillow, especially after he'd worked a hard shift. Darcella laughed inwardly. So much for a proper welcome home, she mused, sorry that Stephen hadn't stayed awake long enough for her to deliver on the romantic evening she'd planned for them.

Darcella's mind raced, as she laid there quietly, thinking about a couple of important things that were going on in her life. It had been a couple of weeks since she'd applied for a new job, one that Stephen didn't know a thing about. A few other issues also came to mind; things she hadn't yet made Stephen privy to.

As Darcella thought about the upcoming medal ceremony to be held in Stephen's honor, she frowned slightly, wondering why women firefighters weren't honored in the same way as their male counterparts. A lot of females had accomplished countless acts of bravery, but seldom were they recognized for such. Unfortunately, men would always have it over women. Some things never change, she thought, getting up to go into the guest room. For so many restless nights sleep was a welcome escape from the world and all its troubles. Darcella said a silent prayer as she climbed into the bed and nestled herself into the embracing arms of the sandman.

Gregory could clearly see that it was time for him to go back to the hotel. He had hoped that Stephanie would've shared with him by now what had happened at her brother's place. Instead of talking to him about it, she had completely withdrawn into herself. Seeing her nodding in and out of sleep caused him to get to his feet. He could tiptoe out without disturbing her, but he knew she'd be upset if he disappeared without saying something to her first.

Stephanie's eyes suddenly popped open. Her hands then flew up to her mouth. "Oh, gosh, Gregory, I'm sorry for falling asleep on you. What time is it, anyway?"

Gregory glanced down at his gold wristwatch. "A little after nine o'clock, time for me to scoot on back to the hotel. You seem to be as tired as I feel."

Stephanie felt totally embarrassed. It wasn't like her to be rude to company, but she was more tired than she'd realized. She patted the sofa cushion next to the one she sat upon. "Please don't leave yet. It's still early."

Gregory grinned. "Yes, it is, but you're very tired. We still have plenty of time to spend together. I'm staying on until Tuesday."

Stephanie patted the sofa cushion again. "I know all that, but please stay. I promise not to fall asleep on you a second time. Besides, there's something I want to run by you."

Gregory dropped back down beside Stephanie. "You've got me hooked, girl."

Stephanie laughed softly. "We're both hooked." Her expression quickly turned pensive. "It's about Darcy, Gregory. She was rather rude to me back at the house. After I tell you what she said to me, you can let me know what you think of it." Repeating the same things she'd told Malachi, Stephanie took Gregory into her confidence without the slightest hesitation.

The sorrowful expression on Stephanie's face told Gregory that she had been hurt deeply by the verbal scrimmage with Darcella. Even though he didn't see the situation as irreparable, he was aware that both women had to want reconciliation before it could occur. He was sure that Stephanie wasn't about to hold this matter against Darcella for petty revenge. His lady had a heart of gold and the nature of her spirit was a forgiving one. There was no doubt in his mind that Stephanie could and would forgive this needless transgression.

In his desire to keep her calm Gregory massaged Stephanie's arm. "I think you two ladies can get past this, especially since it's the first time something like this has happened."

Stephanie nodded. "That's what I'm afraid of, Gregory. That Darcy hasn't said anything to me before now could mean that she's felt this way all along—and that she may have been harboring ill feelings toward me for a long time. An emotional buildup like that can—and will—eventually explode."

Gregory silently admitted to himself that he hadn't thought of it that way, but Stephanie could be right. He still didn't see the situation as out of control, but it had the potential for such if they didn't resolve things between them right away.

After Gregory slid his arm around Stephanie's shoulder, he rested his head against hers. "Go to Darcella as soon as possible and offer her a truce. This issue doesn't have to linger on, not if you don't want it to. Someone has to extend the olive branch first. Even though you're the one who's been treated unjustly, that doesn't mean you can't offer a resolution."

Pleased with Gregory's suggestion, Stephanie smiled at him to show her approval. "I like the idea of a truce. I'll call her first thing in the morning. It seems that this *can* be worked out. Very easily, I might add. Thanks."

As Gregory got to his feet, he smiled back at Stephanie, happy and proud that she wanted to bring the conflict to a screeching halt. "Now that we have that settled, I'm going to leave and let you get some rest. You're going to have one heck of a busy day tomorrow."

Stephanie raised an eyebrow. "How so?"

Gregory laughed heartily. "After you get off work, I have plans for us. I want you to go to the mall with me to pick out a birthday present for my mother. A nice dinner out and perhaps seeing a movie afterward is included in my plans. Does that work for you?"

"I'd say so. However, unless you're really tired, you don't have to go yet. My first in-home appointment isn't until noon tomorrow. I can sleep in much later if I choose to."

Gregory pressed his lips into Stephanie's forehead. "I'm sure that's all true, but I can't ignore the fact that you've been nodding off for a while now. You need to rest. You've had quite an emotional upheaval. That also can be tiring and draining. We still have several days of excitement ahead of us, Stephanie. Love you, sweetie."

Sensing that she couldn't change Gregory's mind about leaving, and not wanting to come off sounding desperate to have him stay, Stephanie conceded. "Sounds like we have a few good plans for your stay. Will you call me once you get back to the hotel?"

Gregory took sweet possession of Stephanie's lips. Holding her at arm's length, he grinned. "Answer on the first ring so we don't wake Uncle Mal."

"First ring, Gregory."

No one could've ever made Stephanie believe she'd one day feel uncomfortable in Stephen's home or at his dinner table, but she felt just that. Before she'd had a chance to extend the olive branch to Darcella, Darcella had called to invite Malachi and her to come to Stephen's home for an early breakfast. Surprising to Stephanie was that Darcella had also called the hotel and had extended an invitation to Gregory. Their uncle Maxwell had been invited, too.

Even though her family was all very well acquainted with Gregory, Stephanie thought Darcella should've had her make contact with him. Stephanie saw the gesture as very manipulative on Darcella's part. Because Stephanie had no desire to remain at odds with Darcella she hadn't passed comment. Stephanie hoped that by accepting the invitation to breakfast that their issues would all be put to rest. The funny thing was that Stephanie really didn't know what their real issues were. All Stephanie knew was that her brother's fiancée had suddenly turned catty on her for whatever ungodly reason.

Stephen looked much better than he had the day before, Stephanie observed. He was back to his usual bubbly, animated self. Her brother seemed so happy to have his family seated around his table. The twins' uncle Maxwell had shown up at Stephanie's very late the previous night, stating that he hadn't been able to get out of New Orleans as early as he'd originally planned on. An emergency situation had come up with one of his semi-trucks and he'd had to take care of it.

Maxwell Trudeaux, a big, tall, dark and handsome man with an even bigger heart, was a long-distance trucker who owned a fleet of trucks and employed a good number of truckers and a trusted administrative staff. While Maxwell's corporation wasn't as large as SSM Trudeaux, it was every bit as lucrative as Malachi's highly successful communications conglomerate.

Stephen passed the bowl of soft scrambled eggs to Maxwell. "I'm so glad you made it in safely, Uncle Max. When I first heard that you and Dad were coming to Houston to see about me, I thought it was ludicrous for you all to drive or fly that distance. I can't tell you how much it means to me or how happy I am about seeing you two big guys...." Stephen had to pause to regain his composure. After picking up a napkin, he wiped the tears from his eyes.

The ongoing confirmation that his father and uncle cared so much about him had Stephen all choked up. Although when he was younger he'd often dreamed that he and Stephanie would one day be united with their father, he had given up hope for that to ever happen a long time ago. The darn near tangible hate he had built up for Malachi had nearly destroyed Stephen. To see them all sitting down taking a meal together was overwhelming to him each time it occurred. Never in his wildest dreams had he thought it was possible for them to become a loving family.

Stephanie's first reaction had been to rush to Stephen's side to comfort him, which she'd been doing all her life. This time she held back. Letting Darcella try to calm her brother was the best course of action. Stephanie knew for a fact that she had given their relationship the utmost respect, but she had to understand that perhaps Darcella didn't feel that she had. It was odd for her to have to think about making any loving gestures toward her own brother, but she now knew it was necessary. A damper had been placed on her readily acting upon her natural instincts where her brother was concerned. That was such a shame as far as Stephanie was concerned.

"Sorry about that," Stephen finally managed to say. "It's just that having all my family around me after so many years of absence is still a very emotional thing for me. Let's all dig into this delicious breakfast my beautiful lady prepared for us." Stephen reached over and covered Darcella's hand with his own. "Thanks, baby. You're the greatest."

Darcella blushed like a teenager. "You're welcome, boo. You know I love to please you."

Stephanie gulped hard at Darcella's last comment, disbelieving a word of it. She then scolded herself. If things were going to go back to normal between her and Darcella, she had to stop reading something sinister into everything the other woman said or did. Darcella just wanted to be the leading lady in her man's life, just as it should be. However, she didn't have to alienate Stephen's only sibling who'd done nothing but champion their relationship from the onset. Stephanie silently prayed that everything would hurry up and get back to normal.

Maxwell laid his fork down on the side of his plate. "With us all here together like this, I guess it's the perfect time for me to announce my intention to retire at the end of the year. I'm finally giving up driving all over the country on my shiny hot wheels."

Malachi gasped. "No! Tell me it isn't so, Max." Malachi had heard this one before.

Maxwell nodded. "Oh, it's going to happen all right, Mal. More to the point, it has to happen. I'm getting too old for this long-distance driving. I can barely see at night anymore. I'm beginning to think I might be a hazard to others on the road. It's time for me to call it quits."

With Maxwell seated right next to her, Stephanie leaned over and gave him a big hug. "If you think you should retire, Uncle Max, then do it. I don't know about the rest of you, but I worry a lot when you're out there on the open road. Congratulations on your decision!"

Everyone else at the table shouted out their congratulations as well.

Malachi laughed heartily. "I hate to admit it, but I worry about you, too. However, I won't get too excited about your announcement. For me, seeing is believing. If you're serious, I'm going to throw you the biggest and the best retirement bash New Orleans has ever hosted." Smiling broadly, Malachi gave his brother the thumbs-up sign.

Stephen nodded his approval. "I think it's a great idea, Uncle Max. Who says you have to wait until you're too old to enjoy life to retire? Fifty-five is the perfect retirement age, and you're two years past that, Unc. Sooner than that is definitely appropriate if you can afford it."

Malachi chuckled. "Since I'm already fifty-five, Stephen, is it your opinion that I should go on and retire, too?"

Stephen looked a bit abashed. "No, Dad, I didn't mean that for you. Both of you guys are full of life, but what good will all that energy do you if you lose it before you can enjoy it?"

Malachi stroked his chin. "You've made a good point. If I decide to retire alongside my big brother here, can I count on you to take hold of the reins at SSM Inc.?"

With everyone waiting with bated breath for Stephen's response, a sudden silence permeated the room. The air also carried a bit of tension. Darcella's mouth was agape as she stared hard at him, concerned with what Stephen might say. The last place she wanted to live was in New Orleans. It was a nice place to visit, but she didn't want to plant any roots there.

Stephen scratched the center of his head. "Now that you've mentioned it, I might consider doing that, Dad. While this last fire isn't nearly the worst I've seen, it shook me up a lot. Since Darcy and I are talking about planning a family not long after marriage, New Orleans may be a good place to raise kids. However, Darcy and I'll have to talk this over in depth. But I promise you, Dad, I'll seriously consider taking you up on your offer."

Malachi couldn't have been happier by his son's response. His broad smile let everyone know his feelings. There was a time when Stephen wouldn't have given a moment's thought to such a proposition. Malachi was glad that they'd come a long way from the troubled place where their relationship had begun. If his son were to take over his business, Malachi would then retire.

Stephanie had intently watched Darcella all through the exchange between her father and brother. It was her best guess that if Stephen's lady had a say in the matter it wasn't going to happen, not ever. However, Stephanie would love to see her brother hang up his fire hose.

Stephen's profession was extremely dangerous and Stephanie constantly worried about him being out on the line. Firefighters also responded to emergency calls along with the medical emergency teams. Responding to gunshot and stabbing victims also came with the territory. Stephanie recalled a lot of harrowing stories about the vicious gang activity they'd run in to during some of the calls. As far as Stephanie was concerned, it was past time for her twin brother to get out of the firefighting business.

Interrupting Stephanie's thoughts was the vibration of her cell phone. After politely excusing herself to the others, she promptly stepped away so that she could hear the caller.

Upon recognizing the baby-soft voice of one her clients, she smiled. "Morning, Maryann. What's up?"

"I need to cancel our appointment. Jaelin is running a raging fever. We're on the way to the emergency room right now. Jaharri's meeting us there. Can I call you later to reschedule?"

Stephanie looked concerned. "Of course you can, Maryann. I just hope your sweet little boy is going to be okay. Please call later and let me know how's he doing."

"Will do, Stephanie. Thanks for being so understanding."

"No need to thank me for being human. I've already sent up a silent prayer for Jaelin."

Stephanie rang off and then sent up another supplication on behalf of the two-year-old. Maryann and Jaharri Rhodes were yet another pair of her young, wealthy clients. Both were architectural engineers. Jaharri was from old money, which allowed Maryann to be a stay-at-home mom. However, Maryann planned to go back to work when the baby was preschool age.

Stephanie slid back into her chair with ease, taking hold of Gregory's hand the minute she was settled in. "My first appointment canceled—an emergency," she whispered. "Looks like we have even more time to spend together."

Leaning into Stephanie, bumping her shoulder playfully, Gregory grinned. "I love it."

As Stephanie looked up, she noticed that Darcella had also left the table. She wanted to ask everyone where she was, but then thought better of it. She hoped her sudden disappearance had nothing to do with the attention-grabbing conversation between father and son. Before Stephanie's last thought cleared her head, Darcella was reclaiming her seat.

Maxwell got to his feet. "Who wants to help me clean up the mess we've made?"

Stephanie quickly raised her hand, but then saw it was all for not. Darcella was already on her feet, looping her arm through Maxwell's.

"Uncle Max and I have the kitchen duties all covered, Stephanie," Darcella announced. "You can just relax and entertain the rest of our guys out in the family room."

Stephanie was genuinely amazed at how cleverly Darcella had pushed aside her offer of help. That she suddenly seemed to be rivaling Stephanie for her own family's attention had her feeling a bit nonplussed. Deciding that she wasn't about to be dismissed like some little child, Stephanie got to her feet. "I'm helping, and that's that." Stephanie's matter-of-fact tone brooked no argument, but Darcella narrowed her eyes at Stephanie to show her dismay.

Stephen immediately noticed the minute clash of tension between his lady and sister. He couldn't help wondering what was going on here. As he thought back on the previous evening, he recalled how strangely Darcella had acted, after she'd come out to find that their guests had left the premises without saying good-night to her. Stephen vowed to get to the bottom of things.

Stephanie did everything but completely take charge of clearing the dining room table first and then loading the dishwasher. No one was going to tell her what she could do or couldn't do in her own brother's house, which he'd already owned before getting engaged. She'd been very careful not to ever step on Darcella's toes, especially after they'd announced their intent to marry, but it obviously hadn't done any good. Darcella should never make the mistake in forgetting the unending bond between her and her brother, Stephanie thought.

Even though Stephanie would make sure she didn't take things too far, she continued to work around the kitchen until every pot and pan was scrubbed clean and put away. She felt the hard looks Darcella doled out to her, but ignoring her impetuous attitude was easy for Stephanie. It took two to wage a war. So much for the earlier truce Darcella had called, Stephanie mused.

Maxwell put his arm around Stephanie's shoulders, squeezing them gently. "Niece, you sure are a whiz in the kitchen. If I didn't know better, I'd think you were working off a head of steam." He lovingly kissed the tip of Stephanie's nose. "Now that everything is done, let me take you back to your lonely man." Maxwell had a good chuckle over his last comment.

Stephanie laughed inwardly, glad that her uncle had no idea how close he'd come to the truth. She *had* been working off steam. As she walked hand in hand into the family room with Maxwell, Stephanie felt sharp daggers digging into her back. Darcella was right behind them.

Gregory stood until Stephanie was seated on the sofa. He then sat down right beside her, drawing her in closer to him. "You guys cleaned up pretty quickly. I feel guilty for not helping."

Stephanie winked her right eye at Gregory. "We did just fine. No need for any guilt."

"Thanks, sweetheart. Are you ready to leave or do you want to stay a little while longer?"

"We'll stay another half hour. I don't want it to look like we're eating and running."

"I don't think anyone will think that about us, my love, but we'll stay on a bit longer."

Once the guys got into a lively conversation about sports, Stephanie groaned inwardly, thinking she should've made the choice to leave. She loved sports as much as any of them did, but all her guys took it way too serious. They loved arguing about whose team was the best.

Malachi, Maxwell and Gregory loved the New Orleans Saints, their hometown heroes; Stephen and Stephanie were lone Texan fans; Darcella doted on handsome Michael Vick, quarterback for the Atlanta Falcons. With football's preseason just getting under way, Stephanie knew she had several months ahead of her to listen to the guys bickering among themselves.

For the past year and a half all the guys had been getting together either in Houston or New Orleans to watch what they called the big games, but only when their individual schedules permitted it. Because Stephen had the most difficult work schedule of all, Maxwell and Malachi did the majority of the traveling. Being in business for oneself did have its fringe benefits. Gregory was always off on the weekends, but seeing Stephanie was more important to him than watching the football games. He'd travel to Houston more often than he did if it were possible. Gregory drove the five or so hours most of the time, but there were times when he flew in.

Since it was still a bit too early for the mall stores and shops to be open for business, Gregory suggested that he and Stephanie take a ride down to one of the beaches in Galveston. Although she wasn't in the right frame of mind for it, Stephanie agreed to it, anyway. As if he could read her mind, he asked if she'd rather go on inside the mall and window shop until the stores opened. Because they'd only have a little over a half an hour to wait, she thought it was a great idea. Window shopping was one of Stephanie's favorite pastimes.

Stephanie nodded. "That works better for me, Gregory. That is, if you don't mind."

"You're really bothered by what happened back at the house with Darcella, aren't you?"

"Why'd you say that, Gregory?"

"I get the impression she's trying to hog up all the attention from Uncle Mal and Uncle Max. She seems insecure about her position within the family. Is that the feeling you got?"

"Right on the money. I don't understand it, though. She's been included in every family outing and her feelings are always taken into consideration on family matters. I think the conversation about Stephen taking over the reins at SSM Trudeaux has her spooked. The look on her face wasn't a very pleasurable one. Do you think that issue was upsetting to her?"

"I definitely saw the unsettled look on her face, but she needs the benefit of the doubt on that one. Pulling up life-long roots *is* scary. I think about that myself, quite a bit. If you and I get married, one of us is going to have to move to another city. Don't you think about it, too?"

Wishing they didn't have to get into this conversation, Stephanie sighed. As much as she wanted to marry Gregory, she didn't like the "if" inference. "If" was too much of an unsettling word. It wasn't the least bit decisive, which always left room for doubt. "All the time, Gregory. But it's probably best if we don't dwell on anyone moving anywhere until everything has been decided between us."

Gregory suddenly swerved the car into the mall parking lot and quickly cut the engine. He then slid his arm around the back of Stephanie's seat and took her hand. "Don't you think it's time for us to decide our future one way or the other? I do. Will you marry me, Stephanie?"

Stephanie was truly astounded by Gregory's unexpected proposal of marriage. This wasn't how or where she'd expected it to happen, but it *had* occurred. Gregory had actually asked her to marry him. She was more than ready to give her answer, but she couldn't seem to find her voice. This was an amazing moment and she felt rather overwhelmed by it. It was surprising to her that he seemed so calm since she was anything but.

Gregory leaned over and kissed her gently on the lips. "The look in your eyes is telling me 'yes,' but the silence of your lips has me confused. Think I can get an answer to my question? I do know I want to marry you, you know."

Stephanie choked back a jagged sob. "Yes, Gregory," she cried excitedly, "yes, I'll marry you! I love you so much."

Gregory was grinning from ear to ear; his arrow-straight teeth gleaming like a brilliant flash of white lightning. "Now, that's exactly what I wanted to hear, sweetheart." He gently squeezed her waist. "Let's start making wedding plans. I'm not interested in any long-drawn-out engagement. I want us to marry right away."

Stephanie gulped hard at Gregory's last remark. "Right away" sounded a bit scary.

As Stephanie and Gregory walked the long corridors inside the huge mall complex, it was hard for her to keep her mind off Gregory's unexpected proposal of marriage. She still had butterflies flitting all about in her stomach. She was as nervous as she was happy—and she couldn't wait to share the wonderful news with her brother, father and uncle. Where they would live still had to be decided upon, but they'd settle that mega issue in due time.

A beautiful bourbon-colored leather sofa and matching chair suddenly caught Stephanie's eye, allowing her to indulge her mind in something other than her engagement. She thought the furniture would look nice in her family room, but she really didn't have enough space for it. Though each of their homes were of adequate size, Stephanie couldn't help wondering if she and Gregory would purchase a bigger one after they got married. She'd really like to have a brand-new house to furnish and decorate lavishly, one she could call her dream home. What fun that would be for her and Gregory to check out model homes together, Stephanie mused.

Gregory grabbed Stephanie's hand and steered her down one of the hallways, not stopping until they reached a reputable jewelry store, where he pointed out the array of diamond jewels in the showcase window. "Does anything in there tickle your fancy?"

Stephanie gasped in awe. "So many beautiful gems to choose from," she breathed. She then laughed. "Look at how many designs the rings come in. I rather like the brilliant cut. The radiant cut is stunning, too. Wow! If I had to choose right now, I'd have a hard time making up my mind." Then she spotted the emerald-shape diamond, which nearly took her breath away.

Gregory stepped up behind Stephanie and wrapped his arms around her waist. "The good news, sweetheart, is that you don't have to choose right now. This can be just the beginning of our search for the perfect diamond. I want your gemstone to sparkle with fiery brilliance, just like your eyes do whenever you look at me."

"Gosh, that was so sweet." Her eyes filled with tears, and she swallowed her fear. "Since I like them all, I guess I'm in big trouble. I'm glad we're going to broaden our search to other jewelers. I'm really excited, Gregory. What about you? Are you as excited as I am?"

"Every bit as much as you are, my love. Our love is a miracle from God. There are a lot of things we have to decide on, but the last thing I want you to feel is rushed. Sound decisions take time, and we have lots of that. I don't relish a long engagement, but I do want everything perfect. Perhaps we could have a double wedding with Stephen and Darcy. Would you like that, Stephanie? I think it would be awesome."

Stephanie was glad that Gregory was okay with not rushing into this marriage, and her eyes lit up. "I can't tell you how many times Stephen and I have discussed that very topic. It would be awesome, but only if Darcy will be a willing participant. I don't want to push her into anything. That wouldn't be good for any of us."

Gregory nodded. "I understand what you mean. You two may have totally different ideas on how you'd want your wedding to be conducted. I can see some problems arising from that."

Stephanie nodded in agreement. "You may be right. However, I'll be content in letting them bring up the idea of a double wedding. If it doesn't come up, so be it. You and I are still going to have our dream day." She kissed him softly on the mouth to reconfirm her commitment.

Basking in the warmth of Stephanie's love, Gregory's heart began to take flight.

Stephen looked very troubled as he stared hard at Darcella. He couldn't believe the things she'd just said. After him asking what was going on with her and Stephanie, she preceded to tell him that his sister was obviously jealous of her—and that she didn't feel Stephanie was at all very happy about their engagement. Darcella had gone on to say that she wasn't going to allow anyone to come between them, especially his twin sister.

Stephen knew that he had to approach this topic with serious caution. He'd never seen Darcella so emphatic about anything, nor did he like this negative attitude she'd posed. No one could ever make him believe that his twin was anything but ecstatic for him. She was in fact the one who told him he was committing a serious infraction by not making a deeper commitment to the woman he'd been seeing for over two years. It was his sister who had convinced him that he should consider taking his relationship to the next level. Only after giving Stephanie's comments a lot of thought had he come to the conclusion that she was absolutely right about everything.

Had he come to the wrong conclusion in getting engaged, and with perhaps the wrong woman? Stephen had to wonder. Warring emotions arose in him. As doubt began to settle into his heart, the icy daggers coursing through his body caused him to tremble from within. It had become obvious to him that he might need to reassess his relationship with Darcella. That pained him to no end, since he'd been so sure that he'd chosen the right woman for his bride.

After a few seconds more of thought, Stephen thought it best not to get any further into this subject right now. He felt that he needed to take some time out, step back and closely observe their relationship in the upcoming days.

For Stephen Trudeaux marriage was a lifetime commitment.

As Darcella continue to sit there in a huffy state, puffing and blowing hot air, she had no earthly idea what doubt she had just placed in the heart of the man she confessed to love. If Stephen thought she was going to play second fiddle to his twin sibling, he had a lot to learn about her. Darcella silently vowed that she'd come in second to no one. She'd already waited too long for Stephen to ask her to marry him, so she'd be darned if she didn't make her intentions clear to him from this point on.

Chapter 3

The rain was falling hard, but the heavy precipitation banging loudly against the windowpanes in Stephanie's bedroom was very soothing to her. It was times like these that she really missed seeing Gregory every single day. Sometimes it felt like an eternity had occurred in between their visits. If he were there, they'd cuddle together and enjoy God's cleansing of the earth. With all the rainfall Houston and New Orleans received, they'd had numerous times to share in the serenity of the rainstorms, although there were times when it was frightening. The unpredictability of hurricane season was upon them and no one ever knew just what to expect.

Stephanie couldn't help thinking of how great their relationship was going. Being engaged to a man of God, even in the absence of a ring or an official announcement to the family, was something she'd always dreamed about. Although his proposal of marriage had come right out of the blue sky, she eagerly looked so forward to the day she'd become Mrs. Gregory Saxton III. Stephanie was in no doubt that she'd make him a wonderful wife, since she and Gregory were definitely evenly yoked. Their love for God was the most important element of their relationship and she truly believed it would carry them far into the future. When God was the head of a household, as well as each of the married couple's individual lives, success in holy matrimony was highly achievable. Stephanie could never forget the things her mother had said.

While the issue of where they'd actually live had yet to be settled, Stephanie was very open to living in New Orleans. She'd absolutely fallen in love with the city and its rich history. She was always eager to make that flight to Louisiana when it was her turn to visit Gregory. Staying in her father's home and spending time with him and her uncle Maxwell were also special highlights of her frequent trips to the Big Easy.

Stephanie no longer felt like a guest in Malachi's home. Her precious father's place was now her extremely comfortable home-away-from-home. And now that Stephen had talked of seriously considering taking over the reins of the corporation, she might not have to be separated from her loving brother. She couldn't imagine living in a different city from him, but Houston and New Orleans were close enough for them to maintain reasonable visitations.

Stephanie's evenings spent with Gregory in New Orleans, especially when they hung out down in the French Quarter, were always utterly amazing to her. Her fiancé was a man of God, a Bible scholar, a true gentleman and a hopelessly wonderful romantic. Stephanie loved Gregory as she loved herself, the same as he loved her, yet God would always be first in each of their lives. Their holy union would be built on the most solid rock of all, not on sinking sand.

Upon hearing the doorbell ringing, Stephanie jumped out of bed, grabbing her robe in the midst of her flight toward the front of the house. As she looked into the tiny viewing screen, she smiled broadly at seeing her dear friend and part-time accountant Farrah Freeman standing there.

Stephanie opened the door wide. "Hey, girl, come on in

and get warmed up. It's so wet out there. It's been a while for us outside of work."

Farrah hugged Stephanie warmly, her nut-brown complexion glowing. She then quickly stripped out of her vinyl raincoat. "It's been too long. I'm jealous of all the time you spend with that fine Muhammad Ali look-alike of yours. You've been so hard to catch up with lately."

Farrah was a slender, sleek and sassy woman, with an amazing riot of reddish-brown curls. Her sense of humor was often off the hook, but it was one of her most endearing qualities. She was also a full-time physical therapist. As she plopped down on the sofa, she patted the cushion beside her in a gesture for Stephanie to sit down next to her.

Before Stephanie could take a seat, the doorbell rang once, then the door opened up. Seeing Stephen coming through the entry caused Stephanie to rush into his arms for a warm hug. The two siblings embraced for several seconds, while Farrah was busy fidgeting all over the place. The sight of Stephen always affected her that way. The man was *it* for her. He'd always been the man of her dreams, but unfortunately, the feelings had never once been mutual.

Stephen took a seat. Much to Farrah's pleasure, he had seated himself on the sofa before his sister could claim her seat. As he acknowledged Farrah with a soft hello and a bright smile, she thought she had died and gone to heaven. The brother was *wearing* that denim jeans outfit.

Eyeing Stephen with open curiosity, Stephanie quickly opted for the large easy chair, which faced the sofa. "What brings you out here in the heavy rain? Something must be up, since you normally call before dropping in." Stephanie could see the stress lines around her brother's eyes. That bothered her because she knew it meant that he was deeply troubled by something. She had a very good idea of what that something might be, yet she hoped she was dead wrong.

Stephen hunched his broad shoulders. "Just checking in on you." Stephen desperately needed to talk to his twin about the troubling situation with Darcella, but once he saw that she had company he knew it would have to wait a bit.

Farrah practically leaped to her feet. "I should go and let you and Stephen talk. I don't want to intrude. I'm like you, Stephanie. I think your brother is here for a specific reason."

From his numerous conversations with his sister, and from their youth, Stephen almost knew Farrah as well as Stephanie did, although they hadn't been in each other's company for a long time. Farrah had been a downright nuisance to him in his teenage years because she had always hung around him looking for attention. He had paid her no mind back then, but there was something different about her today. He couldn't help giving her a covert once-over.

Stephen chuckled again. "You do not have to leave, Miss Farrah. I'm cool. Stephanie and I talk every single day, numerous times. Tomorrow will be no different." He gave Farrah a boyish grin. "And pray tell, what makes you think you have a clue about why I'm here?"

Farrah looked totally embarrassed. "Well, I really don't know why you're here, Stephen, but I sensed an urgency in you. Forgive me for being too forward." Without any further prompting from anyone, Farrah retook her seat, happy to do so. Being in the company of Stephen no doubt would be exhilarating for however short or long it lasted.

Stephen smiled in Stephanie's direction. "Your big brother is starving. Did you cook today? I'm in need of some serious vittles."

Stephanie shook her head in the negative. "I'm afraid not. Why do you always pass all those fast-food places on the way here and not stop and get yourself something to eat? You know I don't cook that often, unless you call and ask me to."

"'Cause I didn't want any fast food. You got something in the kitchen I can rustle up real quick? I want some grub that'll stick to my ribs."

Farrah got to her feet again. "I fixed this amazing ravioli

casserole which I haven't even touched yet. I also tossed a huge salad and grilled a few boneless chicken breasts. I'll run next door and get everything. I took the food out of the oven just before I popped over here."

Stephen rubbed his stomach as he stood. "I'll go with you and help you carry the meal over here. That sounds like a mighty heavy package for such a dainty woman to be packing. I hope you got some French or sourdough bread to go with the ravioli. I'm really hungry."

"You're in luck. I do have some," Farrah responded with a huge grin.

Stephanie's mouth was agape as she watched Stephen and Farrah dash out her front door. If she didn't know better, she would think her brother had been openly flirting with Farrah. Stephen had had some nerve, she mused. She'd never seen him this animated around Farrah, but then again, rarely were the three of them together in one place. Stephanie figured her girlfriend was in seventh heaven by now, but she hoped she hadn't read too much into her twin's actions. The boy was only hungry. *Or was it something more than that?* "No, not a chance."

After all the food was laid out, ready for consumption, Farrah seated herself right next to Stephen at Stephanie's dinner table. Stephen then said a blessing over the food.

Once Stephen bit into one of the chicken breasts, he closed his eyes. "Girl, you *can* throw down. The meat is really tender." Then he popped a piece of ravioli into his mouth. "This ain't half bad, sister. You got skills, girl."

Farrah blushed. "Oh, stop it! You know you're lying."

Stephanie was amused by her brother's comments, but more amused by Farrah's reaction.

For the next half hour Stephanie's head turned between Stephen and Farrah, who were chatting up a breeze. Her brother could barely chew his food for talking so much. When Farrah announced that she had to leave to go and check on her mother, Stephanie thought that Stephen actually looked very disappointed to see her best friend go.

Grinning broadly and blowing kisses all the while, Farrah backed her way out of the room until she reached the exit. Stephen continued to smile and wave at her playfully until she disappeared from his sight.

The moment the front door closed shut, Stephanie dramatically rolled her eyes at Stephen. She continued to stare openly at him without saying a word.

Stephen looked nonplussed. "What?"

Stephanie glared hard at him. "You already know what! What's up with you being so flirtatious with my best friend? You were a maniac at dinner. You're practically a married man."

Looking slightly off kilter, Stephen shrugged. "Yeah, huh, I know. The fact that it felt so good really bothers me. Farrah's a riot, easy to like."

Stephanie gently sucked her teeth. "Please be careful with Farrah. I don't want her to misinterpret a thing. She would be drawing the wrong conclusions about your intentions, wouldn't she? She still has that same mean crush on you from way back in the day."

"After all these years?" Stephen appeared stunned. Then he felt himself smiling within.

On an unexpected rush of sympathy over Farrah's deep feelings for Stephen, Stephanie nodded. "Yep. After all these years you're still the man of her dreams."

"Wow! That's kind of amazing and flattering." Stephen shook his head from side to side. "I can't believe how much Darcy has changed, practically overnight. The girl's been tripping hard. After you tell me what went down between you two, I'll fill you in on all the drama we're having. That's the real reason I dropped in here unannounced. I needed to talk to you badly."

No signs of shock or surprise crossed Stephanie's face as she and Stephen moved into the family room. Though she had almost been sure of his reason for coming by, she refrained from saying she'd already figured out as much. Stephen listened intently as his sister told him the details of her ugly encounter with Darcella.

After Stephen pummeled one of the loose sofa pillows, he got up from the sofa and began pacing the floor. "Is this what happens when a brother puts a diamond on a sister's finger? I'd hate to think that's it, but I can't make hide nor hair of this crazy situation. How's she going to tell me how it's going to be where my family's concerned? I'm not trying to hear that garbage from her. Loving her doesn't mean I have to choose between her and you or anyone else. It's just not going down like that. Blood is always thicker than water."

Stephanie encouraged Stephen to sit back down. He quickly complied. "I think you two can work this out. You've been together too long not to try. Maybe she's just having anxiety attacks over a few things. You *have* been talking about a possible move to New Orleans. That may have also set her teeth on edge. You need to give her a chance to come around, Stephen. Give her every benefit of the doubt. All is not lost."

"It is if she expects me to act any differently toward you. You're not only my sister, you're my twin. We shared the same womb for nine months. You don't get any closer than that."

Stephanie nodded in agreement. "That's true, but God gave specific instructions on how man should leave his family and cleave unto his wife. A wife should always have top billing."

"And she will! She can be the main star of the show, but not the only one. It's always been just you and me. Now we have Dad and Uncle Max. So who'll be the next one on Darcy's hit list if I give into her demands about you?"

Stephanie's eyes grew wide and bright with surprise. "Are you saying you've already given up on you and Darcy?"

Stephen shoved a nervous hand through his hair. "No, I'm

not. I just know what I'll put up with and what I won't. She has no reason to be jealous of you. She's acting like you're a lover of mine. You're my flesh and blood, for God's sake! She has that ring on her finger because of the things you discussed candidly with me about relationships, the things you made me see."

Stephanie saw big trouble in that statement. The things she'd pointed out to him were the wrong reasons for Stephen to have gotten himself engaged. Marriage was about love and commitment. Seeing the light was one thing, but deciding to get married because of it was ludicrous, not unless the chosen one was actually *the one*. Stephanie scowled hard. "I have issues with your last remarks. If you mean to tell me you're marrying Darcy based on the things I said, and not because of how you feel about her, your relationship *is* in big trouble."

Stephen palmed his forehead. "I know how I feel about the woman I thought Darcy was. But I don't even know this weird character that recently showed up. A mean spirit has to reside inside her for her to say some of the things she said. Why I haven't seen this side of her before now is a mystery to me. She has always been so darn sweet and accommodating."

Stephanie exhaled rather loudly. "New challenges have arisen in each of your lives, Stephen, major ones. Marriage is a big step no matter how sure you think you are."

"So, if Gregory were to ask you to marry him, you think you'd turn evil on him like Darcy has turned on me? I don't think so!"

Stephanie couldn't help smiling all over herself. This wasn't the best time to announce her engagement to Gregory, but how could she not when her heart was bursting open with the good news? She was surprised her brother hadn't already read the truth in her eyes.

Stephen looked utterly amazed. "He's already asked you, hasn't he?" Before Stephanie could respond, her brother had her in his arms, sincerely congratulating her as he hugged her tightly. He once again had read her perfectly. "You *did* say yes to his proposal, didn't you?"

Stephanie's eyes sparkled like diamonds. "My heart said *yes,* and my total body and soul are in sync with my decision. Gregory is everything I've ever wanted in a man."

Stephen kissed both of Stephanie's cheeks before he released her. He then looked down at her finger. "Where's the bling, girl?"

Stephanie blushed. "We're still in search of the perfect gem, dear brother."

"Ah, yes, the perfect jewel for the near perfect woman, my twin sister. You know I have to interrogate the boy and then read him his rights before I agree to give you away."

Stephanie kissed his cheek. "I wouldn't have expected anything less." Stephanie bit down on her lower lip as she thought about her father, who'd surely want the honor of giving her away. She then looked up at Stephen and smiled. "I was thinking about Dad's role in my wedding. What do you think?"

Stephen knew exactly why his sister has asked that particular question. "We'll both give you away. I'd never take that privilege from him—and I'm sure he'll understand why I also plan to walk you down the aisle. How many women get two fine black brothers to escort them down to their awaiting Prince Charming? Girl, you're so blessed."

Stephanie hugged Stephen. "I know, huh. Now, let's get back to your situation."

Stephen shook his head in the negative. "No more on that subject right now. I'll eventually get it all figured out. I want to leave here feeling darn good, just as I do right now. Your engagement to Saxton has put me on a cloud, darling angel."

Stephen got up to take his leave. As he stuck his hand in the pocket of his jacket, he felt a piece of paper that he knew hadn't been there before. He quickly pulled it out to explore it. His eyes lit up like fire when he realized Farrah had slipped him her home, work and cell numbers.

Even as he thought of his sister's warning to him about her best friend, he couldn't help how good he felt deep down inside. He'd never use Farrah or hurt her, but she just might be the right prescription to aid in what ailed him. He needed an unbiased friend right now. The girl sure knew how to make a person laugh. Why he hadn't ever paid any close attention to her bubbling personality completely eluded him. And she definitely knew her way around in the kitchen. Her food was the closest he'd ever come to tasting something just as good as his mama's cooking.

As Stephen drove along to his destination, his thoughts were chaotic. He half hoped Darcella wouldn't be at home when he got there so he could put off this confrontation one more day. Strange feelings had a hold of him and he wasn't sure how to shake them. Seeing his father for the first time ever, after twenty-eight years, was the only other personal thing that had had him so unsettled. He'd been through countless fires, but even those involving tragic circumstances hadn't produced the kind of turbulence going on inside of him right now.

Get a grip, he silently commanded himself. "You're much tougher than this. A man not only knows when he has to handle his business, he knows how to handle it. Just lay down the law. Your family is your family; anyone who loves you will have to take them as they are, or just up and leave. There can be no compromises in this area. Darcy can be the first lady in my life, but she has to understand that my first family also mean everything to me."

Stephen's heart raced a little as a vision of Farrah suddenly popped into his mind. *How strange was that?* That disturbing incident caused him to make a quick U-turn and head toward home. Perhaps he had a lot more thinking to do, especially before he got into a showdown with Darcella. The thought that he needed to know more about what God expected of folks involved in personal relationships came as a total surprise to him. He needed to read for himself exactly what God had to say on the subject of love and marriage. That was the only way he'd find out. Perhaps what Stephanie had had to say about God and His theory on marriage had awakened a sleeping giant within him.

After loosening the belt on her robe, Stephanie slipped into bed and plumped the pillows before resting her head. Turning her thoughts on her wedding plans would be a nice diversion from worrying about Stephen and Darcella, which was something she had no control over.

The very idea of her, Stephen and Farrah having dinner together had disturbed Stephanie both during and after the meal. She couldn't help wondering how that would've made Darcella feel had she suddenly popped in for a visit, though she'd never come to Stephanie's house without calling first. It had been innocent enough, at least she thought so, but Darcella may've read something entirely different into it.

Stephanie had made a vow that she would not be a part of any duplicity on Stephen's part, but it was so hard for her to deny the attraction and affection she'd witnessed blossoming between her twin and her best friend. If Stephen and Farrah suddenly decided to hang out together, it would not occur in her home.

Stephanie finally turned her thoughts to her wedding, since she really didn't like dwelling on any negative stuff. She was about to start a new life with a wonderful man and she thought that he should be the center of her attention.

So far Stephanie and Gregory hadn't discussed anything to do with their upcoming nuptials, but she hoped he'd agree to a small, intimate wedding with just their families and close friends. She wasn't up for dealing with all the hoopla of a big wedding. She may've felt differently about the size of her wedding had her mother been there to help oversee all the dozens and dozens of intricate details.

Stephanie just wanted to marry her man and ride off with him to the airport in a shiny white stretch limo. A cruise would make a nice getaway for their honeymoon, but the idea of them lazing together under the Caribbean sun on a Jamaican beach was also very appealing. Heaven was just around the corner, Stephanie mused, waiting for the newly-weds, Mr. and Mrs. Gregory Saxton III, to make their grand entry.

As Stephanie reached over to turn off the nightstand light, she couldn't help smiling at Gregory's picture. Her man was as handsome as they came, yet it was his pureness of spirit that turned her on. She'd never met anyone sweeter than Gregory Saxton. He aimed to please her and she wanted only to return the favor. They were very happy together.

While Stephanie didn't expect them not to have differences from time to time, she was sure they'd always be respectful toward each other. Those boundaries had been clearly defined from day one and would be enforced until in death did they part.

The phone suddenly buzzed in Stephanie's ear. She thought of not answering it until Gregory came to mind. She was feeling very drowsy and wanted nothing more than to slip into the sweet arms of peace, but she loved to hear Gregory's voice just before falling asleep.

"Sorry if I awakened you."

Stephanie heard the sincere regret in Gregory's voice. "I wasn't asleep yet, but I'm ready for it. Did you feel my thoughts of you?"

Gregory chuckled. "I'm sure of it. The urge to call you has been overwhelming me for the past hour or so. Now that I've heard your sweet voice, I'm going to say I love you and good night. Until tomorrow, my love."

A huge grin covered Stephanie's face as she hung up the phone and then slid down under the comforter. "Good night, Gregory. I love you, too," she whispered into the still of the night.

* * *

Gregory held the phone to his ear a few seconds longer before cradling the receiver. It was as if he could still hear Stephanie softly breathing. He loved talking to her, which they often did up until the wee hours in the morning, but more so on the weekends. Their conversations usually ended by eleven o'clock on the weeknights. The workday dictated that.

Gregory was so grateful that God had blessed him with Stephanie. Her pureness of heart never failed to captivate and enchant him. She was a very kindhearted person, giving freely of herself and her many talents. He'd only met a few of her clients, but they'd all sung high praises for her. Her elderly friends thought of her as a daughter and her peer group likened her to a sister. Gregory hadn't heard one bad thing about her other than from her. Stephanie never hesitated in pointing out her numerous flaws to him. Being highly aware of who she was, she knew all of her strengths and constantly worked on her host of easily identifiable weaknesses.

As Gregory's thoughts turned to his mother, he frowned slightly. He often attempted to match up her character against Stephanie's, or do comparisons between the two women. The only likeness between Stephanie and Aretha Saxton was their outer beauty. Although he loved his mother dearly, he detested what she'd done to his father. The relationship between his and Stephanie's parents was another thing the couple had in common. His mother had left her family behind just as the twins had believed their father had done until the truth had come out.

Deciding whether or not to meet his mother over lunch later in the week had Gregory feeling a little shaky. Of course he saw his mother often and rarely failed to call her at least once a day, but this meeting was to be something different. Aretha was trying to gain her son as an ally in getting her husband, Gregory II, to take her back. Because Grant had always been under his mother's thumb, she'd had no problem in convincing him to help her out.

Betraying his father wasn't something Gregory had ever indulged himself in. Aretha had left of her own accord and he thought she should work solo to try to get herself back in, just as she'd done in walking out. His father had been devastated when she'd deserted him, but the devastation had tripled after he'd learned that Aretha had left him for a much younger man.

The man Aretha had run off into the sunset with was only a few years older than Grant, her eldest son. Gregory II's manhood had been severely tested by his wife's unscrupulous move. There was no doubt in Gregory's mind that his father still loved his mother; he'd heard him confess it enough times, but he didn't think his father foolish enough to take her back. But then again, Gregory wasn't so sure.

Love could make women and men do some of the strangest, craziest things.

Gregory then thought of Grant. His brother had been hit the hardest by Aretha's fleeing the nest. He'd counted on her for so many things. Though Grant was the eldest son, he was by far the weakest, which Gregory hated to admit. Aretha had made Grant so dependent on her that he hadn't been able to make the simplest decision without first seeking her advice and approval.

Unable to see his mother every day had caused Grant to withdraw into himself, leaving him vulnerable to all sorts of vices. Despite being an adult, Grant had still been living at home when Aretha had first taken leave. Now thirty-four years old, Grant had been living in his own place for only a few months.

Gregory II had allowed Grant to stay on in the family home because he knew how emotionally crippled Aretha had made their son. Grant also worked on special projects in his father's law practice, those that their father would assign to him. He was paid a generous salary, but Grant normally wasted most of his earnings on wining and dining the fairer sex.

Gregory couldn't help wondering what he'd say to his mother if he went to lunch with her. He'd often wanted to tell her how wrong he thought she was to leave her family behind, but he wasn't sure it was his place to do so. It certainly wasn't his place to judge her, yet he had done just that at one time, harshly so. His anger at his mother had once been out of control. He'd also felt embarrassed and ashamed of her since everyone in the church and community had known about her adulterous affair. It hadn't been enough for her just to have an affair; she'd run off with the guy like some rebellious teenager. Although the odd couple was no longer living together, according to what Aretha had recently told Gregory, the horrific shame and pain that had been brought on the prominent Saxton family couldn't ever be eradicated.

Since Gregory knew that he had a long court day ahead of him, he reached over and turned off the bedside lamp. A smile in his heart for Stephanie came next. Then, there, in the silence of the night, Gregory silently prayed to his God to provide him with the course of action to take in this sticky situation with his mother.

Stretched out on the leather sofa in his den, wearing navy-blue silk pajamas and matching robe, Stephen looked pretty relaxed as he perused scriptures from the Bible. Learning about what God had in mind for personal relationships and family was now his main objective. He'd heard a lot of things from his mother and sister on the subject, but he now needed a refresher course. Thinking it was the best place for him to start, Stephen had turned to Genesis.

And the Lord said, "It is not good that man should be alone. I will make him a helper comparable to him." Genesis 2:18. Companionship was one of the first purposes of the family. In the Garden of Eden God had miraculously formed the first family by putting Adam into a deep sleep, then taking one of his ribs, and closing up the flesh in its place. With Adam's rib God made Eve. And Adam said, "This is now bone of my bones and flesh of my flesh; she shall be called woman because she was taken out of man." Genesis 2:22–23.

After reading about how man and woman were created by God, Stephen then began to read about the Creator uniting in marriage the first man and first woman.

Stephen first closed the Bible and then his weary eyes. As he pondered all that he'd read, he felt as though God couldn't have been any plainer in his intent for personal relationships and family. *Could he be all that God intended him to be as a husband and a father?* If he followed the blueprint God had laid out, he felt that he could. He'd heard all too often that a wife and children didn't come with operating instructions; he could beg to differ now that he'd reread these things for himself. Stephen definitely had gotten a much better understanding of it this time around.

Although Stephen often attended church, he knew there was room for improvement. Many of the firefighters at his station during downtimes sat around and discussed the Bible. There were just as many firefighters who had absolutely nothing to say on the topic of God or religion, but that didn't necessarily mean they didn't believe in Him.

A lot of people were reluctant to get into religious discussions. Stephen was one of them. He always thought of it as a no-win situation, especially when one didn't agree with what was being said. He had actually seen those types of discussions escalate into huge, angry arguments. It seemed to him that no one was going to change their minds on whatever they believed in or didn't believe, so it was all so futile. Then there were some people that just needed to be right.

Once Stephanie poured into mugs two cups of steaming hot coffee, she carefully carried them over to her kitchen table, where Darcella anxiously waited for her. Stephanie was still disturbed by what had gone down between the two of them and she wanted to bring it to a close once and for all. After setting down the mugs, she retrieved the shortbread cookies she'd baked in the early morning hours, after she'd awakened and couldn't get back to sleep.

Stephanie took the seat directly across from Darcella. She collected her thoughts as she prepared her coffee to her liking, one hazel-nut cream and two packets of Splenda. After taking a small sip of the hot brew, she made direct eye contact with Darcella. "I'm guessing that you have a pretty good idea of why I asked you here."

Darcella nodded, hating how nervous she felt. "I think I do. Things have been a little rocky between us, huh?"

"I think that's a safe analysis." Stephanie smiled softly. "I don't know how all this began, or even why, but I'd like to see it end today, right now. I care a lot about you and I've been very respectful to the relationship between you and my brother. Can you tell me what went wrong?"

Looking down into her mug, Darcella nervously stirred the dark liquid around and around with her spoon. Although she'd known this showdown was imminent, she still didn't feel wholly prepared for it. None of this really had anything to do with Stephanie. This all had to do with her strained relationship with her own family. Darcella was disenchanted with her job as a nurse and she also felt pressure over her engagement to Stephen. "Stephanie, I'm going to start by sincerely apologizing to you. You've been very respectful and loving to me. You are not the problem."Darcella went on to explain to Stephanie the issues in her unsettling family life, things she hadn't ever really expressed to anyone before now. Not even to Stephen. As far as her fiancé knew, she came from a very happy family, which was extremely remote from the actual truth. It was easy to hide the truth from everyone since her family lived in Biloxi, Mississippi. Stephen had only been around her family twice in the past year. The Coleman family had put their best feet forward on those two weekends they'd visited them in their home.

Darcella then told Stephanie that she was one of those accidental pregnancies, which had ended in a shotgun wedding of a sort. Her parents' unhappy circumstances had been taken out on her, yet they'd gone on to have two more children, sons Daniel and David.

Darcella sighed heavily. "'If I'd never gotten pregnant with you, I wouldn't be in this unhappy marriage.' I can't tell you how many times my mother, Patsy, said that to me. It felt to me like she was saying 'if you'd never been born.' Patsy and Reginald Coleman are still together and still very unhappy. It's so sad."

Stephanie reached over and briefly covered Darcella's hand. "I'm sorry. I didn't know any of that. I'm sure it's been hard on you. Does Stephen know about your family life?"

Darcella shook her head in the negative. "Very little of it. I've sort of made him think we're one big happy family. He has no idea how strained our relationships really are. We haven't even called them since the engagement party, so I'm sure he's wondering. I hate to say this, but I don't even want my family at my wedding. I don't think I could keep everything so well hidden if they lived here in Houston. My mother couldn't even help me with my engagement party."

"Stephen *will* understand, Darcy. We're no strangers to family adversity. Look at all that has gone on with Malachi and us. The Trudeaux family has also lived with lots of personal pain."

Stephanie *was* surprised by Darcella's family revelations. She had often wondered why the Coleman family hadn't gotten together more often, but she hadn't put too much emphasis on it. As Darcella had said, it was easy for her to hide when her family lived in another state.

The two women continued to talk and talk, until both Stephanie and Darcella realized how much time had slipped away. Stephanie saw that she was really pressed for time as she looked up at the kitchen wall clock. Malachi, Maxwell and Gregory were coming in for the weekend; she had promised to have dinner ready for the guys when they arrived. Getting to the grocery store was an immediate must.

After Stephanie explained her mission to Darcella, Stephanie got to her feet. "Since Stephen is coming over to eat with the family, why don't you come back and join us for dinner? Dad and Uncle Max would love it."

As Darcella made it to her feet, she wrung her hands together, looking rather anguished. "I don't know. I'm going over to see Stephen when I leave here. He may not want me anywhere around him after I tell him everything I need to say. Can we just play it by ear for now and see how it goes between your brother and me?"

"Of course we can," Stephanie soothed, making the hard decision not to ask Darcella any questions about her pending visit to Stephen. "There'll be plenty of food for everyone if you decide to come, Darcy. We're having meat loaf and roasted red potatoes. I hope you come back."

Darcella looked hopeful. "Me, too. The menu sounds delicious."

As if drawn to each other by some magnetic force, the two women went straight into each other's warm embrace, holding each other close for several peacefully silent moments.

Darcella's arms were still around Stephanie when she pulled back slightly. 'I'm so glad we had this heart-to-heart chat. I'm feeling so much better now. Thanks for asking me over to bring everything to a close."

Stephanie brought Darcella back to her for another hug before releasing her hold. "You're welcome. I'm also glad that the air is clear. Darcy, you can always count on me. I'm here for both you and Stephen. Since your family is so far away, we'll continue to be there for you. We all feel as though you're already a part of the Trudeaux family."

Darcella smiled broadly, fighting back her tears. "Family

indeed. Thanks. I really needed to hear that, Stephanie. I've decided to come back for dinner. Since Stephen isn't aware that I'm dropping in on him, I can wait until later to see him and tell him what I have to say to him."

Stephanie looked pleased. "Great. I'll look for you around five-thirty or so."

Nothing else needed to be said between Stephanie and Darcella. The open-and-honest conversation, loving affection and understanding had said it all, healing wounded hearts while restoring their amicable relationship in the process.

Darcella felt so upset and confused that she had to pull her car over and park it. Glad that she was already a few blocks away from Stephanie's place, she sighed with relief. There were so many things keeping her off kilter. She'd had a chance to spill all her guts to Stephanie, but she hadn't since she was her fiancé's sister. When she'd told Stephanie that she was sorry about her attitude, she'd meant it, but there was so much she hadn't told her future sister-in-law.

Marrying Stephen was the one thing she wanted the most, but she was now having second thoughts. Where had all these sudden fears come from? Darcella laughed at her stupid question. Her fears, in one form or another, had been there as far back as she could remember.

Darcella had ended two other meaningful relationships when it looked as if facing the altar was only a few feet away. She never wanted to live as unhappily as her parents had. Patsy and Reginald were downright miserable with each other. She couldn't remember the last time her mother and father had cast a loving smile in the other one's direction. Laughter was practically nonexistent in the Coleman household. The only time her parents enjoyed a laugh was when something incredibly funny was on television.

Playing into her fears was easy for Darcella because they were so real. It seemed to her that once people settled down into marriage they stopped doing the wonderful things that got them to the altar in the first place. That theory didn't include her parents since they were unhappy before marriage, yet it was often the norm and not the exception in other marriages.

The kissing and hugging had a way of stopping all too soon with married couples. The intimate eye contact and nonverbal messages that spoke volumes between lovers abruptly ended. Frowns of dismay often replaced warm smiles of encouragement. She'd heard so much about failed marriages from female coworkers who trusted her enough to share their painful stories.

Patsy and Reginald had dated and had also had an intimate relationship. However, the unwanted pregnancy had ended their dreams and aspirations. The lives of her parents had drastically changed in a twinkling of an eye. *If only you hadn't been born...* The one sentence that would forever remained unfinished in Darcella's head.

Stephen wanting children right away was another big problem for Darcella. Why hadn't she told him the truth from the very beginning, when the subject had first come up, that she wasn't keen on having kids? Now that she'd led him to believe otherwise, she didn't know how to tell him the truth. Stephen would be terribly hurt, but he deserved to know how she felt.

Darcella quickly decided she'd tell Stephen everything after Stephanie's dinner party.

The biggest fear of all for Darcella was that she'd come to resent her child, just as her mother had resented the birth of her daughter. How could she have kids when she knew nothing about what it meant to be a mother? She certainly didn't have a role model in defining motherly love. Telling Stephen the truth was a must.

Well, that wasn't totally true, Darcella mused, wrapping her mind around the truth.

Patsy was a real doting mom to her sons, but even then her love for them was conditional. As long as David and Daniel catered to their mother's every need, they were great sons. The minute they crossed Patsy she labeled them as heathens, but she still managed to lead them around on leashes. Darcella believed that her two brothers would make lousy husbands if they didn't grow backbones before marrying.

Losing Stephen was just as scary to Darcella as getting married and having children. He was her best friend even if his sister held that position over her in his life. She often compared Stephen's relationship with his sister to the troubling one she had with her mother. Darcella wanted to be close to her mother, like mother and daughter should be, but Patsy's world revolved around David and Daniel. Her mother's best friends were her sons, not her husband or daughter.

As much as Stephen desired children, Darcella feared he'd turn all his attention to the kids and leave her out of the family equation. Having no real place in the family was a position she was used to, but one that she positively hated. Darcella never doubted how much she loved Stephen. Love wasn't always enough, though. If marrying Stephen were a guarantee that she'd always come first with him, she'd marry him in a heartbeat.

Life held no such guarantee. At least not for one Darcella Coleman.

Sweat poured heavily from Stephen's face. His body was soaked under his heavily padded clothing. The heat from the fire felt as if it was scorching his eyebrows as he tried to find his way through the burning house. The smoke was so thick he could barely see his hand in front of his face. Smoke stung his eyes badly, causing them to tear up. His hands were too sooty to put up to his eyes to wipe away the moisture.

"Help," he heard a little voice call out. "Please help us!"

Stephen made his way toward the sound of the distraught pleas, struggling to see his way.

Flames charged him as he reached the end of the hallway,

causing him to back up several steps. Then the door a few feet away from where he stood flew open. Standing there were two little girls who were an exact replica of each other. Tears filled their eyes as they reached out to him, crying out for him to pick them up and carry them to safety. The girls practically jumped into his arms as he bent down to scoop them up.

Resembling fields of fire, flames were all around them, licking and taunting ferociously, threatening to devour their very existence. Then a thin path of escape suddenly appeared, parting like the Red Sea, allowing them to walk out of the house unscathed.

Once Stephen and the little Anderson girls made it outside, he hugged them to him with all his might. He then fell down on his knees and began to pray, crying out in anguish, thanking God for sparing their lives, and for giving him another opportunity to get his life right.

Stephen sat straight up in the bed, a wild and crazed look in his eyes. Darkness was all around him, frightening him something awful, until he realized he was in his own bedroom, safe and sound. Once he realized he'd been trapped in a horrific nightmare, he began to sob uncontrollably. If only his dream had become a reality. That he hadn't been able to save the little twin girls, Kelly and Karla, had him sick with grief. This was the greatest personal loss of his entire career as a firefighter. Stephen knew he had to forgive himself, but he didn't know how he'd ever manage such an impossible feat. Forgiving oneself was the hardest task of all.

Chapter 4

The Trudeaux family and all their guests, including Farrah, had thoroughly enjoyed Stephanie's meat loaf, roasted red potatoes and the buttery steamed vegetable medley. Gregory was especially pleased by the delectable dinner his fiancée had prepared. Even though he was a great cook he was happy that Stephanie could hold her own against some of the very best chefs.

Much to everyone's surprise, including Gregory's, his father and brother had come to Houston with him, but Gregory II and Grant had driven a different vehicle. They were to all stay at the airport Hilton in separate rooms. Gregory had mentioned to his father and brother that he planned to officially announce his engagement to Stephanie during this visit. With his son taking such a serious and important step in life, Gregory II wasn't about to miss out on it. That Grant had asked to come along for the ride had been a pleasant shocker to both Gregory II and III.

Gregory II was a tall, sophisticated man, who possessed warm brown eyes and a head full of wavy silver hair. He carried himself in a dignified manner, and Stephanie could only imagine what a powerful presence he exuded in the courtroom when presenting a case. Grant looked a lot like his father, though a much younger version, but he resembled his only brother even more.

All three Saxton men were extremely handsome, but Stephanie was biased. Gregory III was the best-looking man of all and his spirit was so pure. She'd been around the elder Saxton enough to know that he was a good man, a great father and he loved the Lord. Grant, on the other hand, was still trying to find himself. His restless spirit had finally called him into accountability. He was even attending church on a regular basis.

The doorbell rang just as Stephanie got to her feet to retrieve the lemon meringue pie she'd purchased at the local bakery. Baking wasn't her strong suit, but she knew how to whip up a few tasty desserts, especially cookies and cakes. She had yet to master the art of making decent piecrust. When Malachi had mentioned his love for lemon desserts, she then knew why lemon had always been her and Stephen's favorite flavor. Doreen's lemon meringue pies had always been mouth-watering delicious, the crust so flaky that it instantly dissolved in one's mouth.

Upon seeing who was at the door, Stephanie smiled broadly. It was certainly a surprise for her to see Eliza Beth Tobias and Sarah Watson on her doorstep. Eliza Beth was one of her wealthy clients and Sarah was the Tobias family's personal chef and nutritionist. Eliza Beth was married to Lemanz Tobias, a world-renowned cardiovascular surgeon.

Sarah had been a widow for more than seven years and she had also lost her only daughter to death when the girl was in her early teens. Eliza Beth and Lemanz treated Sarah extraordinarily well, claiming her as a much-loved family member. Though no blood relationship existed between them, Sarah treated Eliza Beth and Lemanz as if they were her very own children and she also played surrogate grandmother to the Tobias's one-year-old son, Lemanz II.

After Stephanie greeted the two women with warm hugs, she led them into the formal dining room, where the others were still seated around the table. Stephanie promptly introduced her family to Eliza Beth and Sarah.

"Hello, everyone," Eliza Beth said cheerfully, prompting Sarah to sit down in the only empty chair. "My friends simply call me Liza."

Stephen had just vacated his seat in order to grab a few folding chairs for the new arrivals. The last few times he and Stephanie were in the company of this many people at one time was at their mother's funeral and repast and at the holiday festivities at Malachi's. Seeing how loved his sister was gave him a warm feeling. Being together with loving family members and friends was what life was all about. Stephen reveled in the cozy scene before him.

In a matter of seconds Stephen had grabbed the chairs and returned to the dining room.

As Stephanie once again excused herself to serve dessert, Sarah handed over to her the gift-wrapped package she'd carried into the house. Stephanie had seen the medium-size parcel but hadn't really thought anything about it. "What is this, Ms. Sarah?"

Sarah smiled beautifully. "Unwrap it and see."

Stephanie began to smell delicious food scents the moment she tore off the wrapping paper. Her smile grew wide. "No, you didn't! Peach cobbler?"

Sarah chuckled. "Go ahead and open the lid, Stephanie. I want you to be surprised."

Stephanie was nearly reduced to tears as she remembered the conversation she'd had earlier with Eliza Beth about lemon flavoring being the Trudeaux family favorite. Not only was there a humongous peach cobbler in the box, Sarah had made countless dozens of tiny lemon tarts, which could only mean that Eliza Beth had mentioned their conversation to Sarah.

Stephanie hugged Sarah with one arm, carefully holding

on to the pastry box. "Thank you so much, Ms. Sarah. This is so special."

"You're mighty welcome," Sarah sang out. "When you told Liza that your family was coming into town, and that they loved lemon pastries, I got the notion to bring you some desserts. I already knew you loved my peach cobbler so I added that one, too."

Maxwell got to his feet, grinning from ear to ear. "Niece, let me take this package off your hands so you women can chat as long as you want. I'm ready for what's in the box, and I'm sure everyone else is ready. The delicious scents are killing a brother over here."

Everyone cracked up as Maxwell took the box from Stephanie and set it down on the table. He then ran out into the kitchen for the dessert plates and extra silverware. Stephen joined his uncle in the kitchen, where he went about the task of making a pot of coffee.

Eliza Beth laughed heartily. "This morning, Stephanie, after you told me about your dinner plans, I told Ms. Sarah that this might be a good time to do the desserts for you. She was only too happy to bake the goodies for your family. I hope you're not upset with us for intruding on family time. But we really wanted to meet your father and uncle."

That last statement by Eliza Beth put Stephanie on alert. Knowing that her friend was an incurable romantic and had a thing for matchmaking, Stephanie couldn't help wondering if she was trying to set Sarah up with one of the Trudeaux brothers. By the way her uncle had been eyeing Sarah, Stephanie didn't think Eliza Beth would get a chance to put her plan into action. Stephanie knew what a man's romantic interest in a woman looked like. Since Sarah was an excellent cook, that would be another major attraction for Maxwell, who loved to eat.

Another strange connection seemed to be happening, too, but Stephanie wasn't sure it was a good thing. Grant was chatting up Farrah something fierce. Farrah seemed to enjoy it. All she could do was warn her friend about Grant. But then again, he really had changed a lot, and was no longer drinking and taking drugs. Stephanie knew that Farrah was still very much into Stephen, which had pretty much kept her from moving on over the years. Stephen was engaged now so she hoped her friend would let go of her romantic notions about him.

Stephanie hugged Sarah again and she also hugged Eliza Beth. "There's nothing to be upset about. You two are welcome here any old time. It was really nice of you to drop by. Thanks a lot for the goodies. I'm going to go help out the guys in the kitchen. Be right back."

Stephanie turned and walked away. As she heard Eliza Beth say, "Gregory, it's so nice to see you again," she had to laugh. Eliza Beth had a way with most people so Stephanie wasn't worried about leaving her alone with any of the folks she didn't know. Her friend/client would do just fine on her own. *However, Sarah had better watch out for Uncle Max.*

Stephanie was pleased when she saw that Stephen had made the coffee and that Maxwell had gathered all the dessert plates and silverware. She was amazed by what families could accomplish when they worked together side by side. Seeing that her lemon meringue pies would go untouched for now, she was glad she hadn't removed them from the bakery boxes. Hoping she had enough ice cream for everyone, to go with the peach cobbler, Stephanie opened the freezer door to check. Seeing the full carton of vanilla ice cream made her smile.

"Hey, you," Gregory said, slipping up behind Stephanie. "I thought you might need some more help, but it looks like you guys have it all under control. Is there *anything* I can do?"

Stephanie smiled softly. "Please look in the center drawer and get the ice cream scoop. We're definitely going to need that."

Gregory shrugged. "No problem."

"Drats," Stephanie blurted out, "this carton of ice cream needs to go into the microwave for a minute or two. It's frozen solid."

Gregory came over and removed the cold carton from Stephanie's hands. "I can do this while you guys take all the stuff in the other room. I'll be right behind you in no time."

Fighting off the urge to kiss her man, Stephanie just nodded and smiled her approval.

Everyone was chatting away amicably when Stephanie, Stephen and Maxwell returned to the dining room with the plates, silverware and carafe of hot coffee. Seeing her guests getting along so well gave Stephanie a warm rush inside. If only Doreen were around to enjoy these type of precious moments with family and friends. She knew without a doubt that her mother would've enjoyed herself tremendously. Doreen had also loved to cook for others.

Doreen hadn't had much of a social life, but she loved meeting new people and being around the church folk on the Lord's Day and Wednesday night service. If she, Stephen and Malachi had found one another sooner, Stephanie was sure their parents would've eventually gotten back together. Their love for each other had never ceased despite the long separation.

True to his word, Gregory popped into the dining room a short time later, carrying with him the carton of ice cream and the scoop. He then assisted Stephanie in serving all her guests.

In a matter of minutes expressive moans could be heard throughout the room. Stephanie thought the peach cobbler was divine and it appeared to her that everyone else thought so, too.

"Ms. Sarah," Maxwell said, "this cobbler is downright sinful and the lemon tarts are decadent. These are the kind of delicacies that could keep a man out of heaven. Talking about forbidden fruits!"

The room filled with laughter.

"Why thank you, sir," Sarah responded in kind. "I'm thrilled that you like it."

"*Like* is not a strong enough word for what we're tasting," Malachi chimed in. "A smart businessman would see to it that you got your own pastry shop. If that's what you wanted."

Malachi discreetly bumped Maxwell in a meaningful way. Maxwell's smile let Malachi know his brother had gotten the message loud and clear.

Malachi waved his fork in the air. "I happen to love both the tarts and the cobbler."

"Me, too," came simultaneously from several of the others at the table.

The minutes flew by all too quickly for Stephanie. She loved that everyone was having such a good time in her home. However, she was concerned about Stephen and Darcella. Not much communication had occurred between them. In fact, they'd barely looked at each other.

Stephen had given Darcella a big hug and a warm smile when she'd first arrived, but that had been the extent of their physical contact. Neither of them looked comfortable in the other's presence. Had she made a big mistake by inviting Darcella to dinner without discussing it with Stephen first? She sure hoped the invitation wasn't going to be a bone of contention between her and her twin. Things were going too well within the family for that to occur now.

As Stephanie took note of the way her uncle paid special attention to Sarah, she had to smile. Maxwell was literally beaming all over. The look in his eyes was easy to discern. He was positively bowled over by the stunning lady who cared for the Tobias family. Stephanie couldn't help wondering if this might truly be a love connection, especially since Sarah seemed to be just as smitten with Maxwell.

After everyone had retreated to the family room, Stephen made his way over to where Stephanie was seated. He then sat down next to her and threw his arm loosely about her shoulders. "Are you thinking what I am? Is our uncle infatuated with Ms. Sarah?" he whispered.

Stephanie looked over at her brother and chuckled. "So it's not just the hopeless romantic in me. Uncle Max does show serious signs of being deeply infatuated. From now on we'll have to keep a close eye on him when he comes to Houston." Stephanie reached up and squeezed Stephen's fingers. "Look, he's programming something into his cell phone."

Stephen grinned. "It appears to me that she's calling out the digits to him. Uncle Max is not missing a beat, is he? The brother sure works fast."

Stephanie stifled a giggle. "Oh, I can't wait to talk to him later. That handsome Louisiana uncle of ours is interested in a Texas lady. A very beautiful one." Stephanie then looked over at Farrah and Grant, who were still deeply engrossed in conversation. "Looks like Farrah might also be besotted. She and Grant have barely come up for air since they first started talking. What kind of magic love dust is being spread all around in my house?"

Stephen groaned, causing Stephanie to look closer at him. What she saw in his eyes let her know that he didn't like Farrah being with Grant. If he was so in love with Darcella, why should he care what Farrah did? Well, she thought, she had told Stephen all the bad things she'd heard about Grant. That would make anyone concerned, but she wasn't sure that's where Stephen's concern was coming from. He seemed jealous and discomforted by what he saw.

Darcella joined Stephanie and Stephen. "What's going on here? Something private?"

Although Stephen didn't like the suspicious tone in which Darcella had posed her question, he decided to answer her, anyway. "We're just talking about Uncle Max getting his Mack on with Ms. Sarah. I think he's got the digits already."

Darcella discreetly looked over at Maxwell and Sarah. "I

see what you mean. They're certainly a striking couple. Uncle Max is single, but what about Ms. Sarah?"

"Widowed," Stephanie responded. "She has no children, either. Her daughter died at a very young age. Ms. Sarah is a sweetheart. Uncle Max couldn't do any better for himself."

Darcella sighed. "Too bad they live so far apart. Otherwise, it might work for them."

Stephen moaned his disapproval of Darcella's statement. "Stephanie and Gregory are perfect examples of long-distance love. Uncle Max has been a long-distance trucker since he was a teenager. If he's romantically interested in Ms. Sarah, the miles won't stand in his way."

"I agree," Stephanie said. "Uncle Max will find a way to see her as often as she wants. The timing couldn't be better. He'll have plenty of time now that he's retiring. We all might be jumping to the wrong conclusion about them, but I hope not. I'd love to see them get together."

Stephanie held her breath after Gregory sauntered to the center of the room and then asked for everyone's attention. He quickly summoned Stephanie to come to him by reaching his hand out to her. Smiling, Stephen helped his sister get up out of her seat. He couldn't help laughing at how his twin's legs wobbled as she made her way over to the man she loved.

Knowing that Gregory was probably going to announce their engagement had Stephanie overly excited and scared stiff, all at the same time. Her palms felt sweaty and she felt beads of perspiration forming on her forehead and upper lip. However, she couldn't be any happier. The timing couldn't be more perfect with both the Trudeaux and Saxton families present.

After kissing Stephanie gently on the mouth, Gregory wrapped his arm around her waist. He then cleared his throat. No one would've guessed that he was nervous. He appeared cool and calm. His insides were quivering, but his eyes and smile were on high beams. "Family, friends, as you all know, Stephanie and I are very much in love. So much so that we've decided to marry." Gregory laughed nervously, looking deeply into Stephanie's eyes. "I guess you can say that we're officially announcing our engagement to the ones we love and care about. I hope you'll all be happy for us." He then kissed Stephanie again and again.

In the next instant Gregory was reaching into his pocket for the purple velvet box he'd been carrying around all day. "This was picked out especially for you, my love. The perfect diamond for the woman I love like crazy." Gregory then placed the gem on her left ring finger.

Congratulations, loud clapping and approving shouts rent the air.

Stephanie did her best to hold her emotions in check, but the tears fell, anyway. "I love you, too." Her eyes were all aglow as she stared with wide-eye wonder at the magnificent emerald-cut diamond. *Brilliant* couldn't begin to describe the dazzling facets. The gemstone was also much bigger than the one she'd seen earlier, but she wasn't mad at anybody. "This *is* the perfect diamond," she gushed, pleased that he'd taken the initiative to pick out her engagement ring on his own. "And just think. I'm also blessed to have the perfect man. Thank you, Jesus!"

Malachi wiped away his tears as he made his way over to his daughter and future son-in-law. He was so pleased and happy for the newly engaged couple. He loved Stephanie and Stephen more than anything in the world—and now his precious daughter was to be united in marriage to Gregory, his godson, the young man he loved as if he were his own.

With tears streaming down her face, Stephanie rushed into Malachi's open arms. "Is this a wonderful evening, or what? Daddy, I'm so happy. I love Gregory so much. I don't even want to think about what might've happened had I not accepted the invitation to visit you in New Orleans. Thank you for seeking Stephen and me out. Thank you for two of the most wonderful years of my life. You have no idea what it means to me to have you around. God has blessed us all so abundantly. How do we dare ask for more?"

Malachi was still stuck on the word *Daddy*. His tears ran freely as his wild heartbeat pounded inside his chest. Stephanie had never called him Daddy before. *Dad, but never Daddy*. It sounded like music to his ears. He *was* Daddy and she *was* and would always be her daddy's little girl. "Come here, my dear princess. Let me just hug you tighter than tight. I love you so much."

Stephen couldn't stay in the background another second. He had stayed away just to let Malachi and Stephanie have their special father-and-daughter moments since he'd already known about the engagement. As he was very much a part of this family, he wanted to be right smack dab in the center of all the love and emotions flowing out from them.

After Stephen grabbed his uncle by the arm, the two men walked over to Stephanie and Malachi and immediately formed a family circle. A few moments later Gregory II and Grant joined Gregory III and the Trudeauxs in making a strong showing of family unity.

Now that everyone was gone Stephanie took a moment to reflect on the evening. Most everything had turned out better than she'd ever hoped for. Although there were a couple of things that had disturbed her, she'd made up her mind not to worry too much about them. Stephen and Darcella hadn't left her home together, nor had he walked her to her car. Her brother had stayed at her house an hour or so after his fiancée had taken leave.

Since Malachi and Maxwell were spending the night in Stephen's home, Stephanie was pretty sure the couple wasn't getting together again on this night. These were grown folks and she knew there was no way she could direct the outcome of their personal situation.

Farrah was an adult, too. If she decided to involve herself romantically with Grant, she'd eventually find out exactly who he was. Stephanie had decided it wasn't up to her to tell her best friend anything about Grant, not unless she was asked specific questions, especially since he'd changed so much over the past two years. At any rate, nothing negative would come out of her mouth about her future brother-in-law as long as he was on the up-and-up with Farrah.

Stephanie laughed out loud as she thought of how Maxwell had so graciously offered to walk Sarah and Eliza Beth out to the car. He was gone long enough to have jogged around the block a few times. She thought him being so infatuated at his age was rather sweet and innocent. Maxwell hadn't married in all these years, which might not make him a good candidate for matrimony, but people didn't always have to marry to share good times with each other.

That Sarah might be somewhat lonely was something Stephanie could only guess at. She didn't know if she dated from time to time or not, but Eliza Beth would've definitely mentioned it to her had that been the case. The matchmaker couldn't have kept it quiet. All of Eliza Beth's friends would know every minute detail. Once Uncle Max retired his hot wheels, loneliness just might catch up with him, too, she mused. Even though he was a very active man business-wise, being off the road for good could make him crave more of a personal social life.

It would be really nice to see Sarah and her uncle Maxwell indulge in a meaningful relationship, but Stephanie knew everyone would just have to wait and see what developed between them, if anything. Her father was lonely, too, she knew, but she didn't think he had any heart left to give away to another woman. Doreen had taken Malachi's heart and soul to the grave with her. However, she planned to include the possibility in her daily and nightly prayers.

Man was not meant to live alone. God had proved that by creating Eve for Adam.

Malachi had fixed breakfast for only Stephen and himself. Maxwell had voiced his desire to sleep in late before they'd eventually retired. The three men had sat up talking until the wee hours of the morning. Because of Malachi and Stephen's mental and physical conditioning and work schedules, they were early risers despite how late they went to bed. Father and son had already walked five miles, long before the sun had streaked the sky with brilliant light.

Stephen watched from his seat at the kitchen table Malachi's adept preparation of the morning meal. He was already aware that his father knew his way around in the kitchen. He could also see that his father was very used to multitasking. The coffee was already brewing, the broiler had been turned on to make the kind of toast the twins' loved, and whipped eggs had been set aside for scrambling. Malachi was now busy grilling the turkey sausage links and turkey ham slices. Since meat took the longest to prepare, Malachi always began preparing it first.

The turkey sausage and ham smelled so good to Stephen. The aromas were starting to get to him. He was as hungry as a bear that had just arisen from hibernation. The warm, cozy setting, with a wild dash of color, made him feel really good inside. The fresh red-and-orange rosebuds Malachi had cut from Stephen's backyard rose garden was responsible for that. The scent of the blooms was no match for the food scents, though. Stephen's stomach growled in protest.

Being alone with his dad like this was awesome for Stephen. Malachi was such an attentive man. He seemed to know just what to do and say. He made his son feel really special. Above all, he made his two children feel loved. Stephen hated that he'd lost so much time with his father, time he could never reclaim. But life was funny that way, so unpredictable.

Malachi set down in front of Stephen a plate of food and a mug of hot coffee. He then went back to retrieve his own meal. Once the two men settled in at the table, Malachi passed the blessing. Stephen wasted no time digging in. He had gotten way past hungry.

It wasn't long before Stephen and Malachi had devoured everything on their plates. It was then that Stephen began to talk to his father about his relationship with Darcella, informing Malachi of how things had suddenly turned bad for them. Stephen laid out the issues one by one, starting from the less serious to the most egregious. "Dad, I don't know what to do about any of this. Do you think it's unreasonable for a woman to try to cut off her man from his family?"

Malachi turned down the corners of his mouth. "It's not about what I think, son. You have to go on your gut feelings. Relationships are hard work. Marriage is not easy, but it can be wonderful if both parties work on it. I wish I could advise you, but you know how miserably I failed at mine. I put lust before love. And I've been paying a costly price for it ever since."

Stephen blew out an uneven gust of air. "I think you can advise me for that very reason. You lost the woman you loved because your physical needs got the best of you. I hate to admit it, but I now understand how that can happen." Stephen went on to explain his last comment, sharing with his father how attracted he'd suddenly become to Farrah.

Malachi raised both eyebrows. "Do you think its just lust on your part, son?"

"I don't know, Dad." Stephen shook his head from side to side. "I can't explain the sinking feeling I got last night when I saw Farrah being so chummy with Grant. My stomach was virtually tied up in knots. *Jealousy?* If it wasn't that, I sure felt green with envy."

Malachi nodded his understanding. "Lust can disguise itself very well in some instances. I knew what I did was nothing more than being a slave to my sexual needs. I was never confused about it. I saw that night as a one-time deal. I wish I had considered the lifetime consequences. But we never do that when we're overly heated in the flesh." Malachi still looked so regretful after all these years. "As you know, that one-night stand cost me everything I loved dearly."

Stephen felt a sudden rush of tremendous empathy for his father, yet he felt compelled to address Malachi's decades of deep regret and self-incrimination. It was time for his dad to get over his mistakes and move on. No future existed for those who constantly lived in the past. "Dad, if God has forgiven you, why can't you forgive yourself? It's time, you know."

Malachi shrugged. "I guess it's because your mother could never forgive me, son."

Stephen's expression said he didn't agree. "I think she did forgive you. The love letters she wrote to you were proof enough of that for me. Mama loved you still. It was her pride, Dad, pride wounded beyond comprehension. For her to take you back would've made her feel weak and less than the woman she prided herself on being. She chose to love you from a distance because it was the only way she could keep her pride intact. So sad but very true."

Malachi was surprised to hear Stephen acknowledge such things. The bitterness he once had in him when he spoke on this matter was absent. His son sounded so mature. He actually seemed convinced of what he'd just said. God's miracles never ceased to rain down when least expected. Stephen was right. He had to forgive himself, had to let go of the past. God had given him a second chance by reuniting him with his children, yet he'd continued to wallow in his unyielding guilt and grief. "Son, I really needed to hear that from you. And I will take heed."

Stephen smiled broadly. "I'm glad to hear that, Dad. I want to see you whole. I believe Mama is smiling down on all of us. She's at peace and you need to find tranquillity, too."

Maxwell popped into the kitchen, smiling brightly. "How's a man to sleep in with all these delicious scents drifting up his nose? The devil is always busy. What'd you all cook?"

Stephen and Malachi laughed heartily.

Malachi got to his feet. "Sit down, Max. I'll heat up some food for you real quick."

Maxwell grinned. "You see why I like being around your daddy. I'm the oldest, but he's the one who does all the spoiling. That's 'cause he doesn't have a personal life," Maxwell whispered to Stephen. "That boy needs a real woman to spoil and pamper."

Stephen cracked up. "Looks like you were working on getting yourself one last night. What's up with you and Ms. Sarah?"

Maxwell chuckled. "How'd you manage to keep that question in for such a long time? I was sure you all would've grilled me unmercifully when we got back here last night."

"You weren't volunteering any information so I decided not to get into your business, Uncle Max. Now, that niece of yours, she's probably at home still chomping at the bit. Consider yourself forewarned. Stephanie *will* be all up in your business. You can count on it."

Maxwell chuckled. "I'll be ready for her. If she's anything like her grandmother, she won't be able to hold her wagging tongue. I'm surprised she didn't call over here last night."

Malachi set a plate of warmed food in front of his brother. "That's because she's probably still on cloud nine. Announcing an engagement is a heavenly experience. Stephen, did your mama ever tell you how I proposed to her?"

Stephen regretted that he couldn't say he already knew the story. Doreen had told the children nothing about her and Malachi's love affair or their marriage. "I'd love to hear it, Dad."

The pain in Malachi's eyes was visible. It always hurt him to know how very little Doreen had talked about him, especially since they'd been so crazy in love. That his kids hadn't ever seen a picture of him was still tortuous to his gut. As he recalled Stephen's earlier advice, Malachi quickly pulled himself up out of the doldrums. Believing that Stephen was right about his mother loving him until the day she'd died had brought him great comfort.

Malachi rubbed his hands together. "Well, son, the proposal went like this…"

A very animated Malachi went on to tell Stephen that he'd had Doreen serenaded with a singing telegram. The professional singer he'd hired had come to their favorite restaurant to sing their special love song by Larry Graham, "One In a Million." Once the performance was over, he'd handed her a bunch of helium balloons. Then he'd popped the one that said "I love you" to reveal the black velvet case with the diamond ring inside. "You should've seen the stars in your mama's eyes that night. We were so in love, Stephen."

"Wow! Some smooth romantic you were. I can see Mama's bright smile now." Stephen suddenly felt like crying, but he warded off the urge, not wanting to start a chain reaction. "I wish everything had worked out between you two, Dad. Your love for each other still lives on even though one of you is gone from this life forever. No one can ever change that."

Malachi forced a smile to his lips. "That's life, son. So grab it by the tail and never let go. It may turn you every way but loose, but you just hang on for the wildest and craziest ride ever."

Maxwell cleared his throat to keep from choking up. "Okay, let's get back on a lighter note. I'm too ugly when I cry. You all don't want to see me do that twisted-face thing."

Laughing, Stephen patted Maxwell on the back. "Sorry about that, Uncle. So are you going to tell us what's happening with you and the classy lady you met at Stephanie's place?"

Maxwell nodded and shrugged at the same time. "Yeah, I just might do that, Stephen. But only after you tell me what's up with you and Darcy. If I didn't know better, I would've thought you two were perfect strangers last night. Are you two on the outs or something?"

Stephen frowned. "Was it that obvious?"

"To everyone that personally knows you two," Malachi responded.

Stephen quickly repeated to Maxwell the very same story he'd told his father earlier. "Crazy, huh, Uncle Max?"

Maxwell hunched his shoulders. "Love is pure insanity, man. That's why I've steered clear of it all these years. But my advice to you is to get busy and handle your business. You just can't be attracted to one woman while in love with another. Let me rephrase that. You can be, but it won't work for you. Life is complicated enough without adding even more drama to it."

"What do you mean, Uncle Max?"

"Whatever is going on between you and Darcy, you need to either straighten it up, or let the door hit you in the butt on the way out. Life is too short to be miserable. If the relationship you're in isn't the right one for you now, it won't be right ten years from now. Listen to your uncle, boy. I haven't been running hard from love just to get my exercise in. I have watched your daddy suffer behind love all his adult life. He's still grieving the loss of your mama's love."

"I'm going to handle my business, Dad and Uncle Max. I plan to talk to Darcy later this evening. I'm back to work in a couple of days, so we need to resolve our matters and hopefully get them behind us. Now, back to that lighter note. I want to hear about you and Ms. Sarah."

"Me, too," Stephanie said, as she walked in and passed around hugs to everyone. She then joined the guys at the kitchen table. "I'm just dying to know all the juicy details, Uncle Max. I can barely breathe from the anticipation." Stephanie laughed at how silly she sounded, but she'd already spent a good bit of her time wondering about Maxwell and Sarah. Knowing the truth would set her free from conjuring up a romantic relationship between them.

Maxwell had a good chuckle over the family interest in his personal life. "Guys, don't get too excited. Ms. Sarah just gave me her phone number so I could ring her up when I'm in town. We haven't gone and gotten ourselves engaged or married," Maxwell joked.

Stephanie playfully hit Maxwell on the arm. "That's more than enough to get excited over," she enthused. "Ms. Sarah is such a nice lady, Uncle Max. She's really down-to-earth."

Maxwell nodded. "I've already gotten that impression, niece. I guess that's why I asked her out to lunch today."

Stephen stretched his eyes in disbelief. "You did what?" Stephen gave his uncle a knowing look. "You sure are a fast worker, Uncle Max. You are so darn amazing."

"You haven't said if she's agreed to go out with you or not, Max," Malachi said. "Do you two have a luncheon date or not?"

Maxwell's upper body shook as he laughed at the expression on Malachi's face. "You bet I do! Twelve-thirty sharp." Maxwell suddenly frowned. "However, gang, I've got a problem."

Stephanie looked concerned. "What is it, Uncle Max?"

Maxwell shrugged. "I don't have anything decent to wear. All I brought along in my suitcase are blue jeans, casual shirts and a few changes of underwear and athletic socks."

Stephanie waved off Maxwell's concern. "We have malls all over this large city. I'd love to help you pick out something to wear for your date. You just need to get jazzed up a bit. No major overhauling is needed on you, Uncle Max, since you already have great looks."

Maxwell nodded his approval of his niece's comments. "I'll accept your help, Stephanie, but there's one more problem. As you all know, when I couldn't make my flight, I drove over here in my pickup. Ms. Sarah seems too refined to be riding around in a truck."

Malachi laughed at the pained expression on Maxwell's face. "There are three cars in this family. I'm sure you can use any one of them. Mine, for sure."

Stephanie shook her head in the negative. "I think you should drive your truck, Uncle Max, though you might want to clean it up a bit, especially the inside. Trucks are part of your lifestyle. Any woman who wants to be with you has to accept you for exactly who you are. I don't believe Ms. Sarah would want you to change a thing about yourself for her. Just continue to be the kind, wonderful gent you are, Uncle Max. The Trudeaux men are all winners!"

Maxwell beamed at his family. "Well, it looks as if all my issues have been resolved. Thank you, guys. When can we hit one of the malls, niece?" Maxwell looked down at his wristwatch. "We don't have much time left. The morning is getting away from us."

Stephanie patted Maxwell's hand. "The stores open in twenty minutes or so. All we have to do is get there. Dad can help Stephen clean up the kitchen while we're gone."

Stephen got to his feet. "Thanks for your cleaning suggestion, but the kitchen duties can wait. We're all going on this shopping spree!"

"Great idea, son," Malachi seconded, loving the suggestion of a family outing.

"Look out, mall clerks," Stephanie shouted. "The Trudeauxs are on the loose. Only the very best in clothing for our sweet uncle Max."

Darcella hung up the phone. Frustration had set in on her. This was only the umpteenth time she'd dialed Stephen's home and cell numbers. She wanted to confirm their plans for the evening, but how was she supposed to do that if she couldn't make contact? It wasn't like him not to have his cell phone on, but all she kept getting was his voice mail message. His New Orleans family *was* still in town, so she figured that's why she couldn't get in touch with him.

Although Darcella felt better than she had in several days, she was still worried about her relationship with Stephen. Her optimism was on the rise even though she knew there were a lot of serious issues for her and her fiancé to work through. As she was now considering a significant career change, she couldn't help wondering how he'd feel about it. The job Darcella had in mind would more than likely be totally disapproved of by Stephen. In fact, there was very little doubt in her mind about how badly he might react to the news.

Stephen was such a good man and she'd hate to lose him. Never in a million years would she have expected them to be faced with serious problems. They'd always been of one accord. Now they couldn't seem to agree on the smallest things. Not so long ago, before he'd been united with his father and uncle, Stephen had also been in somewhat of a funk. She had been patient with him back then, and she hoped he'd offer her the same courtesy. Confusion wasn't an easy thing to contend with. Darcella felt confused and torn on a lot of issues to do with her relationship. The discontentment she felt over her job had her confused the most.

Deciding to try Stephen one more time, Darcella quickly hit the redial icon. Bingo, she thought, when Stephen responded on the second ring. For all the loud noise in the background, she could barely hear him. "Where are you, Stephen?"

"In the Baybrook Mall with my family. We're helping Uncle Maxwell pick out some new clothes. Will you still be available later this evening?"

Darcella fought the tinge of anger she felt about being left out of the family outing. She had to wonder why Stephen hadn't called and asked her to join him. She only lived a few blocks from that particular mall. "Our plans for this evening, Stephen. That's what I was calling about. I want to confirm the time and the place."

"Seven-thirty, at my house. Is that okay with you, Darcy?"

"Fine by me. I'll see you then, Stephen."

"Excellent, Darcy. See you later."

* * *

Stephen and Stephanie were beside themselves with joy. Seated in a leather chair outside the men's dressing room inside Dillard's department store, Stephanie was eagerly waiting for Maxwell to make his first appearance. The group had picked out for him a pair of heather-gray dress slacks and a soft black-and-gray lightweight V-neck sweater.

Stephen and Malachi were busy choosing other outfits for Maxwell to try on. Malachi was such a smart dresser, looking debonair in everything he wore. He thought his brother should wear a sports jacket on his first date with Sarah.

On the other side of the coin, Stephen thought a jacket was too stuffy for a luncheon date so he'd chosen a long-sleeved button-down shirt in robin's-egg blue. The temperatures were very hot in Houston, but air-conditioned restaurants also had to be taken into consideration. It was often very cold in most of the dining establishments so perhaps a jacket wasn't too far-fetched, Stephen considered, since he was going to recommend one of the Galveston restaurants overlooking the Gulf of Mexico. If the couple opted to sit outside on the restaurant balcony, Maxwell could always remove the jacket.

After an hour and a half of modeling clothes for his family, Maxwell had had enough. Shopping wasn't a favorite pastime for him. To make everyone happy, he'd chosen one item from each of the outfits presented to him. Maxwell was more than pleased with the blue shirt Stephen had chosen, the heather-grays slacks from Stephanie's contribution, and the gray-and-blue jacket Malachi had picked out for him. Now all Maxwell had to do was purchase a pair of shoes and get a haircut. Stephen had promised to take his uncle to his personal barber.

Knowing that time was of the essence, the group made a mad dash to the parking lot.

Chapter 5

Seated on the sofa in Stephen's den, Darcella fumbled with her keys as she looked into the autumn-brown eyes that looked awfully bleary. As her eyes drank in the silk lounging attire Stephen wore, even though it was only early evening, she had to wonder if he'd forgotten their date. Despite how tired he appeared, he still looked darn good. Darcella then quickly snapped out of her scattered thoughts, reminding herself that she was on an important mission.

What Darcella had to tell Stephen would probably both disappoint and upset him. He would more than likely feel betrayed by her, but she'd deal with that, too. This was her life, not his. While she believed their conversation would affect them both, she still had the right to choose her own path. What she'd told Stephanie earlier was only half of the real story.

Stephen eyed Darcella curiously. "What is it, Darcy? You got me worried over here."

Stephen had high hopes that he and Darcella could quickly straighten things out with each other and then have a pleasant visit afterward. He no longer felt that way. She was way too nervous about whatever was on her mind. Things didn't look good. Stephen missed Darcella a lot, but he knew they had a way to go before things between them got back to normal.

After Darcella smoothed her hands down her jeans, she then made a fist with her left one. "I've applied to become a firefighter. But not just to hold a job as a regular fireman. I'm interested in going into smoke-jumping training. I'm very intrigued with the idea of fighting forest fires." With her insides quaking like a bowl of jelly, Darcella pursed her lips, looking very determined. *How was that for jumping right into the fire with both feet?*

Stephen palmed his forehead, wondering if Darcella had lost the rest of her mind since the last time he'd seen her. It would sure explain her recent strange behaviors. She was a registered nurse, an angel of mercy, which was one of the most important jobs in the world. *Why would she want to give all that up to fight fires?* He couldn't help wondering why she was so suddenly interested in being a firefighter. It wasn't like she didn't have firsthand knowledge of all the traumas he'd been through in the job. Her present career was just as traumatic as any firefighting career since she also treated seriously injured victims of fire.

Stephen bit down on his lower lip. "Intrigued! Girl, you have to be more than just intrigued to want to take on the most dangerous firefighting job of all. You just can't be serious about this, Darcy."

Darcella leapt to her feet. "Why not, Stephen? Why can't I be serious? Is it because you think of me as just a brainless, overly emotional woman?"

Wondering where that sudden outburst had come from, Stephen shook his head from side to side. "It's insane, Darcy. That's why!" As he thought about what her career change might mean for their future, Stephen's expression grew blank. He then winced in pain. "So are the plans off for us to start a family a year or so after marriage?" His eyes narrowed with suspicion. "You never planned to have a baby with me, did you?"

Feeling extremely nervous now, Darcella began to pace the floor. "That's not true. I did want us to have a baby."

"*Did?* I can only take that to mean you no longer want a child with me. What has changed your mind so suddenly?"

Darcella shrugged, not daring to look Stephen in the eye. "Nothing specific that I can pinpoint. I guess I desire to further my career more than I want to settle down into motherhood. We will have our family. Just not right now. Can't you just be happy for me, Stephen?"

"Happy for you? You've got to be kidding me. The job you're speaking about is too dangerous for someone who's never experienced fighting a fire. You do know that you'll have to have firefighting experience first, don't you?"

Darcella nodded. "I do know. I'm also aware that smoke jumpers are responsible for suppressing forest fires by parachuting to remote locations. I realize that we can be deployed at anytime to anywhere. I'm already in the required superior physical condition, which will allow me to withstand the rigorous training."

Darcella went on to tell Stephen that her present job already called for good judgment skills and the ability to work well under pressure. She then told him that she was highly aware that smoke jumpers prided themselves on being first on the wildfire scene to battle harsh environments that might slow down others. She mentioned that organizational skills were crucial and that she already prided herself on being very organized. Darcella also let Stephen know that she was very much aware of the heavy supplies she'd have to carry on her back through the rough terrain she'd have to hike over in order to fight forest fires.

"As you've just heard, Stephen, I'm well aware of what I'm getting myself into."

Stephen laughed derisively. This was just too darn rich for

him. How his fiancée had come to all these serious conclusions without bothering to consult him was pretty darn insulting. He had to also admit that his pride was hurt as much as anything. Most women lived to have children with the man they loved. He'd obviously chosen one who didn't share in that sentiment. Stephen wanted kids badly, but it had to be a mutual agreement between him and the woman he married. He'd never try to force anyone into doing anything they didn't want to do.

"Say something, Stephen," Darcella practically barked out, close to losing her cool altogether. Hoping she could calm down, Darcella reclaimed her seat.

Stephen threw up his hands. "There's not a lot for me to say, Darcy. Even if you're opposed to having children soon after we marry, you need to reconsider this smoke-jumping training. That job is no joke. I can't even imagine you leaping out of planes and helicopters."

Feeling distraught by the entire matter, Stephen put his face into his hands. His dream of first becoming a husband and then a father within the next year or so had just been shattered. He was totally stunned by this unexpected turn of events. The lady seated across from him really had become a virtual stranger. *When and how had this all happened?* A short time ago they'd been happy and so in love with each other. Or at least he'd thought so.

Then he'd proposed to her. Had that been his first big mistake? Then there was Farrah.

Was Darcy fearful of marriage? If so, why? Well, if she was, she wasn't the only one who had anxieties about it. He wasn't taking it so lightly, either. Stephen had once felt that together they could conquer any and all fears, but he was now no longer sure about anything to do with their relationship. Darcella had him wondering if this was the beginning of the end.

Stephen finally lifted his head. Seeing the sadness in Darcella's eyes nearly leveled him. Hurting her was the last thing he wanted to do. She was a vulnerable little thing. No matter how tough she talked, he knew how tender her heart was. This new personality of hers was a cover for something she carried deep down inside of her, a painful something. Until Stephen could find out what was really going on with Darcella, he decided to hang right on in there. She was worth it.

Stephen got up and crossed the room with long, deliberate strides. After he dropped down next to Darcella, he took her into his arms and rocked her back and forth. "Do you think we can get through all this, Darcy? Is our love strong enough to withstand this fiery blaze?"

Darcella wrapped her arms tightly around Stephen's neck and then pulled her head back slightly. "I don't know, Stephen. What do you think?"

Stephen stared into her eyes. "I really wanted to hear what you had to say on the matter, since you're the one who's changed directions in midstream. But let's do this instead, Darcy. We'll continue to talk things over and see where we go from here. We also need to pray about it. Whatever we decide will affect our lives for a long time to come. People planning to spend the rest of their lives together should be on the same page, before the marriage—and throughout. I don't want us to stop being friends and I don't ever want to take you for granted, Darcy."

Darcella smiled weakly. "Thank you, Stephen. I like your plan. I'm glad we're friends."

Stephen kissed her lightly on the lips. "Now that we have that settled, how would you like to help me eat the dozen or so lemon tarts I smuggled from Stephanie's house?"

Darcella threw her head back in laughter. "If you need a partner in crime, you got one. Those tiny pastries are absolutely to die for."

Stephen laughed heartily. "I didn't really steal them. Stephanie packaged them up for me to take home. She always sends me off with a goodwill baggie or two when I eat at her place."

Darcella jumped up. "I'll get the coffee going."

Stephen laughed. "Now, that's what I call teamwork. I'll take care of the plates. Paper and plastic. No washing dishes for me tonight."

It only took a matter of minutes before Stephen and Darcella were seated at his kitchen table. The reheated tarts had caused some delicious scents to drift in the air, smelling as fresh as they'd been the last evening.

Stephen took a sip of his coffee. "How's your day been?"

Darcella shrugged. "Busy, as usual. I got a little shopping done."

Stephen grinned. "Grocery or clothes?"

"Both. You know I'm addicted to shopping, Stephen."

Stephen shook his head. "A straight-up addict is what you are. What's your work schedule like this week?"

Darcella clapped her hands with enthusiasm. "I actually have three days off in a row. I've got several books I'm going to lose myself in. This girl needs a little romance in her life."

Stephen winced, looking a bit stunned. "From in between the pages of a romance novel! That doesn't say much for me, does it? I don't do it for you anymore? What's up with that?"

Darcella immediately regretted her joking remark. "I'm sorry. I didn't mean it like that."

Stephen's expression grew grim. "Then how did you mean it?"

Darcella rubbed her fingers across her forehead. "Stephen, you may not realize it, but it's hard not making out with you. So what if I let myself fantasize over a love story? It's not like we haven't ever been hot and heavy with each other. You suddenly pulled back, deciding we should wait until after we're married to go all the way. We don't even go half the distance anymore."

Stephen raised an eyebrow. "I'm assuming that's a problem for you. But how's a romance novel going to help you out?"

"Just a fantasy, Stephen. Don't make so much of it."

Stephen stood up and then brought Darcella to her feet, pulling her gently into his arms. After lowering his head, he kissed her full on the mouth. "Is this what you've been missing, baby?" He kissed her again and again. Then, as his mouth teased her inner ear, he looked deeply into her eyes. "Can you get this kind a feeling out of a paperback?"

Laughing, Darcella blushed. "No, silly, and you know it."

Stephen smoothed back Darcella's hair from her face. "Tell me what you want from me, babe. Is it this?" He slowly traced her lips and neck with his lips. "How much more do you want? I can deliver, you know."

Darcella backed away from Stephen. "Okay, okay. I get it. I know it's important for you to wait until we're married. It's important to me, too, but a girl can get a little heated up."

Stephen laughed. "In that case, we need to move up the wedding date. What about next weekend or the week after that, but definitely before the end of the month?"

Darcella didn't look too pleased at that joking suggestion. "The fire training, Stephen, will have to come first. I don't want to get married until after that's all behind me."

Stephen closely studied Darcella, trying to make sense of whatever was driving her. He narrowed his eyes. "Could there be another man in your life?"

Darcella looked appalled. "How dare you suggest such a vulgar thing, Stephen? How can you hurt my feelings like that?"

Stephen tried to take Darcella into his arms, but she pulled away. "I didn't mean to hurt you, Darcy. I just can't seem to make sense of all these darn changes in you. One day we get engaged and then this new personality invades your body. What am I supposed to think?"

Darcella glared at Stephen. "You have some darn nerve! I have half a mind to take a swing at you, Stephen Trudeaux. I don't like being insulted that way. Listen, this visit is not going very well. I'm going home. We'll talk later."

Before Stephen could protest Darcella had already made a beeline for the front door.

Stephen felt sick inside. "Well, you certainly handled that well, Trudeaux."

After moving into the living room, Stephen dropped down in a chair and tossed his long legs over the side. Could things between him and Darcella get any messier? He'd sure made a mess out of their visit. He was willing to bet that something more than what met the eye was going on with her. She'd been very moody lately, yet she hadn't shared with him why.

This smoke-jumping gig was beyond the cat's meow. It had come right out of the blue. Never once had he ever heard her talk about taking on firefighting as a profession. It was obvious that they had a lot of things to work through, way more serious stuff than he'd imagined.

Knowing he wasn't going to rest after all that, Stephen ran to the bedroom and slipped into a pair of jeans and threw on a shirt. On the way out the door he grabbed his jacket.

A thorough search of Stephanie's house let Stephen know that his sister wasn't in, neither was his father or uncle. Stephanie was normally home this late even when Gregory was still in town. Perhaps the family had gone out to dinner. He tossed around the idea of waiting before deciding to try and ring her cell. Five rings later the voice mail message came on. He didn't tell her he was at her place since he planned to go on home. "Call me when you get this message."

Just as Stephen stepped off the porch, Farrah appeared before him, looking fresh and stylish in a pair of designer jeans and a low-cut silk blouse, black and seductive. As he drank in her stunning appearance, he didn't like where his thoughts were heading.

Farrah smiled, liking the desirious look in his eyes. "Hey, Stephen, is Stephanie in?"

Stephen swallowed hard, shaking his head in the negative. "She's not. I just called her cell and left her a message. She may be with the family or a client. I really don't know."

Farrah nodded her understanding. "Probably so. You're not waiting for her?"

"I don't know how long she'll be out. I'll catch up with her later."

Farrah nervously shuffled her feet back and forth on the pavement. "I just finished cooking dinner. Would you like to come inside and eat? No strings attached."

Stephen laughed inwardly. There were definitely strings attached. How long and binding was the question uppermost in his mind. "It's a great offer, but I really should be getting on. What'd you cook?" he asked in the next breath.

The look in Farrah's eyes was hopeful. "Chicken-fried steak and gravy. Garlic mashed potatoes and collard greens, too."

Stephen's mouth began to water. He knew he should deny his hunger pangs, but it was hard. "How do you eat fattening foods like that and still keep such a great figure?"

"Plenty of exercise. I walk no less than three miles a day, but I try to get in five. I also have a great treadmill in our spare bedroom. At any rate, I don't eat like that all the time."

"It doesn't take a lot, Farrah. Calories can add up easily. Anyway, I guess I can come in and take some of the fatty stuff off your hands." Stephen knew that Farrah still lived in her childhood home with her mother, Helen. Now that he'd decided to take her offer, her mother being at home should make things pretty safe. Stephen was too smart to ignore the attraction Farrah held for him, but his brain was stuck on *stupid* at the moment. It wasn't like his sister hadn't already confirmed Farrah's feelings for him. Examining his own was also an issue.

Farrah laughed wickedly. "Yeah, right! Come on in and get it, boy."

Stephen raised an eyebrow. "You'd better be careful, girl. A man could misinterpret that last statement." Stephen regretted his asinine comment the second it resounded in his ears. Darcella's image came to his mind in the next instant. He had to wonder how he'd feel about her accepting an invitation to dine with another man. Just the thought of it made his insides curl, yet it did very little to squash his ravenous appetite. *Ravenous for what? The food or the woman?*

Farrah gave Stephen her most flirtatious smile. She knew when she had a fish hooked. Reeling this handsome catch in was the problem, especially since another woman already had her hooks deep into him. She was also aware that the liveliest in bait didn't stand a chance of tempting a well-fed fish. "I think you interpreted my remark just right, Mr. Trudeaux."

Guilt hit Stephen full force the minute he stepped inside Farrah's home. This wasn't something he should be doing. Not by a long shot. He was engaged to a wonderful woman, even if Darcella was acting a little crazy right now. Eating dinner with Farrah, no matter how innocent it may be, was an outright betrayal of the promises he'd made to the woman he loved.

Just as Stephen was about to beg off, Helen Freeman came up and greeted him cheerfully, reaching out and lovingly touching his face. "You and Stephanie are such beautiful children. Doreen would be so proud." Helen then looped her arm through Stephen's. "I hear you're joining us for dinner. I was so excited when Farrah told me you might be dining with us. You are always a welcome guest in our home."

Stephen was visibly surprised by Helen's statement. How could Farrah have told her mother such a thing when she didn't know herself that he'd accept her invitation to dinner until minutes ago? She certainly hadn't been out of his sight since she'd first called out to him. He noticed the slight look of shame on his hostess's face, but that didn't make him feel any better. This wily woman had played on him one of the oldest tricks in the book. What bothered him more than anything was how easily he'd swallowed the bait—hook, line and sinker.

Helen smiled up at Stephen. "Let's go into the dining room while Farrah puts out the food. I hope you brought along a good appetite. My girl can sure burn up the pots and pans."

Literally, Stephen mused, suddenly realizing Farrah had seen his car in Stephanie's drive beforehand. He wondered if Helen knew what her minx of a daughter was up to. He could only imagine she might be a little antsy for grandchildren. Neither woman was getting any younger.

There was no way Stephen could back out now, not without hurting feelings. Farrah's mother being present didn't make him feel any better about staying on. At least this couldn't be seen as an intimate dinner for two. Stephen smiled down at Helen, who was much shorter than him. "Thank you for welcoming me." *But I can't say I'm glad to be here.*

As Stephen and Helen headed for the dining room, the doorbell suddenly rang. Helen then asked him to get the door for her. Although he was uncomfortable in answering the bell, he was somewhat inclined to oblige. As far as he was concerned, more guests at the dinner table would be all the merrier. Stephen felt as if he'd gotten himself into deep water.

Stephanie's mouth fell agape as she looked into the shocked face of her sibling. She'd only come there after she'd learned that Stephen wasn't inside her home and that his car was parked in her driveway. Stephanie had fervently hoped for a different outcome than this one. It was still a shocker for her to see him there even though she hadn't thought he could've been anywhere else. What she hadn't expected was for him to answer the door. *Had her brother lost his mind?* Without comment, Stephanie stood on her tiptoes and hugged Stephen.

Stephen looked absolutely shamefaced. "I can explain," he whispered. "It's not what you think. I promise to tell you later how this all came about."

Farrah making an appearance kept Stephanie from responding. That was all well and good, especially when Stephanie had no idea of what to say.

Farrah stepped forward and gave Stephanie a warm hug. "You're just in time for dinner. We were all about to sit down. Please join us."

Stephanie looked from Farrah to Stephen, wondering if this had been a preplanned engagement. If it had, she didn't think her brother would've been stupid enough to park in her driveway. He had to have known she would've disapproved of his actions, though she didn't want to resort to judging him. Lord knew she had more than enough issues of her own to try to correct. Stephanie was dealing with some things she had yet to discuss with her loving brother, wondering if they had the same type of serious romantic relationship anxieties.

After Stephanie quickly decided that this wasn't the time or place to question things, she swallowed the acid taste in her mouth. "Something smells delicious." Stephanie also smelled a big rat, but she wasn't sure if the bad odor was coming from Stephen or Farrah.

Helen reached out to Stephanie when she sat down next to her, giving her a loving hug. "Nice to see you, dear heart."

Stephanie smiled endearingly at the older woman. "It's good to see you, too, Ms. Helen. You look well today. I'm happy to see you up and about."

Helen beamed at Stephanie. "I feel really good today. This is turning out to be quite a little dinner party. I like it when my daughter gets the chance to entertain a handsome guy. It's a rarity for her, you know." Helen giggled. "I'm very hungry. What about you, Stephanie?"

"Close to ravenous. I'm glad I didn't go with Dad and Uncle Max to Ms. Sarah's for dinner." If I had, she thought, no telling what might've gone down. Stephanie laughed gently, but she felt totally uncomfortable with Helen's comments. The look on her brother's face told her he felt the exact same way. This was the second dinner they'd had with Farrah in a very short time.

Farrah clasped her hands together, looking rather embarrassed. "In that case, let's dig in. Stephen, will you please say the blessing for us?"

Malachi and Maxwell were home and already dressed for bed by the time Stephanie and Stephen arrived back at her place. Although the twins had been at Farrah's home for only about an hour and a half, it had seemed like an eternity to both of them. Helen had kept making references to her daughter and Stephen as a striking couple. Whether her comments were said knowingly or unknowingly, Helen had kept the atmosphere charged with utter tension.

Stephen was happy that his father and uncle were back home and still up. That gave him a temporary reprieve from having to try to explain his last sudden bout of insanity to his sister. Accepting Farrah's offer to have dinner at her place had been downright crazy, he mused painfully, especially under his current circumstances. How could he make Stephanie understand something he himself was so in the dark about? His feelings were all twisted and he couldn't make sense of too much of what was going on in his life. How could he be attracted to Farrah and continue to profess his undying love to Darcella? Stephen knew that something had to give.

After Malachi and Maxwell accepted Stephanie's offer of hot tea, she went out to the kitchen to turn on the teakettle, leaving Stephen alone with their father and uncle.

Stephen looked at Maxwell with deep inquisitiveness. He then smiled broadly. "You haven't even told us how lunch with Ms. Sarah went, yet you've already managed to land an invitation to her place to dinner. How were both events?"

Maxwell grinned, looking like the cat that had eaten the bird. "I'd better hold my tongue until your sister gets back in here. I'm sure she also wants to know every juicy detail."

"You bet she does," Stephanie said from the entryway.

Stephen jumped up and removed the silver tea tray from Stephanie's hands.

Maxwell was dying to tell his story, but he waited until everyone had fixed the tea to the desired taste. There was a lot for him to share with his family and he wanted their full attention.

Stephanie smiled at her uncle. "Okay, Uncle Max, we're ready for you to dish the dirt."

Maxwell chuckled. "No dirt involved, my dear niece. Just fun times and great conversations. Sarah is a delight to be around. She's a very interesting lady and very well educated. When she was referred to as a cook, I had no idea she was a licensed dietician. Although she's a stickler about folks eating right, she laid out some food for us that couldn't even come close to qualifying as healthy. Downright sinful is more like it."

Stephanie laughed. "Perhaps she was trying to impress you, Uncle Max."

"Well, if that was her intent, she darn sure succeeded," Malachi said. "While Max was eating her delicious feast, he looked as if he'd found the fountain of eternal youth. I'd say we have a love connection going on here, and in more ways than one. Max loves to eat and Sarah sure loves to cook. In my opinion, that's a strong common denominator."

Maxwell grunted, rolling his eyes hard at Malachi. "You should talk! Josefina Clayton had you grinning like a Cheshire cat all evening long. This boy acted like a high school kid."

"Who's Josefina?" Stephanie and Stephen asked simultaneously.

"Sarah invited Josefina, a single friend of hers, to dinner for Mal to meet." Maxwell suddenly looked uncomfortable, wondering if he should've divulged that part. These two kids loved their mother; announcing something like that may not have been the wisest decision.

Stephanie clapped her hands, laughing joyfully. "Oh, my goodness! This is wonderful news." She beamed at Malachi. "Sounds as if you liked the lady, Daddy. Am I right?"

Maxwell was happy with Stephanie's response to the situation, but he didn't breathe a deep sigh of relief until after he saw how pleased Stephen appeared by the news.

Malachi knew he couldn't hide his enthusiasm over the lady he'd just met, so he decided not to even try. However, he was very concerned as to how his children might feel about it. He never wanted to do anything that would make the twins feel uncomfortable. Their welfare would always be his first concern. "Right on the money, my dear. Josefina is every bit as lovely as Ms. Sarah. She's a retired school-teacher with a master's degree. From what I gathered, she's also a good Christian woman. I'd like to see more of Jose-fina, but I plan to take things very slow. And if my children aren't happy about this news, I won't pursue the lady at all."

Stephen reached over and patted his father on the back reassuringly. "I think you already know where I stand from the conversations we've had on this topic. You need to have a special someone in your life, Dad. The time has come. You've already suffered enough loneliness."

Tears sprang to Stephanie's eyes. "I agree with Stephen, wholeheartedly!"

Malachi felt like crying, too. Things were turning out bet-ter than he'd ever imagined. He wanted to speak, to perhaps say something to make everyone laugh, but he couldn't. His heart was in his mouth.

Sensing the heady but somewhat melancholy feelings of the emotionally charged moment, Stephanie felt the need to get onto another topic. She quickly launched into her plans for her three-day weekend trip to New Orleans to spend time with Gregory, who'd left early that morning. Malachi and

Maxwell were leaving for home the next day so they were pleased to know they'd be seeing Stephanie again sooner rather than later. Because Stephen was scheduled to go back to work in a few days, he wouldn't be able to make the trip.

Stephen had a strong yen to just drop his head down and bawl like a baby. He was alone now, something he'd hardly been able to wait for. His first day back at work had already been very trying. Despite his request not to have any celebratory ceremony for his part in saving the life of the Anderson infant, Nathaniel, his department had held a small welcome-back reception, and had also presented to Stephen a beautiful wall plaque for bravery.

Marsha Anderson and her remaining family had been in attendance, including baby Nathaniel, who'd wrapped his arms around the emotional firefighter as if he'd known exactly who he was and what he'd done for him. The framed picture that Marsha had given to Stephen of the deceased twin girls, Kelly and Karla, haunted him something fierce. He thought of her gift to him as cruel and unusual punishment. What made her think he wanted every day to see on the firehouse wall pictures of the two beautiful children he hadn't been able to save? It was apparent to Stephen that it probably hadn't even crossed the young mother's mind that the photograph might bring him unspeakable pain and deep sorrow.

Stephen's troubles hadn't just begun with his arrival back at work. He'd slept poorly the past few nights because he hadn't been able to stop thinking about all the negative stuff going on between him and Darcella. The situation he'd stupidly created with Farrah also weighed heavily on his mind. A solution to his complex problems hadn't come yet.

Then a weary Stephen had gotten up out of bed and had once again begun reading more of what God had to say about relationships, marriage and families. He soon discovered from the study guide on God and family he'd received from Stephanie that numerous scriptures addressed God's directives to family.

"Honor your father and your mother that your days may be long upon the land, which the Lord God is giving you." Exodus 20:12.

"You shall not commit adultery." Exodus 20:14.

"You shall not covet your neighbor's wife...." Exodus 20:17.

In Stephen's opinion these were three of the most crucial directives for the family that God had written into the Ten Commandments. Stephen was very impressed with God's comments about His commandments, which came from what he'd read in Deuteronomy.

Stephen had then been guided to the book of Proverbs. After he'd read the suggested scriptures, he realized that they also spoke to relationships within the family, specifically between husband and wife. Stephen couldn't help wondering if he'd ever become a husband.

The last several scriptures Stephen had read had had him really tuned in, since they were ones that were probably the least understood of all. He'd heard many interpretations of them, many of which he was sure God hadn't intended them to mean.

Wives, likewise be submissive to your own husbands, that even if some do not obey the word, they, without a word, may be won by the conduct of their wives, when they observe your chaste conduct accompanied by fear. 1 Peter 3:1-2.

Husbands, likewise, dwell with them with understanding, giving honor to the wife, as to the weaker vessel, and as being heirs together of the grace of life, that your prayers may not be hindered. 1 Peter 3:7.

After several hours of filling his head and heart with the amazing Word of God, Stephen had decided that he and Darcella just might benefit from attending premarital counseling at the church he attended. He'd heard from other betrothed couples that it was a darn good program. Uniting Partners in Marriage With God was the title of the six-week seminar.

Unlike Stephen, Darcella hadn't ever talked about whether she'd been brought up in the church or not. For whatever reason, he sensed that she hadn't received any structured religious or spiritual training like what he'd been exposed to. That she hardly ever mentioned God was a strong clue for him. When he talked about God, she listened, but made no comments.

Stephen had to admit to himself that he hadn't really tried to engage Darcella in any type of conversation on religion. He'd just stated his opinions to her from time to time. That revelation saddened him quite a bit. If people didn't share the Word of God with others, they simply weren't being obedient, nor were they helping nonbelievers to become believers. Stephen knew that he was as guilty of that as anyone who had kept silent on the Word of God.

On a rare occasion Darcella attended church with Stephen, but she did work a lot of weekends, which he considered as a possible contribution to her frequent absence in the sanctuary. She couldn't be in two places at once. He worked many weekends as well, but he and Stephanie had gotten into the habit of attending the Wednesday evening church services as regularly as possible. His sister attended weekend services more often then he did, but she most always called him later to discuss the topic of the morning worship sermon.

Stephen's last thought sparked within him the idea to call Malachi and talk to him about all that he was feeling deep down inside. His father was a good listener, a very understanding person, and he wasn't one to pass unfair or evil judgments on others. Suddenly Stephen had to smile through his falling tears. That he actually had his father in his life so that he could call on him amazed the young man yet again.

A smile brightened up Stephen's sad eyes when he heard

Malachi's soft and self-assured voice. "This is your son, Dad. You got a minute to listen to a young man who's experiencing desperate times so he can hopefully avoid taking desperate measures?"

"I'm all ears, son." Malachi was ecstatic and pleased that Stephen had called on him for fatherly advice. His son was opening himself up to him a lot lately. He no longer seemed afraid to expose his vulnerabilities to the man he'd once believed had callously abandoned him. Malachi felt that Stephen was trusting in him more and more with each passing day. Trust was a good thing between a father and son. Malachi trusted in what the Lord had in store for them.

Malachi listened intently as Stephen unreservedly told him all the details of his troubling experiences, especially those that had occurred within the past forty-eight hours.

Before responding to what Stephen had told him, Malachi took a brief minute to assess everything. He couldn't help comparing his son's current plight to the issues he and Doreen had been faced with so many years ago. He knew that he couldn't just look at this from his son's point of view. Darcella's position had to be considered as well. "Stephen, have you determined without any doubt whatsoever that you love your fiancée?"

Stephen swallowed hard. "The only doubts I'm having are because of what's been happening between us lately. Yes, I do love her. When I asked her to marry me, I was sure that's what I wanted."

"And now?"

"Now I'm not so sure about the marriage part, only because of her reservations. I love Darcy with all my heart. I desire a family, Dad, plain and simple. She doesn't seem to want that any longer. This smoke-jumping training is consuming all her thoughts and time right now."

"Assessing one's life and what's wanted out of it is a wonderful thing, Stephen. You can't fault Darcy for that. Farrah Freeman is not the answer to your problems with your fiancée. You have to be stronger than the lust. Take it from a man who knows what he's talking about. Experience is always the best teacher. But when someone sees another person stick their hand in the fire, and then suffer third-degree burns, it would be foolish to follow suit. Don't you think?"

Stephen nodded. "I see what you mean. Is Farrah only tempting to me because of what Darcy and I are going through?"

Malachi stroked his chin. "Only you can answer that one, son. And I think you'd better try to figure it out rather quickly. In the meantime, you should steer clear of the temptation."

Darcella thoughtfully restudied the literature on smoke jumping that she'd downloaded from the Internet some time ago. The job was a very dangerous one, she admitted quietly, but just the thought of jumping from planes and helicopters excited her to no end. The prestige and glory that this type of career might bring to her was titillating, but only if she was successful at it.

Darcella frowned at her last thought. The *glory* part had bothered her somewhat, making her wonder why she really wanted so badly to get into this particular career field. She'd never been interested in becoming a firefighter in the past. In fact, she'd often wished that Stephen wasn't in the business of fighting fires. She was scared senseless every time he was out on the line. Yet something unexplainable had begun to drive her to that end.

That her job as a nurse was a thankless one certainly played a role in Darcella's desires to make a career change. She also saved lives, but unlike Stephen, she'd never be considered a hero for doing her job. The doctors wrote orders and the nurses executed each one with due diligence, but the doctors received all the glory.

There's that word again, she mused. *Glory.* It sounded awfully powerful to her. But what did it really mean? To find out exactly what it meant, and how she might be applying it to herself and her circumstances, Darcella jumped up from her seat and grabbed the dictionary. After she turned the pages to the G-words, she quickly perused the meaning of *glory.*

Glory had many meanings: renown, honor and praise rendered in worship, something that secures praise or renown, distinguishing quality or asset, resplendence or magnificence. All the meanings made it hard for Darcella to figure out what applied to her circumstances. She simply wanted to be recognized for a job extremely well done. Never would she receive anything akin to praise in her current profession. Despite their dedication, nurses rarely received any glory.

Tears welled in Darcella's eyes as her thoughts turned to Stephen. She'd never forget the shocked look on his face when she'd told him she planned to change careers. The heartrending hurt she saw in his eyes when he'd asked about her intent to have babies with him made her feel terribly guilty. Stephen had never made any bones about his wanting kids.

Birthing children was a scary thing to Darcella. She'd seen more than enough women go through labor, hard labor. Scarier than giving birth was the idea of bringing a child into the world and then absolutely paying it no special attention whatsoever. Babies needed far more than to just be fed and changed. They needed lots of love and tender care. Darcella had no recollection of receiving anything special from her mother. However, her brothers had received plenty of attention from their doting mama and papa. Boys had it all. Males were the kings of the world.

What if she could only give Stephen girls? Darcella knew for a fact that the gender of the child came from the father, not the mother. It really didn't matter. Most men blamed the woman when a son wasn't conceived. It was always the mother's fault, according to the men. How many women had she heard tell her that their husbands would leave them if they didn't produce a son?

There were countless women who'd confessed to Darcella that their husbands were so disappointed in the little girls they'd given birth to, wishing the female children were never born. It was always an emotional upheaval for these women to go through.

Darcella had vowed long ago that she'd never allow any man to put her through that kind of melodrama. It wasn't that she didn't want children with Stephen, she just wasn't sure she could handle the demanding pressures of motherhood. If she wanted to marry the man she loved, and she truly did, she knew that she had to come up with some solutions pretty quickly. Stephen was growing very impatient with her. That much Darcella was sure of.

Chapter 6

Gregory stared openly at his mother, one of the most gorgeous dark-brown-skinned women on the planet, who kept her body in great condition. She stood at five foot six and was a very classy dresser. To keep away the nasty gray, as she referred to it, her beautiful long hair was rinsed a dark chestnut brown. Aretha could still turn lots of heads at fifty-five years of age.

The things Aretha had been saying for the last several minutes had Gregory astounded. Why'd she believe it should be so easy for her husband to take her back? Why'd she think Gregory II should swallow his pride? Where was her pride when she'd decided to run off and leave her family? As far as he was concerned, Aretha's thought process was terribly warped. Gregory just couldn't imagine what made his mother think every man should be a fool for her.

Wanting to keep a close eye on the time, Gregory glanced down at his watch. He had to pick up Stephanie from the airport in less than an hour and he could hardly wait to see her. Being away from her was getting more and more difficult. He was eager for them to get married and live under one roof. The constant commuting was getting to both of them.

Gregory looked up and stared directly at Aretha. "Mother, what makes you think forgiving you should be so easy for Dad?"

Aretha tapped the tabletop with her squared, perfectly manicured fingernails, annoying her son in the process. "He's a Christian man. Isn't he?"

Gregory was slightly caught off guard by Aretha's pointed response. She touted herself as a Christian also, but that hadn't stopped her from making the biggest mistake of her life. "Dad is exactly that. He truly loves the Lord, but he's not perfect. No one is. I believe he's forgiven you, because of his beliefs. But my question to you was why you think it should be so easy for him."

Aretha looked perplexed. "For the very reasons you just stated, son."

"Forgiveness never comes easy, even for Christians. At any rate, forgiving you doesn't necessarily mean he has to take you back, Mother. I just don't think it's going to happen. You really injured Dad by running off like that."

Aretha snorted. "Only his pride, Gregory. Only his pride."

Gregory bucked his eyes in incredulity. "You hurt more than Dad's pride. His heart was and still is broken. If he heard your take on things, he'd never consider taking you back as his wife. I wish I understood your way of thinking."

Aretha shrugged her shoulders with nonchalance. "It's not for you to understand. Your father knows me and everything there is to know about me. Inside and out."

Gregory nodded in agreement. "I'm sure of that. That's why I feel the way I do. If you can't convince me you've changed, how will you be able to convince Dad?"

Aretha ran her fingers across her full lips. "If your dad will give me half a chance, he'll be able to see the changes for himself. I won't have to convince him of anything."

"Mother, I've been listening to you talk about this matter for weeks now. I don't see any changes in your attitude about what you've done. There's not even an ounce of remorse in you."

Aretha sucked her teeth hard, flailing her arms about. "Oh, Gregory, that's because I've forgiven myself. Am I supposed to just sit around and drown myself in my wrongdoing? I've admitted all of it to those that matter. More important, I've confessed my sins to God. Vengeance is His, not yours or your father's. You're still judging me, son. It's so obvious."

Gregory felt totally frustrated. All he wanted to do was get up and walk away. That wasn't an option for him. He'd never disrespect his mother in any sort of way, no matter what he thought of the horrible things she'd done to the Saxton family. "Mother, you need to listen up," he said calmly. "I'm only going to say this once. I *am not* going to try to convince Dad to take you back. I just can't do that. It's not my place."

Aretha narrowed her pecan-brown eyes to tiny slits. "Why not? Afraid of being cut out of the almighty Gregory Saxton II's will?"

Gregory was appalled by Aretha's remarks, yet he had no problem holding his tongue. He instead took out his wallet and removed a couple of crisp ten dollar bills to pay for lunch and a tip. "I hate to eat and run, Mother, but I have to pick up Stephanie from the airport."

"Coward," she shouted, looking her son dead in the eye. "I hope you're going to bring Stephanie around to the house," she said in the next breath. "It's time I get to know my future daughter-in-law better, that is, if you and your father haven't already turned her against me."

Gregory hid his dismay at the ugly name his mother had called him. But he didn't need anyone to confirm for him who he was. He already knew exactly who he was. "I'll try to get together with you while Stephanie's here. I can't say when just yet." He stood and then leaned over and kissed Aretha's cheek. "I'll call you later, Mother. I love you."

* * *

It was a great feeling for Gregory to have Stephanie back in his arms once again. As his fingers gently squeezed her waistline, he kissed her thoroughly. His smile was broad, showing her how happy he was to have her there with him. "How was your flight, sweetheart?"

Stephanie leaned her head against Gregory's chest. "Short and sweet. Just the way I like it. As you can see, we landed right on time." She nodded toward her carry-on bag. "That's all the luggage I have. No need to go to baggage claim this time. I'm learning to pack only my needs."

Gregory kissed Stephanie on the forehead. "Good for you. I know how you women like to have lots of choices in clothing. But you always look super to me no matter what you wear."

Once Gregory picked up the carry-on bag, Stephanie looped her arm through his and they headed for the exit nearest to where he'd parked the car. He had promised Malachi that he'd bring her right over to his place, since he was having dinner prepared in her honor. She always stayed with her father, but Malachi wouldn't get to see that much of her this three-day weekend. He planned to keep Stephanie on the go. Gregory also hoped she'd agree to spend at least one night in one of his lavish guest rooms since she now knew she was safe with him.

They rarely spent a lot of time in his home, but Gregory was okay with that. However, he planned to take Stephanie to a few custom-home sites. It was time for them to begin to make plans to build their very own dream place. There were several custom-model estate homes he wanted her to see before she returned to Houston. A ride down the Mississippi on a steamboat and a visit to a couple of antebellum mansions housed on old plantations was also on the agenda.

Spending time with Aretha wasn't the most important item on Gregory's docket, but he'd definitely keep his word to his mother. Gregory just hoped that Aretha didn't make

Stephanie feel uncomfortable by constantly talking about the possibility of getting back with her husband.

The women had only been together a few times. Each visit had been in a public place, only for short periods of time. Stephanie and Aretha had seemed to hit it off okay in Gregory's opinion.

Only after Gregory saw to it that Stephanie was settled in the car and buckled in safely did he go around and get in on the driver's side. Before starting the engine, he leaned over and gave his fiancée a tender kiss. "Do you have any idea how much I've missed you?"

Stephanie smiled and nodded. "I do, but only because I missed you just as much. It's getting harder and harder being away from you. You are constantly in my thoughts, Gregory."

Gregory loved hearing that Stephanie felt the same as he did. Knowing that it was just as hard for her to be away from him made him feel good all over, making him wish that neither of them had to suffer through the long separations. Her comments lent further credence to all the reasons why he thought they should get married as soon as possible. "How does a September wedding sound to you, Stephanie?"

Stephanie looked momentarily stunned. She then smiled beautifully, hiding the fear she felt deep down inside. "That's a little soon, don't you think? There's not much left of the summer and we still have yet to make definite plans. What about next spring?"

Gregory suddenly felt flat inside. "Are you sure you want to wait that long? I thought the commute was getting to you as much as it is to me. Why do we need to put our wedding off? We both know that marriage is what we want. It's hard being without you all the time."

Stephanie reached over and softly ran her hand down Gregory's right thigh. "It's hard for both of us, but we can't rush things because of it." She lowered her head for a second. "Please don't think I don't want to get married as soon as possible, because I do. I just think September is too close for us to pull everything together in enough time. We want it to be right, don't we?"

Gregory pulled the car off the road. After parking in a safe spot, he cut the engine. He then took both of Stephanie's hands and placed them in his. "I'm sorry if I upset you, Stephanie. It wasn't my intent. I just want us to get married. I need you with me every night. Is that so bad?"

Stephanie gulped hard, forcing a smile to her lips. "There's nothing bad about it. I want the same things you do. Can we compromise and get married the first Saturday in October? That'll give us a bit more time to execute our plans, even though we haven't made any yet."

Gregory fought to control his rising emotions. Stephanie setting a definite date for their wedding had him ecstatic. "Oh, I can't wait for October to get here!" He brought her to him and quickly sealed their plans with a passionate kiss. Nothing else needed to be said on the subject. He had his answer. Stephanie Trudeaux was going to marry him in October.

Stephanie was so happy to see how pleased Gregory was by her decision, hoping she'd have all her issues regarding marriage resolved by the magic month she'd given him. She wasn't going to run from a love so pure and deep forever. She loved this man too much to ever cause him an ounce of pain or a minute of doubt. That he loved her, too, with his whole heart and soul, was the one thing in this life she was positively sure about. The Lord would work out everything else for him and her. After all, God invented the beautiful institution of marriage.

Malachi acted as though he hadn't seen Stephanie in weeks, even though he'd just left Houston a few days ago. The way her father crushed her to him made her feel all fuzzy and warm inside and so deeply loved. "Daddy," she suddenly moaned, "I can hardly breathe."

Malachi looked slightly alarmed as he realized he'd been holding his daughter too tight. "I'm sorry, my dear girl. I didn't mean to hug you so hard."

Stephanie's laughter floated on the air. "It's okay. I'm breathing just fine now, Dad."

Gregory felt his heart overflow with emotion. Knowing his fiancée was so loved by her father and him by her made him give silent praise to God for finally bringing them together in His time. Seeing them embracing with such warmth always made his emotions go a little crazy.

Malachi immediately took the necessary steps to ensure his daughter's comfort. He then had one of his housekeeping staff members take her bag up to the room she loved to stay in, the same suite she'd slept in on her very first visit to his home. When Stephanie quickly expressed her desire to wash up a bit, Malachi told her dinner would be held until she returned.

Malachi then led Gregory into the comfortable but lavishly decorated retreat. "Please have a seat, son. Would you like to have something to drink before dinner?"

Gregory shook his head in the negative. He then changed his mind. "On second thought, that would be nice. I am a little thirsty. What about a club soda with a twist of lime?"

Malachi grinned. "Coming right up. Max is supposed to come by, but he told me not to hold up dinner for him. He can always get something warmed up. He really loves his niece."

Gregory nodded. "It would be hard not to love her. She's a great girl. Hey, Uncle Mal, your daughter has finally set a date for us to get married. The first weekend in October."

Malachi's eye lit up like bright stars. "That's wonderful news, son! I'm happy for both of you. Is this going to be a big wedding? No matter what size you decide on, I'm picking up the tab. Its not every day a man's only daughter gets married. I wonder if she's going to let me give her away. I imagine Stephen will fight for that honor. He's well within his rights to want to give his sister away. He's taken such good care of her. They've been inseparable since birth."

Stephanie stepped back into the room. "You're both going to give me away. Stephen and I have already talked about it, Dad. Is that an acceptable arrangement with you?"

Malachi hugged Stephanie to him. "More than acceptable! I'm thrilled to hear that your brother and you have already discussed it. I'll play any role in your wedding that you need me to, Stephanie. Don't worry about the expenses. I've got it all covered. Are you ready to eat?"

Stephanie rubbed her stomach. "The delicious food scents have my belly growling something awful. I smelled dinner when I came down the steps. What are we having, Dad?"

Malachi smiled gently. "Why don't we just wait and see." He extended his arm to his daughter. "Shall we go into the dining room?"

Stephanie laughed softly, looping her arm with Malachi's. "We shall." Once Gregory joined them as they neared the exit, she took his arm also. "I'm so excited about everything. We've got a lot of plans to make this weekend, Mr. Saxton."

Gregory lifted up Stephanie's hand and brought it to his lips. He then placed a light kiss into her palm. "I'm more than up for it, sweetheart. October seems such a long way off, but I guess I'll have to learn how to practice lots of patience. You *are* worth waiting for, you know."

"I know," Stephanie murmured sweetly. "So are you."

"Everything worth having is worth waiting for," Malachi said. "I wished I'd practiced that in my youth. My wife and I would still be together had I waited until after she'd given birth to have my physical needs met."

Stephanie wagged her finger back and forth in front of Malachi. "Uh-uh, Dad, let's not go there. We're in a celebratory mood. Let the past stay in the past. Okay?"

Malachi nodded. "Okay, my dear. You're absolutely right about where the past belongs."

* * *

The corn-bread-stuffed Cornish hens had been roasted to perfection. Stephanie had labeled them as her favorites during one of her visits to New Orleans, so Malachi had had the kitchen staff prepare the birds in her honor. She couldn't thank him enough for arranging the special dinner for her. Her father always tried to make each of her visits to his home quite memorable.

Stephanie couldn't eat another bite. She knew that the servers were standing by to bring out dessert, but she'd have to pass on it this time. If she wasn't more careful, control of her weight was going to get away from her. She'd been eating a lot lately, especially since her family loved sharing meals together. Seated around the dinner table chatting and eating had become one of their favorite things to do.

There was always so much interesting stuff for them to talk about among themselves, although Stephanie didn't think they'd ever catch up on everything. Twenty-eight years was a very long span of time for them to fill in all the blanks. Malachi and Maxwell had endless stories to tell—and she and Stephen couldn't seem to hear enough of what they had to say. The quality time they spent with their father and uncle always brought about some new revelation.

The air was pretty muggy around the largest lake on Malachi's property. Stephanie and Gregory didn't seem to mind the heavy moisture in the atmosphere as they took a leisurely stroll. Walking off some of the calories was her main intent, but she also enjoyed chatting amicably with her handsome fiancé. When Gregory directed Stephanie to one of the benches alongside the lake, she was happy to sit down for a few moments, since her feet had just begun to ache.

Right at sunset yellowish bulbs from the gas lamps had flickered on all over the vast property, making for a very romantic setting. The walkways, trees and shrubbery were also decorated with tiny white lights, making the dozens of different pathways easy to follow.

The bright illumination in Stephanie's eyes mesmerized Gregory even more than the property lights did, as he eased his arm around her shoulder. Wanting to prepare her for spending time with his mother, he'd decided to tell her what was going on with his parents so she wouldn't be completely caught off guard should Aretha bring things out in the open. "I'd like to talk to you about something very personal. Think you can loan me an ear for a minute or two?"

Stephanie's eyebrows furrowed with concern upon hearing the slight stress in Gregory's voice. "Of course. I hope there's nothing wrong. Your voice sounds a little tense."

"Nothing for you to be concerned about, Stephanie. I just need someone to listen. It's about my mother. Since she wants us to spend time with her during your visit, I think you should know a couple of things. Mother wants me to try to help her get my father back."

Stephanie elevated an eyebrow. "She wants him back in the romantic sense?"

Gregory nodded in the affirmative. "You got it. She's left her boy toy."

"Interesting. Very much so. Do you think you're father will take her back?"

"I have no clue. But I know Dad has never stopped missing her. He has been madly in love with Aretha Blackwell since the first moment he locked eyes with her. Blackwell is her maiden name. Looks like we'll have to wait to see how this weird scenario plays out."

Stephanie reached up and smoothed Gregory's eyebrows with her fingertips. "How do you feel about it? Would you like to see your parents get back together again?"

"Stephanie, marriage is supposed to be sacred. Mother committed adultery. I can forgive her and I'm sure Dad already has. But can she ever again find favor with God?"

"God will forgive your mom. However, there will be consequences."

"Dire ones," Gregory stated strongly.

"Yeah, maybe so. Does Grant know your mother wants your father back?"

"Grant knows everything there is to know about Mother. He's the apple of her eye. Always has been."

"You don't sound the least bit envious. You should be proud of that, Gregory."

"It is what it is, Stephanie. I don't envy Grant anything. I'm just going to sit back and watch this drama between my parents unfold. I don't want to see Dad hurt again. Although Mother says she's sincere, I can't ever really tell with her. Once Dad finds out about her intentions, he may want my input. I have no clue what I'd say to him."

Stephanie certainly empathized with Gregory. Adultery had also impacted her family in a very negative way. "I can only imagine how tough that'll be on you. Just be as fair as you can."

"For certain." Gregory looked as if the entire matter pained him. "I just wanted to give you a heads-up so you'll be prepared if Mother should spring this on you. If I know her, she'll try to gain you as an ally in this. Don't get caught up in the madness. It'll only make you crazy."

Stephanie gently entwined her fingers around Gregory's. "Don't worry. Everything will be okay with your parents. It will turn out just as God intends it."

Gregory dropped a kiss in Stephanie's hair. "I'm sure it will." He then thought of visiting his mother's home this evening, just to get it out of the way. It was just a little before 8:00 p.m. Hoping Stephanie was up to it, he posed the question to her.

Stephanie shrugged. "I'm all for it. Do you need to call and let her know we're coming?"

Gregory removed his cell phone from its holster on his belt. "I'll do that now. I hope Uncle Mal won't mind us cutting out on him."

Stephanie shook her head from side to side. "He won't have a problem with it. Dad knows we plan to be on the go while I'm here. He's really happy for us when we get to spend time together. Dad always reminds me that he was young and in love once upon a time."

Aretha eagerly engaged Stephanie in a loving embrace, greeting her future daughter-in-law with an enthusiastic welcome. She then quietly led her son and his fiancée into the extravagantly decorated formal living room, where a white baby grand piano stood imperiously. It appeared to Stephanie that lots of money had been spent with an interior designer.

The beautiful furnishings were fashioned in simple colors of ebony and ivory, yet the room was gently explosive. Splashes of gold and reds scattered about here and there warmed the space, along with the vibrant oils of the exquisite African artwork. Every corner of the room was well appointed. Space this large was cozy only because the perfect decor had been chosen.

Aretha stood by as Stephanie and Gregory seated themselves side by side on the plush antique satin sofa. "Can I get you two something to drink before we begin our visit?"

Stephanie smiled at Aretha. "Is iced tea an option?"

"It can be. It'll only take me a minute or two to make some, Stephanie." Aretha looked at her son. "I've got your favorite raspberry lemonade chilling in the refrigerator. Would you care for a glass, son?"

"Thanks, Mother. I'd like that. Crushed ice please."

Stephanie raised her hand to get Aretha's attention. "The lemonade will work for me also. I've never had raspberry-flavored. It sounds delicious."

"Two ice cold lemonades coming right up. Make yourselves at home, kids."

Stephanie jumped to her feet. "I'd like to come along and help out. That is, if you don't mind, Mrs. Saxton?"

Aretha took a hold of Stephanie's hand. "Company in the kitchen would be nice. Having you call me Ms. Aretha would be even nicer. That is, until you're comfortable calling me Mom."

"Not a problem," Stephanie assured, glad she hadn't been asked to call Aretha just by her first name. Things she'd been taught about respect as a child by her mother were still with her.

Gregory looked pleased by Stephanie's offer of help. Although he didn't think she was trying to score points with his mother, he knew that she had. Aretha liked down-to-earth people, even though she herself could be a bit snooty at times. His mother still seemed genuinely taken with Stephanie and he couldn't be happier about that.

After Aretha showed Stephanie where she kept her drinking glasses, the younger woman removed three tall ones from one of the cherry-wood cabinets. She then filled them with ice from the dispenser on the front of the refrigerator. Aretha came over and opened the refrigerator door and removed the purple glass pitcher of raspberry lemonade.

Stephanie immediately noticed that the glasses she'd chosen matched the pitcher Aretha held. "This is a beautiful set of glassware. I love the color. All shades of purple are my favorites."

"Grant gave me this set for Christmas one year. I've had it a long time. Maybe I can get you a similar set as one of your wedding gifts. By the way, have you two set a date yet?"

Stephanie grinned broadly. "Yes, we have, and I'd love to have a glass set like this one. First Saturday in October is the big day, but we don't have any concrete plans made yet. We're going to discuss ideas for the wedding while I'm here in New Orleans."

Aretha sucked in a deep breath. "Kind of exciting, huh?"

Stephanie nodded. "Very."

"Do you want a huge wedding, Stephanie?"

Stephanie shrugged. "I don't know what I want, but family and friends is just perfect. I wish my mother were around to help me decide. I know nothing about planning a wedding."

"Well, I do. Would you like me to help you, honey? It would be my pleasure."

Stephanie beamed at Aretha. "Oh, would you really? That would make me so happy."

Aretha clapped her hands. "Sweetie, you just made my day. This wedding will be all the talk around the Big Easy." Aretha put her hand up to her lips. "I'm sorry for making assumptions, especially since you haven't said where you two plan to have your wedding. Wherever you hold it, I'll be there to see you through to the end of your very special day."

"Thanks, Ms. Aretha. By the end of my visit Gregory and I should've decided on whether to have our wedding in Houston or in New Orleans. I'm sure you'll know exactly what to do to help make our wedding day the very best."

Aretha was so excited about Stephanie allowing her to help with the wedding plans. She thought it was a great way to really get to know the stunning young woman her youngest son was in love with. She wanted to be a darn good mother-in-law, especially since she'd failed at being the best mother she could've been to her two boys. Aretha had lots of regret in that particular area of her life. Abandoning her sons, though they'd been adults at the time, had been a grave mistake, one that she was sure Gregory still held against her. "That's for sure, Stephanie. We have that settled now, so what about something tasty to eat?"

Stephanie wrinkled her nose. "We already had dinner at my father's place a couple of hours ago. I ate so much food I didn't have any room left for dessert."

"In that case, you and Gregory can have dessert with me. How does a thick slice of double-fudge chocolate cake sound to you?"

Stephanie licked her lips. "Scrumptious!"

Gregory entered the kitchen right at that moment. "What's scrumptious?"

"The chocolate cake I'm about to serve for dessert. You two have a seat at the table. I'll get the plates for us."

"Sounds like a winner to me, Mother. I'm sure you got it at the Sweet Shop Bakery, because I know you didn't bake it," he said on a chuckle. After kissing Stephanie softly on the lips, he guided her over to the kitchen table, where he pulled out a chair for her to be seated.

Stephanie instantly liked the smooth, fruity taste of the ice-cold raspberry lemonade. She took several small swallows before returning her glass to the tray. "It's delicious. I'd like to have the recipe if it's not a family secret recipe."

Aretha glanced at Stephanie and then smiled. "No secret. I'll get it to you before you leave. It's really quite simple to make. How long will you be in New Orleans, Stephanie?"

"Until late Monday. Being in business for myself affords me a little flexibility."

"Will you be moving here permanently after the wedding?" Aretha asked.

Stephanie nodded in the affirmative. "It seems the easiest solution. Gregory has a thriving practice here with his father. I'm sure I can build up a good clientele list. Since Houston isn't that far away, I'm hoping I'll also be able to retain my current clients. Most of them are in the process of decorating or redecorating so they won't need my services for a few years once the projects are completed."

Aretha was happy that Stephanie seemed to want what was best for Gregory. That she was willing to rebuild her career in order for him to retain his current professional status was very commendable. Many women wouldn't be willing to relocate to another state, let alone sacrifice the business they'd carefully built from the ground up.

Aretha knew all about those types of women, because she

was one of them. She hadn't supported her husband in anything he'd taken on. In fact, she had done everything in her power to show him how independent she was of him; despite the fact she had used his money to achieve her freedom. Aretha got the sense that Stephanie was as selfless as Gregory was, and she was ecstatic that her son had found a good woman, one who was absolutely nothing like his self-centered mother.

As Stephanie stared into the crystal-clear pool water, seated on one of the chaise longues outside on Gregory's flagstone patio, she thought about how well the visit had gone with Aretha. She had been very cordial and was always right up front about who she was as a person. Stephanie couldn't be more pleased at Aretha's offer to assist with the wedding plans, which had actually brought her a lot of comfort. If Stephanie had to rate the visit, she'd give it a ten plus.

There weren't any older women in Stephanie's life that she could turn to, at least none who were as socially well seasoned as Aretha Saxton. Just listening to the things she'd already had to say let Stephanie know that the lady knew how to plan an elite social event. The first and most important decision Stephanie had to make was which state to hold the wedding in.

Houston seemed the most logical city to get married in, because all of Stephanie's life-long friends, past and current clients, and business and casual acquaintances lived there. Asking them to travel all the way to New Orleans for her wedding day might be a bit much. However, she knew people who'd invited their family and friends to weddings in places like Hawaii and the Caribbean. It was a lengthy drive, but only a short flight from Houston to the Big Easy.

Gregory appeared and sat down in front of Stephanie with a cup of hot lemon tea. "About the wedding," he said, taking a seat on a lounge chair, "why don't we have the wedding in one place and then hold the reception in the other? That way, we both get to invite everyone we know."

Stephanie gave a couple of seconds' thought to Gregory's suggestion. "I like the idea, but even that might be hard to pull off." As her brain began to toss around other ideas, she gave serious thought to their dilemma. Then a light bulb suddenly went off in her head. "Why don't we just have a quiet wedding in Houston with just our family members in attendance. Then we can have one reception here in New Orleans and one in Houston. I think it can work."

Gregory scowled. "Are you sure about that one, Stephanie? I thought you wanted the traditional wedding, maid of honor, bridesmaids and all the other girlie trimmings."

Stephanie looked deeply into Gregory's eyes, her love for him shining brightly. "I want you! This is all about us wanting each other, desiring to live together for the rest of our lives. The other stuff is trimmings, just as you said a minute ago. Our wedding day should be all about us."

Gregory looked impressed and uncertain at the same time. "Can it really be that simple?"

Stephanie grinned. "I know it can. We get to make all the decisions. No one but us."

Totally accepting of Stephanie's proposal, Gregory shrugged. "I guess it's on then—Houston for the wedding and both Houston and New Orleans for the receptions. I believe you've come up with a workable solution. Since my mother is helping you with the wedding plans, what if she doesn't like your tale of two cities? No pun intended. Her personality can be pretty overpowering, especially when she wants things to go her way. How will you handle that?"

Stephanie raised an eyebrow. "I'll just have to politely and assertively tell Ms. Aretha that this isn't about her. I agreed to let her help me, not do a complete take-over."

Gregory chuckled heartily. "That's my girl! Mother is strong-willed, but I think you might be a bit stronger on this one. Stick to your guns, Stephanie. Let her know where you're coming from at the very beginning." He came over and sat down next to her on the chaise longue. "Can I get a big kiss to seal this deal?"

Stephanie smiled flirtingly. "How does a dozen big kisses sound to you?"

"I love how you're so willing to compromise," Gregory said, casting her a huge smile.

Stephanie eagerly went into Gregory's arms, ready to cash in on the deal.

"You're so beautiful, Stephanie. I'm really blessed."

Stephanie bumped Gregory with her shoulder. "That makes two of us. Speaking of beautiful, Ms. Aretha looks more stunning every time I see her. She sure keeps her body in tip-top shape. The woman is incredible looking for someone fifty-five. The fifties and sixties today look nothing like the same age group from just a few years back."

Gregory nodded in agreement. "She has always believed in working out. Mother is very health conscious, too. Eats all the right foods. I noticed that she didn't touch the chocolate cake. She's more into counting carbohydrates and fat grams than she is at paying attention to calories."

"Anyone can tell her workout habits in just a single glance. Who's her interior designer?"

"She is. Aretha Saxton knows her stuff when it comes to decorating and such. She has an amazing eye for design. She also decorated our family home. I guess I forgot to mention it when you were raving over the lavish decor at Dad's place. That gives you two something in common. That is, besides me."

Stephanie looked surprised by Gregory's announcement. "How you forgot to mention her design skills is a mystery to me. I only had a conniption fit over your dad's amazing home."

"Sorry about that. The next time you see Mother, please tell her what you think of her design skills. Coming from an accomplished designer, she'll eat your compliments right up."

Stephanie laughed, tilting her head to one side. "You're not suggesting I kiss up to your mother, are you?"

Gregory cracked up. "Not really, but a little kissing up can't hurt. No, I'm just kidding. Mother is going to love you no matter what. I can tell she's already impressed with you. Impressing that lady isn't the least bit easy. She's a hard nut to crack."

"I think your mother and I are going to get along just fine. I feel so blessed by her offer to help me out with our wedding plans. I'm sure we'll become closer. I'd really like that to happen. I know I'm going to ache for my mother all during the planning process, but she's the one who taught us that life always has to go on."

After Stephen sent up a few silent words of prayer, he hesitantly rang Farrah's doorbell, halfway hoping she wasn't in. When the door swung back wide, he knew it was too late for him to catch his hat and run. His heart raced inside his chest as she gestured for him to come in.

Looking terribly nervous, Stephen followed Farrah into the family room, hoping her mother would eventually come out so they wouldn't be alone. However, he first needed only to talk with Farrah about what he had to say. This wasn't a pleasant thing for him, but it was something he needed to do. It was time for him to clear the air.

Farrah slowly dropped down into a chair, keeping her eyes fastened on Stephen, who was already seated in one of the leather chairs. "What brings you over here this evening, Stephen?"

Stephen folded his hands and placed them in his lap. "I came to apologize."

Farrah looked perplexed. "For what?"

Stephen wrung his hands together. "If I've been leading you on, I'm sorry. I am attracted to you, but I'm deeply in love with Darcy. We're having a few minor problems in our relationship, so I guess I allowed myself to be distracted and then become slightly infatuated with you. I don't want to use you like that, Farrah. You're a very special woman and I think there's a great guy out there just waiting for you two to find each other."

Farrah saw her dreams of having a meaningful relationship with Stephen crumbling right before her eyes. But she'd known from the start that Stephen was in love with his fiancée. A little wishful thinking never hurt anyone. *If that was true, then why is my heart in such excruciating pain?* She didn't know what kind of problems he and Darcella were having, but she prayed it would turn out the way he wanted it to. Her feelings for Stephen were deep, but purely unselfish. "I understand. I'll be here if you need me, Stephen. Always."

Touched by her heartfelt gesture, Stephen felt the emotional swelling in his throat. Sensing that the timing was perfect for him to make his exit, so things didn't get a chance to get any heavier, Stephen rapidly got to his feet. "I truly appreciate you saying that, Farrah. I really like having you as a friend."

Farrah laughed through her distress. "'Friends' hasn't ever been my ultimate goal for us, but I respect the position you're in. Darcy is a blessed woman. I only hope she knows it." She softly patted her left shoulder. "If you ever need one of these, they're pretty strong."

"I have no reason not to believe that." He started for the door but quickly turned around and walked over to where Farrah sat. He then bent down and gave her a warm hug. "I'll keep those strong shoulders of yours in mind should I ever need one to lean on."

Farrah laughed. "This sounds just like a Bill Withers' 'lean on me' moment. I hope you know you can always call on me, Stephen." Farrah got up to walk Stephen to the door.

Stephen's heart skipped a beat. "Thanks. By the way, where's your mother?"

Farrah lowered her lashes. "She's in the hospital, Stephen.

Her blood sugar was extremely high when we checked it, so I took her to the ER. Her doctor admitted her."

Stephen felt foolish. His problems now seemed trivial compared to what Helen and Farrah were faced with. "I'm sorry to hear that. Is there anything I can do to help out?"

Farrah smiled. "Perhaps you can keep one of those broad shoulders on reserve for me."

Laughing, Stephen brushed off his left shoulder. "You got it, girl. Seriously, though, if there's anything I can do to help you out, please don't hesitate to ask. I'm positive Stephanie feels the same way. I guess you know she's down in New Orleans. Do you want me to call her?"

Farrah shook her head in the negative. "And spoil her special time with Gregory? Not a chance. Everything is completely under control around here."

"Okay. On that note, I'm out of here." He tenderly kissed her forehead. "Good night."

Stephen was proud of himself for doing the right thing by Farrah. His sister would also be proud of him. If Farrah had been hurt by what he'd said to her, she certainly hadn't shown it. Honesty was always the best policy. Stephen had been honest with her when he'd said that she was a great girl and that he hoped she'd find Mr. Right. Under different circumstances he might've been Mr. Right for her, he considered.

Perhaps something good could come out of Farrah's budding friendship with Grant Saxton. Since Stephanie had informed Stephen that Grant had changed a lot in the past two years, that he was no longer drinking and drugging, he felt better about a possible union between them. Farrah was as loyal as they came and she deserved all the best that love had to offer. Stephen was pretty certain that she'd make some man a wonderful mate. He wasn't sure Grant was the right man for Farrah, but he knew people could change for the better.

As Stephen continued on toward home, he allowed his thoughts to wrap around the possibility of working in his father's company in New Orleans. Even though Darcella didn't seem too keen on the idea of moving to another state, he felt that he at least had to explore all his options. He loved his job as a fireman; practically thrived on the unbelievable adrenaline rushes, but to go into another career field might be a nice change from all the strains and stresses.

There were many questions in his mind about his future with Darcella. A huge drawback for him was that he really wanted kids and she wasn't ready for a family yet. Still, he thought she was the right woman for him. Perhaps everything would work itself out in due time.

Only God knew the beginning and the end.

Chapter 7

Surprised to see Darcella's vehicle parked in his driveway, Stephen couldn't help wondering what had brought her out to see him this late. He prayed she wasn't there as a bearer of more bad news, because he'd already had his fill of the negativity. Eager to find out what was on her mind, he hurried from his vehicle and then ran up to hers. As Stephen tapped lightly on the driver's window, Darcella nearly jumped out of her skin.

The moment Darcella recognized her fiancé, she got out of the car and rushed right into his arms. "Hi. I've missed you so much, Stephen. I hope you don't mind me dropping by like this, but I really needed to see you tonight. I waited all day for you to call."

Stephen squeezed Darcella tightly, loving the tender feel of her in his arms. "I didn't know what to do, especially since our last visit didn't go too well. I wanted to call you, but I was trying to give you your space. I'm glad you're here, Darcy. Come on. Let's go inside."

Once Stephen made the offer to Darcella for something

to drink or eat, and both were declined, the couple quickly made themselves comfortable on the sofa in his media room. His first thought was to turn on the television, but then he thought better of it. He sensed that Darcella hadn't come there just to sit up and watch a movie or program. She had an agenda.

Darcella clasped her hands together. After lacing her fingers into one another, she then turned them inside and out. "We need to talk, Stephen. Serious talk."

Stephen wasn't surprised. "I'm willing to listen to whatever's on your mind, Darcy."

Darcella drew her legs up under her to try to keep herself from fidgeting so much. "First off, I apologize for my bad behaviors over the past days. I'm an emotional mess, Stephen. There's so much you don't know about me. I've misled you in so many ways, about so many things. Where do I begin?" She shrugged. "I guess my childhood would be a good start."

Stephen felt that the dawning of a new day was about to begin for him and Darcella. He had a lot to tell her, too. Confessing to her about his attraction to Farrah and how he'd nearly acted upon it was at the top of the list. He and Darcella definitely needed to get everything out in the open if they ever hoped to have a great future together.

Keeping secrets had killed countless relationships; his parents' marriage included.

Darcella took a deep breath before she began to tell Stephen some of the same things she'd told Stephanie about her childhood. As she discussed her serious issues with her family, she had a pained expression on her face. A few minutes later the painful expression began to look like one of relief. It wasn't easy for her to reveal the truth to him, but she knew there was no other choice. It was time for her to get real about who she was and what she hoped to become.

Darcella was smart enough to know that her very future hinged on how she chose to deal with her disturbing past and also how she ended up handling the troubling matters presiding over her present. If issues weren't managed when they first happened, or shortly thereafter, the past would always collide with the present—and would eventually impact the future. Though surprised at how easily things slipped off her tongue, she continued to let the words fly. Telling Stephen about how ignored she had always felt by her mother made her feel terribly sad.

"As for church, religion and things of the spirit, we weren't taught too much in those areas," Darcella shared with Stephen. "We never attended weekend services." She then told him she thought that her father was horribly fearful of God's punishments. "Dad's a good man, but a miserable spouse. My parents still don't have what it takes to make them happy. They're the saddest couple on the planet. I wish they were happy and madly in love with each other."

Stephen turned his mouth down at the corners. "I was a tad suspicious that you might have serious issues with your family. On the other hand, I had no idea you felt totally ignored by your mother. Your brothers sound selfish and only into themselves. As for the religious stuff, I often wondered if you'd been brought up in the church. I wish I could change your circumstances, Darcy, but we both know I can't. Only you can do that. I can be here for you."

Darcella laid her head upon Stephen's shoulder. "I don't expect you to change them, Stephen. I know I have to do that all by my lonesome. Does it bother you that I'm not baptized?"

Stephen gently smoothed Darcella's hair with the palm of his hand. "I'm not at all bothered by it, Darcy, but are you?"

Darcella gave Stephen's question a couple moments of thought. "Yeah, I guess you could say it bothers me. Doesn't being baptized mean you're saved?"

"Baptism is only the beginning of the long, hard road toward deliverance, Darcy. Believing wholeheartedly in Christ makes the road a lot easier. Even then, it's still very tough. I have been taught about God my entire life, yet I'm still in the dark about many spiritual things."

Stephen saw Darcella's questions as the perfect opportunity to share with his fiancée the things he'd been thinking about. It seemed to him as if she may now be more receptive of going to marriage counseling with him than she might've been had he brought it up before now. First things first, though, he mused. Confessing to Darcella about Farrah shouldn't be put off any longer. There were times when you first had to get rid of the unpleasantness in order to make room for the pleasantries. Darcella deserved to know the truth about everything.

Stephen gulped hard as he tried to make himself more comfortable on the sofa. "You know Farrah Freeman, Stephanie's friend, neighbor and part-time employee?"

Darcella looked perplexed. "Of course I know Farrah, Stephen. Why are you asking?"

Stephen sighed hard, wishing he could skip completely over this part. "Because I've been slightly attracted to her. I believe it's only in a lustful way. I started looking at her differently when our personal problems first arose. Farrah has been around me since childhood, but I never paid her any kind of personal attention until lately. I've had dinner with Farrah twice now."

Darcella's eyes blinked uncontrollably. "Lusting after her! Dinner! Are you sure this is something you want to be telling me, Stephen? And if you call yourself joking, you need to know that I don't think anything you had to say was the least bit funny. Are you feeling me?"

Stephen pressed his lips together. "Abundantly!"

Darcella slightly distanced herself from Stephen. "Now that we're feeling each other, perhaps you can enlighten me about the not one but two dinner dates you had with Farrah."

"I'm no longer sure this is something I want to tell you," he mocked, hoping to lighten the mood. The calculated narrowing of Darcella's eyes told him she wasn't in a joking mood. "Okay, I'm getting it, Darcy. To set the record straight, they weren't dinner dates." He went on to explain to Darcella how he and Farrah taking meals together had come about.

"Are you telling me that Stephanie is a part of this? If so, I find that hard to believe."

"Stephanie's not a part of anything to do with this. I just happened to be at my sister's house when Farrah offered to run next door and get the food she'd just cooked. The second time we ate together was when Stephanie wasn't home one evening, and Farrah sought me out. Neither dinner was preplanned or intimate. Farrah's mother was present at the one in her house."

Darcella glared at Stephen. "So now Ms. Helen is involved! Everyone you've mentioned knows that you and I are engaged. So what part of getting married don't they understand? More to the point, what part of our engagement don't you get?"

"It's perfectly understood by me and everyone else who knows us that we're getting married. I actually went to Farrah's to apologize to her if I've led her on in any way. I wasn't unfaithful to you, Darcy. I'm just guilty of entertaining the very idea of it."

Looking exasperated, Darcella posted a hand on her hip. "I guess that depends on how an individual defines unfaithfulness. You may not have cheated physically, but there has been some mental and emotional cheating going on between you and Farrah. How can you tell me you love me while you're out there lusting after another woman? Your sister's best friend, no less."

Blowing out an uneven stream of breath, Stephen haphazardly pushed his hand through his hair. "I told you because I want everything to be aboveboard with us. I'm in love with you, Darcy. I know you might consider this a funny way of me showing my feelings for you, but I've been checking myself hard on this matter. I think we should go to premarital counseling."

Darcella snapped her neck, rolling her eyes dramatically. "Oh, so you step out on me with another woman, but I'm the one needing counseling. I can't believe you just said that. Stephen, this is so dang messed up. I never dreamed you'd stoop to this level. How can you dare humiliate me this way? Does your family know about your so-called attraction to Farrah? Since you share everything on God's green earth with them, I'm sure they do. Your family knowing about your lustful affair is a problem for me. A big one! You have embarrassed me to no end. How do you expect me to ever be able to look your family in the eyes?"

Stephen reached for Darcella, but she pulled away from him, screaming for him not to ever touch her again. He pulled back as though he'd grabbed hold of a hot wire. "I didn't step out on you, Darcy. The meals I took with Farrah were unexpected and unplanned. I'm not going to discount your feelings by trying to convince you I'm totally innocent in this matter, because I'm not. I made a mistake, a huge one. I'm sorry that I hurt you this way. I feel terrible about it."

"Not half as terrible as I do. Stephen."

As she envisioned Stephen and Farrah seated at a table for two, intimately lit by candlelight, Darcella's heart nearly stopped. Just the thought of him flirting with another woman made her heartsick. Imagining him kissing someone other than her was sheer agony. What she felt was beyond jealousy. It went so much deeper than any emotional envy. There was no way Stephen would want her to have dinner with another man. How had he thought she'd accept something like that from him? He had to be crazy if he thought she'd be okay with his confession.

This wasn't something Darcella had expected from Stephen. Now that it had happened, she didn't know what to do about it. Breaking up with him was an option for her, but not a very attractive one. She tried to tell herself that it was only an innocent flirtation on his part, but her heart wasn't buying into it. Where there was smoke, fire was normally somewhere waiting in the wings. Stephen was a flesh-and-blood man—and Darcella could only believe that he would've eventually acted upon his attraction to Farrah. Men played by a different set of rules than women normally operated on. Men had the tendency to act in an instant and then think about it later.

The agony Stephen felt deep down in his heart was practically unbearable, yet he undoubtedly knew that it couldn't compare to the kind of hell he'd just put Darcella through by his untimely confession. Perhaps it would've been better had he not told her about his juvenile attraction to Farrah, especially when it was nothing more than that. At that very moment Stephen realized that the best thing that had ever happened to him was Darcella and her unselfish love.

The kind of love Stephen had shared with Darcella over the past years had been nothing short of beautiful. Of course they'd had their differences, many of them, but it was the number of things they had in common that had made their relationship work. All of a sudden things had begun to fall apart—and it wasn't getting any better. Why did the truth have to hurt, even when it wasn't the intent? Stephen hated that he'd crushed the heart of the woman he loved.

Stephen had no more intended to hurt Darcella than Malachi had intended to hurt Doreen so many years ago. Not only did he understand the devastation his mother had probably gone through, upon learning that her husband had cheated on her, he was now seeing it up close and personal. He had completely devastated Darcella with his insensitive confession.

The pain of Stephen's callous remarks was written all over Darcella's face. He hated himself for putting the look of utter hopelessness on her pretty face. What had just occurred caused him to wonder how Doreen had found out about her husband's infidelities. Had Malachi confessed to her just as he'd done with Darcella? He made a mental note to ask his father how Doreen had found out about his illicit one-night affair.

Stephen had often heard people say that *"what you don't know can't hurt you."* That statement was certainly applicable in this situation. If only he'd been wise enough to have spared Darcella this kind of unnecessary pain. His regret over causing her so much agony was deep.

Hoping Darcella wouldn't reject him again, Stephen dared to reach over and put his hand on her thigh. "I know how horrible you must feel. I'm really sorry about it all. You may not find any consolation in this, but this has made me realize how much I really love you and how much I want our relationship to work. I'm sure you want to take some time away from us to think about what you want to do. I can understand that. However, since you're so upset, I'd like you to sleep in the spare bedroom tonight. I don't want you driving when you're feeling like this."

Darcella stared at Stephen with distrust. "I think it's you that needs to figure things out and then decide what you want to do. This isn't about me, Stephen. I'm not the one sneaking around and having private dinners with someone I'm physically attracted to. If I had to tell you this very minute what I want to do about this situation, you'd be shocked senseless. Instead of acting on my felonious urges, I'm leaving. Perhaps we'll talk in a couple of days. It's obvious that we both have a lot of soul-searching to do."

Stephen got up from the sofa and followed Darcella out into the foyer.

Just before Darcella made it to the exit, she turned to face Stephen. "I strongly suggest that you really be honest with yourself about your attraction to Farrah. Maybe it's not just physical. If you're interested in her, you should find out before you walk down the aisle with me. I'd hate for you to realize you've made a big mistake after our wedding. That is, if I decide I still want to marry you." With that said, her tears falling rapidly, she rushed out the front door.

A stunned, confused Stephen watched from the doorway as Darcella settled into her car. He wanted to run after her and beg her to stay there with him, but he saw it as adding insult to injury. He needed to respect her wishes and give her as much space and time as she needed. Although he couldn't believe she actually wanted him to analyze his true feelings for Farrah, he respected her for having the courage to say it, especially when her heart was shattered.

Stephen silently prayed that Darcella's heart wasn't broken beyond repair. Considering all that she'd revealed to him about her childhood and family life, before he'd confessed to her, he wouldn't be surprised if she called the whole thing off. Trust was a big issue for Darcella.

The weather was extremely warm, yet a cool breeze fanned the air, making Stephanie feel less heated than she'd been the day before. The area Gregory had brought her to visit today was one of the poorest parishes in New Orleans. This poverty-stricken place seemed to reach out and grab her in the gut. She'd never seen anything as downright wretched as this in her entire life. She instantly felt guilty for feeling bad about the things she and Stephen had been deprived of during their youth. They had been filthy rich compared to how the folks were living down here.

Stephanie had to wonder if the people who lived here knew how poor they were. The smiling faces were hardly a testament to the poorest of living conditions. Kids yelled out with gleeful greetings as they waved enthusiastically from the windows and porch fronts of the dilapidated houses. The pungent smell in the air, smelling a lot like rotten garbage and other unmentionable human waste, had Stephanie fighting hard not to gag. Although she was careful not to show how horrified she was by what she saw, she got the sense that the people didn't need anyone's sympathy. They needed help, love, understanding, and more help.

Sensing Stephanie's inner turmoil, Gregory slipped his arm around her shoulder. "I know exactly what you're feeling. I brought you here because I wanted you to see one of America's darkest, dirtiest secrets. Our people need so much. I do whatever I can down here to relieve some of this poverty, but it's not nearly enough. I wish I could do more. Our law firm sponsors several families and we give heavily to the community at large. Places like this are where most of our tax dollars go, money that we'd otherwise end up sending to Uncle Sam. Are you okay, sweetheart?"

Stephanie leaned into Gregory for a brief moment. "This is overwhelming. But I'm glad you brought me here. There's definitely a lesson to be learned from it. Stephen and I used to cry about holes in our shoes, but some of the folks down here probably can't even afford them. How did things get this bad? Who's responsible for the horrible way our people are living?"

Gregory hunched his shoulders. "That's the problem. No one wants to take the blame. Our government doesn't seem to care about what's going on down here. Very few people are aware of how some of our folks live. They have no idea. I fear so much for all the places like this in New Orleans. There are numerous parishes just like this one. A Category 3 or 4 hurricane could easily wipe these areas off the face of the earth one day. I just can't begin to imagine what would happen to these good folks if something like that were to occur. I believe it would be total devastation. I pray every night that a strong hurricane won't hit here."

As Stephanie thought about all the fresh loaves of French bread that Gregory had just purchased from the bakery, she had to smile. She no longer had to wonder what he was going to do with all the bread and beef sausages he'd purchased. She hadn't asked because she wasn't sure it was her business, since he hadn't offered an explanation. Like Jesus had done, he was going to feed as many people today as he could. But how would he go about it? How could he feed some and not others? How was he going to choose among them? Stephanie had to wonder.

The answer came in the next instant, when Gregory pointed at a stone building down the street. "Want to help me deliver the food to the church? They always feed the people in dire need. There are many other sources that deliver food here on a daily basis, but I like to show my face around here pretty often so people know I care. I have become a friend to many a family."

Stephanie stood on her tiptoes to softly peck Gregory's cheek. "I'd love to help out. You are truly an amazing man. God must be smiling down upon you."

Gregory smiled gently. "Perhaps. But I don't do it for glory. I do it because I care."

Stephanie's admiration for her fiancé had deepened tenfold. He lived like royalty, yet he hadn't forgotten those who practically lived in squalor. It was the laughter of the children that had put Stephanie more in awe. Those little happy voices had deeply touched her heart.

In a matter of minutes Stephanie and Gregory had carried all the bags of food into the church. Everyone inside knew Gregory by name and he knew everyone's name as well. All the folks that worked in the kitchen received him with open arms, male and female alike. It was as if they saw him as their hero. When he proudly introduced them to Stephanie, they welcomed her warmly, too. It also surprised Stephanie to learn that her fiancé also came down to help serve the meals no less than two to three times a month. That was yet another commendable trait of Gregory's. Learning new things about the man she loved always excited Stephanie.

It made Stephanie feel so good inside to be able to help fill the pantry and the refrigerator with the goods they'd brought with them. Other foods, canned goods and staples had also been delivered earlier that day, and a good bit of it still needed to be stored away on the shelves. It didn't matter to her that she wore white pants and a light colored blouse. Getting them dirty didn't concern her in the least. Stephanie felt honored to be a part of such a worthy cause.

The church ladies and volunteers chatted amicably with Stephanie as they worked alongside her, showing her exactly where everything was supposed to go. They asked her a lot of personal questions, and she answered each one without hesitation. When the men and women learned that she was Malachi's daughter, they began to sing to her the praises of their generous benefactor. He had employed many of the uneducated men and women to do odd jobs for his company and around his estate. Stephanie learned that her father was also heavily involved in donating monies and food to the families who lived in the poverty-stricken parishes. He'd also set up a scholarship fund. Malachi was as well known in the parishes as the Saxton family was.

Gregory had also rolled up his shirtsleeves, and began to pitch in as well. His smile was broad and his eyes gleamed as he conversed animatedly with a few of the men who were regular volunteers. The deep respect all the men had for each other was quite apparent.

Hours later Stephanie and Gregory took their leave, each of them sorry to go. It was starting to get dark, and he wanted to get out of the area safely, though there were many young men who had his back. They took special care to see that he was safe, even looking out for his car when it was parked there. Crime was a huge problem in the low-lying parishes, but people were also very happy and had learned to play the hand dealt them. Gregory had deep respect for the families that lived their lives in peace and harmony despite the horrific circumstances.

As Gregory opened the passenger door for Stephanie, she turned into him and cupped his face between her hands. She then gave him a passionate kiss. "You are something very special, Attorney Saxton. I hope you know that. God surely does. I know you've found favor with Him."

Gregory kissed her back. "Thanks, Stephanie, but I just pray that something special could happen for our folks every day for the rest of their lives. No human being should ever have to live this way. My heart aches every time I visit these areas. I'm always looking for ways to bring more money and attention to these places. I've even asked God why He allows this to happen, but I know He has a reason for everything. We just have to wait on Him to answer the call."

"Don't stop praying, Gregory," Stephanie said to him as he settled into the driver's seat. "We can't ever stop praying. There are people all over the world who are living in poverty. With the United States being touted as the number-one superpower, it's a criminal act for this to happen here. Our government should be so ashamed of its indifference to its citizens."

Gregory gave a mighty harrumph as he fired the engine. "Shame is something our government never experiences. The fat cats get fatter and the poor get poorer. It's been that way for a very long time. I wonder how many congressmen and senators have ever visited these poverty areas. I'm sure there aren't many. Louisiana's official representatives know exactly what goes on down here, but they don't seem to care, either. I've even considered running for a political office, but I don't think I have what it takes. The frustration would drive me insane."

Stephanie reached over and placed her hand on Gregory's shoulder. "I think you'd make a wonderful congressman or senator. Maybe you should run for attorney general. I know you can handle frustration and pressure. You're a lawyer, for Pete's sake."

"Thanks for the vote of confidence, but I'd start with city council if I were to run for anything. You need to get some good experience before you run for the higher offices. I think I can make a big difference at the city council level. I'll have to give it a lot more thought before I decide what I should do."

Stephanie grinned. "You do that! I think I'd love being the wife of a city councilor."

"Is that so?" he said on a huge smile. "I'll see what I can do to accommodate you."

The next stop on Gregory's sightseeing route had Stephanie once again amazed. This brightly lit, colorful area was in direct contrast to the drab, depressing place they'd just left behind. They appeared to be at an amusement park of some sort, but Stephanie soon found out that it was a carnival held yearly. Laughter and excitement was all about them. People were running here and there while having the time of their lives. Her heart thumped loudly inside her chest the moment her eyes fell on the numerous carnival rides. When Gregory led her over to the carousel, her eyes lit up like the bright stars overhead. She felt giddy inside at just the prospect of riding the merry-go-round. Stephanie hadn't ridden on one since she was a teenager.

"Two tickets please, for the carousel," Gregory said to the young man in the ticket booth.

Stephanie wanted to jump up and down like an overly excited kid, but she refrained. Riding the carousel would hopefully lift her spirits. Although she'd never forget the experience she'd just had down in the parish, nor could she set aside in her mind the peril of the people living there, a pleasant end to the evening might ease the burden on her saddened heart.

Stephanie had had a wonderful time with the folks at the church, and she hoped to visit them again in the future. She felt as though she'd made quite a few friends there. The time had flown by as they'd worked together in perfect harmony. Since she'd be living in New Orleans one day, she wanted to help do all she could to ease the lives of those who were less fortunate than her. Stephanie couldn't wait to discuss with her father what she'd seen with her own eyes.

After Stephanie chose the most colorful horse on the carousel, one with a pole that went up and down, she allowed Gregory to help her get into the saddle. This was one lady who didn't want to sit sideways. She wanted to ride the wooden horse the way a real one should be ridden, since she was still fearful of riding a flesh-and-blood steed. Malachi had several horses and had offered her riding lessons, but she'd thus far declined because she felt totally intimidated by the beautiful animals. One thing was for sure. The wooden variety wouldn't ever throw her off.

Gregory seated himself on the horse right across from hers. He immediately noticed the glowing embers that had replaced the sadness he'd seen in Stephanie's eyes only minutes earlier.

However, he was glad he'd taken her to the impoverished area. He'd wanted her to see how the other half lived. She'd seen the ritzier areas of New Orleans, but the Big Easy had many other faces. Gregory wanted his wife-to-be to see them all. He was proud of how she'd chipped right in and helped out. She had truly won over the folks down at the church, which made him very happy. Stephanie had shown him that she would be by his side through hell and high water. Like him, she had loads of compassion, and she cared deeply about others. He couldn't ask for more.

In the early morning hours, Stephen's phone rang. As he sat straight up in the bed and then picked up the receiver, he saw it was 5:30 a.m. All that his ear met with was dead silence. Then he heard sniffling, which caused him to listen closer. "Is someone there?" When no one answered, he scolded himself for not checking the caller ID first. "Hello, can I help you?"

Darcella squeezed the receiver tightly. "Stephen, are you in love with Farrah?" she tearfully asked, sniffling still.

Stephen's heart lurched. The pain in Darcella's voice caused him to flinch. "No, Darcy, I'm not. I'm in love with you. Only you. Please stop crying. You have nothing to worry about. I assure you that I'm not going anywhere. I'm all yours, baby."

"Are you sure about that, Stephen?"

"I'm positive. I was just trying to be honest with you the other night. I don't want to hide anything from you. I really didn't mean to hurt you. Where are you? I've been calling you."

"I'm at home. I had to pull off to the side of the road to compose myself that night. I should've taken your suggestion of staying there. That drive was really rough for me."

"That was a couple of days ago, but you still sound a bit shaky. Do you need me to come over there and be with you for a while, Darcy? I don't have to go into work until this evening."

"Could you please, Stephen?"

"I'm on my way. Hold on tight, baby."

Darcella's hands trembled as she hung up the phone. The troubling images she'd had of Farrah and Stephen locked together in loving embraces had disturbed her sleep over the past two nights. Her tears had been endless. Something she rarely did, unless she was in bad shape, she'd called in to work to say she was sick. Heartsick was the same as being physically ill to her.

Not so long ago Darcella had thought she was in total control of her relationship with Stephen, telling him what she was going to do and what she wouldn't. Now all she wanted to do was hold on to him. In trying to gain the upper hand with him, she'd somehow landed on the bottom. Her cocky conversation about wanting to put her career first before motherhood had been ringing in her ears annoyingly. She'd said so many things she wished she could take back.

Now that Farrah posed a real threat to her, Darcella knew she had to do things differently. She was also aware of how attractive the other woman was, but she wasn't about to give up Stephen without a fight. Still, she wished he hadn't told her about his attraction for his sister's best friend. It had only proved to her how insecure she really was. Wishing Stephen would hurry up and get there, Darcella ran to the front window to watch out for him.

The second Stephen's SUV came into view Darcella stepped back from the window. She hoped he hadn't seen her standing by waiting on him like a lovesick puppy. During her wait she'd been able to regain a dab of composure and some of her self-esteem. She wasn't going to allow herself to be walked all over, but taking a contrary stand wouldn't work, either.

As much as Darcella hated to admit it, she really had no control over the outcome of this situation. If Stephen had feelings for another woman, there simply wasn't a future for them. No matter how much she loved him, if he didn't feel the same way, she couldn't make him love her. With that in mind, she quickly realized she had to keep her dignity intact. Begging Stephen to stay with her was absolutely out of the question. There'd be no groveling on her part.

Stephen drew Darcella into his arms as soon as he stepped into the house. He squeezed her tightly, asking her to please forgive him for hurting her. Stephen then took hold of her hand and led her into the living room, where he dropped down on the sofa and nestled her onto the sofa cushion right beside him. His fingers grazed down the side of her face. "Can we start all over again? I don't want to lose you, girl. There is no one for me but you."

Darcella wanted to believe him, just wanted to throw caution to the wind, but the fear in her heart was strong. "How do we do that, Stephen?"

"Remember when I asked you about going to premarital counseling?"

She nodded. "Why is that so important to you all of a sudden?"

"Because we're important. More than that, we need to know how to lead the kind of life God intended for us to live. Reading the Bible and seeking counsel is how we start.

We need to be clear on His instructions for married couples. I've done a lot of reading on the subject, and I think we can definitely benefit from the course. Please say you'll at least try it with me, Darcy."

Darcella looked rather skeptical. "I don't know, Stephen. We can sit here and talk about God all you want, but that's not going to solve our immediate problems."

"It's a start, Darcy. I truly understand how you feel, but you're either going to trust me or continue to let our situation blow up in our faces. "I want us to have a fresh start. Whether we like it or not, getting in tune with God is the only answer to our problems."

The long, drawn-out sigh Darcella blew out clearly showed her frustration with their dilemma. Trusting him again would be hard for her. Since she loved him so much, she was aware that she had to try and regain the trust. She wanted so much to bring up his attraction to Farrah again, but that would be like beating a dead horse. Only Stephen could resolve that issue. He either wanted a lifetime with her or he'd decide to move on to greener pastures.

As much as Darcella wanted to believe that a life with her was Stephen's strongest desire, she was still fearful. However, she was extremely grateful that Stephen and Farrah hadn't already hooked up physically. That particular scenario might be an impossible one for her to forgive.

Physical attractions often had a tendency to win out over love.

Stephen lightly bumped Darcella with his shoulder. "Hello, can we please get back on the same page? Are you willing to take the premarital counseling sessions with me?"

Darcella nodded, yet she seemed a bit reluctant. "I'm willing, Stephen. Just let me know when you get everything set up."

Pleased with Darcella's cautionary response, Stephen kissed her gently on the lips. "I'm happy to hear you say that. You won't be sorry, Darcy. I know it's going to take a minute for you, but I plan to win back your trust. We can regain everything that we lost. Can you get me a copy of your work schedule for the upcoming month so I can compare it with mine? Once I see what days we have off at the same time, I can attempt to get the counseling ball rolling."

"I'll e-mail you a copy of it later on today." Ready to move on to other things, Darcella smiled. "How are you feeling, Stephen? I'd like to hear all about your first week back at work."

Darcella was definitely interested in how Stephen had fared on the job after his extended leave, but she also needed a safe subject to focus her attention on. She knew that locking her mind onto his situation with Farrah would keep her from getting past it. The truth of the matter was that she couldn't wait to get over it and eventually have things back to normal for her and Stephen. Darcella hoped to heaven that it wasn't going to take her too long.

Although Stephen wanted to talk more about the counseling sessions, and what he'd read in the Bible, he drew Darcella closer to him. "I have to warn you that part of my workweek is somewhat depressing. Still want to know?"

Darcella laid her hand against Stephen's cheek. "Absolutely."

The amount of food Stephanie had eaten had her wanting to run ten miles to help burn up some of the calories. Malachi's kitchen staff had done it again. For the evening meal they'd prepared a variety of Cajun dishes, each of them hot and spicy. She wasn't big on hot foods, but she'd had more than just a taste of every delicious morsel that had been put in front of her.

There were several moments during the meal when Stephanie had felt awfully guilty for having so much good food to partake of while many others in the world hardly had a crust of day-old bread. Because all she'd been able to think of was the poverty she'd seen during the day, she'd had a fitful night. Sleep hadn't come for her until the wee hours of the morning. Even with all the food that they'd stored away in the pantry, there were still thousands and thousands of hungry people in New Orleans who wouldn't get so much as a small sample.

In a world where there was so much wealth, as well as an unbelievable amount of waste by both government and civilian sectors, Stephanie couldn't begin to understand how so many folks were living without the bare necessities. It was downright scandalous.

Malachi reached over and briefly put his hand over Stephanie's. "You looked troubled, my dear. Anything you care to share?"

Stephanie looked up at Malachi and smiled. "Lots. I hope you have awhile."

After placing his linen napkin in the center of the plate, Malachi got up from the table. "I have all the time you need, sweetheart. Let's go into the salon, where we can get more comfortable. Sure you don't want dessert?"

Stephanie rubbed her slightly swollen belly. "I'm positive. I'm sure I'll feel differently before I go to bed later on. I smelled and then saw the sweet potato pies when I peeked into the kitchen earlier. If you want dessert, please don't let me stop you. We can talk right here."

Malachi extended his hand to Stephanie. "We'll talk now and do dessert later. Max will be here sometime before the evening is over. We can join him for a slice of pie then."

Stephanie got up from her chair and then placed her hand into her father's. "Sounds like a winner to me. Maybe by the time Uncle Max gets here my stomach can hold something else."

Hand in hand, smiling brightly at each other, Stephanie and Malachi made it down the long corridor and on into the informal salon, where both of them took up residence on the plush creamy-beige sofa. Once she saw that her father had made himself completely comfortable, she began to tell him all about the areas she and Gregory had visited the day before. Holding in her emotions was easy at the beginning, but by the time she finished her heart was on her shirtsleeve.

Malachi reached over and gave Stephanie a comforting hug. "The bottoms are not tourist attractions, my dear. That's for sure. It's mind-boggling to know that people can actually survive in such revolting conditions. It really shows me how much gumption some people have. It takes far more nerve and guts to live poorly than it does to live like royalty."

Stephanie nodded in agreement. "Their stamina is what astounds me the most. It's tremendous. I can't imagine that anyone wants to live like that, yet I've heard that very thing said about the poor. There are some folks who actually believe that people living in poverty can do better if only they wanted to. It takes a hell of a lot more than desire to make a decent living in this world. Mama could tell you a lot about that."

Malachi knew Stephanie's statement about what some folks thought of the poor to be one of fact. He'd have to disagree with her about her mother, though he'd never voice that to her. Doreen could have lived much better than she had off of the large sums of money he sent her every single month. Making a sharp point to him had been more to her liking. Living poorly had been all about her showing her husband that she could make it without him.

The only problem Malachi had with how Doreen had chosen to live was that his children had been deprived of so much in order for her to keep her pride. He would never say an unkind word about his late wife to their children, but there were times when he wished she were around so he could tell her exactly how he felt about what she'd done. He'd never discount the unconscionable wrong he'd done in his marriage, but two wrongs never resulted in right. He was of the mind that Stephanie and Stephen had deserved so much more than what they'd gotten from both parents. Malachi would never fail to shoulder his part of the blame, but he was also grateful to God that he'd been given a second chance to make it right. Doreen hadn't.

Stephanie realized she'd unwittingly struck a nerve with Malachi by mentioning her mother in the same light as the others. She was well aware that Doreen hadn't lived as well as she could have, but she'd forgiven her mother for making the family go through hell when it hadn't been necessary. Her mother was deceased so it wouldn't do anyone the least bit of good to hold a grudge against her. After a second or two of wondering if she should discuss with him the reference to her mother, she decided some things could go unsaid. "A lot of the folks I met at the church sang your praises to me," she said instead. "I was told how much you've helped them out."

Malachi waved off her comment. "I can't do nearly what I'd like to do. There's so much that's needed. It's our government that needs to do more. These are forgotten people, Stephanie. It's like they don't even exist, as far as the powers-that-be are concerned. It's a travesty."

"Gregory said the same thing. Well, I know that individually we can't make a big difference, but we can do more collectively. When I move down here, I plan to make my mark. I'm going to do whatever it takes to open up some eyes. Gregory says he might even consider running for city council. He would be wonderful as a councilor. What do you think, Daddy?"

Malachi chuckled. "That young man of yours is a marvel at everything he takes on. I've encouraged him to run for a political office, even before he graduated law school. He's the kind of person that truly stands up for the people. I'd love to see him run. Gregory would be phenomenal as a city councilor."

"I'll reiterate to Gregory your sentiments." Stephanie suddenly got a proud gleam in her eyes. "Daddy, you should've seen how genuine he was with the people he introduced me to yesterday. He is very much a people-person. For someone who grew up with a silver spoon in his mouth, he has no problem rolling up his sleeves and pitching in wherever help is needed."

"That's the type of men his daddy and granddaddy are. His great-granddaddy was a great man, too, but he wasn't an attorney. He made his wealth off the land. Chesterfield Saxton Sr. was one of the best farmers to ever live. 'Green Thumb' was his nickname. It's been said that he could make anything grow, even in desertlike conditions. They've made a lot of invaluable contributions to the state of Louisiana. The Saxton name is well respected around these parts."

"So I've noticed. Gregory seems to be well known everywhere we go. Mind if I ask you to tell me more about my paternal grandparents? What were they like, Dad? How did they live?"

Malachi's eyes sparkled with mist. "My dear, I could talk about Joseph and Marquisa Trudeaux all night long. They were also amazing people, very family-oriented. They possessed more courage than you could shake a stick at. I wish you and Stephen could've known them."

Stephanie rested her chin on the top of her two fists. "I really missed having grandparents. Stephen and I often wondered what it would be like to have them around."

Malachi choked up a little at the sadness in his daughter's eyes. He wished he could give her back all that she'd missed out on. "Dad was a trucker like Maxwell, but he only did local deliveries. He took us around with him when school was out. Maxwell got hooked on the trucking business at an early age. However, Joseph was an absolute whiz at turning wood into the most amazing furniture. Selling his home-made furniture was the real moneymaker."

Malachi went on to tell Stephanie that his mother was a happy housewife, and that there was nothing desperate about her. It was her creative hands that brought her the most pleasures. She made all sorts of beautiful arts and crafts, hand-painting many of them. Her superb crocheting and knitting skills produced some of the most elegant table-cloths and other fine linens, which she sold to neighbors and friends and anyone who made a request.

Marquisa lived for her family and loved to feed them full meals, three times a day, not to mention the snack and dessert breaks. She was a true helpmate. Canning fruits and vegetables for winter storage and sharing them with neighbors was another favorite pastime for her. He told Stephanie that his mother had always been willing to lend a helping hand to anyone in need. Malachi then referred to his mother and father as Jesus' modern-day disciples.

Malachi twiddled his thumbs. "Ah, reading. Mother and Daddy loved to read to us. Every night before bed Max and I were treated to a bedtime story. None of that fairy-tale stuff, either. They made up their own stories about the true struggles of our people. Most of the endings were triumphant ones. But our parents always warned us that triumphs often came from tragedy. The last thing read to us before the lights went out was a story from the Bible. We were never sent to bed on a sour note. All troubling issues in our house were resolved by bedtime."

Stephanie could almost imagine her grandparents sitting at the foot of the bed reading aloud to their two sons. That wonderful image also brought to mind the first night her father had ever tucked her into bed. That glorious evening had happened more than two years ago, but it was one of her fondest memories of Malachi to date.

"So no one ever went to bed angry?"

Malachi shook his head from side to side. "It was simply not allowed. Max and I had to make up with each other if we were ever mad about something. We had to give one another a hug and an apology. I never realized how much anger a small hug could dissolve. That's why I hug you every chance I get. I never want you to be angry with me, Stephanie. I've held enough anger inside for myself, probably enough to destroy a small country."

Stephanie moved over closer to her father and gave him a huge hug. 'There's no more anger inside me, Dad. Only love. I love you unconditionally. I think my grandparents were onto something really good. Maybe you, Stephen and I should adopt their rule. You think?"

Malachi hugged his daughter back. "I know so. To this day your uncle Max and I never part in anger. We resolve all bad feelings before nightfall—not that we've had any serious issues lately. We're too old for that sort of thing. We get along so well because we love and respect each other. Doreen and I practiced the anger rule in our marriage for quite a while, but the infidelity changed all that. Still, that's one rule you should seriously consider establishing in your marriage, but you have to stick to it. It works."

Stephanie hugged Malachi again. "I already have, Dad. I believe Gregory will, too."

"What's going on in here?" Maxwell boomed. "If my niece is doling out sweet gobs of love, I think I'm entitled to some of it, too. Come here, sweetheart, and give your uncle Max a few of those big hugs. I sure have been missing you."

Stephanie stood and stepped into her uncle's warm embrace. "I missed you, too, even though it hasn't been that long since we last saw each other," she teased. "Come and sit down."

Maxwell laughed heartily. "I'll be back. One or two of those sweet potato pies out on the serving board has my name on it." He cupped his ear. "I can hear them calling out to me."

Stephanie and Malachi laughed, too. "We'll join you for a slice," they said in unison.

Chapter 8

Stephen sat across from his dad in Malachi's private retreat, hoping to find some of the answers he needed. He had flown to New Orleans right after he'd completed his last six-day shift. The situation with Darcella had blown up despite their voiced desires to start fresh. She had changed her mind about the marriage counseling sessions after he'd gotten it all set it up. Then she'd broken off their engagement and had announced that she only wanted them to be friends.

Malachi felt Stephen's pain. Although his son hadn't come close to making the huge mistake he'd made, he was still persecuting himself something awful. The look on Stephen's face, after his father had told him how Doreen had found out about his infidelity, had Malachi wishing the question had never been asked. Guilt had also caused Malachi to confess his sin.

What Malachi had hoped for by coming clean with his wife were understanding and forgiveness, which he now understood was as far-fetched as anything could ever be. Instead of the desired outcome, he'd been thrown out of the house and out of his family's lives. Malachi's sentence had cost him the love of his life and had lasted a long, lonely twenty-eight years without face-to-face contact with his two kids. *And for what?* That question had constantly plagued him.

Malachi didn't even know what the woman he'd cheated with looked like. He wouldn't recognize her if she walked up to him on the street and said hello. The entire evening with her was one big blur, yet no alcohol or drugs played any part whatsoever in the life-changing event. It had all been about his physical desires.

"Dad, do you ever wish you hadn't told Mama about that night?" Stephen had finally found his voice. The initial shock of what his father had said had finally begun to wear off.

Malachi put his finger up to his right temple. "All the time. The confession hurt her and our marriage something terrible. She lost total faith in me and in our love. If I could do that to her, especially when she was pregnant, she said I couldn't possibly be in love with her. I now believe it was the worst thing I could've done, but if I hadn't confessed, I don't know that I could've lived with myself. Guilt had consumed me. Day and night I grieved over what I'd done. Of course I felt worse for your mother than for myself. It took me three weeks to finally come clean with her, but I finally got up enough nerve to confess. It wasn't a pretty night."

Stephen stroked his chin nervously. "I regret telling Darcy about Farrah. Like you, I thought I was doing the right thing by putting the truth out on the table. Now all I can ask myself is can we move on from here. I really flubbed this relationship badly. I felt horribly guilty for just flirting with another woman, so I can only imagine how you must've felt. Now I feel the worst kind of guilt for killing Darcella's spirit with my confession. It has caused nothing but pain. I don't know how to deal with our broken engagement. I can't believe it's come down to this."

"Love is unpredictable, Stephen. You've heard your uncle

Max say that on more than one occasion. No truer statement was ever spoken."

Malachi hated seeing Stephen in such pain. The agony he felt was written all over his face. Unfortunately, the excruciating pain he was in was of his own making. When his son had called to say he was flying to New Orleans, Malachi had instantly known trouble brewed.

"Stephen, let me ask you something. Have you ever really assessed your feelings for Farrah? There may be more to this thing than just a physical attraction. Is that possible?"

Stephen looked shocked by the question, though it was the same one he'd asked himself at least a hundred times. "That's what's so crazy about this whole thing, Dad. I still think about Farrah even though I try hard not to. I can't figure it out. I feel so out of control about all this."

"That's because you *are* out of control, son. Either Farrah has badly affected your libido, or you have genuine feelings toward this girl. Your job is to figure out which one it is. No one can solve this dilemma for you. I can only tell you about my experiences and give you guidance. I can't keep you from making the same mistake I did nor can I make you take my advice. I just don't want to see you go through a lifetime of pain over what might be just sexual urges."

"I know all that. Still, I'm struggling with this issue. If I really do have feelings for Farrah, how do I find them out?" Stephen hunched his shoulders. "I guess I already know the answer to that question. Getting to know her is the only way. But I know it's not fair to Farrah, Darcella or me to explore this issue. Someone is bound to get seriously hurt."

"Someone has already gotten terribly hurt. I'd dare to say that this has hurt all of you. I only know of your history with Farrah because of what you and your sister have told me. It seems like the once pesky nuisance in your life has turned into a woman you find very attractive, physical or otherwise. Like it or not, this woman has turned your head something fierce."

Hating to have the truth confirmed for him, even though

he'd come there seeking just that, Stephen lightly pounded his thighs with his fists. "The truth sucks. I've lost the girl I was so sure I was in love with, all over my attraction to another woman. How crazy is that? Why is everything suddenly so complicated? I just don't understand any of it."

"I don't think it's all of a sudden, Stephen. I believe you've just discovered your unrest with your relationship with Darcy. Something important was missing. It's best that you find this out now rather than after the vows. It's time for you to step back and take a real hard look. Just as I told you before, assessing one's life is a good thing. Take your own inventory, son."

Stephen sighed hard. "I know what you're saying, Dad. I think I'm just afraid of what I might find out about myself. It's so easy to take everyone else's inventory. Looking at the man in the mirror is difficult at best. I'm sure I won't like what I see."

Malachi nodded in agreement. "Difficult but very, very necessary, son."

Stephen knew what had to be done before he could get on with his life. Doing it was the hard part. He'd always thought of himself as a good person, but his character was now in question—and mostly by him. For some reason he was equating flirting with adultery, yet he wasn't married. He could blame his father for his own way of thinking, but he hadn't even known that Malachi had cheated on his wife. He'd flirted before, plenty of times, had taken phone numbers from women while involved with Darcella, but they hadn't been engaged then.

Forget the fact that Stephen had never gone through with anything akin to being out with another woman. Still, the guilt was on him like the plague. The pain he'd seen in Darcella's eyes was unforgettable. He'd seen that very look for years in his mother's eyes. His dilemma was growing. Malachi had given him so much to think about, had put even more burdens on his heart. How could he possibly act upon his attraction to Farrah? What would happen if he did act upon it, only to find out it wasn't what he wanted? What would he think of himself then? He had lost everything he believed he wanted in a wife, but what if there was something important to gain? How many people had to get hurt before he dealt with his demons? So many questions had been posed to him by himself and others, but Stephen didn't relish the idea of seeking the answers. Darcella had left him cold, but what if she had a change of heart later?

The road ahead of Stephen was very difficult and terribly winding. He knew that without a shadow of a doubt. God's instructions on relationships came to mind once again. It was one thing to read about it in the Bible, but Stephen was finding out that it was an altogether different matter to practice obedience. *Was he a hopeless sinner or what?*

Malachi empathized with his son, but his hands were virtually tied. Stephen had to seek the truth for himself. There was no other way out for him, nor was there an easy resolution. He had to choose his love and then love his choice— and he had to do it with all his heart and soul.

Malachi got to his feet. "What do you say to us putting our troubles aside long enough to go and visit Max? I know he's eager to see you. He was excited when I told him you were coming. Then he grew concerned when I told him I thought you had big troubles. Because he felt we might need some time alone, he made the decision to wait a day or so before dropping by."

That Malachi thought of this as *their* troubles filled Stephen emotionally. Having someone who understood his dilemma made things a bit more bearable for him. Happy for a break from this troubling situation, he jumped to his feet. "That's a great idea, Dad. I'd like to take both you and Uncle Max out to dinner. I'm in the mood for some good old Louisiana cooking. My appetite hasn't been the best lately, so I really could use a tasty meal."

Malachi grinned. "I know just the place, son!"

Stephen clapped his hands enthusiastically. "Okay. Let's get this party started."

Café Le Beaux was a cozy little restaurant with a great selection of Cajun dishes. Malachi and Maxwell frequented the animated, colorful place, where both were known on a first-name basis by the staff. Jazz played softly in the background as the three men enjoyed their delicious meals. Maxwell had ordered a big bowl of gumbo and an order of jumbo fried shrimp. Stephen had chosen shrimp Creole on the recommendation of his father, who'd ordered the same dish.

Stephen couldn't help noticing how beautiful all the waitresses were. He even wondered if their good looks and great figures were covert requirements for employment. There wasn't a single male waiter in the cafe. It was interesting to him that he wasn't all that keen about paying too much personal attention to the opposite sex. Of course, he always took a cursory glance at females, but he now avoided making any sort of eye-to-eye contact with them, especially since his relationship with Darcella had landed hard on the rocks. He certainly wasn't interested in making a casual acquaintance or jumping right into another serious relationship.

Now that Stephen was a jilted fiancé, he didn't know what to do with himself or all the free time he suddenly had on his hands. Although he still thought there might be a chance for him and Darcella to reconcile, he figured it was rather a slim one. She had seemed so sure of her decision not to marry him or even continue their relationship when she'd given him back the engagement ring. It had hurt like the dickens at the time, and it still did, but he couldn't allow himself to dwell on it twenty-four seven. It was too depressing.

Getting answers from Malachi and discussing the breakup were not the only reasons Stephen had flown down to New Orleans. Further checking out the day-to-day operation of his father's business was also on his agenda, since he was seriously considering changing careers.

Stephen took a long gulp of his iced tea and then set the glass back down. "Hey, Uncle Max, how are things going with you and Ms. Sarah?" he asked, feeling anxious.

Maxwell chuckled. "I'd say we're getting on pretty well. I talk to her on the phone no less than three times a week. We're even talking about her paying a visit here. She said perhaps she'd like to make the trip the next time Stephanie comes. She's never been here before."

"That would really be nice," Stephen remarked. "I'm sure Stephanie would love to have her as a traveling companion. She thinks a lot of Ms. Sarah."

"She certainly does," Malachi offered. "Since we're back and forth to Houston so often now, Max and I are considering purchasing a home there. We've been looking up properties for sale on the Internet. There are some great steals to be had in your city."

"Yeah, but the property taxes in Texas are off the chart, Dad. However, I'm sure that's not a problem for you two business moguls. Are you thinking of purchasing one place or two?"

"Just one place, preferably accommodations with two master bedrooms," Maxwell responded. "We've checked out the prices on homes, condos and town houses. We're actually looking into properties right around the area you and Stephanie live in."

"We're also interested in a couple of places in Galveston," Malachi added, "but of course we definitely have to be concerned about hurricanes and flooding. That's a huge problem here in New Orleans, so we don't want to buy anything in or close to a flood zone."

Stephen nodded. "I know what you're saying. I don't live in a flood zone, but I sure have flood insurance. Lately some areas in Houston have flooded that never took on water before. Does buying property in Houston have anything to do with your relationship with Ms. Sarah?"

Maxwell shook his head from side to side. "Not really.

It's more to do with you and your sister. It would be nice to have our own place when we come to visit you two. Living out of suitcases is a drag. However, if things continue to progress nicely between Sarah and me, I'll at least have a place to entertain her in. It would also be nice to cook her a meal for a change."

Stephen smiled knowingly. "I hear you, Uncle Max. But it looks like Stephanie might be moving here after she gets married—and I'm considering it also."

Maxwell raised an eyebrow. "You are?"

"Surprising, huh? I've recently developed an interest in possibly working with Dad. He and I have been tossing it around. Since the engagement is off, I'm not so bound to Houston."

"What if Darcella changes her mind about things?" Maxwell inquired.

Stephen shrugged, trying hard not to show how raw his emotions were. "We'll cross that bridge if we come to it. But I have the feeling there'll be no change of heart. Darcy seemed pretty adamant about not wanting to marry me. And I really don't think her decision is all to do with what went down with Farrah and me. I believe something else is going on with her. Darcy's parents are in a very unhappy marriage and I think she fears the same thing might happen with us. I believe that's what I've been reading between the lines. In fact, I'm almost sure of it."

Malachi nodded. "It's certainly possible," Malachi said. "Darcy may be using your attraction to Farrah to hide her own fears about marriage and kids. She's already admitted being fearful of both. In my opinion neither of you are ready for marriage, Stephen. It would do both of you good to take this time off to reassess your lives. If God has ordained marriage for you two, He'll put your relationship all back together again."

"I agree with your dad, Stephen. Taking some time away from each other might help."

Stephen shrugged. "You're right. At any rate, Darcella has already seen to that plan."

* * *

Darcella's hands trembled as she reread the letter of resignation she'd drafted over a week ago, yet she still hadn't turned it into personnel. She had become so indecisive about everything affecting her. As hard as she tried to blame Stephen for the downward spiral of her life, she knew better. She was just plain unhappy with life and herself. The unhappiness had increased dramatically without Stephen there to lift her spirit.

Before Stephen had had a chance to break it off with Darcella, she'd beat him to the punch, because she'd been so sure that he was eventually going to end things with her. He was now free to pursue the stunning Farrah or any other woman he so desired. She'd tried to convince herself she'd broken off her engagement out of nobility, but it really had nothing to do with being noble. Just the thought of them as no more hurt her like crazy, but it would hurt her even more if he chased other women after they'd married. Fear was behind every negative action in her life. How to overcome those fears was Darcella's biggest problem.

Darcella was well aware that she allowed her family life to influence every aspect of her existence. Despite the fact that she rarely saw them, she allowed herself to be controlled by what she'd experienced while living at home. It was hard for her to figure out how events of so long ago still affected her to this day. *Shouldn't she be over all that already?*

It wasn't like Darcella's parents had argued or fought physically, because that wasn't the case. To this day they just had absolutely nothing to say to each other and even less to do with each other. The silence between them was deafening. To live in a house where there was no communication was like being darn near deaf. Darcella's failure to communicate all of her feelings to Stephen had caused her to sacrifice the relationship instead. Even though she had tried to exorcise the demons living inside her head, it had been virtually impossible.

The doorbell suddenly pealed, startling Darcella momentarily. Wondering who could be out there, she hurried from her den/office and made her way out into the hallway. Seeing Stephanie's car in her driveway came as a surprise. She couldn't help wondering if Stephen had sent his sister there to talk with her. After tossing that ridiculous thought aside, Darcella quickly opened the door to allow her guest to gain entry.

Stephanie smiled brightly. "Hi, Darcy. Sorry for not calling, but I feared you might not let me come by had I done so. You're back to being distant again."

Darcella hadn't been answering her phone, so she knew that Stephanie was somewhat right in her assumptions. Trying to avoid any calls from Stephen had been futile, simply because he hadn't called since she'd seen him last. Their fatal evening together had occurred a week ago.

Darcella gestured for Stephanie to follow her. "Come on into the living room. I assume your brother has told you we're no longer engaged," Darcella said flatly, as she and her guest took a seat on the beautiful gold-and-white brocaded sofa.

Stephanie's gasp was rather loud, her eyes wide with shock. "You assumed wrong. Stephen hasn't told me a thing about this."

Darcella raised an eyebrow. "That has to be a first. I thought he confided everything in you." Darcella's expression clearly showed her stress. "I'm sorry for that barbed comment. I shouldn't be taking my frustrations out on you."

Stephanie got to her feet. "I think I should leave. This is an awkward situation for both of us." Stephanie quickly turned on her heels and headed back toward the hallway.

"Please, Stephanie, don't go," Darcella shouted after her. "I could really use someone to talk to. I know you're Stephen's twin and I certainly don't expect you to take sides."

The stress in Darcella's voice had caused Stephanie to stop dead in her tracks. As she turned around to face her hostess, her heart crumbled at the excruciating pain in Darcella's eyes. Knowing she couldn't leave Darcella like this, Stephanie reclaimed her seat. "I wish I knew what to say, Darcy, but I don't. I'm truly at a loss for words."

Darcella nodded her understanding. "You don't have to say anything. I just need an ear. I'm curious, Stephanie. If Stephen didn't tell you about us, why'd you just suddenly drop by?"

With her heart pounding hard, Stephanie smiled weakly. She had come there to ask Darcella to be in her wedding. It would be insensitive of her to reveal her motivation under the circumstances. "It was nothing, really. We haven't talked in a while and I wanted to know how you were doing." That was true enough, but Stephanie still felt uncomfortable with her response.

Darcella looked skeptical. "You don't expect me to believe that was your only reason, now do you, Stephanie?"

Stephanie felt totally embarrassed. "No, I guess not. The truth is I came here to ask you to be in my wedding party. I wouldn't have come to you with the idea had I known about you and Stephen's broken engagement. I'm really sorry about it, Darcy. Did he tell you why he suddenly doesn't want to get married?"

Darcella was genuinely surprised by that question, but she hid it well. "He didn't. Did he tell you why?"

Stephanie cast Darcella a strange look. "I just told you that he didn't tell me a thing about it. Why do you find that so hard to believe?"

"Then why did you ask the question you did? He must've said something to you about not marrying me for you to ask me that."

Stephanie was growing impatient. The last thing she wanted to do was get into an argument with Darcella, but she wasn't about to allow herself to be verbally attacked, either. "Look, Darcy, I don't know what's up with you and Stephen, but I won't be caught in the middle of it. And you're right about one thing. This is a first for my brother not to share with me something so serious. I'm afraid I'm totally in the dark on this one. I only heard about it when you told me."

Darcella stared at Stephanie in disbelief. "I never thought you'd be the type to play games. You know all about your brother's attraction to your best friend. He told me all about the dinner you had together with Farrah. Whatever you do, please don't commit the mistake of trying to make a fool of me. Your brother has already done enough of that."

Stephanie suddenly realized she'd stepped into a minefield. Getting out of it without one blowing up in her face might not be possible. She felt caught between a rock and hard place; darned if she did and darned if she didn't. "I have no desire to make a fool of you, Darcy. Once again, I'm not going to caught in the middle of Stephen's and your battles."

"Stephanie, you're already in the middle of it. How could you be a part of Stephen and Farrah's duplicity? I didn't think you capable of that kind of deception."

Stephanie felt terribly affronted. "I'm not a party to anything to do with Stephen and Farrah. The dinners we had together were innocent. There was no duplicity. I'm in no way responsible for what goes on between you and Stephen, so don't try to blame me for any of this. I'm not the enemy here."

Stephanie got up from the sofa. Without uttering another word, she turned on her heels and walked away. Before she could reach the front door, Darcella whizzed past her, and then blocked the exit by covering it with her body.

Fuming inside, Stephanie sighed hard, furling and unfurling her fists. "You don't want to do this, Darcy. Get out of my way or I'll move you out. You can't intimidate me."

Darcella actually thought Stephanie would make good on her threat, which was so unlike Stephen's mild-mannered twin. The look in her eyes proved to Darcella that Stephanie was ready and willing to do battle over her right to leave the premises. It was hard for Darcella to imagine Stephanie getting physical with her, but she quickly decided she didn't want to find out. "I'm sorry, Stephanie. This is my fault. I guess you can see how desperate I am."

"Darn right it is!" Stephanie shot Darcella a dagger-sharp look and then walked out the front door. This entire episode with Darcella had been totally unexpected by Stephanie, but she wasn't about to step in as a scapegoat for anyone, including her twin brother.

Stephanie now knew why Stephen had suddenly flown off to New Orleans. She just wished he had told her what had happened between the two of them so she could've avoided this ugly confrontation with his fiancée. Their shattered relationship was something for them to work out, not her. Stephanie felt bad for both parties, but she was adamant about not taking sides.

After Stephanie pulled her car into the garage, she got out of the vehicle and ran into the house, where she quickly grabbed the telephone. Stephen needed a large piece of her mind. That he hadn't told her about the broken engagement had her incensed now, only because she could've avoided what had happened at Darcella's. *How had everything gotten so messed up?* This should've been the happiest time of all their lives, but it seemed as if it was anything but. Getting engaged to the people they loved had once appeared to her as the perfect scenario.

Once Stephanie dialed the memory code to connect her with Stephen's cell phone, she quickly cradled the receiver. Calling him in New Orleans and then upsetting him wasn't the right thing to do. She could wait until he came back home to give him a chilling blast of reality.

Upon Stephanie spotting Farrah coming up her walkway, she sighed heavily, wishing this visit could be put off indefinitely. She hoped her friend didn't want to talk about Stephen. Stephanie just wasn't in the mood for another dark episode of pure drama. She regretted that she'd threatened

Darcella in a menacing way, but at that moment she'd seen it as necessary.

Stephanie opened the door before Farrah had a chance to ring the doorbell. "Hey, girl. What's up with you?"

Farrah hugged Stephanie warmly. "Not much. I just came over to see how you were doing. I also need to ask you about one of your accounts. A check has bounced on us."

Stephanie looked totally surprised, since most of her clients had money to burn. "Which account is it?"

Farrah dropped down in a chair. "The Tobias one."

"No," Stephanie shouted, "that can't be. Eliza Beth would never give me a bad check."

Farrah shrugged. "I beg to differ. That sister's five thousand dollar check is bouncing around like a rubber ball. I've put it through twice already. Plus we've been charged a bad-check fee. You might want to call her on it."

"Don't worry, I will. But I need to have in front of me the proof of what you're talking about. I'll pull the account up on the Internet before I call her."

"That's a good idea. I know you and she have become friends. I hope it's just a mistake."

"Come into my office with me while I check it out. I can't believe this is happening. They have plenty of money. Lemanz is one of the best cardiac surgeons in the country."

Farrah laughed. "It appears that he might be a broke one," she joked. "I guess you'll have to see it for yourself to believe it."

Stephanie didn't like Farrah's joking inference, but she let it slide past her. She didn't have enough strength to champion another cause. There was a darn good reason why the Tobias check bounced. She was willing to stake her reputation on it.

As Stephanie sat down at her desk, she turned on her computer. Farrah took a seat on the straight-back chair facing the desk.

In a matter of minutes Stephanie had pulled up the questionable transaction. "This is so bothersome," Stephanie squealed. "This will be a hard one for me to confront because of our friendship. I hope I don't regret mixing business with pleasure, but my gut tells me this isn't intentional. There has to be a reasonable explanation for this."

"I can handle it for you, Stephanie. I *am* the accountant so it wouldn't be anything out of the ordinary. This is a business matter."

"Thanks, Farrah, but I'll check it out myself. I think our friendship is solid enough to deal with this without encountering a major problem."

"I'll keep my fingers crossed, Stephanie. Anything new going on with you?"

Stephanie smiled broadly. "Gregory and I have set our wedding date. First Saturday in October. I hope we're ready by then. We have so much to do to prepare for our big day."

Farrah laughed with enthusiasm. "Congrats! I know I have the maid-of-honor gig sewed up, but have you decided on the size of your wedding party?"

"Small and intimate. Just our families and close friends. Gregory's mom, Ms. Aretha, wants it to be the wedding of the century, but I think not. Too much stuff to do for a large one. Of course I still want you as my maid-of-honor. But will that be awkward for you?"

Farrah shrugged. "Why would it be?"

Stephanie saw that she had stepped into the very arena she had hoped to avoid. However, it was only fair that Farrah knew she had asked Darcella to be a bridesmaid. She'd certainly want to be apprised of something like that. "I've asked Darcella to be in the wedding party, too."

"And? What does that have to do with me?"

"Come on, Farrah. You darn well know that I'm aware of your feelings for Stephen." Farrah looked cool and calm. "You don't think I anticipated this happening, Stephanie? Darcella is only your brother's fiancée. It didn't bother me before and it won't bother me now."

"Would it bother you to know that Darcy knows you and Stephen have been flirting with each other and that she also knows about the dinner the three of us shared?"

Farrah was obviously rattled now. "She does? Did you tell her that, Stephanie?"

"Stephen did."

"That's interesting he'd confess that, since he has made things very clear to me."

"Clear how?"

Farrah told Stephanie all about Stephen's visit to her house, leaving nothing out.

Stephanie whistled. "That *is* interesting. Stephen probably confessed to Darcy out of guilt. It was the right thing to do, though. At least I think so." Stephanie grew quiet for a second. "On the other hand, it might not have been such a good idea. I can only imagine the pain of hearing that from someone you love. I learned today from Darcy that their engagement is off."

Farrah's eyes widened with disbelief. "You're kidding! Don't say that, Stephanie."

"Why not, Farrah? It's true."

"Did they break up over me?"

"I don't know, Farrah. Darcy didn't say. I can't believe that the flirting is all there is to it, but it shouldn't be discounted. Stephen has yet to mention a thing to me. That is so not like him."

"You can say that again, Stephanie. It's hard for me to believe he didn't confide in you. You two tell each other everything."

"Apparently not," Stephanie remarked.

"You sound disappointed over it. Are you?"

"A little. Since Stephen now has our father and uncle to confide in, he's obviously not telling me as much as he used to. I guess that's pretty normal. Man-to-man stuff."

"Probably so, Stephanie. You're not jealous of their relationship, are you?"

"Heavens no! I'm glad Stephen has them to talk to. There are probably some things a guy can't or shouldn't tell his sister and vice versa. I've been keeping a few secrets of my own."

"Like what?" Farrah inquired, highly curious about the nature of the secrets.

"For one, how scared I am of getting married. I'm afraid it might be too soon to jump the broom. I haven't worked out all my issues yet, either."

"What issues?"

Stephanie began to tell Farrah about her fears. It seemed they had begun to grow right after she'd witnessed the problems Darcella and Stephen were faced with. The flirting between Stephen and her best friend had also impacted her. The failure of her parents' marriage was largely responsible, too. It was very scary for her to know the truth about Malachi and Doreen.

If Stephanie was to be honest with self, marriage had always been a troubling issue for her.

Farrah was deeply concerned about what she'd just heard from Stephanie. "Have you talked any of this over with Gregory?"

Stephanie looked slightly abashed. "Not so much as a word. I should've discussed it with him before we got engaged. I don't know how to bring it up now. He might think I'm being silly and juvenile. I hate that I haven't talked to him about my mountain of fears. His parents' marriage is in shambles, too. Infidelity is an issue there also. The divorce rate today is so darn high. I don't know too many marriage success stories. Uncle Max said he never got married because of my father and mother's ill-fated relationship. Go figure."

Farrah easily sympathized with Stephanie's situation. "I don't think you should take one step down that aisle until you've discussed this with your fiancé. Seriously."

Farrah went on to tell Stephanie that she was walking into something she knew very little about and that if she didn't take the time to explore and then conquer all her issues that she'd more than likely end up in divorce court, too. Marriage wasn't something anyone should take lightly. She then told Stephanie that she believed Gregory would want to know about her fears so he could help allay them. Just because there was infidelity in other marriages didn't necessarily mean it would happen in theirs. It sounded like Farrah had the recipe to happily ever after.

"I think you're right, Farrah. Gregory will be here over the weekend. I can discuss everything with him then. I hope he isn't crushed by it. Stephen told me he's been reading what God has to say about relationships and marriage. I guess I need a refresher course, too."

"Do whatever it takes to make yourself comfortable with the lifetime commitment you're about to make. There's no time like the present to back out of the deal if you're not sure about marriage or even ready for it. As opposed to much later, be sorry before you take the plunge."

Stephanie made direct eye contact with Farrah. "Thanks for the advice." She then bit down on her lower lip. "I want to say something to you. Because of the way you feel about Stephen, I know it may be very difficult for you to participate in my wedding. I'll truly understand if you want to back out."

Farrah frowned. "It sounds to me as if you're the one that's not comfortable with it, Stephanie. If that's the case, then you need to tell me so. I don't want to do anything to ruin your special day. I love you too much for that."

Stephanie felt awful that her friend had misunderstood her. "Farrah, please don't think like that. I've always wanted you as my maid-of-honor. We discussed this as teenagers. My wedding wouldn't be complete without you in it. I just don't want you hurt."

Farrah rushed over and gave Stephanie a big hug. "It's okay, girlfriend. I won't be hurt. I promise you that. Like I told you earlier, Stephen has made everything clear to me. I know there's no future for us."

Stephanie couldn't help wondering if that statement was untrue. Stephen might not want to admit it, but she believed her brother's interest in Farrah was genuine. He talked about Farrah to her a lot, but she didn't think he realized how much. Stephanie knew that she wasn't the only one who needed to get things out in the open. Stephen needed to get real honest with himself.

Although Stephanie didn't want to see anyone get hurt, she wanted her brother to be happy with his choice in a mate. Stephen and Darcella no longer seemed happy and content with each other. If the strong feelings of dissatisfaction and unrest with their relationship were mutual, then perhaps it was time for them to really end things and move on. Stephanie wouldn't want their marriage to end in divorce any more than she wanted her own to end up that way.

Stephanie had invited Farrah to stay over for dinner and she had accepted. The two friends had then gone into the kitchen where they'd joined forces to pull a quick meal together. White rice, steamed vegetables and grilled teriyaki chicken had been the quickest foods to prepare. In less than forty-five minutes the women were seated at the kitchen table.

Halfway through the meal, Farrah laid down her fork, already feeling full. "Thanks for inviting me to stay over and eat with you. I'll help you with the dishes and then I have to get back to the hospital. I've only been away from there for a few hours, but I'm sure it feels a lot longer than that to Mom."

"I can do the dishes later. I'll just stack them in the dishwasher until I get back."

"Where do you have to go, Stephanie?"

"To the hospital with you. I've only been up there twice this week to see Ms. Helen. I wish I could've done better than that, but I've been swamped. Too many days off has put me a little behind. I'm glad Ms. Helen loved the flowers I sent her."

Farrah smiled warmly. "She really had a fit over the color-ful bouquet. The get-well helium balloon the florist added was also a very nice touch. She loves you like a daughter, Steph-anie. My mother has been through so much this past year, but I think she'll pull through this crisis, too. Her blood sugar has come down considerably and she's feeling much better."

Stephanie sighed with relief. "That's such good news. I've been praying for her a lot. I even sent a prayer request to everyone in my e-mail address book. I also asked the recip-ients to pass it on to the folks on their lists."

"Thanks, Stephanie. I'm glad you're always here for me. I don't know what I'd do without you. Our close friendship has definitely withstood the test of time."

Stephanie closed her hand over Farrah's for a brief mo-ment. "The feelings are mutual. You've never let me down, either. I don't think anything can pull us apart."

"I hope not. I know you're nervous about your wedding day, but I can assure you I'll step aside if things become awk-ward. Your wedding ceremony will be very special. Your comfort is my first concern. I'm not worried about Darcy or Stephen. Only you, my friend."

Stephanie shook her head from side to side. "You won't have to do that. Darcy hasn't made a commitment to be in my wedding. When I mentioned it, she didn't respond one way or the other. She may not even want to be a part of it, especially if she and Stephen don't get back together. How-ever, I don't want to lose her as a friend. I thought she and I had become close, too, but she obviously has some under-lying issues with me. I'm surprised they're only surfacing now. Stephen and I were closer than close when they first met. That's never going to change."

Farrah got up from the chair and began cleaning off the table. "And it should never have to change. You guys are blood, family. Don't fret over what happened at Darcy's house. You and I both know you haven't done anything to her. To lose you as a friend would be her loss."

Stephanie frowned. "I'd feel the loss, too, but I hope it doesn't come down to that."

Stephanie then joined Farrah to finish cleaning off the table. After the table was completely cleared, despite Stephanie's earlier statement, Farrah rinsed off the plates and utensils with hot water and handed them to Stephanie to stack in the dishwasher.

Once the kitchen was back in order, Stephanie ran off to her bedroom to change into something more comfortable and to also change her shoes. She knew how anxious Farrah was to get back to the hospital so she hurried through her personal preparations.

Stephanie drummed her fingers on the desktop as she impatiently waited for someone to answer the phone in the Tobias household. Getting this problem dealt with was something she wanted over in a hurry. Sleep hadn't come easily for her because of it, making her lie awake well into the night trying to form in her mind what she would say. She smiled nervously when she heard Eliza Beth's voice. "It's Stephanie. How's it going, Liza?"

"Good. How are you?"

"I'm just fine. Busy as heck, though."

"What's on your mind this morning, Stephanie?"

Stephanie drew in a calming breath. "Listen, I called to let you know that we couldn't cash your check. It came back to us. Do you know what happened?"

"Are you saying my checked bounced?"

"Yeah, I'm afraid so." The silence on the other end made Stephanie even more nervous. Perhaps this exchange might not go as well as she'd expected it to.

"I don't know what to say, Stephanie. I don't have an answer for you right now. I'll have to check with Lemanz when he gets home. He's out of town right now and I can't reach him."

Stephanie didn't think she could get any more nervous

than she was, but her hands had begun to tremble. She'd written checks off the amount of money that she thought was in the account. That meant her checks could also bounce. "When will he be back?"

Eliza Beth cleared her throat. "To tell you the truth, I don't know. There's been some other strange happenings around here. I'm in fact really worried about my marriage. I can't use my credit cards, either. Do you think he purposely closed my accounts?"

How did Eliza Beth expect her to answer that question, Stephanie wondered. She wasn't privy to their private affairs. "I wouldn't have a clue," she finally responded. "If you don't mind me asking, what makes you think he'd do something like that?"

"Well, he's been on me about my spending habits, but I didn't think it was that out of control. Lemanz is at a medical symposium in Africa. That's why I can't reach him. I've been absolutely crazy the last couple of days. He normally would've contacted me by now, but he hasn't. Like I said, there are a lot of unexplainable things going on with the finances. I promise to get back to you as soon as he contacts me. Is that a problem for you, Stephanie?"

Stephanie scowled hard. "It could be. I wrote checks on the money from your check. Since I never had a problem with your account before, there was no reason for me to think otherwise. I have enough money in my savings account to do a transfer. I'll go ahead and do that and you can square things with me when you get everything straightened out."

"No, Stephanie, you shouldn't have to do that. I have enough pin money to cover the check. I'll bring the cash over to you around noon. Can you wait that long?"

"Sure I can. I still think I should cover the check out of my savings, though. I'd hate to have my checks bounce, too. That could be a real mess. I can then put the money back in my savings out of what you give me. I'll see you at noon."

"Thanks, Stephanie, and I'm really sorry about this. Please

send up a prayer for us. I hope Lemanz isn't considering divorcing me over the amount of money I spend. I couldn't deal with that. I love him so much. Cutting off my cash flow without telling me is out of character for him."

"Don't jump to any hasty conclusions, Liza. There may be a plausible explanation."

"I sure hope so. See you later, friend."

Stephanie was totally puzzled by the time she got off the phone with Eliza Beth. As she made an electronic bank transfer from her savings to her checking, she couldn't help thinking how weird their conversation had been.

Why would Liza Beth suddenly jump to the conclusion that Lemanz might want a divorce? Was there more to their personal story than her friend had dared to reveal? It didn't make a bit of sense that a man would cut off his wife's finances without prior warning. Doing that could actually cause a lot of problems to arise for both of them.

Stephanie hadn't seen anything in Lemanz to indicate he'd ever be that callous toward Liza Beth. If anything, all he ever showed her was how much he truly adored his wife. He was the one who'd spoiled her to no end so a sudden change in him just wasn't adding up for Stephanie. Just as Eliza Beth had requested of her, Stephanie closed her eyes and said a silent prayer for the Tobias family. Only God could sustain the strength of the Tobias marriage.

Chapter 9

Adrenaline pumped wildly through Stephen, making him feel as if streaks of hot white lighting had taken over his entire body. Sweat dripped from his face as he'd raced for the fire pole. From the moment the firehouse gong had sounded, his blood had been rushing through his veins at breakneck speed. This was his first fire since his return to active duty and he wasn't looking forward to what dangers that might lie ahead of his team.

Stephen's initial response to the fire alert had him terribly worried. How he'd react when the team finally arrived at their destination gave him cause for concern. Despite the adrenaline rush, he felt as though he was moving in slow motion. For what should've been routine to him was anything but. It felt as if his heart were going to punch its way right through his chest cavity. His steady inhaling and exhaling wasn't calming him down in the least.

As the fire engine pulled up in front of the burning office building, acid bile arose in Stephen's throat. He hadn't had this kind of reaction since his very first fire run. He'd become physically sick that day, but only after he'd done his job. The later thoughts of him trekking through a house of fiery flames had caused his stomach to go berserk. Determined not to let that happen again, Stephen willed himself into a state of calm. He then put on his game face.

It was showtime and time for Stephen to set all his fears aside. This was a new day in his life as a firefighter. He couldn't let the past influence this moment or the moments to come. There was a lot riding on his performance. How he handled this situation would speak volumes about his readiness for duty, or his lack thereof. It was his desire that no one else would ever expire on his watch. The pretty faces of those two little girls might haunt him for the rest of his life, but he couldn't let that hold him back from doing what he was highly trained to do. With that in mind, Stephen quickly whipped into action, prepared to take firm charge of the situation.

Stephen felt totally relieved now that everyone had been safely evacuated from the building. He had immediately thanked God for the favorable outcome, though he'd been praying right on through the entire ordeal. The upper floors of the office building hadn't fared as well as its occupants, but structures could most always be rebuilt. That wasn't always possible with human beings. Even when people survived the burning flames, there were always emotional scars to contend with if not physical ones.

As Stephen's cohorts congratulated him on a job well done, he knew they'd meant it, but he was also aware that his buddies wanted to keep his confidence high. He was sure that his fear had been strong enough for them to smell. Several of the firefighters, at one time or another, had experienced the same uncertainties and fears Stephen had. It was difficult for firefighters to come back after tragic circumstances had occurred on their watch, yet the majority of them did just that, those that had been blessed enough to survive the traumatic ordeal.

Moments later, before the Southeast Houston Fire Department could leave the current fire scene, another call had been put in for them to handle another fire emergency at a nearby hospital. It was a one-alarm deal, according to what had been transmitted, which was a much lesser degree of fire. Still, the sirens roared to life as the shiny red truck rapidly made its way to the next incident. Fires could be controllable one moment and in the next instant they could become uncontrollable. No one ever knew exactly what to expect from one fire scene to another.

The hospital fire was easily extinguished, but it could've had a dire outcome. A patient in a private room had violated the nonsmoking ordinance by lighting a cigarette in bed. The elderly guy had fallen asleep, more than likely from the medication he'd been given earlier, and he had then somehow knocked the cigarette from the end of the tray table and onto the bed, where it had fallen onto the mattress and had eventually burned a hole into it. The slightly charred wood at the end of the tray table was the evidence that the cigarette had been situated there. The door to the private room had been closed so no one had smelled the smoke. The fire alarm had finally alerted a few of the personnel to the emergency situation on the hospital floor.

Since it was mealtime, the crew had decided to grab a bite to eat in the hospital cafeteria. This particular hospital also served food from a popular fast-food franchise, Chick-fil-A.

After the cafeteria worker had given Stephen his order of fried chicken strips, he took his large plastic cup over to the soda dispenser and filled it up with crushed ice and Minute Maid lemonade. He then retrieved eating utensils, napkins and a straw for his drink.

Just as Stephen was about to join his coworkers at a large table, he spotted Farrah. As it normally did when he saw her, his heart began to beat fast. His first thought was to act as if he hadn't seen her. He dismissed that idea rather quickly. There was no reason for him to be rude to her, especially since he also considered her a friend. He then took a deep breath and proceeded toward her table. Stephen planned to say a quick hello and then be on his merry way. But when it appeared to him that she'd been crying that plan also flew right out of his mind.

Stephen looked at Farrah with concern as he greeted her in a soft tone.

As Farrah looked up at Stephen, a single tear escaped from the corner of her right eye. She wiped it away, feeling a bit embarrassed by it. "Hi. You're the last person I expected to see in here. The uniform says you're on duty. How are you, Stephen?"

Stephen smiled with empathy. "You stole that question right out of my mouth. You look distraught so I need to know how you are first. Is it your mother? Tell me what's happening." Without giving any thought to the fact he'd come there with his coworkers, Stephen set his tray down on the picnic bench-style table. He then took a seat directly across from Farrah.

Farrah sighed hard. "Mom is not doing very well. Her blood sugar is extremely high. Her heart is also in trouble. Things had gotten better for a minute. I thought she'd be back home with me by now. It doesn't look too good for her, Stephen. I came down here to force myself to eat so I can keep up my strength. I haven't taken very good care of myself during this family crisis."

Stephen reached over for Farrah's hand, holding on to it for a brief moment. "I'm sorry to hear that. I'll keep both your mother and you in prayer."

"Thanks so much, Stephen. We need all the prayers we can get. So what's been going on with you lately?" Farrah didn't think Stephen would bring up his broken engagement to her, but she'd like to hear about it from him. If he needed consoling, she'd like to be there for him. Not in a romantic sense, though. Just as a good friend. Everyone needed a friend at one time or another.

Stephen stretched out his hands and turned up his palms. "Same old, same old. Work, running errands, working out at the fitness center and then chilling out at home when I'm off. I did just get back from New Orleans visiting my dad and uncle. We had a good time hanging out together as boys. I really needed that quick break. I wish I could've stayed another few days."

"That must've been nice, Stephen. Your sister and I like hanging out as girls. I'm sure you've seen Stephanie since you got back."

Stephen chuckled at that. "Of course I've seen her. She was yelling all up in my ear when she first saw me, but I recognize sisterly concern when I see and hear it. In fact, I'm having dinner at her place tonight. My dad and uncle are here for the weekend and they've invited a couple of ladies over to eat with us. Those two old boys are out on the prowl. I'm happy to see them having the time of their lives. I imagine it's hard to start dating after the age of fifty."

Farrah giggled softly. "It's hard to begin dating at any age. Is Gregory here also?"

"I think he'll be here this evening. Did Stephanie tell you they've set a wedding date?"

"I've heard from her already. I'm sure they can hardly wait for October to roll around."

"I don't know. You'd think so. Stephanie has some fears, but she's working it all out. Marriage is a difficult pill for us Trudeauxs to swallow."

The conversation lapsed into silence as Stephen resumed eating his food. Minutes later he spotted one of the guys coming toward him, thinking it was probably time to go already. It seemed as if he'd just sat down. "Looks like I have to run. I came here with the firehouse crew."

Stephen then excused himself for a moment so he could meet up with Tim Baker before he made it to the table. He was pleased to learn they'd be there another twenty minutes or so. With that in mind, Stephen returned to Farrah. "Looks like we have a few more minutes to chat. If you're free this evening, you should come by Stephanie's for dinner. I'm sure she'd love to have you drop in."

Stephen was aware that having dinner with Farrah was somewhat behind his breakup with Darcella, but no one would ever convince him that there wasn't much more to it than that. One day the real truth of the matter would come out, but he'd decided not to pursue it. If Darcella wanted to share her reasoning with him, she'd eventually seek him out.

Farrah shook her head. "I'll probably be up here all evening. I go home to shower and change in the mornings and I often don't get back to the house until late evening. Mother's health has taken a turn for the worse. I don't want to be too far away from her during this difficult time."

Stephen thought back to when Doreen had been ill. She had passed from this life rather quickly, but that hadn't eased their grief and pain one iota. "We'll all say a special prayer for her health to be restored when we get together this evening. I'll see to it."

Before Farrah could respond to Stephen's considerate comment, the overhead loud speaker came on, announcing a code blue. When Farrah recognized the floor being coded as the same one her mother's room was on, she jumped up and took off running, leaving behind a bewildered Stephen. All he could do at this point was look at Farrah's retreating back.

As Stephen gathered up his trash to toss in the metal bin, he saw that Farrah had left her purse behind. He knew that he couldn't leave it there for someone to steal, but he didn't know if he should take it home with him or try to find her. Figuring that she'd more than likely need her purse, especially after thinking her car and house keys might be inside of it, his decision was an easy one. He'd get her mother's room number and then take Farrah her handbag.

After Stephen filled the guys in on what had just occurred, he asked them to please bear with him. His coworkers then told him that they'd wait for him out in the parking lot.

* * *

The moment Stephen heard the loud screaming his heart sank to the soles of his feet. His mouth moved rapidly in a silent prayer as he walked away from the elevator and then ran toward the room number he'd been given by the volunteer manning the hospital information desk. As he reached his destination, the medical personnel had just begun to file out of the room. He waited until the room was completely clear of all equipment and personnel before he entered.

Memories of Doreen's death flooded his mind as he watched Farrah holding her mother so tenderly in her arms, tears streaming down her pretty face. Her screams had now been reduced to low moans of agonizing grief. There was no doubt in his mind that Ms. Helen was deceased.

Oh, God, what was he to do now, Stephen wondered. His feet felt rooted to the floor. He couldn't seem to move forward or backward. This was an awful situation for anyone to be in. He knew Farrah wasn't going to let go of her mother until someone forced her to. He didn't want to be that someone, but no one else was available. Farrah had no other family members around. In fact, Stephen suddenly realized he'd never met anyone else in her family.

It had taken Stephen and a couple of nurses to finally pull Stephanie away from their deceased mother's body. His sister had eventually collapsed in his arms on that fateful day, but not until all her strength had been depleted. She'd had no fight left in her when she'd given in.

Stephen was finally able to step back out of the room, knowing that he had to alert his crew to this dilemma. After reaching Tim on his cell phone, he told him what was going on, advising them to head on back to the station. He'd call someone to pick him up once Farrah's mother was taken down to the morgue. Someone had to be there for her.

Stephen was the only friend she had right now. Since he'd been in her situation before, he knew she was going to need all the compassion and tender care he could muster. Stephen then rushed back into the hospital room to offer as much support to Farrah as he possibly could.

What came next had Stephen wishing Stephanie were there to help him console her best friend. He had left his sister a voice message to call him right away, but he hadn't been able to bring himself to speak of Ms. Helen's death into the recorder. That would have been insensitive of him. He already knew that his sister was going to be terribly distraught and that she'd take this death very hard. Ms. Helen had been involved in Stephanie's life for what seemed like forever. His sister had spent countless nights with Farrah in Ms. Helen's home while growing up.

Farrah was back to screaming at the top of her lungs, her body writhing all over the place. Her pain was obviously excruciating as her uncontrollable tears flooded rapidly down her face. Two nurses were now in the room with her, but they had to wait on a doctor's order before a sedative could be administered to the grieving woman. Farrah's screams grew louder.

Stephen saw that Farrah was in as bad a shape as Stephanie had been under the same set of circumstances. He fought hard to maintain his own composure. The death of Farrah's mother had brought back to his mind the death of his own mother and the recent demise of the Anderson twins. The devastation he felt was hard for him to bear, yet Stephen knew he had to find a way to put his grief aside in order to assist Farrah in hers. This moment wasn't about him.

Once a morgue attendant finally wheeled Ms. Helen's remains from the hospital room, Stephen immediately nestled Farrah in his strong arms, allowing her to cry her eyes out against his chest. As he whispered comforting words into her ear, he gently stroked her hair, wishing he could take away all of her pain. If folks hadn't said what they needed to say to the people they loved before their demise, there were no second chances. Death was final.

At this moment Stephen was grateful that he'd told his

mother every day how much he loved and appreciated her. The three of them had been extremely close. Both he and Stephanie had had a special bond with their mother. Stephen was aware that Farrah had the same kind of bond with Ms. Helen and he was sure she'd often heard her daughter confess her love to her.

Stephen suddenly realized he didn't know a thing about Farrah's father, which he thought was rather strange considering they'd lived next door to each other all those years. He didn't remember ever seeing a man over at the Freeman house, but that didn't mean a whole lot since Stephen only paid close attention to the things he was keenly interested in. Still, he should have some recollection of a man hanging out in the yard over there, but he didn't.

Stephen was certain he'd find out about Farrah's dad before this was all over with. Stephanie hadn't ever mentioned him, either, but that didn't mean she didn't know of him. If nothing else came out of it, her dad's name would probably be listed in Ms. Helen's obituary.

Stephen had driven Farrah's car to the firehouse, but with her as a passenger. Since this was his last shift, he was going to take off early so she wouldn't be alone. After he'd failed to get her to come inside with him, he rushed away to do what he had to do. He planned to leave his car there. Someone in his family would bring him back to the firehouse later to pick it up.

Glad to know that everything was quiet at the firehouse and that there'd been no emergencies during his extended absence, Stephen told his supervisor the situation he'd found himself in. He then explained to the man in charge that Farrah was a family friend and a lifelong neighbor, telling him that no other member of her family had been at the hospital with her. His boss had given him his blessings once he'd approved of Stephen leaving the job early.

* * *

Stephanie was right there to meet Stephen when he pulled Farrah's car into her driveway. His sister came running out of her front door the same moment she'd spotted the vehicle. The twins had had a chance to talk briefly over the phone when she had returned her brother's call. Stephen was glad that Stephanie had called in before he'd left the firehouse. It would've been difficult for him to tell her about Ms. Helen's death right in front of Farrah.

Once Stephanie took Farrah into her warm embrace, hugging her tightly, she carefully guided her friend inside her house. After making sure she was comfortable on the sofa, Stephanie went to Farrah's master bathroom to retrieve a couple of Tylenol for her aching head. Farrah had also requested her house slippers. Stephanie planned on making her friend a cup of hot tea and was also of the mind to coax her into lying down for a spell. She knew firsthand that Farrah would have to preserve her strength to get through the trying days ahead.

Grief was draining: emotionally, physically and mentally.

Stephen stayed in the family room with Farrah while Stephanie went out to the kitchen to brew the hot tea. Before turning on the flame under the teapot, Stephanie stashed inside her purse the prescription for sedatives that her brother had handed her. Once she had her friend settled into bed, she'd run out to the pharmacy to have the prescription filled. On second thought, Stephanie decided she'd stay with Farrah and ask Stephen to run the quick errand. There was a CVS Pharmacy right around the corner from their homes.

Minutes later, heeding the call of his sister's voice, Stephen made his way into the kitchen. Upon seeing that everything was ready to be carried into the family room, he lifted with ease the heavy tray. "I'll carry this in for you."

"Thanks, Stephen." Stephanie frowned slightly. "I don't know what to do about dinner tonight. Dad and Uncle Max are cooking for their friends, but they expect me to be there to help out. How can I leave Farrah at a time like this? She's a basket case."

"Don't sweat it right now. You and I can take shifts keeping an eye on Farrah. You can be there for the beginning of the dinner and I'll show up near the end. Does that sound okay?"

Stephanie nodded in agreement. "Sounds great."

Stephanie followed along behind her brother, toting her purse under her arm. After entering the room, she sat down next to Farrah on the sofa. Stephen sat in one of the plush chairs. The threesome drank the tea in total silence, each one lost in their individual thoughts.

Thinking that she should tell Farrah about her dinner plans, Stephanie began to do so.

Farrah waved off Stephanie's concern. "I should be fine, Stephanie. I know I have to deal with the grief. Unfortunately, life has to go on. Mother wouldn't want me to fall totally apart."

Stephanie smiled sweetly. "Of course she wouldn't." Stephanie then told Farrah about the plan Stephen had come up with.

"Stephen told me about the dinner earlier, Stephanie. I'm not sure your plans to watch over me are necessary. But thanks for caring about me, guys. If I feel like I need to be with someone, I'll just call over to your house. I'm exhausted so I'll probably sleep for a long while."

The look on Stephen's face said he didn't agree. "We're doing it the way I said. You don't need to be alone, Farrah. You'll sleep better with one of us here. No one will disturb you."

Farrah could tell she was in a no-win situation. She didn't want to ruin their plans for the evening, but she was also very grateful that the twins cared so much about her. Being alone would be very hard on her, but she'd have to get used to it. Her mother wasn't ever coming home. Helen was heading for her new mansion. The one Jesus had gone before her to prepare.

"I'm taking first shift," Stephen informed Farrah. "Stephanie has to help out next door."

Stephanie reached into her bag and pulled out the prescription. She then waved it in the air. "I need you to fill this at CVS, Stephen. It shouldn't take too long."

Stephen got up and walked over to Stephanie, taking the script from her hand. "The doctor should've called this one in. It would be ready by now. Is there anything else I can get for you two while I'm out?"

Both women shook their heads.

Stephanie and Farrah's eyes stayed on Stephen until he'd disappeared from the room.

Stephanie then turned her attention to Farrah. "How are you doing?"

Farrah's eyes filled with moisture at the caring gentleness in Stephanie's tone. "I'm downright miserable, but I'm happy for Mother's peace. She's no longer in pain. I wish I could say that about myself. I am hurting something awful, but this shall pass, too. You've been where I am so you know what I mean."

Stephanie slipped her arm around Farrah's shoulder. "I do know. I still grieve my mother. There isn't a day that goes by that I don't think of her or wish she were still here with us. We can become very selfish in our grief. I experienced anger, too, so don't be surprised if that happens. I was angry because I felt Mama had left me alone in this big, bad world to fend for myself. Then one day I realized she had equipped both Stephen and me to deal with anything. And we have."

Farrah wiped a tear from the corner of her eye. "Yes, you have. About Stephen's plan to be here alone with me for a short spell, is that going to cause him problems with Darcy? I don't want to make things any worse."

"Nothing has changed in their relationship and it doesn't look like it will. But don't you worry your pretty little head about any of that. Stephen is a big boy. He knows how to handle his business, Farrah. Stephen is all grown up, all man, just the kind of man Mama raised him to be."

Farrah smiled softly. "Okay, then I won't worry. Could you come in the bedroom with me? I want to slip into something more comfortable."

Stephanie laughed, raising an eyebrow. "How comfortable?"

Farrah instantly caught Stephanie's drift. "Don't even go there, girl. I'd never entice Stephen with provocative clothing. But that's not a bad idea, especially for a bad girl. I just happen to be one of the good ones, yet I do have an incorrigible imagination."

Both women laughed over that.

Farrah began to rummage through her chest of drawers. She pulled out a couple of articles of clothing and then held up a pair of cotton pajamas and a matching robe. "Does this meet with your approval, Stephanie?"

Stephanie cracked up. "No one said you had to look like Grandma Gump. Even Forrest liked to see Jenny in something soft and pretty."

"Stephen isn't Forrest Gump and I'm not Jenny." Farrah put her finger up to her temple in a gesture of thought. "Hmm, maybe that's not such a bad analogy after all, especially since Forrest finally got the woman of his dreams. Look at all those years he pined away for her."

Stephanie rolled with laughter, glad to see that Farrah was laughing, too. Her dear friend's laughter wouldn't last for very long, though. Her bitter tears would return full force. But it was such a nice reprieve for now. Stephanie knew there'd be long absences of Farrah's laughter.

Of course, Stephanie already knew Ms. Sarah, but this was her first introduction to Josefina Clayton, the woman her father seemed genuinely interested in. In Stephanie's opinion Josefina was a very attractive woman. Her jet-black hair was long and wavy with lots of bounce. Her physical body was every bit as fit as Malachi's, which meant she was no stranger to the gym. Every part of her anatomy appeared very firm. As a whole, she looked very healthy.

Instead of taking Stephanie's extended hand, Josefina had brought the younger woman into her for a loving hug. She had then smoothed back Stephanie's hair, telling her how beautiful she was. A lot of people may have deemed Josefina's friendliness as a bit much for a first-time meeting, but Stephanie thought the older woman was very sincere. Her hug had certainly broken the ice, not that things had been chilly between them. Stephanie felt the lady was very warm.

The dinner menu consisted of tender brisket, delicious barbecued ribs and grilled Alaskan halibut. Potato salad and corn on the cob were also served, along with baked beans and fresh yeast rolls. The very capable hands of Malachi and Maxwell had prepared everything.

The extremely tasty halibut had been a gift to Malachi. One of his young Texas friends, Preston Hesselgesser, had gone fishing in Alaska with his father, brother and a lifelong friend. He had caught quite a bit of the fresh halibut himself. Preston then had it cleaned, vacuum-sealed and shipped back to Houston, where it finally ended up in his home freezer.

When Malachi had stopped by Preston's house to see him and his wife, Connie, and their baby daughter, Emma, Preston had given him several packets of the frozen halibut to take with him. Preston had rounded out the visit by telling Malachi one of the biggest true fish stories he'd ever heard. To fish out in the wild in Alaska had been an absolute dream come true for Preston.

On the way to Stephanie's place Malachi had decided to grill the fish for dinner.

Much to Stephanie's surprise and pleasure, Malachi and Sarah had invited Eliza Beth and Lemanz over to the house as dinner guests. This was the first time Stephanie had seen her friend/client since the bad-check incident. True to her word, Eliza Beth had brought Stephanie the five thousand dollars that very afternoon, but there'd never been any explanation for why it had bounced. Stephanie figured her friend would tell her about it if she wanted her to know.

Stephanie couldn't help observing how well Maxwell and Sarah got along. The couple really seemed very much into each other. Sarah appeared to hang on to Maxwell's every word and he looked at her as though he simply adored her. Periodically their hands would touch and then their fingers would entwine. A time or two Maxwell had even brushed the length of her shiny hair with his flattened palm. The smiles passing between them appeared very intimate. Maxwell and Sarah certainly weren't lacking in subject matters for great conversation.

As much as Stephanie was enjoying her guests and the animated dinner chitchat, her mind kept returning to Stephen and Farrah, holed up together. She hoped her friend was faring as well as possible, wondering if her brother had felt it necessary to give her a dose of the medication he'd had filled for her at the pharmacy. No matter how exhausted a person was, the death of a loved one made it very hard to find peace, even in sleep.

Stephanie had had many sleepless nights when she'd been in the same position as Farrah. It was hard to relax, let alone slumber. When she had finally fallen off to sleep, nightmares had plagued her, causing her to awaken in worse shape than she'd been in when she'd first gone out. Fatigue had set in on her, too, making it very difficult for her to concentrate on anything. Even after Doreen's funeral, not much had changed in that area. Stephanie had felt tired all the time, noon and night. The moment the phone rang Stephanie quickly excused herself to the others, hoping the call was from Stephen. She really needed to know how Farrah was doing. Besides that, it was time for Stephen to come be with his family, as well as eat dinner.

Stephanie perched herself on one of the bar stools at the breakfast nook to continue her conversation with Stephen. "Are you sure everything is okay over there?"

"Farrah's knocked out cold. She's had a few jagged crying spells, but they didn't last very long. How are things going at your place?"

"Very well. So far everything's been a charm. I really like Ms. Josefina. She knows how to keep it real. I can see that Dad is genuinely interested in her. Are you hungry, Stephen?"

"Are you kidding?" Stephen chuckled. "I'm famished. All I can think of is the barbecued ribs. Are they off the hook, like the last ones Dad fixed for us?"

"Yeah, and then some. As soon as I hang up, I'm on my way over there. Everyone has been asking when you're going to join us. I'll be right there, Stephen."

"Wait a minute, Stephanie. Why don't you just fix me a plate and bring it over here? I want to be around when Farrah wakes up."

Stephanie was surprised by her brother's request. The deep concern lacing his voice wasn't lost on her. He seemed to really care a lot about Farrah. "Are you sure?"

"I'm positive."

"Okay. Whatever you want. Do you think I should bring a plate of food for Farrah, too?"

"I think that's a great idea, Stephanie. I hope she'll be hungry when she wakes up."

"Don't count on it, Stephen, but I'll bring enough food for her. See you shortly."

"Bring me a couple of sodas, too. I don't want to rustle through her refrigerator."

Stephanie delivered two plates of food to Farrah's house, but she only planned to stay a couple of minutes, long enough to try to convince Stephen to go over to the house so he could see everyone before they left. She would then come back and stay with Farrah until he returned. Stephen reluctantly agreed to her suggestion, but only because he didn't want his father to think he was uncomfortable with meeting his date. He was very curious about Josefina—and the only way of having his curiosity satisfied was to meet the lady and have a nice little chat with her. It would be rude of him not to make an appearance at all.

"Why don't I go over to your place now. I'll take my food back with me and eat it there."

"That's fine with me. Tell Dad about the change of plans." She lifted Stephen's hand and kissed the back of it. "Have a good time and don't rush to get back here. We'll be okay."

Stephen looked down at his wristwatch. "It's getting late. I don't intend to stay long. If Farrah gets up, please tell her I'll be back. I don't want her to think she's alone."

Stephanie playfully punched at Stephen's arm. "Alone! What am I, invisible?"

Stephen ruffled Stephanie's hair. "You know what I meant. At any rate, I'll be back."

It was only a matter of minutes before Eliza Beth showed up at Farrah's door. Since Farrah was still asleep, Stephanie was happy to have someone to talk with. Eliza Beth had brought along with her two mugs of hot, freshly brewed coffee. She hadn't brought along three drinks because Stephen had told her Farrah was completely knocked out.

Eliza Beth took a seat on the sofa. "I'm sorry about your friend's mother," she whispered. "This has to be really hard on Farrah. Was Ms. Helen's death totally unexpected?"

Stephanie took a small sip of her coffee before setting the mug down on a decorative wooden coaster. "Ms. Helen has been ill for long time, a diabetic, but no one expected her to die. This last diabetic episode was the worst one yet, but having it end in death was very much unexpected. It's so sad for everyone who knew and loved her. Farrah is taking it really hard, which is certainly understandable. I'm glad Stephen and I can be here for her."

"If I can do anything to help, please let me know. Stephen seems deeply concerned about Farrah. Is something going on between those two?"

"Yeah. They've discovered they really like each other. They're building a solid friendship. They're not rushing into anything. Who knows where it'll go from here."

"I was sorry to hear about him and Darcy. But if he's over it already, perhaps he wasn't really in love with her. If that's the case, they're lucky to find it out before marrying."

"I don't know that's he's over it, but his hands are virtually tied. Darcy seems to be serious about not wanting to marry him. Speaking of marriage, the last time we talked you were worried about yours. Have you and Lemanz worked everything out?"

Liza Beth put her hand over her mouth to stifle her laughter. "Girlfriend, you are not going to believe what happened with that. But I'm going to tell you, anyway. This is so unreal."

Eliza Beth could hardly contain her laughter as she told Stephanie that Lemanz had closed down all of their accounts because of identity theft, and not because of her out-of-control spending habits. When one of his charge accounts had been compromised, he was instructed to shut everything down. He'd learned about the problem in Africa, so that's why he hadn't had the chance to tell his wife about it. It had never dawned on him that she'd be without means since they kept a lot of cash in the house. Lemanz had finally called her from Africa to clue her in.

Stephanie chuckled softly. "I bet that news came as a huge relief. You really seemed worried about your marriage on the phone that day."

Eliza Beth nodded her head up in down. "Mega worried! If my spending weren't a problem, I probably wouldn't have thought about it like that. In a way I'm glad I did see it in that light. I've learned a very valuable lesson from this experience. I was guilty of taking Lemanz's generosity for granted, but not anymore. He was only concerned about my spending because he feared that if anything happened to him, I might not be able to pay off the huge debts. He was right to think like that. This issue made me realize I hadn't been thinking about our future. It's all resolved between us now. But never once did Lemanz consider cutting me off financially."

"I'm glad to hear it, but I never thought he'd do something like that, not without talking to you about it first. He only adores you, Liza. You have a wonderful man in Lemanz."

"Tell me about it! That's why I need to ever be mindful of what I do have in him. The last thing I want to do is take Lemanz for granted. He's so darn good to me. Men like that don't come along every day."

"I can attest to that," Farrah said, walking into the family room. "I'm still looking for Mr. Right, but he hasn't turned up yet. Still, I haven't given up hope."

Stephanie rapidly jumped to her feet. "Hey, sweetheart. Come join us. I'm glad you were able to get some sleep. You look far more rested now."

"I feel better, too, Stephanie. Hi, Liza. How are you?"

Eliza Beth smiled warmly at Farrah. "I'm fine. But it's you that we need to be concerned about. You have my deepest sympathy on the loss of your mother, Farrah. If there's anything I can do to ease your burden, financial or otherwise, please don't hesitate to call on me."

"Thank you, Liza. I promise to keep that in mind." Farrah looked over at Stephanie as she seated herself next to Eliza Beth. "Did Stephen go on home?"

"He went over to my place to visit with our dinner guests. He told me to tell you he'll be back shortly. He really didn't want to leave, but Dad was counting on him meeting Ms. Josefina. She's the lady I told you my father was romantically interested in."

Farrah smiled inwardly about what she'd just heard. It made her feel really good. It had bothered her that Stephen wasn't in the room when she'd entered. She knew she had to be careful about not reading too much into how he was treating her lately, but it was hard not to let herself go with him. She really trusted him, too. Stephen had become a good, reliable friend.

"So what were you two ladies discussing, besides the fact that you both have wonderful men in your lives?"

"Identity theft was the other thing we were talking about. Liza's husband's personal information has been compromised. That's why the check bounced, Farrah. Lemanz had to shut down all his accounts. I know that had to be one big hassle."

"Oh, my. I'm really sorry about that, Liza. Is everything okay now?" Farrah asked.

"We were very blessed. Luck had nothing to do with it. God had a hand in this. From what we were told, identity theft is very prevalent these days. Usually bank accounts are emptied and charge cards are maxed out before the owner even finds out about it. Only one of our charge accounts was compromised. Thank God it was only for a couple of hundred dollars, which we're not liable for. Talk about blessings. No one can tell me God isn't watching over us."

Farrah began to sob. "He's watching over my mother, too, but I wish He was doing it with her still down here. Mother is in God's hands now. How am I going to live without her?"

Stephanie was now glad that Farrah had agreed to let her dinner guests come over to her house for a visit. When Stephen had called to say that Malachi and Maxwell wanted to come see Farrah, Stephanie hadn't been sure it was a good idea. Once she'd posed the idea to Farrah, who thought is was an okay proposition, Stephanie began to see the good that might come from it.

Ten minutes later Farrah's house was filled with well-wishers and sincere offerings of sympathy. Malachi had brought over to Farrah's the delicious desserts he and Maxwell had prepared. Malachi had baked a large, two-tiered red velvet cake, a southern favorite. Maxwell had baked four divine lemon cheesecakes. Josefina and Sarah had made a fresh pot of coffee in Farrah's kitchen, after the hostess had given them the okay to do so.

Stephen kept a close eye on Farrah. He didn't want her to get too tired out. The nap had done her a lot of good, or so it seemed to him. It was nice to hear her laughing, especially after hearing her earlier wails of grief. He had thought it was a great idea for the dinner party to visit her when his father had first approached him about it. Farrah needed all the cheering up she could get. It had been hard for Stephen to think of her being sad and upset while everyone at Stephanie's house was having a good time.

As Stephanie and Gregory approached Stephen, their hands entwined, Stephen smiled. Seeing his sister so happy made him feel good. He liked how well Gregory treated his sister. The deep respect the couple had for each other was also a good thing. Relationships couldn't possibly survive without respect. Too often disrespect was the reason for the high rate of divorce.

Stephanie briefly took a hold of Stephen's hand. "Hey, man, you look a little tired. How are you doing, Stephen?"

Stephen and Gregory shook hands even though they'd done so earlier.

"I'm good. Just keeping an eye on Farrah. She seems to be holding up pretty well. What do you think, Stephanie?"

"She's doing just fine. The company has been good for her." Stephanie took a glance across the room, where Malachi and Josefina were seated. "What do you think of Dad's date?"

"I like her," Stephen responded. "She seems like a really nice person."

"Uncle Mal likes her, too," Gregory offered. "He's normally very uncomfortable around women. I've had the opportunity to closely observe him in hundreds of social settings. He usually steers clear of the ladies in attendance. But that doesn't ever stop them from trying to get his attention. Even women a lot younger than himself have become deeply infatuated with him."

Stephanie grinned. "He's only one of the handsomest men in New Orleans. Being rich doesn't hurt his chances with the fairer sex, either. I'm glad he's finally coming out of his shell."

"I'd have to agree with that assessment. Do you think something serious might develop between him and the lady?" Stephen asked Gregory.

"Your guess is as good as mine. The fact that he's seeing anyone at all is a miracle. I'm not saying he didn't date other women from time to time, but I've never known him to get close to someone. There's never been a steady lady in his life that I know of."

Stephen grunted. "Probably because he was still wrapped up in Mama. According to their letters, they saw each other and talked plenty over the phone. If he'd thought they'd get back together someday, that would explain why he wouldn't get too involved with someone else."

Stephanie nodded in agreement. "I think they got together for more than an occasional dinner. At least I'd like to think that. If only Mama could have forgiven him completely."

"Wishing and hoping isn't going to change anything, darling angel. Mama's gone now. But thinking of them continuing their love affair despite their issues is a nice thought. I'm sure Dad holds on to all of his good memories of their time together. He looks happy right now."

"Very happy, "Stephanie seconded. "Uncle Max looks happy, too. I believe it's already serious between him and Ms. Sarah. They look like they're ready to ride off into the sunset."

Gregory chuckled. "That relationship is a miracle, too. Uncle Maxwell hasn't ever been in a serious relationship, either. When he came in off the road, he used to tell us stories about the ladies he met. Most of them were short-order cooks and waitresses that he met at truck stops. He really enjoyed the time he spent on the road. I can't imagine him retired."

"I can," Stephanie said. "He thoroughly enjoys himself every time we all get together. Since he and Dad are looking to buy a house here, it looks like he's serious about retiring."

Stephen bumped Stephanie with his shoulder. "Farrah is summoning you, Stephanie. I hope she's okay. Maybe we should clear everyone out now."

"Let me see what Farrah has to say first, Stephen." Stephanie kissed Gregory lightly on the mouth. "I won't be long, sweetheart."

Stephanie looked back and waved at the two men as she reached Farrah. "What's up?"

Farrah took hold of Stephanie's hand and began moving toward the kitchen. "We've run out of coffee. I just want you to come in the kitchen with me while I fix some more."

Once inside the kitchen, Stephanie insisted that Farrah take a seat at the kitchen table. She would prepare the coffee. After tossing away the old coffee grounds, Stephanie rinsed and dried out the cone-shaped holder before filling it with fresh grounds. "How are you holding up, Farrah? Are you ready for everyone to leave?"

Farrah shook her head from side to side. "I'm enjoying everyone. I'll be alone plenty in the coming days. The nap restored my strength. Sitting around the hospital all day and evening is very tiring." Farrah sucked in her bottom lip. "I don't know how I'm going to get through Mother's funeral. I'm glad she was wise enough to preplan everything. She has one of those preplanning policies with the Turner Brothers Mortuary. I believe she even picked out her casket and all. Can you please help me get it all done, Stephanie?"

"Of course I can, Farrah. We'll start taking care of everything first thing in the morning. I'm sure you're in possession of all of your mother's important papers. Is there an insurance policy? If so, we need to start with notifying them of her death."

"Mother has two life insurance polices besides the policy that takes care of the funeral expenses. We'll have to contact social security, too. Since it's the middle of the month, I don't think I'll have to return the last check she received."

"There's also a social security death benefit, but I don't think you qualify for it, Farrah. I think only a spouse, minor or disabled child can file for it. It's not that much, anyway. At any rate, we'll get it all checked out tomorrow. Most funeral homes give their patrons a packet of valuable information on making arrangements. It should have a very helpful checklist in it."

Stephen stuck his head in the doorway. "Are you ladies okay in here?"

Farrah smiled broadly at him. "We're fine. We just needed more coffee."

"Is there anything I can do to help out?" he asked.

Stephanie looked over at her brother. "We're all done now, but you can let everyone know there's fresh coffee brewing. It'll be ready any second now."

"Will do," Stephen said, ducking out.

Stephanie walked over to where Farrah sat and helped her up out of the chair. She then brought her friend into her warm embrace. "You're going to get through this. I promise to be here to help you oversee everything. Stephen wants to be here for you, too. Don't hesitate to tell us what you need us to do, no matter how big or small it may be."

Farrah squeezed Stephanie tightly. "Thank you. I couldn't do this without you. I thank God that I have you for a friend. You've always been here for me."

"We've always been there for each other. I'm only doing the same as you did for me when I went through this. Shall we go join the others?"

"Let's do it."

"Okay, but just give me a nod when you're ready for everyone to go home. I don't think they'll stay much longer, anyway. It is getting late."

"I'm very grateful for the company, but I'll let you know if I start to get overwhelmed."

The two friends hugged each other again before leaving the kitchen.

Chapter 10

Farrah sat perfectly still between Stephanie and Stephen on the front pew of the Everlasting Arms Chapel, located on the cemetery grounds where Ms. Helen's remains were to be interred. Each twin had an arm wrapped around the shoulders of their grieving friend as the presiding minister read masterfully from the Bible the Twenty-Third Psalm.

Ms. Helen's casket was now closed. Once the lid had been lowered, Farrah had nearly fallen apart, knowing that she'd never again see the lovely face of her mother. All Helen had ever wanted in this life was to live long enough to see her daughter married and to have at least one grandchild. Rarely had she asked much of her daughter. Helen knew it hurt her daughter not to have a man of her own. Farrah was among the unfortunate nice girls who often finished last.

Farrah felt as though she'd failed her mother in regards to being married and having children. Yet she knew without a doubt that she'd been a loving, devoted daughter. Her mother had known it, too; she'd often praised Farrah for that very thing. Helen's daughter was her pride and joy, her most precious treasure.

There was no mention whatsoever of Farrah's father in the obituary or the memorial program, but the twins now knew as much as there was to know about the man, which was hardly anything at all. A nondescript, nameless man who'd only been passing through town had raped Helen. Rumor had it that he'd left the city on a Greyhound bus on his way to only God knew where, never to be punished for his horrific crime against an innocent young woman.

This cowardly man had been faceless to a young, virginal Helen, simply because she hadn't had a chance to lay eyes on him. He'd come up behind her on that fateful evening, as she'd walked home from choir rehearsal. After he'd dragged her into a deserted house, he'd had his way with her, leaving her twenty-year-old body and spirit broken and badly bruised.

Farrah thought of her mother as a very brave woman to have kept her child and to have raised her alone. Helen had actually told her daughter all that had occurred to her back then. Farrah was about sixteen years old when she'd first heard the story of Helen's rape. When Helen had opted to have her child rather than abort the fetus, her parents, both deceased now, had disowned their daughter because of the embarrassing decision to carry her child to term. Helen's parents had died without ever again speaking to their only child, without every laying an eye on their only grandchild. Her parents had crucified Helen in the worst possible way.

No family members had rallied around Farrah during this family crisis because she didn't have any. If she had family members out there in the world, none of them had ever come forward to make themselves known to her mother or to her. However, Ms. Helen had earned the love of a host of dedicated friends and a huge church family. She had been quite an upstanding pillar of the community. Stephanie and Stephen were definitely accounted among her loved ones.

Stephen's heart trembled as he recalled how emotional Farrah had become when she'd told him and his sister the sad story of how she'd actually come into existence. Stephanie had always believed that Farrah's father was dead because that's what she'd been told by her friend. She and Stephen had heard the true story at the same time. Farrah had literally bared her soul to both twins during the time her grief had been most overwhelming.

Stephanie and Stephen had learned so much about who Farrah was as a person. They were extremely proud of her unyielding strength and courage, proud to call her their friend. In the twins' opinion Farrah Freeman was an incredible woman in every sense of the word.

Malachi and Maxwell had also attended Ms. Helen's funeral service. Malachi had known her when he and Doreen had first met. Although Doreen and Helen had been friends, the two women didn't become neighbors until after the twins had become toddlers. Doreen and Malachi had long since been separated by then so he hadn't gotten to know Ms. Helen well.

Now that the deeply touching funeral service was over, Stephen helped Farrah and Stephanie into the black limousine, which would transport them the short distance to the cemetery plot, where Ms. Helen would be interred in her final resting place. The Turner brothers, who owned the Turner Brothers Mortuary, had conducted the funeral service. One of the three brothers had graduated from high school with Ms. Helen.

Troy Turner had also been very fond of Helen in a romantic way. The two schoolmates had dated off and on throughout their teen years, but after the rape had occurred, Helen did very little socializing with the opposite sex. However, she had allowed Troy to pay her a visit a couple of times a month up until he'd married at the ripe age of forty. Helen remained a loner after that.

Stephanie was hosting the repast in her home. Ms. Sarah

had offered to prepare all the food for the meal, which Malachi and Maxwell had insisted on paying for. The Trudeaux family had also donated the beautiful casket spray consisting of dozens and dozens of white roses and large yellow and white mums. Farrah was grateful for all their generosity.

Ms. Sarah had outdone herself on preparing the food for the repast. The fried chicken was crisp on the outside but tender inside. The huge baked turkey breasts were browned to perfection and were also juicy and tender on the inside. Candied yams, macaroni and cheese, green beans and buttered mixed vegetables were served as delicious accompaniments. A large bowl held tossed salad greens, cherry tomatoes and thick slices of cucumber. For dessert was Ms. Sarah's delectable peach cobbler and her mini lemon tarts. A fruit punch garnished with lemon and lime wedges was the refreshing drink served.

It appeared to Stephanie that Farrah was in a daze. The medication had been prescribed to help to keep her calm, but Stephanie figured that her friend was hysterical inside. That's what she had experienced during the death of her own mother. Much of that time was still one big blur to Stephanie, most everything but the unyielding pain. She had remained terribly unstable for several months after Doreen had been buried.

Farrah had eaten very little of her food, which also concerned Stephanie, even though she knew her appetite would eventually return. Stephanie also noticed that folks were starting to leave already. As soon as the house was empty, except for her family, Stephanie hoped Farrah would lie down in her guest room. Malachi and Maxwell were staying with Stephen this go-round, so that left the room available.

Gregory would be leaving late Sunday evening, but he always stayed at the Hilton hotel. He'd never spent a single night at Stephanie's place. They each felt that him staying at the hotel was more morally correct, though they were very much in control of themselves.

Stephanie thought about Darcella as she looked over at her brother, who appeared deep in thought. She had seen his ex-fiancée at the funeral service, but she hadn't come to the house for the repast. At least she hadn't shown up yet. Stephanie was sure that it had been hard for Darcella to see her fiancé being so attentive to another woman, and her heart went out to her. If she still had feelings for Stephen, she was keeping mum about it.

Stephen had told his sister that all of his calls to Darcella had gone unreturned. He just didn't know what to do about her refusal to communicate with him. Stephen still cared about Darcella, but he'd come to realize they were incompatible. He also had come to understand that he couldn't ever compromise on the issue of children. Plain and simple, he wanted at least two babies. Adoption would have been their alternative solution if Darcella hadn't been able to bear children, but that wasn't the case. Darcella didn't want children and that was her prerogative.

Seated on the other side of the room from where Farrah sat in Stephanie's home, Stephen quietly observed Farrah. He didn't like to see her eyes so red and swollen, but it was the afteraffect of so many tears. He'd also noticed that she had barely eaten enough to keep a bird alive, but like his sister, he knew her appetite would return in due time. Death of a loved one was enough to take anyone's appetite away. He had certainly lost his desire to eat when his mother died and so had his sister. Stephanie had continued to lose weight long after their mother's funeral was over.

Stephen saw that Farrah smiled at everyone who stopped to chat with her, but he could tell that her heart just wasn't in it. Her smile was actually forced. That would return, too. Right now she had very little to be happy-faced about. Grief didn't leave any room for happiness.

Outside of the fact that her attire sensuously hugged her every delectable curve, Stephen really liked the soft-looking dress Farrah wore. It was a beautiful but simple white silk sheath. The long sleeves were fashioned in lace. The color white was a symbol of the will to live; that's what Farrah had told him and Stephanie. She'd also told the twins that she thought black was too dark and depressing. If Farrah had her way, she'd said she'd never wear black again.

The trembling of Farrah's hands, when she'd lifted the glass of fruit punch to her mouth, let Stephen know how hard she was struggling to get through the repast. It was time for her to excuse herself and get some rest, he mused. He knew she'd be too polite to do what was best for her so he quickly decided to take control of the situation himself.

On Stephen's way to where Farrah sat, he stopped for a moment and pulled Stephanie aside. "Farrah has had enough. I'm taking her next door. Will you announce her departure to the guests? She won't do it on her own. That would be too socially incorrect for her."

Laughing softly at his comment, Stephanie reached down and squeezed Stephen's fingers in a reassuring manner. "Of course. She does look ready to drop." She smiled up at her brother. "Thanks for being so sweet and considerate to Farrah. You've become a good friend to her. I know that for a fact because she told me so."

"Farrah is a great girl. I'm glad she considers me a friend. Right now I'm going to exercise my rights in our special bond by getting her out of here. See you in a little while."

Stephen then bent his head down and kissed his sister on both cheeks. "Keep it under control."

Stephanie went to the center of the room and then asked for everyone's attention. As she made the announcement that Farrah had to leave due to sheer fatigue, she watched her brother and dear friend slip out the front door unnoticed. She was happy that Farrah hadn't protested Stephen's plans for her to rest. If anything, Stephanie thought she probably felt relieved by his goodwill gesture. Stephen had been taking very good care of Farrah. He was to be commended.

* * *

Gregory had seriously listened to what Stephanie had had to say regarding her fears about their upcoming nuptials. There wasn't a thing she'd said that he hadn't understood. His mind had also turned over many of the same issues she'd addressed. He had come to the conclusion that it was natural to be fearful of a drastic life change. Making the transition from single to couple, me to us wouldn't be so easy. Now that Gregory was ready to make his comments on the subject of fears in entering into lifelong partnerships, he first gave Stephanie a reassuring hug.

"Stephanie, I'm sure we'll run into obstacles in our marriage. That's pretty normal. It's how we deal with it that counts. If we keep the line of communication open, we'll be okay."

Gregory went on to say that he'd try very hard not to take her or their love for granted. He promised to respect her and to always include her in the decision-making process. With God as the head of their household, he was confident they wouldn't get too far off the right track. He felt that once they identified each other's weaknesses and strengths, and then if they worked on each area accordingly, their marriage would grow even stronger. He vowed not to lie to her, even when it might prevent her from getting hurt. Spending quality time with each other was also a must. His desire was to be a faithful husband, one who loved and cherished his wife above all else. God was the only exception. As the head of their household, the Lord had to come first.

Stephanie was in utter awe of what Gregory had had to say. "If we can stick to all that, there's no reason why we can't make our marriage work. I'm glad we've become good friends to each other. Can you make the promise that we never go to bed angry with each other?"

Gregory nodded. "That's so important, Stephanie. We don't have to agree on everything, but we do have to respect each other's point of view. I can definitely make that commitment. Uncle Mal once told me that that was a rule that his parents had practiced in their marriage. I'm sure he shared it with you, too."

"He did. I think it's a wonderful rule. I'm slow to anger, but when I get that way sometimes it's hard for me to let go of it. It was very hard when Stephen was angry with me over my decision to see our father. It wasn't a good feeling to go to bed at night knowing he was upset with me. Stephen and I rarely display anger toward each other. And when we did have problems, we most always worked it out right away. I guess our mother instilled that into us, too, now that I think about it. Dad said they used to practice that rule until the infidelity had occurred."

Stephanie was amazed by how just simply communicating with Gregory had eased her fears. They had a good foundation. She now felt confident that they could make their marriage work. She liked it when he'd said they shouldn't borrow other folk's troubles or their drama. People didn't always handle their issues in the same manner. He was right about that.

Darcella had chosen to close herself off from Stephen by not communicating with him at all, which was exactly what Darcella had accused her parents of. Doreen had also cut Malachi off. Though they'd communicated plenty in the past, Doreen had refused to open up her heart to him again.

According to Gregory, effective communication had also been a big problem with his parents. Aretha had gone for days without talking to his father when they'd disagreed on one thing or another. Communication was the major key in all relationships. People had to talk to each other.

Laughing inwardly, Stephanie thought of Eliza Beth and Lemanz. The lack of communication between them had had Eliza Beth thinking all sorts of things. Because she'd feared the answers, she hadn't gotten her needs met by asking him what was going on with the finances. As important as it had been, a husband had forgotten to communicate to his wife that the credit cards and bank accounts had been compromised. Thank God that it had just been one huge misunderstanding between the loving couple. Each of them had learned a valuable lesson.

Stephanie leaned into Gregory and then gave him a passionate kiss. "I love you," she whispered softly.

Gregory smiled broadly. "I love you more."

Knowing he'd found his soul mate, Gregory held Stephanie tightly in his arms. At one time Gregory II had thought he'd found his soul mate, too. Then his heart had been shattered to smithereens. "Dad knows about Mother wanting to get back with him. He was very surprised."

"How's he taking it? What did he say?"

Gregory squeezed his forehead with his forefinger and thumb. "He was pretty much in shock at first. Once the initial reaction wore off, he thought the idea was a ridiculously funny one. Soon after he felt anger over it. He then took time to give it some serious thought."

"Sounds like he went through a range of emotions. I feel for him over that, Gregory. What did he decide on after giving the idea more thought?"

Gregory pursed his lips. "That the relationship would work much better with them as just friends. He doesn't think it's a good idea to take Mother back as his wife. He thinks that would be disastrous, mainly for him. He's still pretty hurt by what happened."

"Is Ms. Aretha disappointed?"

Gregory explained to Stephanie that he really didn't know how Aretha was taking the rejection from Gregory II. She'd thus far offered very little information on the matter, yet she was totally opposed to them as just friends. "Aretha Saxton doesn't let too much get her down. She may cool her heels for a bit, but I suspect that she hasn't given up completely. Mother is downright tenacious. She's been known to fight to the death for what she wants."

Stephanie chuckled. "That's how you have to be when you

want something badly enough. I think it's a good idea for them to build a new friendship, though. What about you?"

"I second that. Friendship would be like a fresh start for them. Grant would also like to see them become good friends." Gregory paused a moment. "Speaking of Grant, he called Farrah to offer her his condolences. He'd like more than just a friendship with her, but she made it clear to him that she was in love with someone else. It's Stephen, isn't it?"

"How you'd know, since I haven't mentioned anything about them to you?"

"By the way Farrah looks at Stephen. Her feelings for him are there in her eyes. It's my best guess he feels the same way about her. I wouldn't want to be in his shoes."

"I agree with you, Gregory. They've become very close friends, according to him. Stephen's still a little gun-shy. Even though the outcome of his relationship with Darcella may be for the best, he wishes she hadn't been hurt. He thinks he's hurt her as much as Dad hurt Mama. But that's not even close to being true. Stephen never really acted upon his attraction to Farrah. Outside of a little flirting, he's innocent. They haven't shared so much as a little kiss."

"Regardless, Stephen feels totally responsible for Darcy's pain. At least he's been a man about it. Unlike my brother, the old Grant, he would've trampled all over a woman's feelings. Perhaps Darcy will one day come to see that Stephen has handled this in a very manly way."

Stephanie nodded. "That would be nice. As long as she's not communicating with him, he feels like they still have unfinished business. That keeps him from really moving on. I wish Darcella would find it in her heart to talk to Stephen about things one more time. He needs to be sure she's really through with him. He's not all the way there in accepting that it's over."

Stephanie and Gregory slipped off into a comfortable silence, her head resting against his chest. Each felt unconditionally loved by the other. Fears often pulled apart couples.

In this case, it had strengthened both Stephanie and Gregory, bringing them even closer together.

Farrah picked up one of Stephanie's sofa pillows and lodged it against her abdomen. "Darcella asked me to meet her over here. She didn't call to tell you about it, Stephanie?"

Stephanie's eyes widened at what she'd heard. "Not so much as a peep, Farrah. I just heard it for the first time." Stephanie looked over at Stephen. "Did she ask that of you, too?"

Stephen nodded. "She said it was urgent that she see me. She never mentioned Farrah's name. I figured you would be present only because it's your house."

Stephanie shrugged, a light coming on in her eyes. "Which is not necessarily a neutral setting. I have a pretty good idea why she's asked to see you both. I may be included, too. Darcy has had plenty of time to stew in her own juices. I sense a serious confrontation coming on."

Farrah jumped to her feet. "Not with me. This is between you and her," she said to Stephen. "I have nothing to do with this."

"You and I both know the truth, Farrah, but Darcy doesn't seem to believe me. Maybe we should indulge her. I guess she has a lot to say because she hasn't been saying anything lately. I say let's hear her out. What do you think, Stephanie?"

"I say not," Farrah shot back. "No good can come from this. I have enough grief on my plate at the moment. I shouldn't have to deal with Darcy's anger, too."

The doorbell rang. Everyone looked at one another, as if they didn't know what to do.

Farrah pointed toward the back of the house. "I'm out the back door."

Stephanie gave Farrah a pleading look. "If you leave, it's only going to further fuel her desire to confront you, if that's her intent. You should stay, especially since you're not guilty of anything. If you run away, Darcy will then be assured of your guilt."

"Maybe you're right, Stephanie," Farrah said, retaking her seat. "I guess I should get all this behind me. I wonder if Darcy is angry with you, too, Stephanie."

Stephanie sighed hard. "I don't know, Farrah, but it looks like we're about to find out. I'll get the door. Be right back."

Stephen was disturbed and it upset him to see the fearful look on Farrah's face. He didn't think she was scared of Darcella, just fearful of confrontations. Farrah was such a peaceful person.

Why Darcella had waited until Farrah was in the throes of a tragedy to make her voice heard was beyond him. For her to do something like that seemed rather cruel. But then again, Darcella wasn't a cruel person. However, his ex-fiancée had become an angry, unhappy being.

Stephen knew he'd just have to wait to see how this weird situation played out. He suddenly felt like he was sitting on pins and needles. Pinpricks of fear also had him sweating.

Stephanie ushered Darcella into her family room, gesturing for her to have a seat.

Darcella put her feet together and folded her hands out in front of her at mid-waist. "I prefer to stand. Thank you. What I have to say won't take long." She drew in a deep breath. Then a look of uncertainty crossed her face, as if she was asking herself what she was doing there.

Darcella shuffled her feet slightly. It was easy to see that her hands were shaking, even with them folded together. "What I have to say goes for all of you. That you three people would plot and plan against me sickens me more than I can express. I never dreamed you all would form an alliance to hurt me like this. Stephen, you're the guiltiest of all. You've practiced the worst kind of deception, telling me you loved me all the while—"

Injured by Darcella's remarks, Stephen leapt to his feet. "Wait a minute here—"

"Sit down, Stephen," Darcella shouted loudly. She lifted her hand in a halting gesture. "I have the floor now. I can tell by the hundreds of messages left on my answering machine that you've been anxious for me to speak, Stephen. Now that I'm speaking out, you're trying to shut me up. I won't be silenced."

Looking totally bewildered, Stephan sat back down. Although he didn't know how much more he could listen to without exploding, he'd do his best to respect Darcella's wishes. He still thought she had some nerve bringing them all together so she could beat them down verbally. That she'd decided to do this in his own sister's house had him the most incensed.

Darcella refolded her hands and placed them back in the same position, as if she thought they would somehow keep her anchored. "Stephanie, I'm surprised by your actions more than anyone else's. I thought you were a wonderful person, a fair one. By you letting your brother use your house to cheat on me, I now see you in a totally different light. In fact, there's no light at all in you. You are a very dark person in my eyesight. I know I've shown jealousy toward you over your relationship with your twin, but that doesn't give you the right to campaign against me to help another woman win his heart. Even if that same woman is your best friend. I find your actions deplorable. You can't imagine how bitterly disappointed I am in you as a person."

Stephanie was wounded and angry, but she never flinched, her eyes remaining steadfastly on her accuser. She also saw that it would do her no good to protest the things said about her. If Darcella had yelled at her to sit down, like she'd done Stephen, Stephanie was afraid she just might throw the woman out of her house on her butt. Remain still and calm, she told herself.

Stephanie thought it was best to just let Darcella go ahead and vent. Her rage would eventually eat her alive if she didn't learn how to promptly expel it. Stephanie only wished that the lady would find a more constructive way to blow off steam. This wasn't the healthiest way.

Darcella turned and looked directly into Farrah's eyes. She then pointed her finger right at the woman she believed responsible for her broken heart. "I don't know you all that well, but from the little I've learned about you, you're not the type of person I'd even want to get to know. When a woman sneaks around with a practically married man, she's nothing more than a tramp in my opinion. You knew Stephen and I were engaged, but you pursued him, anyway. It doesn't matter that you've had a crush on him since childhood. What you did was plain wrong. I guess the old adage, 'the way to a man's heart is through his stomach,' worked for you. You fed him your brand of food, as if he were a starving man, all in hopes of getting him into your bed. Did that part work as well? Were you able to lure him into your bed with your cheap tactics, Farrah?"

Farrah saw red. As she got to her feet, her eyes dared Darcella to tell her to sit back down. Darcella had asked specific questions and Farrah was going to give her specific answers.

Stephanie looked alarmed. She'd never before seen a murderous look in Farrah's eyes. What might happen in her family room between the two women had the hostess scared stiff. Farrah had always been meek and mild, but Stephanie had always feared that she wasn't someone to be messed with. Quiet, gentle people could be deadly when forced into a corner. It appeared to her that Darcella had her best friend cornered. Stephanie was gravely concerned about the method Farrah might decide to use to come out of that corner.

Stephen had already moved to the edge of his seat, praying that he didn't have to get in between these two fire-breathing women. He'd never seen either one of the ladies lathered up like this. Of course he'd seen Darcella angry before, but never beyond rage.

Farrah stopped within mere inches of Darcella's face. "Yes, I fed Stephen a couple of times, but I'd feed anyone who expressed hunger to me. No, getting him into my bed didn't work, simply because I never tried to get him there. It wasn't on my agenda."

Farrah drew in a shaky breath, trying to control her anger and her heart rate. "If I had gone after Stephen in that manner, you can rest assured that I wouldn't have stopped until I accomplished my mission. It wasn't and still isn't like that with us. Stephen and I are only friends. You would've found that out if you'd been woman enough to just ask me face-to-face."

Farrah backed up a few paces when it looked like Darcella might strike her. The furling and unfurling of Darcella's hands had given Farrah a clue. Farrah knew that she wouldn't take a hit without retaliation. It was above her to get into a physical altercation with someone, especially over some man. However, if Darcella dared to hit her, what she'd get in return wouldn't be about Stephen.

For Farrah it was all about self-defense.

Darcella slapped her right hand on her hip. "Are you through yet?"

Farrah glared at her accuser. "No, I'm not finished. You had to bring us all together and then hurl awful accusations at us, like we've done you so wrong. It's not my problem that you feel inadequate where your man is concerned. You're fearful of something. That's what's really going on here. You're just using a couple of dinners between friends as lame excuses. You don't want to look deep into yourself for the answers because you're probably fearful of what you might find. Stephanie, Stephen and me are not plotting against you. It's all in your head."

Stephen was on his feet now, pacing back and forth on the side of the sofa. He wasn't about to let this verbal battle turned physical. He could clearly see that his sister was very uncomfortable with what was happening in her home. It was starting to get out of hand. He was the only one big enough to keep this verbal confrontation from turning into flying fists.

Farrah laid her hand against her chest. "I can admit I have feelings for Stephen, strong ones. That doesn't make me a horrible person. He's been nothing but a perfect gentleman and he certainly hasn't come close to cheating on you. Not with me. I'd be concerned about my man if he didn't indulge in a little flirting, instead of blowing it all out of proportion. When you're pointing a finger at someone, just remember there are four pointing back at you."

"What man?" Darcella shouted. "You don't have a man. I've never seen you with a male, period. That's why you're busy running after mine. Face it. You can't get a man of your own."

Farrah actually laughed in Darcella's face. "If I can't get a man, then why are you so worried about Stephen and I eating together, especially when others were present at the time? These are your insecurities, Darcy, not mine. I refuse to own them."

Farrah began to walk away, then she quickly turned back to face Darcella. "From what I've heard Stephen isn't your man. Didn't you recently set him free? Free men are always fair game. At least that's my understanding of how the game is played."

Farrah hated what she'd just said in defense of herself, but Darcella had really provoked her to the boiling point. Still, Farrah knew she was the only one responsible for what came out of her mouth. There would be consequences for her comments, but she'd be darned if she'd take back any of what she'd just said, because she'd meant every word of it.

Stephen put his hand on Darcella's arm, hoping to quash her next comment. The look on her face told him his ex had plenty more to say. The thought of covering up his ears came next.

Darcella jerked her arm from Stephen's light grasp. "Don't

you ever touch me again, Stephen. This is happening all because of you. You go out and cheat on me and then you leave me high and dry. I don't know what I ever saw in you in the first place. You're a lowlife."

Stephen winced at the pain in his heart. He couldn't understand why Darcella continued to accuse him of cheating on her. Farrah had just told her nothing had happened between them beyond a little flirting, but he could tell that she still wasn't ready to face the truth. "Don't worry, Darcella, I won't touch you again. But we have to take this nonsense away from Stephanie's house. It's not fair that her and her friend have to listen to our mess. Your beef is with me. Let's go outside and sit in the car. We're not going to resolve anything like this."

"It's always about Stephanie with you, isn't it? Your need to always protect her is sickening and abnormal. She's not the Goody-Two-shoes you make her out to be. Any woman that sets up a convenient way for her brother to cheat on his fiancée is no woman at all. All of you can go straight to hell. I'm though with this entire matter." She got right in Stephen's face. "Stop calling my house. I don't want to hear from you. That should've already been apparent."

Stephanie realized she'd been quiet long enough, perhaps too quiet, period. After all, this was her home. Stephen was her brother and Farrah was her best friend. All of them were under siege. Darcella had taken things too far. The situation was clearly out of control. "Darcy," Stephanie called out to her, staying planted in her seat. She thought that getting up might appear too confrontational. "I've had enough of this. You're dead wrong about all of us. Won't you please take a seat and listen to what we have to say? Can't we reason with you?"

Darcella rolled her eyes at Stephanie. "Why would I listen to any of you? Especially you, Stephanie. You're just as bad if not worse than your brother and friend. Birds of a feather are known to flock together."

It was hard for Stephanie to remain seated, but she did so, not wanting to make things any worse. "This is my house, Darcy, and I get to call all the shots. Either calm yourself down or leave. The choice is yours to make."

"Don't worry. Your request will be granted, darling angel," Darcella spat out at Stephanie with heavy sarcasm. "Once I'm finished with my say I'm out of here."

Stephanie moved to the edge of her seat. "As far as I'm concerned, you're through now. We've all tried to tell you that nothing happened between Stephen and Farrah, but you're not trying to hear that. It seems easier for you to think the worst of people. I wonder why that is."

Stephanie had struck one of Darcella's exposed nerves. The look on her face said she'd taken a direct hit right where it hurt the most. If Darcella had had a weapon, Stephanie feared she would've used it in a heartbeat. The angry young woman had lost her objectivity. Something was eating her up terribly on the inside.

"This is all about your family life, isn't it, Darcy?" Stephanie inquired, aware that she had trodden onto sacred grounds. "The sad things you told me about are killing you. You're an adult now. When do you plan to set aside the childhood hurts? You know it's time, don't you?"

"Shut up, Stephanie!" Darcella balled up her fists and held them rigidly down at her side. "You have no idea what you're talking about. Neither do I. But leave my family out of this."

"Why should I? You're not cutting my family any slack. You really need to seek counseling to help you deal with your past."

"And you need to go straight to—" Darcella rapidly bit down on her tongue, cutting off the inflammatory expletive. She'd already voiced that unsavory sentiment earlier.

Stephanie had hit the nail right on the head, but Darcella wasn't about to acknowledge it. Getting out of this house without losing any more ground was her top priority. She'd told Stephanie far too much about her family life. She didn't need to have repeated what she already knew. Her family was her biggest drawback—and no one knew that better than she did.

"You don't need to say anything about my family life, Stephanie, not with all the troubles you've had in yours. Like father, like son. I'm sure you get my meaning. What I said to you was in strict confidence, but that just goes to further prove what kind of person you are. Using my confidences against me is downright cowardly."

With that said, Darcella headed for the front door, leaving the others in a state of shock. In the next instant Darcella's loud sobbing reached Stephen's ears, making him feel that he should run out behind her to try to calm her down before she began the drive home. As he left the room, his eyes conveyed to Stephanie and Farrah his sincere apologies.

Stephanie looked over at Farrah. "I really feel terrible about this. I'd never set Stephen up so he could cheat. Besides, he has his own place, and he didn't cheat. Why would he need to come over here for that? Farrah, I'm not guilty of anything I was accused of."

Farrah nodded. "I know. You don't have to convince me of that. I know you'd never do anything like that, anyway. Darcella knows it, too."

Frustrated by it all, Stephanie threw up her hands. "Then why all the theatrics? Why was it necessary for her to confront us this way?"

"Probably because she can't come to terms with their broken engagement, even if she is the one who broke it off. Trust me, it's not about cheating, 'cause nothing happened." Tears began to fill Farrah's eyes. "But Darcy's right about one thing. I *can't* get a man, at least not a decent one. I keep wondering if it's because I'm a product of rape."

Stephanie looked horrified by Farrah's last comment. "Why would you say something like that? I can't believe you think like that. How would anyone even know about that?"

"Gossip has a way of passing down through the generations. People nowadays talk about stuff like that in front of their kids. Not much is kept hidden these days. My mother was the target of a lot of malicious gossip back then. Some folks treated her like a leper. The really sad part is that my grandparents led the charge against their daughter when they disowned her. Mother went through hell before her skin thickened. Rape is a dirty act, so some people may see me as a dirty by-product. Houston is a large city, but Mother's community was very small then. There was no problem in closing the distances with phone-to-phone gossip. The story of my mother's rape probably reached ears all over the country—one relative or friend telling another."

"I've never thought about it like that, and I'm sorry that you've had to. As far as that goes, I've never really had a good man, either, not until Gregory came along. God has a man all picked out for you. He will reveal who it is in His time. Don't grow impatient, Farrah."

Farrah laughed softly, wiping away her tears. "My biological clock is about to run out of time. I don't want to be a forty-something mother. I don't want to be old and worn out when my children are born. I want to be able to romp around with them and run and jump and play."

"I understand, Farrah, but that's a long time from now, nearly ten years away. We both just turned thirty this year. You have a few more years left before your fortieth."

"I guess. Have you and Gregory discussed having children?"

"Not in any depth. We both definitely want children. We've discussed that much. I'd like to have a daughter and a son, but what I want most are healthy children. Gregory told me that Grant is romantically interested in you but that you told him you were in love with someone else. Gregory easily guessed Stephen as being that someone. How did Grant take what you told him?"

"Of course he wasn't happy with it. If he thought it was

Stephen, he didn't mention it. I had to tell him something because I didn't want to lead him on. He's nice, but just not for me."

"Are you saying that you lied to him about being in love, Farrah?"

Farrah closed her eyes for a brief moment. "It wasn't a lie. I am in love with Stephen. I've always had a romantic thing for him. But it takes two. Stephen is not in love with me. I wish Darcella could see that he loves only her, but her eyes are blinded by whatever is going on with her personally. I only want what's best for Stephen. Although I'm now convinced that Darcy is not the right woman for him, I'm not the one who gets to decide."

"Decide on what?" Stephen asked upon reentering the room.

Farrah looked embarrassed. She wasn't about to clarify her statement for Stephen, but she was having a hard time thinking up something passable to say. "Uh…"

"Decide on what to eat," Stephanie quickly interjected. "We're both hungry."

"Hungry? After all that drama! I was hungry beforehand, but now my appetite is gone."

"How *is* Darcy after all that was said in here?" Stephanie asked.

Stephen looked troubled. "I'm beginning to believe she's convinced herself that what she's saying is true. We all know better. I wished I hadn't confessed to her, especially when I'm not guilty of what I'm accused of. The more I think about it, the more I realize it was the wrong thing to do. She doesn't seem capable of grasping the truth about what I told her. I've stopped blaming myself for the flirting, but it looks as if she can't let it go. Since she's already broken things off with me, I don't see why she has to keep going."

Farrah sucked her teeth. Probably because she doesn't have anything else to do, Farrah mused, not daring to make that sort of malicious remark out loud. "Perhaps it keeps her connected to you, Stephen, even if it's in a negative way. She's not ready to let go of you. Continuing to bring this up may be the only way she feels she can hold on to you."

"Well, it's definitely not working. I've had a hard time accepting the fact that it's over between us, but I've come to accept it now. Darcy hasn't returned a single phone call to me in days, and now she comes over here making all sorts of nasty accusations. I'm through trying to figure her out. Regrettably, what we had is over and done with. I have to move on with my life. Do you guys want to go out to eat or should I try to find something in the kitchen to cook?"

"We have to go out," Stephanie responded. "There's nothing in my refrigerator to cook. I haven't done my grocery shopping for this two-week period. I'd like to eat at Chili's."

"Chili's it is." Stephen looked at Farrah. "You are going to join us, aren't you?"

Farrah laughed gently, wringing her hands. "The three of us eating together is what got us in this mess in the first place. Are you sure it's a good idea for me to tag along?"

"It's the best idea I've come up with today," Stephen said. "How much time do you ladies need to get ready?"

"A half hour," Stephanie remarked.

"That's enough time for me, too," Farrah said, getting to her feet. "I'll run next door and change into something nicer. Phone me when you're ready to leave and I'll meet you outside."

Now that both women had left him alone in the family room, Stephen thought back on what had happened earlier, wishing he could make sense of it all despite saying he was going to stop trying to figure it. Even though he no longer thought it was up to him to figure out, he'd still like to know what was really behind all of Darcella's sudden bouts of insanity.

Running outside behind Darcella hadn't been such a good idea. She was even far less cooperative outdoors than she'd been inside the house. He couldn't believe it when she'd told him she hated him. At any rate, he'd been hurt by her tear-ful outburst. He didn't want anyone to hate him, least of all the woman he had once planned to marry.

Stephen knew deep down in his heart that it was really over for them. No wedding bells would be rung in their honor. They no longer had a romantic relationship, but he still wanted Darcella to be his friend. Keeping their friend-ship alive also seemed impossible, but that wasn't going to stop him from trying. Stephen just didn't want things to re-main on a bad footing.

Darcella could kick herself for the way she'd behaved in front of Stephen, Stephanie and Farrah. They must've thought she'd lost her mind. All the way to her place she'd imagined the threesome talking about her and laughing their heads off. She had made a downright fool of herself. She had shown the insecure side of her to everyone, something she wished she could've kept hidden. It was embarrassing enough that Stephen was aware of her insecurities. Now Stephanie and Farrah had also gotten a dose of her self-doubting, a double dose.

Darcella was sure she'd really blown it with Stephen this time. It was almost like she kept sabotaging their relation-ship on purpose. Telling him she hated him had been an awful thing to say. She wouldn't blame him if he never talked to her again, but she hoped that wouldn't happen. If noth-ing else, she owed him and the others an apology. How many times had she apologized to Stephanie only to go off on her again? Everyone was probably sick and tired of hear-ing her apologize, especially since her regret over each inci-dent didn't last but a hot minute.

As Darcella lay down across her bed, she thought about the phone call she'd received earlier from her brothers. Their mother was ill. It was suggested that she come home to help take care of Patsy. The last place Darcella wanted to go was Mississippi. But how could she not go? Even her father had voiced his desire to have her come home and help out. He didn't think a nurse should be hired when they already had a very capable one in the family.

It didn't seem to matter to Darcella's family that she had a life in Houston. The Colemans needed her and expected her to jump at the opportunity to meet their every desire. They really wanted a slave, someone to do all their bidding. She wouldn't just be taking care of her mother. Cooking, cleaning, and laundry duties would also be her chores to perform. Hers alone.

Moving back home would solve one of her problems. She wouldn't have to worry about running into Stephen around town or seeing him on his emergency runs to the hospital. Perhaps it would be easier for her to get over him if she lived elsewhere. There were so many reminders of him there in Houston. They had made a lot of memories together. Wonderful reminiscences.

The thought of moving back into her parents' home was a scary one for Darcella. She didn't want to live there. She'd have to get an apartment of her own, but it had to be within walking distance of the Coleman house so she could come and go at will. As much as she dreaded living near her family, she knew she needed to make amends with each of them. Someone had to be the bigger person in this. It was all up to her to get it done.

Darcella still hadn't turned in her letter of resignation to the personnel department, but she'd already taken the firefighters entry-level exam. It would be another two weeks before she'd find out if she'd passed it or not. At any rate, fighting fires from the air was growing less and less appealing to her. She'd also begun to recognize the real danger in it. She was no hero.

Stephen hadn't been exaggerating about how dangerous smoke jumping could be. He'd known exactly what he was talking about. Darcella had already read for herself the statistics on casualties in that particular career. The numbers were rather harrowing.

Chapter 11

Stephen smelled Farrah's perfume on his clothes as he removed them to hang up in his bedroom closet. Taking a firm hold of his jacket, he held it up to his nose, inhaling deeply of the tantalizing scent. The fragrance she wore smelled so darn good. It was delicate and sensuous, just like Farrah. This woman continued to amaze him. She kept him absolutely intrigued. Her sweet innocence blew his mind also. Farrah was such an innocent person for a woman her age.

Stephen and Farrah hadn't shared so much as a kiss, yet he saw shooting stars every time he imagined it happening. Once he had begun to pay serious attention to her, the flirting between them had pretty much stopped. It was as if they had drawn an imaginary line in the sand, one that shouldn't be crossed. Their conversations were always lively and they could make each other laugh uncontrollably. Their friendship was very special. So much so that it seemed if they tried to be more than friends it would ruin everything. Stephen didn't want that.

The couple never considered the few things they'd done

together as dates. They merely saw it as good friends sharing a meal, watching a show on television or taking a leisurely stroll in the park. They had held hands on two occasions, but that only had come about in her grief.

Neither had seen it as an act of intimacy.

However, Stephen had begun to check his sanity a lot lately. He was more than slightly interested in Farrah, but for him to tell her that was scary. The possibility of ruining their friendship was what had kept him from sharing with her how he felt. What they shared as friends was too good for him to go and blow it. *Keep it simple* was what he constantly told himself. *How did one keep it simple with something so darn complicated*?

As if he had a choice, Stephen thought. Farrah wasn't exactly exposing how she really felt about him, either, at least not since she'd said something about it when they'd had the little heart-to-heart conversation the night he'd apologized to her for possibly leading her on. Yet he was sure she felt something special for him. Apparently she hadn't mentioned anything more to his sister about her feelings for him. Stephanie hadn't said a thing to him if Farrah had.

The tiny velvet box on Stephen's dresser suddenly caught his eye and he walked across the room and picked it up. He carried it back to his bed, where he sat down on the side of the mattress. After opening the jewelry case, he stared at the diamond ring he'd purchased for Darcella, loving how it sparkled and winked at him. The marquis-cut diamond was exquisite.

Making up his mind to keep the gem or take it back to the jewelry store for a refund was hard for Stephen to decide on. He had wanted Darcella to keep the ring, but she'd refused in no uncertain terms. In all good consciousness, she'd said that she couldn't accept it as a mere gift.

As Stephen thought more about what he should do with the diamond, he realized he really couldn't afford to pay for something that would lie in his drawer unused. He had also gone into debt to purchase it. The ring could never be given to another woman, so returning it to the store was really his only option. As Stephen recalled the conditions for the return of a purchase, he knew it was way past the three-month deadline placed on store returns. He realized he'd just have to try to sell it himself.

After Stephen had given it a lot of thought, he was satisfied with his decision to run an ad in several local papers to try to sell the ring. As Stephen slid into bed, he hoped he could get some sleep tonight. Trying to be there for Farrah had kept him sleeping with one eye open. He hadn't wanted to miss her call in case she had needed him so he hadn't turned the ringer off, which was something he did when he was dead tired and didn't want to be disturbed.

Seeing Darcella earlier in the day had confirmed a couple of things for him. Not taking his calls or returning them had been by design. He had known that she was physically okay because he'd finally called one of her coworkers to find out. It had hurt him something awful when Darcella had told him to stop calling her house, that she didn't want to hear from him.

It came as a relief for Stephen when he'd found out that she hadn't yet resigned from her job at the hospital, which made him wonder if she'd given up on her desire of becoming a smoke jumper. He sure hoped so. Darcella was strong, but he didn't think she was tough enough for that killer of a job. He didn't even think he was strong enough to handle it.

As Farrah's image popped into Stephen's head, he couldn't help smiling. It appeared to him that she had begun to dream again. Her eyes were now lucent and the puffy bags beneath them were gone. A healthy glow of color had also returned to her complexion. Her smile once again looked as if the sun had kissed it. Farrah's appetite had returned, too. During their meal at Chili's she had eaten everything on her plate and had even ordered dessert and a cappuccino.

The numerous memories of the evening had Stephen smiling within. Farrah was good for him. Even through all her grief she had found a way to lift his spirits. He was in no doubt that he would've fallen hard after Darcella had ended their relationship. Instead, he'd risen above the agony. He had Farrah to thank for that, because she hadn't let him fall prey to deep depression.

After dinner the three friends had taken a walk in the park across the street from Stephanie's and Farrah's houses. The place had been filled with animated kids and adults. Stephen's heart laughed with glee when he recalled the little children at play. Their giggles had excited him, freeing his spirit even more.

Much to his surprise, Farrah had joined in the fun, revealing yet another side of her.

When Stephen had first spotted the tiny plastic container of liquid bubbles that Farrah had taken from her purse, he'd thrown his head back in laughter. The girlish smile on her face had shown her pleasure in making him laugh. Her joy had rung out after she'd blown her first set of bubbles. Then the kids had crowded around Farrah, making her the center of attention.

For the next half hour or so Farrah had had the children chasing around after all the bubbles she had such fun blowing. Both he and Stephanie had thoroughly enjoyed watching the kids try to catch the elusive bubbles. It had been a wonderful sight for him to behold. It was yet another confirmation of Stephen's strong yen to have babies. Seeing those little children having such a great time had been like an energizing shot in the arm. Farrah's pure spirit had touched everyone who was lucky enough to have been present—and the kids had absolutely adored her and had also loved the entertainment she'd provided for them.

With a huge smile pasted on his face, Stephen pulled the comforter up over his head. He then said a silent prayer, asking for peace and harmony in his life and in the lives of everyone he cared about. He also asked that the Lord make a way for him and his ex-fiancée to come to an amicable understanding. Most of all he wanted forgiveness from both the Lord and Darcella.

After Stephanie poured raspberry lemonade into two ice-filled glasses, she joined Malachi at her kitchen table. This was her first time trying out Ms. Aretha's lemonade recipe and she hoped her father liked it as much as she did.

Once Stephanie was comfortably situated, father and daughter entered into a conversation about Stephanie's wedding plans. Malachi saw how pleased she was with the progress being made. It sounded to him as if Aretha had been a godsend for her. The miles between them obviously hadn't mattered. The two women were getting the job done despite the distance. Malachi was extremely pleased that Aretha was being such a tremendous help to his daughter.

As Malachi's eyes misted up, he cleared his throat. Reaching into the pocket of his sports jacket, he pulled out a small gray velvet jewelry box. After opening the lid, he set the box on the table and pushed it in front of Stephanie. "I want you and Gregory to have these special gifts."

Without having to ask any questions of her father, Stephanie knew exactly what the two solid gold bands represented. Tears sprang to her eyes at the generous sentiment. "Yours and Mama's wedding bands." She picked up the smallest ring and then kissed it. "Knowing Mama wore this band on her finger makes it very special to me. I'll wear it proudly, Daddy."

"Thank you, my dear, for accepting the rings in the same spirit in which they were given. I know Doreen would want you to have hers." Malachi's eyes suddenly filled with sadness. Recalling the evening Doreen had thrown her ring back at him was a very painful memory.

Stephanie could easily tell by Malachi's expression that he was recollecting a sorrowful incident. She didn't have to ask him about that, either. The agonizing pain he felt was as plain as the nose on his face.

After Stephanie slid the gold band onto her ring finger, she picked up the larger one. "I'm sure Gregory will feel honored to wear your wedding band. I haven't picked out his ring yet, so I can hardly wait to present him with yours. As far as I know, he hasn't picked out a band for me, either, only my engagement ring. These are perfect wedding gifts, not to mention how precious."

Stephanie got up from her seat. Positioning herself behind Malachi's chair, she wrapped her arms around his neck and pressed her cheek against his. "Thank you for thinking of this idea. It's wonderful. I love you."

Malachi covered his daughter's small hands with his large ones. "My pleasure, daughter. I want Doreen to be a part of this wedding day as much as possible." With that said, he reached into his other pocket and brought out a small gift-wrapped package. "Please come and sit back down, Stephanie, before you open this gift."

Stephanie instantly honored his request, eyeing the package with open curiosity. Since she couldn't guess at this one, she'd just have to wait and see. For whatever reason, her hands shook as she unwrapped the package. Her breath suddenly caught. Tears spilled onto her cheeks as she fingered the lacy blue garter. "Mama's?"

Malachi swallowed hard. "Mama's."

For several seconds Stephanie and Malachi sat in stony silence, each deeply feeling the weight of the sentimental moment. He was pleased by her response to all the gifts and she was ecstatic with his loving overtures. Wearing her mother's wedding ring and her blue garter would indeed make Doreen's presence felt on her big day. Stephanie couldn't have been more thrilled.

Stephanie looked up and then made eye contact with Malachi. "Thanks again, Dad." She paused a moment, biting down on her lower lip. "I'm concerned about Stephen, Daddy. How's he going to feel on my wedding day knowing that his big day has been called off? I feel really sad for him."

Malachi shrugged his shoulders. "You shouldn't feel that way, my dear. Stephen will be just fine on your wedding day. We should all be thankful that he and Darcy didn't take sacred vows with each other. It has become obvious to me that they're all wrong for each other, especially when one mate wants children and the other one doesn't. That can't be a match made in heaven. Being at odds about children is a very difficult obstacle for anyone to overcome."

Stephanie lifted an eyebrow. "Yeah, I see what you mean. Still, Stephen's bound to feel something that day. He is taking all the brunt for the breakup. I don't think he's solely to blame."

"Of course he's not. Whenever something fails that two people are involved in, both have to shoulder a portion of the blame. It may not be a fifty-fifty deal, but both parties are in part responsible for the outcome," Malachi explained.

Malachi went on to say that Darcella had made a very big mistake in trying to alienate Stephen from his family, especially Stephanie. He believed it would have gotten even worse after the marriage despite her numerous apologies over it.

"That *was* a huge mistake on her part. Stephen would never stand for something like that, no matter how much in love he is. What do you think about Farrah, Daddy? Do you like her?"

Looking thoughtful, Malachi stroked his chin. "She's a sweet girl and she truly loves Stephen. The depth of what she feels for him is written all over her face. To answer your question, I like her very much. She's also very compassionate, stunning and quite intelligent."

"I love Farrah, Dad. We've grown up together and we've always had each other's back. That's for sure." Stephanie then launched right into the story of how Stephen used to beg her to keep Farrah away from him.

Stephanie smiled broadly as she relayed an incident where Farrah had written her brother a love note and had somehow managed to sneak into his room and slip it under his pillow. Stephen would go the other way or slip out the back door whenever he saw Farrah coming. He hated it when she stayed overnight, because if he wanted to watch television, they had to do it as a group. Only one television was in the house back then. Farrah had watched him more than she viewed what was on the boob tube. Her eyes on him had made Stephen awfully uncomfortable.

Malachi laughed heartily. "He doesn't seem to mind her eyes on him now. They really do make a stunning couple, even though they don't see themselves like that. Stephen is way more into Farrah than he wants to admit. But I think he still feels a certain loyalty to Darcy."

Stephanie pursed her lips. "I know he does. He can't seem to shake the responsibility he feels toward her. But if all he feels is responsibility, they can't build a life together on just that."

"You've got a point." Malachi looked down at his watch. "Stephen should be home from work by now. Let's give him a call so he'll know I made it here safely."

"Good idea."

Stephen stood by patiently as Farrah placed a colorful bouquet of summer flowers on Helen's gravesite. Even when her shoulders began to shake from her grief, he kept his distance. This was her private moment with her mother and he didn't want to intrude upon it. However, he silently prayed that Farrah's broken heart would soon begin to mend. Her pain had become his.

Only a few minutes earlier, as Stephen was driving Farrah to the cemetery, he'd asked her what she was daydreaming about. He recalled how she had looked up at him and smiled.

"Life in general" had been her response. "It feels good to be back," she'd said. "I've missed living, Stephen."

"That's a good sign," Stephen had told her. "Life missed you also. The sun in your eyes appears brighter now that you've returned. I'm happy you're smiling again."

"I'm experiencing a joyful healing, Stephen. Things are really getting better for me."

The sorrowful scene before Stephen seemed to belie their earlier conversation. It didn't look to him as if things had gotten any better for Farrah at all. She was downright miserable at the moment. As Stephen said a silent prayer for her, his heart also went out to her.

Farrah became so overwrought with anguish that she suddenly fell to her knees. Her trembling hands then reached out and touched the granite headstone. "I miss you, Mother. I wish you could come back home. I am so lonely without you...." Gut-wrenching sobs took her over, causing her to rock back and forth on her haunches.

Stephen couldn't stay back any longer. After he knelt down beside Farrah, he took hold of her hand, gently squeezing her fingers. "It'll be okay, Farrah. We just have to give it time."

The softness of Stephen's voice caused Farrah to lean her head against his chest. This man's voice had comforted her quite often in the past few days. He had been at her side to help her through the tough spots, which had allowed her to rely on him, possibly too much. For several moments they remained down on their knees in an uncomfortable silence. Her hand suddenly reached up and lovingly stroked his face. Then her lips softly caressed his cheek.

Stephen was stunned by Farrah's overt affection toward him, but he wasn't offended. Her hands felt so good on his skin, causing his body to tingle all over. He felt her desperate need to belong to someone. This woman was starving for love and affection, but it was obvious to him that she was very choosy about who she gave her love to. He admired her for that.

Although Stephen longed to give Farrah exactly what she desired, he couldn't. At least not right now. There were too many unsettled issues in his life. How could he get emotionally involved with Farrah when he was seriously considering moving to New Orleans? That would hardly be fair to her. He himself also needed something rather desperately— a new beginning, for starters. Even though Stephen believed he could love Farrah liked he'd never loved anyone before, fear held him back once again. The fear of getting hurt again was overpowering.

As Farrah attempted to get to her feet, Stephen rushed to his first so he could help her up. Taking a handkerchief from his back pocket, he wiped her face free of tears. The liquid sadness in her eyes was nearly his undoing. If only he knew how to take away her pain without causing her more, he'd be only too glad to do that.

Farrah pressed her lips against Stephen's, dying for just a small show of affection from him. She had surprised even herself. Losing the battle of self-control, Stephen deepened the kiss, giving her more than what she'd imagined. His hands entwined in her hair as he drew her head onto his chest. He instantly knew that he shouldn't have allowed this to occur, but he wouldn't allow himself to regret it, either. It was as if their coming together like this was inevitable. Something inside of him had broken free and he no longer felt the steel bands of restraint.

Farrah's eyes were as soft as a cloud as she looked up at Stephen. "There are no strings attached to that kiss, Stephen. I just needed to feel close to you. I hope you're not upset."

Stephen gently kissed Farrah's forehead. "We both needed what occurred." He laughed softly. "Why would I be upset over receiving something so sweet and innocent? I just don't want either of us to get hurt, Farrah. We need to take things very slow."

Farrah felt as if her heart was bursting open from the un-bridled joy she felt. Did Stephen's remarks mean that he wanted the same for them as she did? Was it really possible for them to have a romantic liaison? She could go as slow as he wanted her to. There was no need to rush into anything. They'd already established a solid friendship. Besides, she'd only been waiting on him for umpteen years.

Although Farrah knew that Stephen could possibly be on the rebound, she wasn't going to allow herself to become overly concerned. If they were truly meant to be, they would come together in God's time. Farrah believed that with her whole heart and soul.

Farrah kissed Stephen lightly on the mouth. "I can do slow. Is a snail's pace slow enough for you, Stephen?"

Stephen smiled brightly. "Slow it is, then." As if to seal their winsome pact, he kissed her again. "Are you hungry?" he asked in the next breath.

Farrah nodded. "I could eat a little something."

"Good! I recently discovered this little café in Nassau Bay. They serve the very best in Mediterranean food. In fact, it's called Mediterraneo Market & Café. Want to try it out?"

"Absolutely, Stephen. The place sounds interesting."

Stephen drew Farrah to him once again. He first kissed her gently and then he kissed her thoroughly. As his heart took flight, Stephen began to feel utterly free.

Farrah also felt free. She couldn't fathom what was happening, yet it made her believe that fairy tales did come true. More than that, she believed that God answered prayers. She'd lost count of the times she'd prayed to have something special with Stephen. No matter where the journey took them, she was ready to take the ride that would hopefully land them in paradise.

After several attempts Stephanie had given up on reaching Stephen at home or on his cell phone. Just when she felt sure that they wouldn't see him this evening, he had called to invite her and Malachi to join him and Farrah at the Mediterraneo Market & Café.

Stephanie didn't know what had happened between Stephen and Farrah, but she was certain that something wonderful had occurred with them. Just the way they constantly looked and smiled at each other was enough evidence for her. Both of them were all starry-eyed. She would later get all the 411 from either her brother or best friend, but right now she was content to watch them closely for any other interesting clues.

Stephanie's eyes were also aglow as she shared with Stephen and Farrah the story about receiving from Malachi the wedding bands that had once been worn by their parents. Stephen was happy to see his sister so excited. Knowing that her deepest fears about marriage had been allayed, after she'd talked them over with her fiancé, pleased him also. Stephen really liked his sister's choice for a husband, certain that Gregory Saxton III was the perfect man for her.

"So what have you two been up to today?" Stephanie asked Stephen and Farrah. "I couldn't reach either of you by phone."

Stephen rubbed his chin. "Right after work I went grocery shopping. I then took Farrah to the cemetery to put flowers on Ms. Helen's grave."

The expression on Stephanie's face showed her regret for asking. Farrah was having a hard enough time with her mother's death without any reminders.

Farrah sensed that Stephanie felt bad. "It's okay, Stephanie. We can't continue to tiptoe around the subject of my mother's death. If we do that, I'll never get used to her being gone. I know I have to stop being so sensitive about it. Talking about her helps me tremendously."

Malachi smiled at Farrah with empathy. "Talking about our dearly departed is the best way to keep them alive in our hearts and minds. It would be such a shame not to talk about them at all. To do that would be like totally erasing their very existence."

"I agree with you, Mr. Trudeaux. I don't want to do that. I have so many warm, loving memories of my mother to keep me company when I'm feeling lonely." Farrah looked up at Stephen, her eyes clearly thanking him for also helping to ease her loneliness.

Stephen acknowledged Farrah's nonverbal communication with a wink and a nod. "I don't know about you all, but I'm ready to order. I haven't eaten since noon."

The others also voiced their desires to get on with ordering their meals.

Both Stephanie and Farrah ordered lamb kebobs and Greek salads. Stephen had a taste for the roasted chicken while Malachi was interested in tasting the chicken-lamb kebob combination. The two men also requested Greek salads to go along with their entrées. Everyone ordered iced teas for their beverage.

Conversation continued on as the small group waited for their hot meals to be served.

Once Stephen had walked Farrah to her front door, he'd seen her safely inside, after kissing her lightly on the mouth. Then he'd returned to Stephanie's house for a cup of hot coffee and further conversation with his sister and father. Seated at the kitchen table, father and son waited for Stephanie to serve the hot drinks.

"Farrah appears to be doing much better," Malachi remarked. "Is she?"

"At times." Stephen mentioned the events that had occurred at the cemetery earlier.

Stephanie set down two cups of coffee before retrieving a third mug. Seconds later she took the chair right across from her brother. "If I may put in my two cents," Stephanie said, "there are days when Farrah is very up and optimistic. Then, without any prior warning, she suddenly falls apart again. Her emotions will be up and down for some time to come. Ask someone who knows exactly what she's going through. At least I had you to lean on, Stephen. Farrah doesn't have any family to see her through the tough spots."

"That's why Stephanie and I continue to be there for her, Dad."

Malachi smiled knowingly. "I commend both of you

for constantly tending to Farrah's needs. You have grown very fond of the young lady, haven't you, son?"

Stephen tucked his lips inward, sighing heavily. "I think we all know that I care a lot about Farrah, Dad. She has become very important to me. I don't know where our relationship is heading, but I'm happy with how things are progressing. We've actually decided to explore our feelings. Taking things very slowly is our plan. Nothing will be rushed."

Stephanie felt happy and sad. She was happy for Farrah and Stephen but sad for Darcella. "Are you sure it's over between you and Darcy?"

Stephen shrugged. "I think Darcy has made things very clear to me. It's over, Stephanie."

Malachi looked concerned. "Despite what Darcy has or hasn't made clear, I'd like to know if it's over for you, son. Are you sure you're emotionally ready to move on?"

"No doubt about it. My emotions are stable. I want children, Dad. Darcella doesn't. That alone is something I don't feel we can overcome. I'm not willing to compromise on that issue. Darcy has yet to put all the cards out on the table, and I'm not sure she ever will. As I see it, I have no choice but to close this chapter of my life. I want to move on."

Stephanie felt terribly sorry for her brother. Knowingly or unknowingly, she believed that Stephen was still torn between the two women, but she was sure he'd eventually be okay. What he needed most was for him and Darcella to have final closure. As bad as she felt for Darcella, she'd also seen how good Farrah and Stephen were for and to each other.

Stephanie was pleased that Stephen and her best friend weren't going to rush into a romantic relationship. However, she hadn't seen either of them any happier than they were right now. She would not openly champion the possibility of Stephen and Farrah becoming a couple, not until her brother and Darcella achieved closure, but she was positively excited about it.

From all indications, Farrah's lifelong dream just might come true.

The threesome began to discuss Malachi's plans for his stay in Houston. He smiled broadly as he told his kids that he planned to see Josefina once Maxwell arrived. The two couples had made plans to see a stage play and have dinner afterward. Malachi was still uncomfortable seeing his lovely lady friend alone. He liked her a lot, thought they might have a chance at happiness, but he never wanted to marry again.

Stephanie looked puzzled. "Why not, Dad? You're too young to live out the rest of your life alone. Everyone needs companionship."

Malachi nodded. "Companionship is one thing. Marriage is another animal entirely. I took those sacred vows with your mother long ago. Nothing will ever compare to what Doreen and I had before I blew it. For your information, Josefina isn't too much interested in marriage, either." He chuckled. "She has only hinted at her feelings on the matter, but I was able to read between the lines. I don't think she wanted to hurt my feelings by saying it as a matter of fact. She's very independent and lives well off her pension and the one her late husband left her."

Stephanie understood, but she wasn't too thrilled about Malachi never getting married again. She wanted to see her father happy and settled down with a life partner. He deserved all the joy in life he could find. Perhaps he *was* okay living just as he was, she considered. Marriage the second time around wasn't for everyone. Stephanie decided to respect his decision, but she couldn't help hoping he might one day have a change of heart.

"How's the house hunting coming, Dad?" Stephen asked.

"We've narrowed it down to three places. One is in South Shore Harbor. The other two properties are in Clear Lake. Max and I are having a hard time choosing. Each house is unique. We plan to make the final decision when he gets here. All of them are spec homes. We don't want to waste time building from the ground up. It takes four to six months in most cases."

Stephen was really happy for his father and uncle. They seemed content enough to him. He loved the fact that the two brothers got along so well, just as he and his sister did. "Dad, I've given a lot more thought to moving to New Orleans. I really think I'd like to go there to work for you. However, I plan to keep my home in Houston so I can come back here whenever I want.

Can you give me three months to make the move? I'd like to give the department at least a month or two notice."

Malachi beamed at his son, ecstatic over his decision. "You can take all the time you need, Stephen. The company isn't going anywhere. It's very strong and solvent. I plan to work alongside you until you're ready to take over the reins on your own. You should be ready after about six months of steady training. You can't imagine how much help you'll receive."

Stephanie giggled. "Well, it looks like all the Trudeauxs will be putting down roots in the Big Easy. We'll all be homeowners in both states since I plan to only lease out this place."

Malachi lifted his coffee cup and held it up. "I think we should toast to that. The Trudeaux family members are going to take Houston and New Orleans by storm!"

As Stephen's cell phone began playing music, he quickly excused himself from the table. When he saw who the caller was, he started toward the front of the house, wondering if Darcella's ears had been burning or if she could read minds. Stephen chuckled inwardly.

"Hi, stranger! How are you?"

"Good, Stephen. Real good," she lied. There was nothing good about what is going on with me, Darcella thought. "I know I'm the last person you expected to hear from, especially after I've been so unreasonable, but I needed to hear your voice. Are you okay?"

"I'm doing just fine, Darcy. Nothing for you to be concerned about."

"Glad to hear it. I'd like to see you again, Stephen. I think we both need some kind of closure. Our issues seem like they're still up in the air. Would you consider meeting with me?"

Stephen wasn't sure meeting with Darcella was such a good idea, but he was also aware that they needed closure. He couldn't begin his life anew until he truly came to grips with the demons from the old one. "Of course, Darcy. Will tomorrow evening at my place be okay?"

"Is seven good for you, Stephen?"

"The timing is perfect, Darcy. See you tomorrow."

As soon as Stephen disconnected the line, he went back into the kitchen and took his seat. "That was Darcy. She wants us to meet to try to bring closure to our situation."

Stephanie's eyes widened. "Did you agree to it?"

Stephen nodded. "Yes. I think it's for the best."

"So do I," Stephanie and Malachi said simultaneously.

Darcella was so happy that Stephen had agreed to see her one last time. The time had come for her to finally set the record straight. Now that she was moving back to Mississippi to take care of her ill mother, she wanted to tell him goodbye and to also thank him for the countless good times they'd shared. Darcella also knew she owed Stephen a huge apology.

As Darcella turned her car onto Stephen's street, pangs of deep regret hit her hard. Tears floated in her eyes, as she thought of this being the last time she'd ever see him face-to-face. Giving her final farewell to the man she loved manically wasn't going to be easy. In fact, this was the hardest thing she'd ever had to do in her life. Fear continued to rule her heart.

After Darcella parked her car in Stephen's driveway, she cut the engine and got out. She then opened the back door and retrieved the small colorfully wrapped package containing a special gift for Stephen. She hoped he would like what she'd done to try to make him think of her in a positive way, once she was gone from his life for good.

Darcella needed Stephen's forgiveness every bit as much as he needed hers.

Stephen opened the door before the bell rang. Although he'd been nervous all day about Darcella's visit, he had been eagerly awaiting her arrival, periodically watching for her from the bay window. As Stephen smiled brightly at Darcella, he appeared genuinely pleased to see her.

Stephen led Darcella into the media room, where they both took a seat, the erratic beating of his heart indicating to him that he was still extremely nervous. Instead of sitting together on the sofa, each of them had opted for chairs. The distance between them still felt odd to Stephen. It was easy for him to recall how close they'd been to each other at one time.

Hoping to keep a froglike sound from taking over his voice, Stephen cleared his throat.

"How're things going for you, Darcy?"

Darcella forced a smile to her generous lips. "Not as well as I'd like them to go, but I'm dealing with everything. I came over to tell you goodbye, Stephen."

Stephen looked puzzled. "What does that mean? Are you going somewhere?"

"Back home to Mississippi. Something I never dreamed I'd ever do. My mother isn't well. I need to help out my father with her personal care."

Stephen's expression clearly showed his deep compassion for her situation. "I'm sorry. Is it serious, Darcy?"

Darcella nodded. "I'm afraid so. Cervical cancer. After surgery, Mom will have radiation and then chemo. I need to be there to take care of her."

"That's certainly understandable. She'll need a good nurse and she'll have the very best one in her own daughter. I'll keep you and your family in prayer."

"Thank you for that, Stephen." She wrung her hands together nervously. "I also came here to apologize for everything I've done to you and your family. I think the worst of it was attacking you and Stephanie at her home. I probably should apologize for my bad treatment of Farrah, too, but I still don't feel very generous toward her."

Stephen looked Darcella right in the eye. "Farrah was never our problem, Darcy, and I think you already know that."

"Are you saying you don't have feelings for Farrah, Stephen?"

Stephen sighed hard. "I didn't at the time you're referring to. I must admit that I do now."

Darcella sucked up the pain from his confession. "So I was right when I said it was just a matter of time before you acted upon your attraction to her. Are you two seriously involved now in a love affair?"

"We're taking things really slow. Farrah knows how I feel about her. I was afraid to tell her for a long time because I thought it might ruin our great friendship. As both you and I have found out, relationships are very fragile. When do you leave for Mississippi?"

Darcella licked her bottom lip. "Next weekend. I've already leased out my house. I decided not to sell in case I ever want to come back here. I'm leaving for home next Friday."

"Are you driving to Mississippi?"

"Of course. I'll need my car to get around. I'm sure I'll have plenty of errands to run while I'm at home. Besides, I'd never want to be without my own transportation. Relying on my father and brothers to take me places isn't the least bit appealing."

Stephen understood. "I guess I hadn't thought of all that. I don't like the idea of you driving down there alone. I could go with you to help you drive and then fly back to Houston. Is that okay with you, Darcy?"

Darcella gave a short laugh, shaking her head. "It's not okay with me, Stephen. It's only a five- or six-hour drive. I've driven there alone many times. You have to stop feeling responsible for me. What happened between us is not all your fault, quite the contrary. My fears about our relationship grew bigger than me. The truth is I feared that we'd end up just like my parents, married but hating every second of it. We really have to let each other off the hook. You can't help how you feel about Farrah any more than I can stop the fears from ruling my world."

"I may not be able to help how I feel about someone, but you can get a grip on your fears. You don't have to be afraid. You're not your parents, Darcy. Stephanie has conquered her fears and so have I. I was fearful just like you because of my parents' troubled marriage. I didn't want my marriage to end up like that, either. That's why I suggested premarital counseling for us."

Darcella smiled weakly. "It wouldn't have done us any good, Stephen. Our love for each other wasn't strong enough to overcome what ailed us. I'm too darn insecure. I know that much about me now. The insecurity alone was already seriously getting in the way of our happiness. Perhaps I'll one day get over my fears of a permanent commitment. Maybe I'll also find with someone what you and Farrah have found. I wish you only the very best, Stephen."

Stephen blew out an unsteady stream of breath. "Don't go jumping to conclusions, Darcy. You sound as if Farrah and me are already involved in a mad, passionate love affair. As I said before, we're not. I care deeply about her and she truly cares about me. We're taking our relationship very slow. Neither of us can afford to rush headlong into an affair, but I do believe we're falling in love with each other. We have yet to acknowledge the depth of our feelings."

Darcella looked thoughtful. "Kids. Do you think if I wanted children we might've had a different outcome?"

Stephen came over to where Darcella sat and reached down for her hand. "The facts are in. You *don't* want children so I'm not going to speculate. I'm just sorry it didn't work for us, Darcy. I never imagined that it wouldn't, at least not until it began to fail and then continued to get worse. Can you ever forgive me for the way things turned out between us? I need forgiveness from you, Darcy. I need that from you more than anything else."

Darcella stood up and wrapped her arms around Stephen's neck, laying her head against his chest. She loved the calming sound of his heartbeat. It had hurt her to hear him say he was falling in love with Farrah, but oddly enough she was also happy for him. Farrah was obviously able to give him what she hadn't been able to. Darcella felt that she had really failed Stephen.

Darcella pulled back slightly from Stephen and looked right into his eyes. "Oh, Stephen, you have my forgiveness. And I need the very same from you. But I guess it's God's forgiveness we should be the most concerned about. I wish I could hate you, but it's not in me, nor do you deserve that from me. You were good to me, often better to me than I was to myself. I still love you, Stephen, but I really don't think we would've been happy married to each other. If I thought there was a ghost of a chance for us to have marital bliss, I'd fight for you like crazy. It's just not in the cards for us, Stephen. The fact that I don't ever want children really seals our fate."

Warding off the pain from Darcella's last statement, Stephen squeezed her tightly. It was still hard for him to accept that she didn't want him to be the father of her kids. But then again, she didn't want any man for that purpose. He guessed she could really love him despite that fact, yet he found it hard to believe that she had truly loved him.

"Thank you for coming here so we could put things right between us. You have my forgiveness as well. I'll never forget all the great times we had together. I'm sorry we didn't have all that it takes to share a lifetime, because you're a wonderful person. Please fight hard to overcome your insecurities. I see them as your only serious drawback. Thanks for forgiving me, Darcy. I wouldn't have been completely happy without it. I would've always regretted that we weren't able to end things on a positive note. I'll always be here for you. I want us to remain friends, Darcy. I really want that."

"Me, too, Stephen, me, too. Can I have one last kiss, for old times' sake?"

Stephen kissed Darcella gently on the lips. "For old times' sake, Darcy."

Darcella definitely felt the absence of any kind of passion in Stephen's kiss. It had been nothing less than a friendly peck from his lips to hers. If he had allowed more than that, she would have seriously questioned what he'd said he felt for Farrah. The type of kiss he'd given her had also reconfirmed for her their incompatibility. It saddened her that they weren't right for each other and that they'd wasted so much time in finding it out. Still, Darcella would be eternally grateful that they'd discovered all their true issues before they'd gotten married.

Darcella returned to her seat and retrieved the gift she'd placed beside the chair. She handed the gaily wrapped parcel to Stephen. "This is for you. I hope you like it."

Stephen looked from her to the package, wondering what was inside. He ripped the paper off, eager to find out what she'd given him, hoping it wasn't something he'd have to turn down. The last thing he wanted to do was hurt her again.

As Stephen looked down at the oil painting of himself and the people he loved without question or thought, without rhyme nor reason, his eyes filled with tears. The painting of him with his arms around his mother and twin sister had touched him deeply. Seeing that Malachi and Maxwell had somehow been added to the painting had him feeling overwhelmed. "How did you ever manage to get this done, Darcy?"

Darcella looked a tad sheepish. "I borrowed the original

picture of you, Stephanie and your mom from your photo album. After I took it home and scanned it into my computer, I sent an electronic copy to an artist friend of mine who lives in Salt Lake City. Much later I sent along the digital picture I'd taken of Mr. T. and Uncle Max. I put your photo back into your album without you ever knowing it was gone. I was going to give it to you for Christmas. Since we're no longer a couple, and I'm leaving town, now is the best time to present it to you."

Stephen gulped hard to clear the lump in his throat. "It's beautiful, Darcy. The intricate details are exquisite. Your friend is quite an artist. I'll cherish the family painting always. I didn't know something like this could be accomplished. I'm glad you thought of it. Thank you, Darcy."

"You're welcome, Stephen." Darcella stood up again. "I'd better go now. I have a lot of things to accomplish before I leave town. I'm on duty up until the day before I get on the road."

Stephen briefly took Darcella by the hand. "I hope you get plenty of rest before you get behind the wheel. By the way, have you heard anything about the smoke-jumper training?"

Darcella gave a low, guttural laugh. "Just another pipe dream gone up in smoke. No pun intended. To tell you the truth, I was beginning to chicken out. I began to see the real danger in the career change I was applying for. Then I got the emergency call from my family. I guess we can say that it was the deciding factor. I don't know which one is my worst fear. The training or being around my family on a regular basis. Either way the fear factor weighs in heavily."

There's that all-consuming word again, Stephen thought. *Fear.*

Darcella turned into Stephen and gave him a warm hug. "If you're ever in Biloxi, please give me a call. I plan to keep the same cell number."

Stephen smiled. "I'll keep that in mind, Darcy. You do the same. If you ever need anything, don't hesitate to call and let me know. I'm glad we're able to stay friends."

Darcella began to make her way to the front door and Stephen followed behind her. As she reached the exit, she grabbed hold of the doorknob. "Thanks for being so understanding with me, Stephen. Remaining friends with you means a lot to me. I wish you and Farrah the best. I really mean that." Before stepping off the porch, Darcella looked back at Stephen and smiled.

"Please be safe, Darcy." Completely happy with the outcome of their final and amicable farewell, Stephen blew Darcella a kiss.

Closure had finally been achieved for the once happily engaged couple.

Chapter 12

A major hurricane had slammed full-force into the city of New Orleans and the surrounding areas. The storm, Hurricane Katrina, once recorded as a Category 5 hurricane, was being reported as one of the deadliest, costliest hurricanes in the history of the United States. The storm had weakened considerably before making its second landfall as a Category 3 storm in southeast Louisiana.

The storm surge alone had caused major or catastrophic damage along the coastlines of Louisiana, Mississippi and Alabama, to include the cities of Mobile, Biloxi, Gulfport and Slidell. Levees separating Lake Pontchartrain from New Orleans were also breached by the surge, flooding approximately eighty percent of the city and many areas of neighboring parishes.

Stephanie still couldn't believe what travesties had happened over the past few days. The things she had constantly viewed on television had her heartsick. The continuous bad news was downright startling, not to mention horribly upsetting and mind-boggling. Never before in her life had she seen such total devastation. Although she'd heard serious weather warnings throughout the past week or so, she really hadn't expected what had actually occurred.

Malachi, Maxwell and Gregory had also voiced their deep concern over the possibility of New Orleans being trounced by inclement weather months before it had occurred. However, Stephanie had known firsthand about all the weather forecasts that had gone totally unrealized in past years. People just seemed to want to remain optimistic rather than prepare for the worst.

Stephanie's biggest dilemma was her missing family. She hadn't heard a word from her father and uncle or her fiancé. Stephen had been deployed to Louisiana less than seventy-two hours ago, but she had only heard from him twice since he'd left her home that morning. He had stopped by to see her and Farrah before leaving for New Orleans with the rest of his crew.

As Stephanie reached for the telephone, she kept her eyes fastened on the television set, repeatedly cringing at what was happening before her very eyes. After dialing the stored code for Malachi's home phone number, she lifted the receiver to her ear. Hearing the recorded message for the umpteenth time, which informed her that the circuits were still busy, made her crazy. Even though she knew she wasn't going to get through she made several more attempts, feeling as if she had to keep trying regardless of how futile it was. It was the only way to keep her sanity.

Stephanie nervously chewed on her lower lip as she sat back to continue listening to the news. This can't be happening, she thought. But it was. And it wasn't over yet, not by a long shot. She would never forget Hurricane Alicia, another major hurricane that had left behind a lot of major destruction all over the Houston area in 1983.

Feeling that she needed to talk with someone before she went completely crazy, Stephanie phoned Farrah, who answered on the second ring. "Are you watching the news?"

Farrah sighed with dismay. "Yeah, I am. It's awful. I've

been waiting to hear from Stephen but to no avail. Have you heard from any of your family members or Gregory?"

Stephanie sighed. "Not a word. Katrina is a killer hurricane, Farrah. I'm so freaking scared. What am I going to do if I can't get in touch with my loved ones over there?"

"Pray, Stephanie, pray. The other line is beeping. Maybe it's Stephen. Hold on."

It wasn't Stephen. Farrah's heart fell. The call was from Janie Erie, a physical therapist who worked at the same health care center as she did. Janie began to tell Farrah that her husband, Darren, was thinking of going to New Orleans to look for his family. The lady sounded terribly fearful for both her husband and his unheard-from family members. Farrah felt bad for not being able to talk to Janie in depth at that very moment, but she promised to call her coworker back as soon as she finished her conversation with Stephanie.

"No, Farrah," Stephanie cried into the phone upon hearing Farrah's voice. She hated the news she'd just heard. "Oh, my God," she screamed, "it's getting much worse over there. They're reporting power outages all over the city. The levee has caused impossible flooding since it first gave way. A good portion of the city is underwater."

"I'm listening to what's being said on the television. I'm going to have to go in a few minutes, Stephanie. I really need to call one of my coworkers back. Her husband's family lives in New Orleans. Janie is beside herself with worry because he's talking about going down there to try to locate the missing members."

"Going there may not do him any good, especially if the authorities won't let him enter the area where his family resides. It may no longer exist. Wow. Just talking about this makes me ill, so I can only imagine how the people feel who are actually living inside this nightmare."

"I know what you mean. I'm going to go now, but I'll call you back shortly." Farrah felt so sorry for Stephanie. The depth of her agony was easy to discern in her voice. Farrah prayed that her dear friend wouldn't suffer the kind of loss she had. "Will you be okay, Stephanie?"

"I sure hope so. Please don't forget to call me back, Farrah." Stephanie instantly disconnected the line. Once she heard the dial tone buzz in her ear, she tried Malachi's phone number yet again. Same recording came on, continuing to frustrate her to no end.

Stephanie's heart was emotionally full now. As she let the tears roll down her cheeks unchecked, she tried to imagine what was happening with her father, uncle and her fiancé. *Where were they?* Upon realizing she hadn't even tried her uncle Max's phone numbers, she did just that. Circuits were still busy. With all the downed power lines, it looked as if she might never get through to her family, sure that she wasn't the only one trying to get a read on their loved ones. Phone calls to homes, businesses and cells would all be in vain. All calls would go unanswered.

Stephanie looked over at the wall calendar, tracing it back to the date of infamy. *August 29, 2005.* She wanted to forever remember the date that Hurricane Katrina had unleashed her wildest fury against the gulf coast.

New Orleans was being utterly destroyed and Stephanie's family was out there lost somewhere in the destruction. The loss of numerous lives had already been reported. Malachi, Maxwell and Gregory were either dead or alive. She prayed for the latter. Her father and the Saxtons lived in one of the wealthiest areas of the city, but that didn't mean a darn thing.

Hurricane Katrina obviously was no respecter of wealth or the lack thereof.

SSM Trudeaux Inc. was located in one of the low-lying parishes, Stephanie recalled, which could mean that it was probably already under water. The building housing the corporation was more than likely a goner. Ten acres of land surrounded the business site, where future developments had already been planned out for more expansion. According to Malachi, the company had grown tremendously over the past ten years, though he had purchased all the land at the same time. God only knew the fate of the communications conglomerate.

Stephanie realized she had another long night ahead of her, like countless of other folks. There were probably people all over the country, possibly all over the world, who were worried about what had happened to family members who resided in New Orleans. The city had been seized by a powerful storm. It was hard to believe that wind and rain could wreak this sort of havoc against the southern coastlines. It was even harder to see it unfold right before your eyes.

Stephanie hated that communication wasn't possible between her and Stephen. He had promised her he'd look for their loved ones whenever an opportunity arose. He was as devastated as his sister was. To lose their folks now, after just being united with them, would be a terrible loss that neither sibling wanted to endure. Both twins felt that their father and uncle were still alive, but they desperately needed affirmation. The Trudeaux twins would not rest until their beloved family members were accounted for.

Gregory had been in Houston just a few days before the hurricane had hit his native city. The entire Trudeaux family had had breakfast with him the morning of his departure. He had known the possibility of pending danger before he'd made the decision to return to New Orleans, just as Malachi and Maxwell had known about the dangerous situation. There was no way Gregory could've stayed behind knowing his family was there.

Stephanie would have gone home with Gregory had he allowed her to, but he'd seen it as far too dangerous to take that kind of risk, especially if the pending threats just happened to become a reality. She couldn't help wondering if the Saxton suite of offices had also been lost in the storm. It was hard for her to recall which part of the city they were located in. It was difficult for her to remember a lot of things in her harried state of mind. At any rate, offices could be rebuilt. The loss of human life could never be restored, at least not until the Second Coming. God only knew why this indescribable disaster had struck her fiancé's beloved city.

As Stephanie's thoughts turned to Ms. Aretha, just someone else near and dear to her heart, she fought to remain calm. She and Gregory's mom had been getting along famously, which had caused her to look forward to their daily telephone conversations. She had grown very fond of her future mother-in-law and could hardly wait to see her again. If only she could hear from someone down that way. If only the phone lines would miraculously come back up. Stephanie would give anything to speak to any member of her family or Gregory's.

"God," Stephanie cried out, gripping the arm of the chair, "please bring everyone back safely. I need my fiancé and my family. All of them."

Gregory had done his level best to calm Aretha down, but nothing had worked. His mother was completely distraught, nervous and extremely tearful. Not knowing where Gregory II and Grant were had taken its toll on her. For a lady so strong, Aretha was unable to hold it together in this instance. Gregory had kept his out-of-control mother from slugging a police officer earlier. The officer's attitude had been terrible, but she couldn't just go around punching out cops. Thanks to the Saxton prominence, she'd been spared. Of course there was no jail left to lock up anyone in. That made New Orleans an even higher security risk.

After a physically exhausted, emotionally drained Aretha had finally fallen asleep in Gregory's arms, her son had placed her on one of the makeshift cots they'd been assigned to inside the Superdome. The conditions inside the humongous sports arena were darn near unbearable. He'd heard there were major leaking problems there and that they might have to move everyone to another location. It was hot and muggy and folks were crammed up together like canned sardines. Gregory was grateful for what little they did have in the way of accommodations because there was a host of people who had been left with nothing, zilch.

It was unbelievable to Gregory that crime was running rampant in a city under siege, crippling it even more. Rather than being of assistance in this horrific situation, criminals were taking advantage of the city's vulnerability. Looting was taking place all over the city. Rifling through and stealing salvageable items from residents and businesses was beyond criminal. He'd lost count of the folks he'd seen running down the streets with things they'd stolen from one place or another. It was such a shame that folks were committing crimes at a time like this.

Gregory was terribly worried about how Stephanie was holding up. He hadn't been able to get through to her by phone and he was almost sure she'd been trying her best to contact him.

Communication was just another huge problem for the city. He didn't know how long his fiancée would be able to hold up if she didn't hear from him relatively soon. If she hadn't heard from her father and uncle, either, he figured she was driving herself crazy with worry.

No news was definitely not good news in this particular instance.

Gregory's longtime fears had come home to roost. It hadn't been so long ago he'd told Stephanie what would happen if a Category 3 or 4 hurricane hit New Orleans. Practically the entire Gulf Coast region had been manhandled by a destructive weather pattern named Katrina.

Although it had been inevitable, he still wished it hadn't occurred.

As Aretha began to stir, Gregory rushed to her side, kneeling down in front of the cot. Her hand reached out and held his in a death grip. Her eyes were wide with fear and desperation.

"Son, I'm terrified. What if we've lost your dad and brother? What will we do?"

Gregory gave Aretha a soothing hug. "We can't allow ourselves to think like that, Mother. We just have to continue to pray." Seeing his mother out of whack like this had him gravely concerned. This was a woman who had no problem tackling and pinning down anyone and anything that dared to come up against her. She was a fierce competitor.

Gregory had to wonder how much of what was happening with Aretha was caused by guilt. She had treated her estranged husband with total disregard—and now he was missing. If she was capable of feeling any guilt at all, Grant had to be included in it. She'd done her oldest son a great disservice by spoiling him to the point of nearly making him totally worthless.

Although Grant was recovering nicely from his addictions and finally doing things the right way, he still had a lot of serious issues to overcome. Gregory felt confident that his brother would be fine, but he also knew how much hard work it was going to take. He had just told Grant how proud he was of him during the meal the family had shared together last evening. He'd also let his brother know how much he loved him. Gregory was grateful for that conversation.

It was funny how things could change in a twinkling of an eye. The Saxton family had taken a meal together last evening for the first time in nearly three years. That his father had actually accepted Aretha's invitation to dinner had been quite surprising to both her and her two sons. She had later admitted to Gregory that she hadn't expected Gregory II to darken her doorstep again, not in this life. Aretha hadn't ever been one to give up on something easily.

Had the Saxton family dining together been an omen of some sort? Was it a good sign or a bad one? Gregory could only speculate.

Aretha had thoroughly enjoyed herself. She'd even made mention of how much it pleased her to have all three of her handsome men together under one roof. That she had prepared her husband's favorite foods hadn't gone unnoticed by Gregory II or his two sons.

Aretha had been in her element for sure, spicy and pert as ever.

"Stephanie? Son, have you been able to reach her yet?"

Gregory shook his head from side to side. "Lines are still down. I was getting beside myself with worry over her so I had to turn it over to God, Mother. She's at least safe. I know that much. It's her emotional state I'm concerned with. Her family means everything to her. If she were to lose them now, I hate to even think of what'd she'd go through."

Aretha smiled gently as she clicked her tongue. "Follow your own advice, son. We can't think anything but positive thoughts. But I do need to say this. I'm terribly sorry for the way I've treated my husband and you children. I know I don't wear remorse well, but I do feel it. It's hard for me to express what's in the depth of my soul. Please know that I'm trying to make things right with God, son. I pray for His forgiveness on a daily basis. I know there are consequences for me to bear and I'm willing to accept them no matter how dire. If I get another chance at it, I promise to show your father how sorry I am. Really show him my deep regret."

Gregory kissed Aretha on her forehead. "I'm sure he'll appreciate that, Mother. I think your failure to show any amount of regret is the one thing that holds Dad back from you. Pride always goes before a fall. As for taking my own advice, I promise to try to stay optimistic. I just desperately need to hear Dad's, Grant's and Stephanie's voices. That also goes for Uncle Mal and Uncle Max. Everything will be all right with me once I know where they are."

"We're going to find them all. We have to believe that, Gregory."

"I agree, Mother. We also have to pray incessantly. God *will* hear us."

Gregory took a good look at their surroundings. In this huge place were some of the saddest faces he'd ever seen. People appeared to be lost and without hope. Babies and little children were crying and mothers were doing their best to console. Teenagers seemed dazed. Men paced the floor, looking both worried and fearful, as if they didn't know how to begin to help their families. Tears in his eyes, Gregory bowed his head to pray for God's tender mercies.

Stephanie couldn't stop sobbing as she slipped into a pair of white shorts and a T-shirt. She still hadn't heard a word from her family members or Gregory and she just couldn't take the deafening silence any longer. Thinking she had to pull it together long enough to make it over to Farrah's house, she dried her eyes with the heels of her hands. She had to talk with someone and her next-door neighbor was the nearest person and her dearest friend.

Josefina and Sarah had also called Stephanie earlier to voice their concerns about the residents of New Orleans and to ask questions about the two men they cared so much about, but she hadn't been able to offer them a smidgen of information. The two ladies had sounded as miserable as she felt. She had been praying fervently to at least hear something from Stephen, but he had warned her that his work shifts might be endless and that communication might not be possible for days in a city with no power. All she knew how to do to help out was keep praying.

Stephanie grabbed her keys off the hall tree as she headed for the front door. Not bothering to set the house alarm, she walked the short distance to Farrah's home. After ringing the doorbell, she waited with bated breath for her friend to respond. When it seemed as if it were taking her forever to come to the door, she became agitated and antsy. Just as

Stephanie thought about going around to the back entrance, Farrah finally answered the bell.

"It's your sister," Farrah said into the mouthpiece of the phone she held in her hand.

Realizing that Farrah had Stephen on the line, Stephanie began to babble incoherently.

Seeing her friend's distress, but unable to understand a word she'd said, Farrah stepped outside and handed Stephanie the portable phone. "Calm down, sweetie. The lines are really weak and your brother won't understand what you're saying if you're crying."

Stephanie's entire body trembled as she put the phone to her ear. "Stephen," she cried, "are you okay? Do you have any information on Dad and the others?"

"I'm fine, but I don't have any news on our family or Gregory and his. I do know that Dad's house is a bit damaged, but Uncle Max's is a total loss, a goner. We made it over to both places earlier today. You'd never believe what's going on down here. I can't even find the right words to tell you how bad it really is. It's much worse than anything you can begin to imagine. Uncle Max will probably be devastated by what's happened to his place."

"Losing a home would devastate anyone." Stephanie felt awful for Maxwell, but if he was alive everyone could live through the loss of his home. "Oh, Stephen, are you really okay?"

"Just fatigued beyond comprehension. The entire crew is frazzled down to the bone. I'll be glad when this is all over, but we can't think of leaving here until things are under control. You'd be surprised at how many city employees have walked off the job, from police officers to bus drivers and a host of others. Listen, I've got to get going. I'm on radio communication. Let me say goodbye to Farrah before this connection is lost. I love you, dear sister."

"I love you, too, Stephen," Stephanie sobbed. "Please stay out of harm's way."

Feeling somewhat relieved, Stephanie handed Farrah the phone before seating herself on the top step of Farrah's front porch. She put her face into her hands and cried, thanking God all the while for Stephen's safety.

Knowing that at least her brother was safe had lifted a tremendous burden off Stephanie's heart. If it were in his power, she knew Stephen would do his very best to find the others. He wouldn't stop until he found them or learned something about their whereabouts. As Stephanie fervently prayed for the Saxton family, she felt optimistic that all of them were alive and well. She couldn't allow herself to believe otherwise. Their fate was solely in God's hands.

Farrah sat down on the step next to Stephanie and looped her arm through her friend's. A few moments of silence seemed necessary in Farrah's opinion. Stephanie was still completely overwhelmed by the lack of news regarding the rest of her family, though it seemed she'd found some semblance of relief in hearing from her brother. Yet her tears hadn't stopped falling.

It was hard for Farrah to think of all the sadness that had occurred in such a short span of time. The death of the Anderson twins had brought Stephen to his knees. He had also lost his fiancée to her fears. Helen had gone home to be with the Lord. Then there was the horrific Hurricane Katrina whirling into New Orleans, devastating thousands and thousands of people.

So many folks residing on the Gulf Coast had been left homeless and alone. Children had been separated from their loved ones, along with other family members. Just the thought of not having electricity or phone service was horrifying. Farrah had to wonder if the end time was near. Was Jesus preparing for His return? She knew that she'd be one of many who'd welcome Him with open arms. It was high time for all the pain and suffering to end.

Stephanie reached out and briefly rested her hand on Farrah's knee. "You can't imagine what's going on inside of me. I'm overcome with fear and grief at the loss of so many precious lives. What's being reported on the news is absolutely gut-wrenching. How will our people ever rebuild their lives? So many of them have lost everything."

Farrah lightly bumped Stephanie with her shoulder. "Don't forget how resilient us black folks are. If anyone can make a comeback, we can. Slavery didn't get us so far down that we couldn't arise again, and neither will Katrina. Of course it won't be easy to regroup, but I'm confident in the courage and fortitude of our people, Stephanie."

Stephanie had to nod in agreement. Farrah's comments had certainly caused her spirit to suddenly soar. Optimism in the face of adversity and tragedy was alive and well. Farrah had just lost the person nearest and dearest to her, yet she was hopeful. Stephanie was amazed by all the possibilities that still existed. "You've said a mouthful, Farrah. I feel empowered by it. We can't ever give up, even when it looks hopeless. Can we have a moment of prayer?"

Without passing comment, Farrah bowed her head and closed her eyes.

"Lord," Stephanie began, "we need you today and every day. Your children are suffering, yet we know you'll take care of us. The citizens of New Orleans and the other affected cities need to feel your powerful presence. Please touch each and every one of us right where we are, right now, at this very moment. Give us the strength and courage to do whatever it takes to help those caught up in our nation's tragedy. Let us willingly open up our hearts and our bank accounts to those in need. Let us not turn away our brothers and sisters who are in desperate need. Lord, I ask that you grant us peace that passes all understanding. In Jesus' name I pray."

Farrah hugged Stephanie warmly. "That was beautiful. We should start an Internet prayer. We can have people all over the world praying for everyone affected by Katrina."

"That's a good idea, Farrah. We can send out the first prayer later on today." Stephanie gripped Farrah's hand tightly. "How did Stephen really sound to you?"

"Overwrought, but he sounds as if he's coping. He called you first, but he got your answering machine. He was hoping you were over here. He was terribly worried about you. Stephen is also worried about the family. He sounded better to me after he spoke with you."

"I'm happy about that, Farrah. He's been through so much lately. It can't be easy for him to be away from home at a time like this, especially when our family is also missing. He's dealing with death once again. We definitely have to keep him in constant prayer."

"Did Stephen tell you that he's worried about Darcella and her family? Biloxi, Mississippi, was hit pretty hard, too."

"He didn't mention anything about it to me, but I'm glad he said something to you. Stephen is trying hard to be real honest and up front about everything, especially his feelings. He's no longer afraid of the truth. I'm not surprised that he would care what happens to Darcella and her family. That's just the kind of person my brother is."

Farrah smiled gently. "Neither am I surprised. That's why he's so special. I've seen a lot of personal growth in Stephen. He's such a caring individual. He didn't want his concern for Darcella to upset me, but he thought I should know that's he's going to try to reach her. Lucky for him, he has her parents' phone number. He doesn't remember how it came into his possession, since he's never called them. But he has it stored in his cell phone."

"It might not do him any good since the phone service is so out of whack. But that won't stop him from trying to find some means of communication," Stephanie commented.

Stephanie informed Farrah that she knew how Stephen had come into possession of the phone number. When he and Darcella had visited Biloxi a while back, he had gone out to

the store for something. Darcella had stored the number in his cell just in case he'd gotten lost.

"That makes sense," Farrah remarked. "Anyway, I hope he's able to reach out to her. He really needs to know if the Colemans are okay. I also know he still cares for Darcy."

Stephanie smiled. "That's Stephen for you. I'm glad they ended their relationship on a positive note. I really hope Darcella gets her life back on the right track. She hasn't called me but once since she left, and that was to apologize for how she acted at my house."

"I recall you telling me about it. I hope Darcy finds happiness, too." Farrah blushed. "I can't believe how nicely things are going for Stephen and me. We agreed to take things slow, but I'm ready to hit the speed-dial button. But I won't. Losing his friendship is not in my plans."

Stephanie chuckled despite her melancholy mood. "Smart girl. I just want you both to be happy, apart or together. Happiness is all I've ever wanted for my brother and my best friend."

"We both know that, Stephanie. I admire the fact that you didn't take sides with any of us in this situation. Even though there's no longer a love triangle, Stephen and I will continue to move at a snail's pace for as long as he wants it that way. We love being friends."

Stephanie looked doubtful. "Giving him limitless time isn't such a good idea. You've already waited on him forever. You can't let him think you're at his beck and call. He won't respect that. Most men don't. You have to set boundaries if you want more than friendship."

"I want more, but I'll wait on him, Stephanie. Patiently. I want it to be right for both of us. If we're to have a future together, we can't rush it. I'm glad we're taking Bible study classes together. He says if we try to do everything God's way, we can't go wrong."

Stephanie grinned. "Okay, okay, I concede. Only Farrah knows what's best for Farrah." Stephanie wrinkled her nose.

"I'm suddenly hungry. I haven't been able to eat all that much since this hurricane nightmare began. Let's go to my house and grab a sandwich or something."

"I can definitely agree to that, Stephanie. Can I suggest that we not watch the news while we eat? It's only going to take away our appetites."

"It'll be hard, but I think it's a great idea. My brain is already oversaturated with too much information. I just want my family back home safe and sound, Farrah. That's all I want."

Smiling, Farrah lifted Stephanie's chin with her two fingers. "That's what we all want."

The smell of death was all around Stephen. His nerves were stretched to the absolute limit and he was so tired he could hardly see straight, but he knew he had to keep up with the others. The numerous teams had been in a rescue mode for the past thirty-six hours. He'd lost count of how many dead bodies they'd found. How many more deceased persons would he have to look at before this was all over with? His heart broke every time they made a recovery, but it also rejoiced later, after Stephen saw that it wasn't one of his or Gregory's family members.

Stephen truly didn't believe his father and uncle were dead. In fact, he was sure that he'd actually feel it deep down inside if it were true. Malachi and Maxwell Trudeaux were alive somewhere in this godforsaken place. He was willing to bet his life savings on it.

Stephen figured his father couldn't be dead. God wouldn't allow that to happen, not after he'd moved mountains and erected bridges to bring them together. God had crumbled all the concrete walls that Stephen had built around his heart to keep Malachi out. The Lord hadn't brought them together just to tear them apart. That was too cruel of an act for a loving God.

Stephen desperately needed Malachi to be alive. He

wanted his father alive and well as much for Stephanie as for himself. He wouldn't be able to stand seeing his sister devastated yet again over the loss of a parent. If the truth was known, neither of them was over their mother's death. "No, God, not Dad, too. Please bring everyone home," he cried, not caring who heard him.

Nightmares had forced Stephanie out of bed much earlier than she would have normally arisen. The menacing scenes that had played out in her sleep had been terrifying. Images of dying people all around her had scared her the most. The heart-piercing screams inside her head had caused her to awaken with a start.

After Stephanie had showered and dressed in loose, casual clothing, the next thing she'd done was to grab the morning newspaper off the front porch. She had then headed straight for the kitchen, where she'd made herself a cup of coffee and a slice of toast under the gas broiler.

The bold headlines in the newspaper spoke to the mass destruction of New Orleans. Stephanie thought she should wait until later to read the news so she wouldn't be depressed this early in the morning, but her curiosity instantly got the better of her. She had to know what had gone on down in New Orleans throughout the night. One thing she already knew was that her brother was struggling badly. Stephanie had felt Stephen's pain in spades all night long.

On August 28, shortly after Katrina had been upgraded to a Category 5 storm, Mayor Ray Nagin ordered the first ever mandatory evacuation of the city, calling Katrina "a storm that most of us have long feared." The government had also established several "refuges of last resort" for citizens who could not leave the city, Stephanie read from the *Houston Chronicle*.

After reading for several minutes, Stephanie was thoroughly disgusted and deeply saddened by the entire matter. She laid down the newspaper and pushed it aside. The urge to go into the family room and turn on the television was overwhelming, but she knew she'd only hear more bad news. Nothing good would probably ever come out of this tragedy. Too much had been lost and the statistics were still mounting.

As Stephanie's thoughts turned to her loved ones, she got up and removed the portable phone from its wall station. Before she could begin dialing, the phone rang. Upon hearing Gregory's voice, she fell to her knees from the sheer shock of it. *He was alive. Thank God he was alive.* "Are you okay? What's going on down there? How's your family? Has anyone seen my father and uncle?" Stephanie had gushed all that out without taking a single breath.

"Whoa, slow down, my love! My mother and me are the only ones I can speak about. We're both fine. I don't know where anyone else is. We're at the Superdome, but we're going to be transported elsewhere sometime today. I don't know where we're going yet."

Gregory's voiced had cracked and he needed a moment to compose himself. He tried to speak again, but nothing came out. His emotions were burgeoning out of control. This was so unlike him, but he couldn't hide his vulnerability. Facing death and destruction was no joke.

"Are you still there, Gregory? What's happening? Is something bad going on?" Stephanie gripped a section of her hair, tugging gently at it, as if it might bring her some comfort. "Gregory, please talk to me!"

"I'm…here, Stephanie. Just suddenly hit by some powerful emotions. We're okay right now. I need you to hold on to that thought. I need and love you so much. I'm trying to get to Houston. Is it okay for me to bring my mother with me?"

"Are you kidding?"

The line suddenly went dead.

Stephanie panicked instantly, staring at the phone in utter disbelief. She then became upset with herself for not an-

swering his last question in a more direct way. A resounding "yes" would've worked nicely. Of course he could bring his mother to her home. Had he really expected her to say anything but yes? She couldn't imagine him thinking otherwise.

Looking as if she was scared to put the phone down in case it rang again, Stephanie held on to it like it were a lifeline. Praying for Gregory to call back just might work, she considered. Although moments earlier she had believed no good could come from the hurricane, she felt differently now. Gregory's and Aretha's lives had been spared. She quickly reminded herself to continue looking for the silver lining in every situation, just as she'd done pre-Katrina. There *was* always a silver lining, though it was difficult to see it in the throes of a catastrophe.

Despite Stephanie praying for such, the ringing phone had her heart beating wildly inside her chest. She wasted no time in answering the bell, hoping it was Gregory calling back. If it wasn't him, she hoped the caller had good news. "Gregory," she cried out. "Before we say anything else, yes, please bring your mother here with you. I know it hasn't been all that long, but have you found out where you're going yet?"

"They are sending a lot of people to the Astrodome there in Houston. We're on the list for the next bus, which leaves in less than an hour. I'll call you from there so you can pick us up. I find it hard to believe I'm coming home to you."

"I can't wait to see you. Give your mother my love. I'll have everything prepared for your arrival. Got any special requests?"

"Only one. I need for you to leap into my arms and never let me go. Stephanie, we need to get married as soon as possible. We shouldn't wait much longer. Life is so fragile. So is time."

"I agree with you, Gregory. We'll work that all out once we're back together. Any word on your father and Grant?"

"None. What about your family?"

"No news."

"The line is breaking up again. God is the only one who could've hooked this call up. There was no other way to get through. I love you, Stephanie. See you later. God willing."

God *was* willing, Stephanie thought, dropping down on the sofa. That He'd saved Gregory's life was evidence enough of that. She ran a nervous hand through her already disheveled hair, silently thanking God, tearfully praising the Master for delivering her fiancée and his mother from the dark shadows of death. "If it's not too much to ask, please let me hear something from my family. My sanity is hanging by a mere thread. I desperately need answers."

Hoping to hear news about the caravan of buses from New Orleans coming to Houston, Stephanie picked up the remote control and turned on the television. Was it possible that Malachi and Maxwell could be on one of the buses? She sure hoped so. That would be another miracle.

Stephanie had to ask herself why she believed the two brothers were together when the storm had hit. After thinking about it, she assumed it was because they'd been together the last time she'd spoken with them over the phone. It seemed to her that all families would come together at a time like this, especially since there'd been numerous warnings, televised and otherwise. Stephanie imagined families scrambling to be together.

Malachi and Maxwell were so close to each other that Stephanie couldn't imagine them not riding out the storm in one place. Who's place had it been? Maxwell's had been leveled, according to Stephen. "God, please give me a sign that they weren't inside Uncle Max's house." Malachi's home had been spared, but there was no one found there. She felt sure he would've relieved his staff so they could go home and prepare for the pending storm.

Mandatory evacuation didn't mean a thing, Stephanie now knew, since so many had failed to adhere to Mayor

Nagin's order to get out immediately. People had been afraid to leave their homes yet they had to have been terrified to stay behind. Folks' worldly possessions were all inside the residences, which was one of the main reasons people hadn't left as ordered. No transportation to get away in seemed to be another valid excuse for folks to stay put.

Chapter 13

The sudden sound of the doorbell ringing had Stephanie scurrying for the foyer. Although she didn't know who was on the other side of the door she would welcome the company. Being alone at a time like this was absolutely the pits. Seeing Sarah and Josefina standing outside her door instantly brought her a great deal of comfort. "Ladies," she greeted with enthusiasm, "please come on in. It's really good to see you both."

"You sounded so sad on the phone when we talked with you earlier. I told Josefina we should come over and try to cheer you up," Sarah said.

The older women took turns hugging Stephanie warmly, offering her gentle words of encouragement and support over her missing loved ones. Once the greetings were out of the way, Sarah told Stephanie she had to go back outside to bring in the hot meal she'd prepared for the three of them. Stephanie was surprised and pleased so she offered to go outside with Sarah to help out, telling Josefina she could go ahead and make herself comfortable in the family room.

* * *

Stephanie removed three glasses from the kitchen cupboard and filled them with crushed ice from the dispenser located on the refrigerator door. The ladies had asked for Cokes, but she herself was in the mood for the fresh lemonade she'd mixed up earlier. Stephen, Malachi and Maxwell loved her lemonade also and she couldn't help wishing they were there to enjoy a cold glassful with her and Josefina and Sarah. She was sure the two ladies had come to see her because they were as fearful as she was. Neither of them had heard from Malachi or Maxwell.

Stephanie couldn't believe her eyes as she looked at the food Sarah had laid out on the breakfast bar. "You remembered my favorites! Two thumbs-up for you, Ms. Sarah."

Liver and onions were Stephanie's very favorite foods. That Sarah had remembered what she'd told her such a long time ago was astounding to her. With Stephanie's favorites in mind, Sarah had prepared the dinner with all the delectable trimmings. Large buttermilk biscuits to sop up the gravy had been a must in Sarah's opinion. Sautéed spinach also went well with the meat entrée. Thickly buttered mashed potatoes were another great addition. To round things out and bring in a touch of healthier foods a tossed salad and fresh low-cal dressing had been prepared.

As much as Sarah was a stickler for healthy eating, she thought that splurging every now and then was okay, as long as it was done in moderation. There definitely were times when folks needed comfort foods. This sorrowful ordeal was a perfect time for such. This was Sarah's way of trying to comfort Maxwell's only niece, whom Sarah knew he simply adored.

Stephanie was hungrier than she'd initially thought. The sandwich she'd had earlier with Farrah was long gone. She'd been so sure that she wouldn't be able to do justice to Sarah's fine home-cooked meal. That would have been such a shame since everything had tasted so good.

Once the meal was consumed, Josefina and Sarah helped Stephanie clear the table. Because Sarah had brought everything over in throwaway plastic containers, there wasn't anything to wash but the glasses and silverware, which Josefina loaded into the dishwasher.

The three ladies then retired to the family room, where Stephanie turned on the television.

Everyone was eager to hear the latest news on the dire situation in New Orleans.

Five minutes into the news coverage it appeared that things were still going from bad to worse to incredibly unbelievable. It was like watching a horror picture show. Seeing folks being airlifted into helicopters on some sort of shaky ladders had the women on the edge of their seats.

Josefina got out of her seat and went over and sat down next to Stephanie on the sofa. She took hold of the young woman's hand. "You look so pale, dear. Are you all right?"

Stephanie pursed her lips. "I don't know if I'll ever be all right again. I'm trying so hard to be brave, but I'm not doing such a good job of it. I can actually feel my insides shriveling up."

"I know the feeling, Stephanie," Josefina soothed. "I'm terribly worried about your father and uncle, too. I know they would've called us by now had they been able to. That fact scares me even more."

Sarah sighed heavily. "We're all scared and we all have good reason to be. What we're seeing on the television is not a theatrical performance. What's happening is all too real. Still, we have to believe that Maxwell and Malachi made it through the storm okay."

Stephanie smiled weakly. "I'm holding on to that belief with all my strength. It's been a long time now since I heard from Stephen. At least it seems so. In reality, only several hours have passed since we last spoke. Still, I hope to hear from him soon."

As if on cue, the phone rang.

It was Gregory calling again. Stephanie knew he couldn't be in Houston already, not unless they'd put him on a flight. "Are you guys on the road to Houston yet?"

"Not yet. There's been a horrific development that will delay us for quite some time." Gregory went on to tell her specifically what the tragic development was.

Stephanie covered her mouth to stifle the scream rising like acid bile in her throat.

The grief-stricken expression on Stephanie's face let Sarah and Josefina know that something else had gone terribly wrong in the personal world of this young woman. The tears falling rapidly from her eyes were further evidence of such. The two friends gripped each other's hands, fearful of what was being said on the other end of the phone line. Both women hoped and prayed that bad news regarding Malachi and Maxwell wasn't the reason for Stephanie's obvious sorrow, yet they knew the possibility of such was very great.

For the next several minutes Stephanie listened carefully to all that Gregory had to say, only nodding every now and then. The story she was being told was overwhelming to her. The horrendous events of this unbelievable nightmare just kept on growing and growing.

Absolutely stunned out of her mind, Stephanie hung up the phone, wondering what else she could've said to Gregory that might've made a difference. Not a darn thing, she concluded. Telling him how sorry she was for him and his family hadn't seemed nearly enough. If only she could be there where he was, to hold him in her arms, to comfort him and let him know how much he was loved. She had a long list of "if only" things she could readily voice.

At the moment, being there with Gregory and for him was an utter impossibility.

Stephanie wiped her eyes before addressing Josefina and Sarah, who looked quite anxious to know what had happened. How she was going to get through this story without breaking down was anyone's guess. "Gregory's brother,

Grant, is dead. He died trying to rescue a young boy who couldn't swim." She stopped for a moment to gain control of her emotions.

According to what Gregory had been told by Reginald Childress, Grant's high-rise apartment manager, who'd seen it all, the kid was thrashing about in the floodwaters, on the verge of drowning, when Grant had jumped in after him. They had both ended up drowning when a powerful under-tow had dragged them below the surface.

Stephanie further explained that both bodies hade been recovered and that Gregory now had to make a positive ID. Gregory had run into Grant's manager inside the Super-dome shortly after he'd talked to Stephanie the second time. That's when Reginald had told Gregory what had happened to Grant. Reginald had also been able to tell Gregory where the remains of his brother had been taken because he'd assisted the fire-rescue team in the recovery mission.

There still was no word on the whereabouts of Gregory II. However, it seemed evident that father and son hadn't been together right before, during or after the tragedy. Reginald had only seen Grant during the evacuation process that had been conducted at the posh high-rise apartment complex. He couldn't recall seeing the senior Saxton, whom he also knew by sight, since Gregory II often visited with his son at his place. Grant had introduced both his father and his brother to Reginald when Grant had first moved into the recently constructed building.

Gregory had said that everything was so screwed up in New Orleans. He told Stephanie that he had no idea how he was going to tell his mother about the death of her first-born. Aretha was already in bad shape over not knowing the fate of her estranged husband and son.

This personal tragedy was going to make things much worse for Aretha. She truly adored her eldest son. Grant's death made no sense to Gregory, since his brother had begun to find himself. That he'd died trying to save a life was a tribute to the man he was striving to become.

All of Gregory's feelings were perfectly understandable to Stephanie. She was heartsick for the entire Saxton family. There was no comfort to be found in the death of a loved one. Stephanie and Stephen had already experienced what the Saxtons were about to go through.

Through the haze of sleep Stephanie looked over at the bedside clock. The large red numbers were normally easy to see, but her eyes were still half closed. The phone ringing at this hour was terrifying to her at 3:16 a.m., even more so with all that was going on with her family.

Hoping for good news rather than bad, Stephanie sucked in a deep breath at the same time she picked up the phone. "Morning," she said, sounding very drowsy.

There was a long moment of silence. Then…

"My dear, it's Dad."

The emotion-filled voice rang resoundingly in Stephanie's ears. She gulped hard. As she opened her mouth again, nothing came out but gasps of air. Her heart was palpitating like crazy. Malachi was on the other end. Her daddy was calling. "Daddy," she finally managed to cry out, "thank God you're okay! You *are* okay, aren't you? Uncle Max, is he with you?"

Malachi choked back his emotions. "We're together, my dear, and we are just fine, although extremely rattled. We're at a rest-stop right outside the city limits of Houston. The bus driver is taking us to the Astrodome, where we'll be temporarily sheltered."

Stephanie tried to stay calm, fighting hard not to lose it emotionally. She knew that a miracle was happening at this very moment. "I'm there, Dad, as soon as I can slip into some clothes. No shelter for you and Uncle Max. I'm coming down to the Astrodome to get you."

"It's so late, Stephanie. We can stay in the shelter until daylight. I don't want you out and about this time of morning. It's still dark outside."

"Nonsense! Besides, Josefina and Sarah spent the night with me. We all needed to be together for support. I'm sure they'll be willing to come down to the Astrodome with me."

Malachi was glad that his daughter wasn't alone. "That'll be a tight squeeze, daughter. Five people crammed into one car might be a little uncomfortable. Don't you think?"

"We'll manage, Dad. In fact, I can use Stephen's SUV since he left it here in my driveway. I even have my own set of keys," she said on a chuckle, wanting to lighten things up.

"Daughter, Uncle Max and me would like to have a private family reunion. If you insist on coming out so early in the morning, maybe you can leave the ladies asleep. Leave them a note if you think they'll awaken before we get back."

Stephanie understood now. She'd finally gotten it. Her father wanted their first moments back together to be private. A family reunion! She liked the sound of that. Yes, she thought, I can do that. "I finally got your drift, Dad. Can you call my cell when you reach the Astrodome? I'll be somewhere in the vicinity by then. I'm sure there'll be a lot of traffic around there."

"From where we are right now, Stephanie, I guesstimate our arrival time to be about forty-five minutes after we leave here. I should probably call you as soon as we get on the road."

"Call the cell so as not to wake the others. I can't wait to see you and Uncle Max."

"Same here. Hold on a second. Maxwell wants to say hello."

"Hello, my sweet niece. I've missed you so much. Can hardly wait to see you."

The sound of Maxwell's cheerful voice caused Stephanie to start crying. He always operated on a positive note. Knowing that her uncle and father were safe and together made her heart leap with joy. "Missed you, too. I'm looking forward to a big old bear hug, Uncle Max."

"You got it, sweetheart. Drive carefully. Please take your time. No need to rush. Whoever gets to the Astrodome first will wait on the other. We've come through the worst of it already. God has all of our backs. He's been in control of everything from the onset. I love you."

The moment Stephanie disconnected the lines she jumped out of bed and fell down on her knees beside the mattress. She began to pray feverishly. She couldn't thank God enough for keeping her family safe. Everything would really be okay for the Trudeaux family once she heard from Stephen again. Stephanie's tearful prayer of praise lasted for several minutes.

Stephanie was already seated inside her car when the cell phone rang. She didn't have to wonder who was calling at this hour. Malachi had said he'd call her back. "Daddy, I'm pulling the car out of the garage right now. Has the bus started moving toward Houston yet?"

"We're on our way, dear girl. I forgot to ask you earlier if you've heard from Gregory. Also, how's your brother? Trying to communicate during this storm has been a bear, even for a man who's made his fortune in the communications business."

"Tell me about it! Both of the guys are fine, Dad. Stephen has actually been deployed to New Orleans, but he's safe. Gregory is safe, too. I'll fill you in on everything when I see you. Love you. Bye for now."

Stephanie was relieved that Malachi hadn't asked about Grant and Gregory II. She wouldn't think of telling her father about Grant's demise over the telephone. That would've been too painful for all of them. There'd already been enough stress and strife in the lives of the two Trudeaux brothers. The bad news would just have to wait until later.

There had definitely been more bad stuff going on than anything good, but nothing compared to God's goodness. He had spared the lives of her loved ones. For that act of love, kindness and mercy, Stephanie would always be grateful to the God she loved and served.

* * *

Although it had taken Stephanie a good bit of time to locate her loved ones among the throng of folks milling around the Astrodome, she had finally accomplished her mission. The cell phones had allowed them to keep in close contact, but Malachi had feared his batteries would run down before they finally reached each other. Stephanie had a car battery charger.

The Trudeaux family members embraced one another as if they were long-lost relatives, which had actually been the case not so very long ago. Malachi felt every emotion imaginable as he held his daughter in his arms, squeezing her tightly. He knew that Stephanie had no idea how close she'd come to losing him and her uncle Maxwell. It was a miracle that they had escaped New Orleans with their lives. God was solely responsible for the final outcome.

Malachi and Maxwell had nearly been killed because they'd dared to venture into the Orleans and St. Bernard Parishes to help out some of the Trudeaux friends, employees and their families. The force of the hurricane had ripped the roof right off one of the houses they'd all gathered in to try to make a difference and a smooth transition. What had occurred after the wind had torn through the roof was one big blur to both men, but they'd managed to get out of the house safely, which had been destroyed only minutes later. A lot of prayer and careful machinations had gone into the group of folks reaching higher ground, thus a safer place.

The two brothers had known how much danger some of the areas were in, yet they'd gone there anyway, to coax people into leaving the city. The men had even come there prepared to finance the evacuations, bringing along with them lots of cash. In anticipation of the hurricane hitting New Orleans hard, Malachi and Maxwell had previously withdrawn lots of money for themselves and to distribute to all of those who needed it.

The brothers had also planned to go back to Malachi's

house once they had assisted their friends and employees and anyone else who needed help.

The estate home was a very sound structure and had already weathered many a strong storm so Malachi and Maxwell were sure they'd be safe staying there. Maxwell's house had also withstood strong weather systems, but it was the flooding and the gale-force winds that had wiped it out. Maxwell still wasn't aware that his house had been lost in the hurricane, but he probably wouldn't be the least bit surprised to learn that it had been completely destroyed.

Malachi and Maxwell had to sign a set of papers refusing the shelter as temporary living accommodations before they could leave the area. Lots of precautions had been put in place to safeguard the whereabouts of residents of New Orleans who'd been evacuated to Houston and numerous other places. People had also been required to sign up for the transportation out of New Orleans before the officials had allowed them to board the buses.

The chatting-happily Trudeaux clan held hands as they made their way to Stephanie's car, which was parked a few blocks away. Droves of other folks were arriving as they were leaving, making Stephanie wonder if their loved ones had called them to inform them of their whereabouts, just as her father and uncle had done.

In Stephanie's estimation the entire past several days leading up to this moment had unfolded strangely. No one could've made her believe what had happened to New Orleans and the other coastal cities. No one could've convinced her that her family would be lost for days.

Once everyone was seated and seat belts were securely fastened, Stephanie carefully maneuvered the car out of the tight parking spot. As she headed for Beltway 8, the quickest route to her home, she silently thanked God for everyone and everything. Stephanie was aware that her family being there with her had only been possible through the mercifulness of the Master.

* * *

Sarah and Josefina quickly scrambled for the front door upon hearing the key inserted. The two women were aware of what was going on because Stephanie had left them a detailed note about where'd she gone, just as her father had suggested. However, it was the phone bell that had startled the two ladies out of their peaceful slumber.

Stephen had called to tell Stephanie that he and the rest of the crew were scheduled to depart for Houston later in the day. Instead, he'd told his plans to Sarah, who had only answered Stephanie's phone because of what was going on with the Trudeaux family.

Stephanie, Malachi and Maxwell became overcome with joy at the wonderful news Sarah had shared with them. Knowing that Stephen was safe and sound made their hearts rejoice. All of them were eager to see him; grateful that he would also make it out of New Orleans alive and well. The pending news of Grant's death was still very heavy on Stephanie's mind, but she planned to share it only after she'd fed her family and had made them comfortable.

More heartfelt greetings and hugs were exchanged before Stephanie hustled everyone into the kitchen, where she planned to rustle up some coffee and breakfast. No sooner than she had everyone seated at the table, the doorbell rang. Although it was daylight now it was still only 6:00 a.m. Stephanie figured that it could only be Farrah leaning on her doorbell this time of morning. With her friend in mind, she rushed out to the foyer and threw open the front door.

Farrah, still in her silk pajamas and robe, embraced Stephanie warmly. "Sorry for coming over here so early, but I just got off the phone with your brother. He's coming home today and I wanted to tell you the good news in person. I hope he didn't call before I made it over here."

Stephanie smiled broadly. "I already know about it. He called here extremely early this morning, but I wasn't home."

Farrah scowled. "Where in the devil were you at such an ungodly hour? It was terribly early when Stephen called me."

Stephanie grinned mischievously. "Come on into the kitchen so you can see what I've been doing, Farrah. I think you're going to be pleasantly surprised."

Farrah *was* totally surprised to see Malachi and Maxwell seated at Stephanie's kitchen table, more astounded than anyone would ever know. She was also very pleased about it.

The two men wasted absolutely no time in getting out of their seats and embracing Farrah with warmth and deep affection. Tears of joy slid from Farrah's eyes as she enthusiastically welcomed home Malachi and Maxwell.

Instead of Malachi sitting back down, he walked over to Stephanie and took her hand. "My dear, could we have a moment in private, please?"

Stephanie looked curious. "Of course, Dad. Let's go back into the family room."

"Why don't we just step out here on the back porch? This shouldn't take long."

Stephanie nodded in agreement and then excused herself and Malachi to the others.

Outside where the birds were chirping up a breeze Malachi asked his daughter what was weighing on her mind. He had sensed that there was something wrong and he hadn't been able to wait another second to find out. Stephanie seemed very nervous to him, as well as a bit sad. Since everyone in their family, including Gregory, was alive and accounted for, he wasn't sure what type of misery his daughter was going through, but he knew something had her off kilter.

After Stephanie summoned Maxwell and Farrah to come outside, thinking she should tell everyone at once, she briefly laid her head against Malachi's chest, praying for strength in courage. Once everyone was outside, Stephanie positioned herself in a way that she could address everyone present.

Stephanie folded her hands together and placed them out in front of her. "I'm afraid I have some bad news for you all. It's Grant. He drowned while trying to save a little boy from drowning in the floodwaters. A strong undertow was responsible for their deaths. Gregory called me with the bad news. He and Ms. Aretha are just fine, but they still don't know where Gregory II is. The last time I spoke with Gregory he hadn't yet told his mother about Grant's death."

Farrah had muffled a scream, her heart racing rapidly inside her chest. She felt horrible for the young man who'd done his level best to impress her during their first meeting, glad that she'd been kind to him. Thinking of his grieving family nearly caused her resolve to crack. She knew exactly what they were going through. Although her mother's death couldn't be compared to the tragic way in which Grant had lost his life, it was a significant loss all the same.

Malachi and Maxwell were stunned to the point of speechlessness, looking dumbfounded. This was excruciating news for both brothers. Each of them had witnessed the changes for the better in Grant, had seen his positive growth blossoming right before their eyes. It was awful that his life had been taken away when he was just discovering all the good inside of him and all the wonderful possibilities the world had to offer him.

With tears streaming down his face, Malachi asked everyone to join hands. He then led the small group in a powerful prayer. His love for God was evident in every word that he spoke. Never once did he blame the Almighty for what had occurred in New Orleans or in the other cities. God's will for His children should never be questioned, though it was, all too often.

Stephen's homecoming had been just as wonderful and heartfelt as Malachi's and Maxwell's was. He looked tired and a bit thinner from when he'd first left Houston, but he was alive and in a cheerful mood. Stephanie couldn't help smiling as she watched the interaction between Stephen and Farrah. There was no doubt in her mind that they had fallen in love with each other. The love they held in their hearts for each other was in their eyes.

Stephanie's thoughts quickly turned to Darcella. Stephen had been able to talk with her and she had shared with him that she and everyone in her family was fine. Their residences had also been spared, though there had been some minor damages. Her mother was now receiving chemotherapy and things had gone relatively well for her during and after the surgery. Stephen was happy that Darcella sounded happy and content with the new life she was building in Biloxi. Knowing that she'd be wrapped up in Gregory's tender arms in a short time from now had Stephanie quite excited and fidgety. They'd been apart a long while, way too long for her comfort. Aretha was also coming there with Gregory and she was going to need loads of compassion and understanding from her son and his fiancée.

Grant had already been cremated, but the Saxton family planned to have a private memorial service for him once Gregory II got out of the Houston hospital he'd been sent to from New Orleans. Gregory had finally tracked down Gregory II from information he'd received from some of his father's neighbors. That he'd been relieved to find his dad was an understatement.

Gregory II had gotten his back badly hurt while trying to help some of his elderly neighbors evacuate their home. He would fully recover, but it would take time. Healing from the tragic loss of his firstborn son was going to take much, much longer.

Stephen had his arm around Farrah's shoulders as they sat on the sofa in her home, discussing the time he'd spent in New Orleans. In painstaking detail he had relayed to her all the devastating destruction he'd witnessed down in the Big Easy. It was hard for him not to emote because of all the pain he felt, but he somehow managed to keep a tight rein on himself.

Farrah gently caressed Stephen's face with her fingertips. "I'm so glad you're home. I really missed you. A lot."

Stephen smiled softly. "I missed you, too. I never knew what hell might be like, but I now have a pretty good idea. It can't be much worse than what we saw in New Orleans. Hell on earth is the only way to describe it."

Farrah empathized. "I'm sorry you had to go through all that. You're home now, where things are much better."

"You would think so. Some of the things I experience on my job can also be a lot like hell. I'm alive, though. That's what's important. Gregory's brother wasn't so blessed. It is too bad Grant had to die, especially like that."

"I know what you mean. Did you have a chance to do anything besides all the hard work you did down there?"

"I did a whole lot of thinking, Farrah."

Stephen felt compelled to tell Farrah about some of the things he'd given a lot of thought to. For one thing, he'd given their relationship a lot of consideration. Even though he believed they should still take things slow, he was ready to take things to the next level. He really wanted them to explore what might be in store for their future. Stephen made it a point to stress the fact that he wanted a godly-like relationship, the kind he'd read about in the Bible.

Farrah had liked what Stephen had had to say. She was most interested in his comments about him wanting to take things to another level. She was all for that. "Are you still studying the Bible like you were before your deployment?"

"Every single day. I'm determined to get it right. How about you, Farrah?"

"I don't read the Word every day, but I get a good bit of studying in during the week. We can get back to studying together now that you're back. The scriptures you recommended to me have been very helpful. It looks like there really is a blueprint for personal relationships."

Stephen chuckled. "Following God's plan for us is the problem. But we have to continue to strive for perfection even though we'll never attain it."

"We *can* get close, Stephen. But you're right. We'll never achieve perfection. Has Stephanie mentioned anything to you about her wedding plans?"

"My sister is in a pickle, so to speak. Gregory wants to marry right away and she thinks it might be considered an insult to Grant's memory. However, Grant's parents are all for it."

Farrah nodded. "I can see why she'd be concerned. A wedding so soon after a funeral might be tasteless to some."

"Life goes on, Farrah. Gregory doesn't want to waste any more precious time. Grant's untimely death proves that life can be really short. I can clearly see Gregory's point."

"I see it, too, but I also understand Stephanie's point of view," said Farrah.

"They'll eventually figure it all out. Stephanie and Gregory love each other too much to let anything come between them. They won't let this issue stand in the way of their happiness."

"I agree." Farrah looked into Stephen's eyes. "Are you really over Darcy, Stephen?"

Stephen was genuinely surprised by the pointed query. "That's an interesting question and I'm not sure I know how to answer it."

"A yes or no would take care of it."

Stephen raised an eyebrow. "Yeah, but I think it goes much deeper than that, which requires a more in-depth response. Being over her is different from being over the relationship."

Stephen explained to Farrah that he still loved Darcella as a friend. Sharing a friendship with her would prevent him from being through with her. As for their love affair, he had definitely moved on past that. It had been hard for him to accept their incompatibility issues, but he had now done so.

He went on to say that he was fully accepting of the fact that they wouldn't have had a good marriage because of the children factor. In that regard, he was over Darcella.

This was a good a time as any to talk about all the things that had occurred in each of their lives, Stephen thought. Stephen began telling Farrah that even though there had been a lot of bad things that had happened, there was also much good that had occurred. "You and me, for one." He went on to reveal everything for her.

Stephanie had found the man of her dreams, a godly man. They *would* be married sooner or later. It was just a matter of them deciding on the proper time. Stephanie's business was going very well and was constantly growing. She had experienced a lot of personal growth and she was happier than she'd ever been in her entire life. Life was really good for Stephanie Trudeaux.

The Saxton offices had been lost, but Gregory was willing and able to start all over again. He hadn't ruled out the possibility of starting a practice in Houston, since many of his clients had relocated there. He was also going to help his father rebuild and maintain the New Orleans office. He would have to take the Texas bar, which he wasn't opposed to doing. In Stephanie he had found the love of his life and he wanted to spend the rest of his being in love with her. Gregory Saxton planned on being a wonderful husband to his wife and an extraordinary father to the children in their future.

Malachi and Maxwell were two of the strongest, confident black men that Stephen had ever known. These two brothers had lived incredible lives, thus far. Although Maxwell had lost his home, he wasn't letting it get him down. Maxwell had said that the purchase of the Houston home had been a wise decision, as well as a blessing in disguise. He'd lost his home in New Orleans, but he had his Texas home to reside in. He'd also lost many personal things near and dear to his heart, but nothing was more precious to him than life. Maxwell Trudeaux felt incredibly blessed to still be alive.

Malachi's physical corporation had also been destroyed, but he felt confident in taking on the rebuilding process. Because of the smart businessman he was all of the personnel records and other pertinent information pertaining to the communications conglomerate was stored on his home computer. He had also kept several backup disks inside his home office. Malachi Trudeaux was extremely pleased with his new life.

The Trudeaux brothers had also established solid friendships with two beautiful women, Josefina and Sarah, who had been widowed for years. Even though neither woman had given much thought to remarrying, nor was Josefina even sure she was down for such, they had found happiness again. Life was really good for Josefina Clayton and Sarah Watson.

Farrah had lost her dear mother, but she'd regained another best friend in Stephen. She was a good woman, not to mention how beautiful she was inside and out, yet she'd never known love from a man before. Men had seen her kindness for weakness, but Stephen had caused her to recognize her own strengths and her inner beauty. Loneliness had been her constant companion. Stephen had brought her back to life just by showering her with kindness and attention. Farrah Freeman was very optimistic about the future.

Gregory II and Aretha had lost Grant to the hurricane, but through all their grief they'd found each other again. Like his younger son, Gregory II didn't want to waste another precious second to being without the woman he loved. He was also of the belief that life was too short to spend time being miserable. He *had* been miserable without Aretha by his side. Forgiveness was always hard to achieve, but it was much easier when true love was involved. Aretha had finally learned humility. No longer was she the pompous woman who hadn't given a darn about other's feelings. Through her son's death she had come to know the true meaning of pain and suffering. Aretha now knew exactly what her family had felt when she'd walked out on them. It looked as if Aretha and Gregory Saxton II had a brighter future ahead of them.

Then there was Darcella, who had lost herself and Stephen to all her phobias. She'd told Stephen that things were good between her and her family. Because she'd dared to face her demons by going back home to live, she'd finally made a love connection with her mother, father and two brothers. For the first time ever, Darcella's family was able to see her for the beautiful woman she was. Her pain had temporarily separated her from her spirit, but the old Darcella was back and had decided that being a nurse was the perfect job for her. Darcella Coleman now looked forward to the day when she'd find love and happiness with a special someone.

After Stephen pulled Farrah closer to him, he hugged her tenderly. "We can't change anything that has occurred in our lives. We shouldn't get all caught up in the past. That is, not if we want a future together. Do you want us to have a future together, Farrah?"

Farrah reached her hand up and laid it atop Stephen's. "More than anything, Stephen. I also want to follow the blueprint God has designed for His children."

Stephen leaned forward and kissed the tip of Farrah's nose. "I have literally been surrounded by fields of fire in my lifetime, but being a firefighter is what I do best. I plan to help Dad rebuild his company, but I'm not going to retire my fire hose just yet. Experiencing the ominous situation in New Orleans helped me to see how much firefighters are really needed. Farrah, are you willing to go through the fire with me?"

Farrah kissed Stephen lightly on the mouth. "With you and for you."

"So be it. May we always be on the same chapter and on the same page. We should toast to all that we've said the next time we have a glass in our hand."

Farrah laughed. "Is there any reason why we can't seal it with a kiss?"

"None at all." With that said, Stephen kissed Farrah thoroughly.

Stephen held up his hand and made a mock toast. "With God leading the way, we can be confident in taking our relationship to the next level. Here's to us surviving the fields of fire!"

Epilogue

This marvelous day was a dream come true for Stephanie and Gregory III. The bride and groom were all smiles as they stood before the minister inside the tiny wedding chapel they'd chosen to exchange their vows. Stephanie was stunningly beautiful dressed in traditional white. Gregory III was quite stylish and looked very handsome in his black tuxedo and white shirt.

Malachi and Stephen had just placed Stephanie's hand inside of Gregory's. True to their words, both men had given away the lovely bride to the man of her dreams. Now that his job was done, Malachi took a seat on the front pew. Standing in for Grant as the best man, Stephen walked over and stood next to Farrah, the gorgeous maid-of-honor.

Gregory squeezed Stephanie's fingers. "As God will be the head of our household, to you I pledge my life. I will be your friend, your confidant, your lover, your husband and your hero. In the midst of stormy weather, I will be your shelter. Through war and peace, I will be your protector and your safety net. Your smile is my sunshine, my umbrella during the rain. Your kiss is my anchor, keeping me strong and steadfast. Your compassion is my warmth, making it easy for me to lose myself in your love. Nightfall will always find us at peace with each other. All these things I promise to you. I love you, Stephanie Trudeaux."

Stephanie smiled into Gregory's eyes. "Gregory, I will be there for you through thick and thin, through the good times and the bad. I will honor and respect you. You will always be able to count on me. I will be your friend, lover and your spouse. May you find peace in my arms at the end of each day and may they serve as a comfort to you in times of trouble. I promise to always communicate my feelings to you in a calm, effective manner. Nightfall will always find us at peace with each other. All these things I promise to you. I love you, Gregory Saxton III."

The minister gazed upon the loving couple, smiling broadly. "I now pronounce you man and wife. You may kiss your bride."

Gregory took Stephanie into his arms and sealed their vows with a staggering kiss.

The minister held up the hands of the bride and groom. "I hereby present to you, Mr. and Mrs. Gregory Saxton III."

Stephen paired off with Farrah as the wedding party prepared to exit the chapel. Smiling up at Stephen, Farrah linked her arm though his, wondering if this would ever happen for them. Marrying Stephen would make her the happiest woman on the planet. There was a time when she had thought she'd never find a good man, but God had had other plans for her life.

Farrah and Stephen's relationship had been built on solid rock.

Inside the reception hall Malachi gathered together the Trudeaux and the Saxton families and had them join hands for a word of prayer. He first thanked God for making possible such an extraordinary occasion. He then asked the

Lord to bless the holy union between his daughter and her husband. "Let's begin the celebration of the joining of these two lives," he said in closing.

* * * * *

Dear Readers:

I sincerely hope that you enjoyed reading FIELDS OF FIRE from cover to cover. I'm very interested in hearing your comments and thoughts on the sequel to The DEVIL'S ADVOCATE, featuring the Trudeaux and Saxton families. I love hearing from my readers and I do appreciate the time you take out of your busy schedule to respond. Please enclose a self-addressed, stamped envelope with all your correspondence and mail to: Linda Hudson-Smith, 16516 El Camino Real, Box #174, Houston, TX 77062. Or you can e-mail your comments to LHS4romance@yahoo.com. Please also visit my Web site and sign my guest book at www.lindahudsonsmith.com.

Born in Canonsburg, Pennsylvania, and raised in the town of Washington, Linda Hudson-Smith has traveled the world as an enthusiastic witness to other cultures and lifestyles. Her husband's military career gave her the opportunity to live in Japan, Germany and many cities across the United States. Linda's extensive travel experience helps her craft stories set in a variety of beautiful and romantic locations. It was after illness forced her to leave a marketing and public relations career that she turned to writing.

Romance in Color chose her as Rising Star for the month of January 2002. ICE UNDER FIRE, her debut Arabesque novel, received rave reviews. Voted as Best New Author by the Black Writers Alliance, Linda received the prestigious 2000 Gold Pen Award. She has also won two *Shades of Romance* magazine awards in the categories of Multicultural New Romance Author of the Year and Multicultural New Fiction Author of the Year 2001. Linda was also nominated as the Best New Romance Author at the 2001 Romance Slam Jam Conference. *Shades of Romance* magazine named Linda as Best New

Christian Fiction author in 2003. In September 2004 she was the proud winner of the African American Literary Show Awards in the romance category. Linda has earned the title of national bestselling author for her story THE DEVIL'S ADVOCATE, her literary contribution to the anthology THICKER THAN WATER, which earned a spot on the Essence Bestselling list in February 2006.

Linda's novel covers have been featured in such major publications as *Publishers Weekly, USA Today, Upscale Magazine, Black Romance, Lupus Now,* and *Essence Magazine.*

Linda is a member of Romance Writers of America and the Black Writers Alliance. Though novel writing remains her first love, she is currently cultivating her screenwriting skills. She has also been contracted to pen several other novels for Harlequin's Kimani Press.

Dedicated to inspiring readers to overcome adversity against all odds, for the past five and a half years Linda has served as a national spokesperson for the Lupus Foundation of America. In making lupus awareness one of top priorities, she travels around the country delivering inspirational messages of hope. Her Lupus Awareness Campaign was a major part of her ten-day book tour to Germany in February 2002, where she visited numerous U.S. military bases. In November 2004 she was awarded the key to the city by the mayor of Crestview, Florida, for the numerous contributions she's made to educating others about lupus.

Linda is also a supporter of the NAACP and the American Cancer Society. She enjoys reading and writing poetry, entertaining, traveling, and attending sports events. The mother of two sons, Linda resides with her husband in League City, Texas.

Acknowledgements

I want to thank each and every one of you for all the encouragement and support you've given me during the year. It has meant so much to the continued success of my literary career.

Evelyn Moore – Borders Express – Fox Hills Mall, Culver City, CA

Stephanie Kuykendall – March Air Force Base, Riverside, CA

Jennifer Johnston – Feldheym Central Library, San Bernardino, CA

Denise Noe – Walden Books – Moreno Valley Mall, Moreno Valley, CA

Karen Ferraro – Walden Books – Inland Center Mall, San Bernardino, CA

Wallace Allen – Westside Story Newspaper – San Bernardino, CA

Beverly Jimerson

Daylin Philyaw

Bob Jenkins

Willie Brown & Woody
Judyann Elder
Ken & Debra Ross
Melville, Etona, Evonte & Elexus Campbell
Carlos, Kevin & Kelsey Ortiz
Leilia Jones
Bonnie Holman
Bill & Renita Anderson